Love Letters

KATIE FFORDE

Love Letters

CENTURY · LONDON

Published by Century in 2009

2 4 6 8 10 9 7 5 3 1

First published in Great Britain in 2009 by
Century
Random House, 20 Vauxhall Bridge Road
London SW1V 2SA
www.rbooks.co.uk

Addresses for companies within The Random House Group Limited can be
found at: www.randomhouse.co.uk/offices.htm

The Random House Group Limited Reg. No. 954009

A CIP catalogue record for this book
is available from the British Library

ISBN 9781846054471

The Random House Group Limited supports The Forest Stewardship
Council (FSC), the leading international forest certification organisation. All
our titles that are printed on Greenpeace approved FSC certified paper carry
the FSC logo. Our paper procurement policy can be found at
www.rbooks.co.uk/environment

Mixed Sources

Product group from well-managed
forests and other controlled sources
www.fsc.org Cert no. TT-COC-2139
© 1996 Forest Stewardship Council

Set in Palatino by Palimpsest Book Production Limited,
Grangemouth, Stirlingshire
Printed and bound in Great Britain by
CPI Mackays, Chatham ME5 8TD

To Ireland and Irishmen, this is for you!

Acknowledgements

To the lovely Laura Flemming, who really did organise a literary festival while a toddler, and was so inspiring. To fellow writer Lesley Cookman for introducing me to the golden voiced Louise Cookman and incidentally, Lindy Hop.

To the wonderful Irish writers I met while doing an event over there, including Sarah Webb whose beautiful boots I also borrowed for this book.

To all the people who have unintentionally inspired me during the writing of this book. Some of you can't be mentioned for legal and embarrassment reasons, but if you read this, and are in it, thank you!

To all my wonderful agents! In no particular order, Sarah Molloy, Sara Fisher and Bill Hamilton. Thank you! Only you know how much I owe you!

To everyone at Random House. Kate Elton and Georgina Hawtrey-Woore for their wonderful editing, inspiring suggestions and infinite patience. Thank you!

To the behind the scenes people who do the work, but don't get the glory.

To Charlotte Bush and Amelia Harvell who are the best fun to go out with and give me wonderful treats (and parties!).

To the shameless marketing and sales departments who force people to buy my books, Claire Round, Louise Gibbs, Rob Waddington, Oliver Malcolm, Jay Cochrane and Trish Slattery.

To lovely Mike Morgan who took me on road trips for many years. So sad we won't be going again.

To Richenda Todd, who has protected me from myself for so many years, I am so grateful!

To the creators of my brilliant covers which I love! None of it could happen without you all, I'm so lucky to have such a brilliant team behind me.

Chapter One

Someone murmured into Laura's ear, making her jump. 'So, what do you think of him?'

The bookshop was crowded: the area they had cleared for the reading was full; the queue to the desk of people clutching recently bought books was long and chattering enthusiastically. Laura had felt a post-Christmas event was a bit of a risk but now she was watching the people with a combination of relief and satisfaction. However carefully you prepared for a bookshop event you could never really tell until they turned up how many people would come. Nor could you be sure whether the author would perform well. Writing was a very private occupation and Laura often thought it was cruel to make them stand up on their hind legs before an audience. But even by her high standards this event was a success.

With all this in her mind, however, she hadn't noticed anyone coming up behind her. She turned round swiftly and saw a short, late middle-aged woman dressed in clothes designed to attract attention. Laura instantly remembered seeing her when she came through the shop door with the rest of the author's party. Her jacket looked as if it were made of tapestry and her jewellery could have been home-made by a grandchild with a welding kit, or by a hot new designer, it was hard to tell. The most startling thing about her close up was her intense, penetrating stare. She had eyes like green agate.

'Very good, of course,' said Laura, startled, but polite

as ever, feeling drab in her ubiquitous black trousers and white shirt.

This answer didn't seem entirely to satisfy the green eyes boring into her. 'And have you read the book?'

'Of course.' Laura was firmer now, indignant at the woman's combative tone. She worked in a bookshop. It was her job to know the stock.

A pencilled-in eyebrow was raised. 'No "of course" about it. What did you think?'

Laura opened her mouth to say 'wonderful' and then decided to tell the truth instead. She had nothing to lose now, after all: her beloved job was going to be taken from her – she might as well put aside her habitual tact and say what she really thought. 'I didn't think it was quite as good as his first but I will be really interested to see his next one.' She was an avid, enthusiastic but critical reader; she could tell when a writer wasn't on top form. Then pennies tumbled in her brain, like coins from a fruit machine when someone wins the jackpot. 'Oh my goodness, you're his agent, aren't you?' Embarrassment turned her from hot to cold and back to hot again.

The woman narrowed her gaze in acknowledgement of this fact, but Laura couldn't tell if she was smiling, or expressing disapproval – her mouth didn't move. 'I do have that pleasure, yes.'

Still blushing, Laura tucked a stray curl behind her ear and looked across at the young man who was now signing books for a long queue of fans. Every book-buyer, she noted, got the charming smile, each book a little personal message as well as a dedication. Not one but two publicists had come with him from his publisher's, and not just for crowd control, but because they adored him. Writers like him were rare.

It was because he had two young women only too eager to open the books at the right page, put them into paper bags and keep his wine glass topped up, that Laura was propping up a pillar; they didn't need her help. And Henry, the owner of the shop, had been firm. 'You set all this up, got all these people here, ordered the wine, opened the polystyrene snacks: take a break.'

'He's a star,' said Laura after watching him for a couple more moments. She wasn't buttering up her formidable companion; she was telling it as it was.

'I know. I'm Eleanora Huckleby, by the way.'

'I know – now,' said Laura, relaxing a little. Agents didn't often come to bookshop events, but Damien Stubbs was special. 'I'm Laura Horsley.'

'So, do you read all the books of the people who come and do events here? I gather this shop is – was – famous for the amount of them it puts on.'

'Yes,' said Laura, not wanting to say 'of course' again, and sound prissy. She felt she was prissy, in fact, but didn't want to advertise the fact. Although talking to this woman made her wish she'd had time to straighten her hair. She felt her rather wild ringlets belied her professional air.

'So how do you get so many members of the public through the doors and buying books?' Eleanora added, looking at the queue leading to the signing table. 'At this time of year, too. I've been to so many where only two men and a dog turn up, and they're staff. Not a single member of the paying public present.'

Laura recognised that sort of book signing; Henry had sent her to one when she first suggested having an event. She had been determined to do it better and had. The shop was fairly well suited to holding events, being big enough to be able to clear the right sort of space. She tried to have something on every month, so people thought of the book-shop as a place to come for a good night out.

'I have a huge database of our customers,' she said to her companion, 'and I hand-pick them. If I think they'll like the book I invite them personally. They almost always come. I also run a book club from here. Did run a book club from here.' She sighed as she corrected herself. 'I expect it'll go on when the bookshop is closed. I really hope so.'

'You sound like a treasure. I'm sure another bookshop will snap you up. It's so sad that this one's going. I suppose it's threatened by the supermarkets?'

Laura nodded. 'And Henry wants to retire.'

Eleanora Huckleby took a bottle of wine from the table and tipped some into both her and Laura's glasses. 'Even the wine is drinkable.'

'I'd love to find another bookshop, but it would have to be a quirky independent shop like this one,' said Laura. 'I'm not sure I could cope without all the autonomy Henry allows me. He's been great. Lets me order extra copies of books I think will do especially well, read all the proof copies, all the fun stuff.'

Eleanora snorted, possibly at the thought of reading proof copies being described as fun. 'I should think he's grateful someone wants to read them.' She paused, pressing her lips together in thought. 'So who do you think is the rising literary star?'

Laura raised an eyebrow. 'Apart from Damien Stubbs?' She indicated her companion's client, who was still signing and being charming.

'Yes. What do you think of Anita Dubrovnik?'

The fact that Laura rarely expressed her true opinions out loud didn't mean she didn't have them. Now, when she was about to lose her job and had a glass of wine in her hand, she decided to say what she thought. 'A great writer but lacks narrative thrust.'

The older woman's eyes narrowed in agreement. 'Who else have you read recently?'

'Bertram Westlake?'

The women exchanged speculative looks. 'Worthy but dull,' said Laura firmly.

'Oh God! Such a relief to find someone who agrees with me. I mean, there's some great writing in there but whatever happened to plot! OK, what about Janice Hardacre?'

'Well, I loved *The Soul-Mate*, but haven't liked any of her others.'

'Me neither. And that last one went on for ever.'

'It was shortlisted for a prize,' Laura pointed out.

'God knows why!'

They talked about books, tearing apart the current literary masterpieces and raving over the unsung heroes that sold under a thousand copies, until the more senior of the publicists came over and addressed Eleanora.

'Fifty books sold!' She turned to Laura. 'This has been such a good event. Henry told me you organised most of it. Brilliant! Thank you so much!' Then she turned back to Eleanora. 'We thought we'd push off to the restaurant now, if you're ready.'

'Mm. May I bring a guest?'

'Of course! I booked a huge table. Who do you want to bring?'

'Laura here.'

Laura, her habitual shyness coming back in a rush, felt totally thrown. 'No. No really, I can't come. It's terribly kind of you to ask me. But there's so much to do here.' Never in the three years she'd been organising bookshop events had she been to dinner with the author afterwards. Her place was in the background, making things happen. It was where she felt most comfortable. Talking to a whole lot of strangers was not her thing. 'I've got to help clear up. Wash the glasses, get rid of the chairs . . .'

'Don't move!' said Eleanora firmly and strode off in the direction of Henry.

'You'd better not move,' the publicist advised. 'She's known as the Vixen in the trade. Easier to do what she says, really. I'm Emma, by the way, Emma Bennet.'

'But I can't imagine why she would want to ask me to dinner.'

'Maybe she enjoyed your company?' Emma smiled, amused by Laura's incredulity at this suggestion.

Laura could see Eleanora, followed by Henry and her colleague Grant, coming over to where she and Emma were chatting.

'She's got reinforcements,' muttered Emma. 'You've got no chance.'

Both her boss and her colleague came to a halt.

'You know perfectly well none of this would have happened without your very hard work,' said Henry, who was tall, balding and distinguished-looking. If he hadn't been forty years older than her and married already, Laura would have fancied him. 'You go and have a nice dinner. You've earned it. Grant and I will clear up.'

'But really . . .' She bit her lip. Panic that she was going to be taken out of her comfort-zone, aka the bookshop, made her look urgently at her friend.

Grant, interpreting her expression, shook his head, determined that she should take this opportunity to mingle with people other than her colleagues for a change. 'That's right,' he said firmly. 'You go and enjoy the ball. Cinderella here will clear up after this one.' He put his hand on her forearm. 'Have a great time and tell me all the goss tomorrow. And don't forget, we're going to the Sisters of Swing gig tomorrow?'

'Oh yes.' She clutched at his arm for a moment.

'Go on! You'll be fine!' Grant, the only other full-time member of staff and her closest colleague, gave her hand an encouraging pat. He was on a you-must-get-out-more mission with Laura and was taking her to a club to hear 'an incredible new girl band'. He teasingly described her as his 'beard', which made her laugh. Nothing and no one could make Grant look anything other than openly

6

gay. But he did have her best interests at heart and she knew he was right and that she should go.

Now Laura had been officially dismissed – or in her eyes, abandoned – Eleanora grasped her arm. 'Show me where the coats were put and get yours. You'll need it. The wind is bitter!'

Instead of a coat, Eleanor had an item that looked like a cross between a hearthrug and a small tent. It enveloped the wearer in red, prickly wool: not a garment for the faint-hearted.

Seeing Laura's slightly startled reaction, Eleanora said, 'I always think I could camp out in this all night if I had to. And I can only wear it in deepest winter, or I sweat like a pig.'

Laura felt her own navy blue overcoat was pathetically drab. She'd bought it from a charity shop while she'd been at university and still hadn't worn it out. Alas, working in a bookshop didn't give one huge amounts of spare cash for clothes.

'Well, come along now,' said Eleanora. 'Take my arm. I can't really walk in these heels but I refuse to wear ballet slippers at my age. And lace-ups would ruin my image.' She looked down at Laura's shoes, which were almost completely flat. 'I rest my case.'

In spite of her disapproval of Laura's footwear, which was comfortable if unglamorous, Eleanora talked to her all the way to the restaurant, grilling her for her opinions of all sorts of books.

Laura read a lot. She lived alone in a tiny bedsit and her television was so small and snowy she didn't watch it much. But she read all the time: at bedtime, while she ate, while she cooked, while she dressed and while she brushed her teeth. She would have read in the shower if she could have worked out a method that wouldn't completely ruin the book. In the same way she could read anywhere, she could read anything, and if it was good, enjoy it. There wasn't a genre or an author that Eleanora quizzed her on that Laura didn't have some knowledge of. Still in the reckless mood engendered by losing her job and finding in Eleanora someone who cared about books as much as she did, she let herself speak her mind without holding back.

Eleanora was impressed. 'Darling! You're a phenomenon!' she declared. 'I'm so glad I've found you.'

At the restaurant Laura was introduced again to the young literary lion, Damien Stubbs. He'd said hello briefly when he arrived at the bookshop and had been as charming then as he was now. He thanked her for arranging such a good event and she muttered a few words of praise for his book. But he didn't seem to need reassurance. Confidence shone from him, and everyone around him basked in its warmth. He was the young writer of the moment and the world loved him.

Laura, who in the confusion of deciding where everyone should sit, which she took no part in, had an opportunity to wonder why she didn't fancy Damien Stubbs. Everyone else, men and women alike, seemed to. Several reasons occurred to her, but the one she felt most likely was that she didn't really admire his writing. When it was allocated to her, she took her seat gloomily. I'm a literary snob, she concluded. My emotions are more wrapped up in books than they are in real life. She felt slightly depressed and not only because she was about to lose what seemed the best job in the world. When had she become so boring? And was it too late to change?

While everyone else sat down, got up again, moved and then ended up back where they'd started, Laura had time for her life to flash before her eyes. Since university, which she had loved, she had only had two jobs, both working in bookshops. Once she'd joined Henry Barnsley Books she hadn't wanted to work anywhere else. Although she was usually shy in her personal life, she enjoyed finding the right book for the right customer. She was popular with them. They asked for her if they wanted a book as a present and didn't know what to buy. Some of them asked her out on dates and sometimes, nagged by Grant, who'd worked at the shop longer than she had and so was her superior, she even went. But it never came to anything. If they enjoyed books and reading as much as she did they quite often had soup stains down the front of their cardigans. She might be a bluestocking bookworm, but she had some standards.

Eleanora handed her a menu. Laura hadn't noticed her sitting down next to her and felt rather cheered. At least she would be able to talk to Eleanora, or if not, sit in silence, observing the other diners, something she loved doing. She much preferred to be safely on the outside of life, watching, than deeply involved. Thankfully there was no one on Laura's other side.

'So dear,' Eleanora said later, and inevitably, Laura felt, 'any plans for your future? Do you want to be a writer?'

'Good God no!' said Laura and then, realising that perhaps she may be shouldn't have sounded so horrified, went on: 'Sorry, I didn't mean to be so vehement, but I would hate to be a writer. I love to get lost in other people's books, but I really don't want to write one myself.'

'Such a relief!' said Eleanora. 'I felt I had to ask, but I'm really pleased. Any other plans for gainful employment?'

'Not really.' She sighed. 'I've hardly had time to think about it, and I've got a couple of months before I'm on the dole. I'm sure to find something.'

'You don't sound very sure.'

Laura tried to make herself clear. 'I'm sure I won't starve – there are always jobs for willing workers – but it's unlikely I'll find anything book related, which I love so much. Not in this town anyway.'

Eleanora narrowed her eyes in thought. 'I might have something.'

Laura turned to her, not sure if she'd heard properly. 'Have you?'

Eleanora leant in. 'Mm, something frightfully exciting!'

Laura's little flicker of hope died. She didn't do 'frightfully exciting'. She wouldn't be right for the job. It would probably involve marketing, or starting a business from scratch – not her sort of thing at all.

'Well, don't you want to hear what it is?' Eleanora demanded through a slice of tomato and feta cheese.

Laura speared a black olive with her fork. 'Of course. It's so kind of you to take an interest.' She hoped Eleanora wouldn't hear her apathy.

'It is, actually,' agreed Eleanora, possibly slightly annoyed by Laura's lukewarm response. 'And if it wasn't in my interest as well, I wouldn't bother. Too busy. But what it is, is this!'

At that moment a phalanx of waiters descended on the table, whipping away Greek salad and taramasalata and replacing it with sizzling platters of moussaka, sinister fish dishes and more bottles of wine.

While all this was going on, Laura framed an elegant and polite refusal for whatever Eleanora might be about to suggest. She didn't think anything this brightly coloured parrot of a woman could offer her could possibly be up her street. They were too different as people.

'I want you to set up a literary festival!' Eleanora announced with the assumption that this would be greeted with clapping and shrieks of delight, as if she was a conjuror who had just produced a particularly endearing rabbit. 'Well, help set up one, anyway.'

Visions of the major festivals – Cheltenham, Hay, Edinburgh, with their phalanx of stars, many of them famous for something quite other than writing books – made her feel weak. 'I don't think—'

'But it's not just an ordinary lit. fest.' Eleanora flapped a heavily ringed hand as if it were boredom that made Laura doubtful. 'There's a music festival going on too. It's at my niece's house.'

'Oh. Big house,' said Laura. For a moment, her wayward imagination was distracted by the notion of a two-bed semi with a literary lion in one room and an *X Factor* entry-level band in another.

'Huge. A monster, millstone round their necks, but lovely, of course. They're trying to make it pay its way so they can keep it. The music festival should make them a bit, but my niece, Fenella, wanted a literary festival too, to make it a bit different.'

'I think there is a festival already that combines—'

'Doesn't mean they can't have one too, does it?'

'Of course not. I was just saying—'

'The music side of it is all going fine but they've got no one to take over the literary festival bit. You'd be perfect.'

Laura shook her head. She wasn't the right sort of entrepreneurial, feisty woman who could blag big firms into sponsoring huge events for ex-presidents who had written heavily ghosted autobiographies. 'I don't think so.'

'Why on earth not?'

Why didn't Eleanora – obviously a very bright woman – get it? 'Because I've never done anything like that before. I wouldn't know where to start!'

Eleanora took a moment and then lowered her voice and spoke slowly, as if to a bewildered child or a frightened horse. 'But, sweetie, you *have* done things like that before! What do you think a bookshop event is? You get the authors there, you get them to speak, you make sure people buy their books. Just the same!'

'But we don't have to make vast amounts of money out of the bookshop events, or hire a venue, or anything.'

'Look, I can tell losing your job has knocked your confidence. It would. But don't turn this down until you've had a proper think about it. Fen said there's some sort of meeting at Somerby – hang on, I'll tell you when it is.' Eleanora took a big gulp of her wine and then started burrowing in her handbag, which had a Mary Poppins quality: it was enormous and possibly contained a standard lamp. She produced a Filofax the size of a family Bible and riffled through the pages. 'Next week. Two o'clock. At Somerby. Do you know where that is?'

'No,' said Laura firmly, although a small part of her wanted to find out. Despite her reservations – and they were strong ones – she felt a flutter of interest. Anything to do with books had that effect on her.

'I'll get Fenella to email you some details. You are on email?'

'Well, at the shop.'

'You'll need a laptop. Better get one with your redundancy money.'

Laura inwardly bristled. She didn't like being told how to spend her as yet unspecified redundancy money. She might need to pay a gas bill or her rent with it.

Eleanora hadn't got to be a top literary agent without knowing how to read body language or how to get people to accept challenges. 'You might as well go to the meeting, at least. If your only other job opportunity is stacking shelves in a supermarket . . .'

Struggling to stick to her original reaction that running a literary festival was not what she wanted to do, Laura kept up her argument about practicalities. 'That's not my only job opportunity, and I'm working at the shop for the next two months!'

'What else are you going to find that involves books, except another bookselling job?'

'I do realise that I might have to broaden my search a bit but that's probably a good thing.'

'Do you want to move house as well as change your job?'

Laura visibly shuddered. Her tiny flat was not a palace but it could have been far worse and, more importantly, she could afford it. 'Not really, but I suppose I may have to.'

'Then far better quit while you're ahead. Run the festival for my niece and you won't have to move. You can live on-site, there's plenty of room. And I'm sure you'd be brilliant at it.'

'Honestly, I may be able to set up a reading in a bookshop but I couldn't do the other stuff – such as how to calculate how big a marquee I'd need for the events. There's nothing worse than a tent for two hundred and only twenty people in it.' Laura had experienced this for herself – she had nearly frozen to death.

'You won't have to do that sort of thing,' said Eleanora confidently. 'There are others who can do that. We – they – need you for your knowledge of books and writers.'

Trying to clamp down on the stirrings of interest this flattering statement aroused, Laura said, 'Will it pay well?' The answer was bound to be no and then she could just say no. Eleanora was the sort of woman who would understand this practical approach.

For once, the forthright Eleanora didn't instantly reply. Instead, she fiddled with her cutlery for a second. 'There'll be some sort of fee, I imagine. To be honest, I'm not sure exactly.'

Laura felt on solid ground at last, although she didn't find it as comfortable as she would have thought. 'Well, that settles it. I can't possibly afford to work for nothing.' She felt a little sad to have got out of it so easily, then shook herself. She didn't exactly get a king's ransom working in a bookshop, but at least it paid the bills and she couldn't be reckless and agree to something on the basis of an as yet unspecified fee.

'But you said! You've still got your job at the shop for the next two months! And all the big festivals are mostly run by volunteers.'

'I can't afford to be a volunteer, I need paid work,' she gently reminded Eleanora.

'As I said, you've got that!'

'But Miss—'

'Eleanora.'

'Eleanora . . .' she blundered on, not quite happy with calling this woman she didn't know very well by her first name. 'I'm paid to work in a bookshop. That means I have to be there, doing my job.'

'Oh, your boss will give you time off to run the festival! I'm sure he will! He seemed such a nice man.'

She was probably right about this, Laura acknowledged. Henry would be as helpful as possible and give her as much time off as she needed if it involved her getting paid work. But she wouldn't do it unless there was money involved. It would be gross foolishness and unfair to Henry. And when she thought of what her parents would say if she admitted to working for even less than she was currently earning, she reached for her wine for support. They still hadn't quite forgiven her for doing English at university instead of studying something that would give her a job that paid 'proper money'.

'All that student debt,' they had said, 'and you'll never be able to pay it off!'

When she'd told them that if her wages were so low she wouldn't have to pay it off, they weren't remotely impressed. Nor was she, really. She didn't like being in debt to the government but she still wasn't going to study to be an accountant.

'Just go to the meeting,' said Eleanora. 'If your boss doesn't want to give you time off, I'll speak to him. Once you've seen the house and met my niece, you'll want to do it. I promise you.'

'I'd better not go then,' muttered Laura. Eleanora didn't hear, but then Laura hadn't intended her to.

Chapter Two

'So,' said Grant in the shop the next day, before he'd even got his coat off, 'did you sit next to the wunderkind?' They were in the stockroom that combined as a staffroom, in the basement of the building.

'Oh, you mean Damien?' As usual, Laura had got in early, and had finished the clearing up that Grant and Henry had promised they'd do, before going downstairs and putting on the kettle. 'No. He was surrounded by beautiful young women who worked in the publicity department.'

'Jealous?' asked Grant, tipping half a jar of instant coffee into a mug. He was the sort of person who always wanted to know how everyone felt. Laura often told him he should give up bookselling and become a counsellor – it would be his ideal job.

She shook her head, squishing her peppermint tea bag against the side of the mug with a spoon. 'No. Not my type.'

'So what is your type?' Grant poured boiling water on to the coffee.

'I don't know really.' Laura scooped out her bag and dropped it into the bin-liner she'd just put in place. 'I don't fancy many people.'

'You must have some idea. If I'm going to help you find a boyfriend, I must know what I'm looking for.'

Laura laughed. 'I don't want you to find me a boyfriend! I'll find my own if I want one!'

Grant made a face of utter revulsion as he sipped his

coffee. 'Of course you want one, darling, we all do. I just need to know the type. Pipe and slippers? Snappy dresser? Yoghurt-knitter-and-dedicated-recycler? Actual cycler?'

'I think the word you're looking for is cyclist.'

'You're such a pedant sometimes, Laura. And you must have some idea of your basic type.'

'Oh, I don't know.' They'd had this sort of conversation before and it never led anywhere. Although she had no particular ambition to end up a lonely spinster with the regulation cat, she did sometimes feel it was inevitable. She sighed. 'We'd better get upstairs. It'll be time to open soon.'

'No hurry.' Grant was rummaging in a tin of short-bread left over from the staff party. 'I need breakfast and everyone's at the sales, buying tat or taking back the tat they were given for Christmas.' He frowned. 'I see your mother is still giving you "slacks" for Christmas, and you're still taking them back?'

Laura glanced down at her new black trousers. 'My mother can't see why I'd rather wear clothes that need ironing instead of nice, easy-care polypropylene or some such. She doesn't understand about static and how it's just not cool to create sparks when you walk quickly.'

Grant laughed. 'It is in some circles, sweetie. At least mine has stopped giving me diamond-pattern golfing sweaters.' He gave her sweater a disparaging look.

'I know black is dull but clothes get filthy working here.' She gave a wry laugh. 'Maybe I'll have a nice nylon overall for my next job.'

'You and me both, ducky! Now are you going to open up, or aren't you?'

Laura went upstairs to the shop. Henry came through the door just as she was turning round the sign.

'Good morning, sweetheart,' he said, as he always did.

17

'How did you get on last night? Eleanora Huckleby's a piece of work, isn't she?'

'She certainly is. She—'

'Wants you to run a literary festival, I know.' He took off his hat and threw it deftly to a row of pegs where it obligingly landed. 'She phoned me. First thing.'

Laura was used to the hat trick but this was surprising. Henry wasn't a 'first thing' sort of person. It was, he claimed, why he wanted to run a bookshop. She felt instantly guilty. 'Oh goodness! I can't believe that!'

Henry shook his head, smiling down at her. 'She's not a top literary agent because of her lack of tenacity, that's for sure. So if you need time off for this meeting, you can have it. But if you do decide to go for it, and actually help set up the literary festival, I insist on providing the books.'

He was being so generous Laura couldn't help feeling a twinge of conscience. 'But supposing it isn't until after the shop is closed?'

'I'll still have my contacts, and I think a lit. fest. would be splendid fun!'

Was everyone determined to get her involved whether she agreed to or not? They certainly seemed to be conspiring to erase any possible objections she might have. She supposed she ought to feel grateful they believed in her so much. Now all she had to get through was her monthly visit to her parents.

'So how did it go?' asked Grant as he came through Laura's door barely an hour after she'd got back from what had proved to be the usual frustrating visit home. At least she had the thought of her night out with Grant to keep her going. He'd made a duty visit that day too, to his aunt's.

'Oh, OK, you know. Quiet.'

'You didn't tell them about the bookshop closing then?'

'No. I thought I'd wait until I'd got something else lined up. You know what they're like. My father might insist that I retrain as an accountant or a book-keeper. Did you tell your aunt?'

'Yup, but as she's not my mother I felt she could take it. She offered me some money if I wanted it.'

Laura smiled. Grant always went through agonies of guilty conscience when his aunt offered him money although he did sometimes accept it. 'So did you say yes this time?'

'Certainly not! I don't need it at the moment. If I'm out of work for ages I might say yes then.' He tutted. 'Don't look at me like that! I'm her only relation and she's loaded. She likes giving me money!'

Chuckling, Laura drew him into her flat and shut the door behind him. 'I know she does and I'm not the one feeling you shouldn't take her handouts. She's got more money than she knows what to do with and you're her only nephew. I don't think you should feel guilty at all. Hey! Why don't you ask her for a really big lump and you could open your own bookshop. Then we'd both be back in gainful employment!'

'What makes you think I'd give you a job?'

'Because I'm the best and you would.'

Grant sighed. 'OK, I would, but I wouldn't like to ask her for real money. She might need it for her care home or something. I'll be all right anyway. I don't mind working for a big chain.' His attention wandered from his possible next job to Laura's outfit. 'Sorry, sweetie, you can't wear that.'

'Why not? I thought I'd put on a skirt for once, look a bit smarter than usual. For our big night out.'

'Well, you look like you're dressed as a secretary in an am. dram. production of something with a secretary in it, only not as sexy.'

Laura was used to Grant's less than enthusiastic

reaction to her clothes. 'Thank you very much for your vote of confidence. I love you too.'

'Don't get huffy, you actually look nearly OK, only you need to wear something a bit fuller, or trousers.'

Laura threw up her hands to express her incredulous frustration. 'Usually you're trying to get me out of trousers! But actually I spilt something on my black ones at the restaurant yesterday, which is why I'm wearing a skirt.'

'I thought you had about five pairs of black trousers – six since Christmas?' It was quite clear how he felt about the working-woman's staple.

'All either dirty or too worn out to be worn out, if you get my meaning.'

Grant sighed. 'Enough with the puns. Have you got a skirt you can dance in?'

'I can bop about in this.'

'I don't mean bop about, I mean dance. Lindy Hop to be precise.'

'Why? We're going to hear a band. We don't have to dance in the aisles if we don't want to. It's usually voluntary.'

'But it's at a club. It's a Lindy night.'

Laura growled at him. 'Grant, why didn't you tell me this before I agreed to go? What is Lindy Hop anyway?'

'It's a dance. A bit like jive or rock and roll but with more moves. You'll find out, anyway. And I didn't tell you because I knew you wouldn't agree to go. Now I'm here I can manhandle you into something you can move in and into the car.'

The thought of Grant manhandling her into a pair of trousers made her relax and giggle. After all, clothes were not a big part of her life and she didn't really care what she wore. The whole Lindy Hop thing was a bit more of a jolt. Although she was perfectly happy bopping about in her kitchen, on her own, she didn't usually do it in public. On the other hand maybe it was time to do things differently. Grant had certainly been trying to get her to do so for long enough. 'You'd better come and look at my wardrobe then.'

'I was hoping you'd say that. And well done for not digging your heels in.'

'I would have done,' Laura confessed, 'but I'm not wearing heels.'

Grant groaned.

'But seriously,' Laura went on, 'the event the other night made me realise just how boring I am. I've got to open myself to new experiences.'

Grant nodded, obviously totally agreeing with her. 'But were you always boring, or is it only since you've been working in a bookshop?'

Refusing to be offended at his agreement that she was boring, she considered. 'I think I've always been what you'd call pretty boring. I had friends at uni, of course, but I didn't go out much, unless I was dragged.'

Grant tutted. 'Such a waste!'

'To be honest, it was such bliss not to be nagged at for reading so much, I just . . . well, read mostly, and wrote essays, of course.'

'And you say you had friends?' Sceptical didn't cover it.

'Yes! I was always there to take washing out of the machine, I always had milk, aspirin, and I could dictate a quick essay if one was needed at the last minute.' She chuckled. 'It really pissed me off if they got a better mark than I did, though.'

'They used you!' Grant was indignant.

'No. Well, a bit, but I didn't mind. And as I said, they did drag me out from time to time. We had a lot of fun together. I just mostly preferred to stay in and read than shout myself hoarse at a lot of drunk people.'

'What about boyfriends?'

'There were a few. They never really came to anything.

21

Grant, I'm sure we've been through all this when I first came to the bookshop and you gave me your standard interrogation.'

'Maybe, but it was obviously all so boring I've forgotten. And I don't interrogate people. I'm just interested in the human condition.'

'You mean nosy.'

'Well, OK, nosy. Now let's look in here.' He pulled open the door of her small wardrobe, expecting the worst. 'Laura, are all your clothes black or white?'

'Pretty much. I've got my summer clothes in a plastic bag somewhere. Here.' She withdrew it from the bottom of the wardrobe. Grant emptied it on to the floor as if he were sorting laundry.

'You should really let me come round and go through all this for you,' he muttered, tossing garments behind him like a picky burglar.

'I would if you were more like that Gok person.'

He stopped. 'I thought you never watched television!'

She laughed, pleased by his surprise. 'I don't but I went round to one of the book group women with a copy of that month's book and she had it on. She persuaded me to stay and watch it. Very brave, all those women. Fancy sitting in a shop window naked?'

'I can think of worse fates actually, but I can see for you it would be torture.'

In the end he found a tiered bo-ho skirt in cream broderie anglaise, a black V-necked cardigan and a tight black belt. 'It's quite sweet but still very monochrome,' he said. 'Where's your jewellery?'

Laura opened her dressing-table drawer and revealed her few bits and pieces, mostly presents from university friends, and a pearl necklace left to her by an aunt. Grant sorted through it dismissively.

'What about scarves, belts, things like that?'

They were stuffed in with her knickers but he rifled

through them until he found a scarf that had been round a sun hat Laura had bought through necessity, the last time she'd been on holiday with her parents, several years ago.

'Here.' He tied it round her neck. 'It looks nice, but your hair needs to be in a higher ponytail. And it needs an iron.'

'What, my hair? I know, the trouble is straightening it—'

'Not your hair! I like that curly, frizzy look, it's cute. No, I meant your skirt! Have you got an iron?'

She nodded, and put on a smug expression. 'Another reason I had friends in my student house was I had an iron and knew how to use it.'

'No wonder you won Miss Congeniality three years in a row.'

Laura giggled. 'How do you know I didn't? I was popular. Sometimes people prefer someone who's a bit quieter.'

'Who could iron.'

Aware she wasn't going to convince Grant that her university days weren't spent reading and ironing her friends' clothes, or if they were, she'd really enjoyed them, she said, 'My mother used to get me to do all the ironing.'

'It's a useful skill,' he said, refusing to be sympathetic to this potential tale of childhood cruelty. 'I'll do it while you do your hair.'

'You're terribly bossy,' Laura objected, getting out the ironing board.

'I know. It's why I'm the manager of the shop and you're not.'

'I'm not sure having one full-time assistant and a couple of part-timers makes you the head of a vast empire . . .'

'Of course it does. Now hurry up, we don't want to miss the first set.'

Laura's efforts with her hair meant that while the bulk of it was in a fifties-style ponytail, there was still a lot of stray hairs, giving her a dark gold aura round her head. 'It's not very tidy.'

'It's not supposed to be tidy! It's supposed to be a bit laid-back. You don't have to look like Sandy in *Grease*.'

Laura stopped trying to smooth her hair. 'Grant, I don't mind dressing the part but I'm not actually going to do Lindy Hopping. You do know that, don't you?'

Grant smiled at her. 'Come along. It's going to be a great night.'

Together they walked down the road to the minicab office. Grant was going to sleep on Laura's sofa that night so he could drink.

'I hope it's not the sort of place where you have to get legless just to get through the evening,' said Laura.

'Have you ever been legless?' Grant demanded.

'Not often, no,' said Laura meekly. 'I really am boring!'

The club was already full and buzzing when they arrived. They made their way down the steps to the basement and Grant paid. A band was playing wonderful old numbers that made Laura's foot tap even though she'd sworn she wouldn't dance.

Grant bought her a glass of wine and put it into her hand. 'Let's see if we can find somewhere to sit, before the girls come on.'

'The girls', he had reminded her on the way, were the band called the Sisters of Swing he'd been bending her ear about for the last couple of weeks. They sang traditional swing numbers and Grant was very keen to see them live.

Laura followed Grant as he headed for a cluster of tables and chairs, taking in what was going on around her. All sorts of people, wearing quite a variety of clothes, were dancing hugely energetically. Slipping easily into her favourite role as observer, she found the crowd fascinating. There were young men dancing with much older women and young women dancing with older men, not (she felt sure) because anything was going on between them, but because they could both dance well. Age was no barrier; dancing was all.

Grant found a couple of seats and they sat down, Laura unable to stop watching the play that was going on around them. Every so often someone from the stage issued instructions to 'freeze' and then say if it was the men or the women who should choose new partners. Laura was fascinated.

'Look at the shoes!' said Grant, indicating a pair of brown and white corespondent shoes.

Once they'd spotted the first pair, they realised women were wearing similar shoes, only with heels and T-bars. There were what even Laura knew as jazz shoes, ballet slippers (they looked a bit vulnerable), character shoes, and ordinary street shoes.

'This is fun!' said Laura, surprising herself.

'Glad you can recognise "fun"!' said Grant and then his complacency fell away. 'Oh God, we may actually have to do this.'

Laura turned to where he was looking and saw a determined girl coming towards Grant. Highly amused at the thought of her gay friend being swept off by a young Amazon, she didn't spot the man heading towards her. Before she knew what was happening she found herself pulled to her feet. Her potential partner was about her age, with curly hair and eyelashes to match. He was wearing baggy trousers and a striped cotton shirt, braces and a pork-pie hat on the back of his head.

'Hi!' he said. 'What's your name?'

'Laura! But I'm only here for the band!'

'So, dance?'

She shook her head, from habit as much as anything.
'Oh no, I said, I'm only here for the band.'

'Nonsense. Come on!'

Laura found herself getting to her feet at the insistence
of her partner. At first she could only stand, bemused, but
then some dance lessons, given by a friend of her mother's,
years ago, came back to her. She began to enjoy the feeling
of flippancy and fun the music and the dancing gave her.
Her partner didn't seem to care that she was more or less
making it up as she went along. She found herself whirled
around, held, pushed away, brought back again, all in
minutes. When she was allowed to sit down again she
was exhausted. 'Thank you so much! That was such fun.'

'You should come more often,' said her partner. 'You've
got real talent!'

'I don't think so. I really—'

'—only came for the band,' he finished for her. 'I know.
I'm Jim, by the way. I'll look out for you next time.'
Although she eventually managed to persuade him to
leave, which he did with a tip of his hat, she had enjoyed
the feeling of being chosen and danced with.

'Well, that was a turn-up for the books!' said Grant,
as they both sipped wine, wishing it was water. 'We both
pulled! And I never thought I'd see you on a dance floor,
being hurled about by a strong man.'

'Back at ya!'

'Mine wasn't a strong man, more's the pity. I did tell
her I was gay, but she said she knew already.' He paused.
'I think the band's going to be on soon. Better get to the
bar quickly.'

Laura, recognising her cue, got to her feet. 'More of
the same?'

He nodded. 'And a pint of tap water.'

There were a few more energetic routines, which
Grant and Laura sat out, mainly to give their feet a rest,

and then three girls came to the front of the stage. They were wearing very full tulle skirts with tight waists and fitted bodices. They all had amazing pink beehive hairdos and the one in the middle had a huge flower behind her ear. They looked fantastic and for the first time that evening, people stopped dancing and turned towards the stage.

'We were lucky to get a seat,' said Grant, and then the lights went down and the singers were spotlighted.

They started with 'The Boogie-Woogie Bugle Boy' and everyone stamped their feet and clapped in time to the music. Several upbeat numbers followed and, in spite of the fear of clapping at the wrong moment that always afflicted her, Laura cast off her inhibitions and clapped and hand-jived with the best of them.

And then the tone quietened right down and the lead singer, the girl with the flower behind her ear, began to sing 'Smoke Gets in Your Eyes'. She followed this with something equally sad and romantic, sending Laura into an unaccustomed mood of nostalgia. She began to think about her own love life, now long in the past. There had really only been one possible serious contender. Why hadn't it ever got any further than a couple of drinks and a snog that didn't go on long enough for him but was as much as Laura could stand? Either she was too young, or she just hadn't loved him. She could barely remember his name.

While her mind was free-ranging she found herself thinking how one thing subtly changing, such as her getting notice from her job, could set in train other small changes. She still had her job, she wasn't out on the street, but since hearing the news that she was going to lose it, she had spoken to Eleanora far more freely than she would have done normally, and she had been asked to help run a literary festival. Then, coming here with Grant, instead of just listening to the band, she had got up and danced and really enjoyed herself. There was probably a scientific name for it, like the theory that said a butterfly flapping its wings in Brazil caused a hurricane somewhere else very far away. Perhaps she should just accept her fate and go with the flow, as Grant would say. Going to the festival meeting didn't mean she actually had to agree to help run it, after all.

'Are you all right, chook?' asked Grant, when the band had gone back into a dance number and people took to the floor once more with abandon. She was still staring thoughtfully at the stage.

'Oh yes. I'm fine.'

'Another drink?'

'Would you think I was awfully sad if I said I just wanted to go home?'

For once Grant accepted this without comment but in the cab back to her flat he said, 'You've gone all thoughtful on me. Have you been thinking about the literary festival thing?'

'Yes. Yes, I have.'

'And?'

'I think I'm going to go to the meeting, anyway.'

'Good for you! You see? A bit of Lindy Hopping and you're a changed woman!'

Chapter Three

Laura was wearing her interview suit, which was now a little tight over the hips. It was the day of the meeting. The entire bookshop was rooting for her, possibly anxious, she suspected, that she would back out. Henry had given her the afternoon off, ordering her to use it wisely, and Grant had offered her the use of his car. Now, Grant came round the back of the shop with her, to help her get it out.

'I haven't driven for ages, Grant,' said Laura, suddenly nervous about it. 'The last time was when I was staying with my parents and Dad wanted me to drive back from a restaurant.'

'And you didn't hit anything?'

'No, but it was my home patch! I could have driven those roads blindfold on a bicycle!'

'All roads are much the same really. And you've had your practice run.'

Laura nodded. 'I know.'

'I just wondered if blind panic had wiped your memory.'

She shook her head, trying to dislodge the blind panic that was washing over her with alarming frequency. 'It's only natural to be nervous. This is a big deal! I don't go to meetings and before you say anything, I don't count what we all do when we get together in the staffroom. That's quite different.'

Grant did his best to be reassuring but as she'd been fretting all week, he was obviously getting just a bit tired of it. 'Just take some deep breaths, you'll be fine.'

'But supposing this Fenella woman is just like her aunt? Scariness is bound to run in the family!'

'Laura dear, are you like your parents? No. I rest my case.'

'But genetics don't always work that way.'

'So Fenella will be a perfectly nice woman. She sounded nice on the phone, didn't she?'

'Yes, but—'

'But nothing. Just get in and drive, girl!' he said. 'It's insured for any driver. And you're insured if I've given you permission to—'

'I'd feel happier if I had a letter saying you've given me permission, or something.'

'Oh for goodness sake! You're far too law-abiding! Go to your meeting and tell us all about it when you get back. Remember, you don't have to agree to anything if you don't want to but I'll want to know why! Now, here's your route.' He handed her some sheets of paper. 'This one's off the computer, and this is mine. Here's the map Fenella faxed through.' He paused. 'You've got a sleeping bag, an ice axe and a boxful of emergency rations in case you're stranded overnight.'

Anxiety had slowed her reactions and it took her a nano-second to realise he was joking. She pushed his arm and got into the car. Then she hooked her curls back behind her ears and turned the key. Grant patted the roof and she was off.

She found she liked driving his little Fiat Punto. It was light and nippy and she soon forgot to worry about handling it. Now it was only getting lost she had to concern herself with. Fenella's map looked perfectly straightforward but as she got nearer, all her nervousness came back and she started muddling up left and right. But at last, after a brief unscheuduled detour around the village, it was before her, on a hill, as described in the directions.

Somerby was a truly lovely house. Surrounded by pasture, currently grazed by a few picturesque horses well rugged up against the winter cold, it looked like a calm, benign being surveying the countryside it presided over.

Although it was still early afternoon, the January day was thinking about closing. The leafless trees stood out clearly against the pale sky and a faint glow from the sun lent a soft glow to the scene, as in an old oil painting.

Laura, who had stopped to double-check she had the right place before going up the drive, took a few moments to enjoy the picture. Some days in January, she always felt, teetered between the melancholy of winter and the optimism of spring. This matched her own feelings: sadness about losing her beloved job, but a stirring of hope at the prospect of something that might be quite exciting. She just had to be brave enough to take the leap. She spent a few moments enjoying the view, wondering just how courageous she was.

Then she noted the several cars drawn up in front of the Georgian façade and glanced at her watch, worried that she was late. In fact she was exactly on time, her watch confirmed this, but she liked to be punctual – early, Grant called it – and turned the car into the drive.

She found somewhere to park it and then, when she could put off the moment no longer, got out. Up until this point a meeting to her meant an informal event held in the staffroom of the shop and consisted of Henry, Grant, the part-time staff and her discussing things. There was no agenda and everyone said what they wanted to say and no one wrote anything down. It worked fine. Laura knew this was going to be different. It was likely to be extremely nerve-racking – if she had any nerves left to rack, that is; she was nearly all racked out simply from the journey!

The doorbell jangled and the door opened swiftly on

a tall young woman with blonde hair, wearing a Cavalier shirt, velvet trousers tucked into fabulous pale green suede boots that nearly reached her thighs and a worried expression. Spotting Laura, she smiled and looked slightly less concerned. 'You must be Laura Horsley?'

'Yes. Am I the last? I got a bit lost towards the end.'

'No, there's still another couple of people who aren't here. Come in.' She closed the big oak door and ushered Laura into a large hallway with a sweeping staircase. Laura tried not to feel too intimidated. It was all so grand.

'I've heard such a lot about you from Eleanora,' the woman went on. 'Isn't she terrifying?'

'Well . . .'

'Heart of gold, of course, but tough as old boots in some ways. She thinks very highly of you and she's very perceptive.'

'Oh no, now I'll have to live up to her expectations!'

The woman chuckled. 'I'm sure that won't be a problem. Do you want the loo or anything or shall I take you straight upstairs where the meeting is being held? I'm Fenella, by the way. It was my mad idea to have a festival here.' She glanced round to check that Laura was following her up the staircase. 'The trouble with having such a massive house is that it's very expensive. It has to earn its keep and if we need to do more renovations – and we always do – we have to do something big. We mostly do weddings. Here we are.'

She opened the door to a room with floor-to-ceiling windows and, Laura guessed, fantastic views. There was a huge table in the middle with chairs all round. Most of the chairs were occupied; voices bounced off the parquet floor as people chatted animatedly. Laura licked lips that had gone dry, certain she would never be able to open her mouth in such circumstances.

Just as Fenella was about the introduce her, the

doorbell jangled and she gave Laura a worried look. 'Do you mind if I answer that? Sorry to abandon you.'

'No, not at all, I'll be fine,' said Laura, feeling anything but fine.

One young woman, who seemed somehow familiar, had looked up as Laura entered and raised her eyebrows in greeting, waving her fingers. 'Another girly,' she called across the table. 'What a relief!'

Laura hadn't ever thought of herself as a 'girly' before and found she rather liked this new status. She waved back.

'Find an empty chair,' said Fenella. 'Here, between Rupes and Johnny. They'll look after you. Rupert is my husband. Johnny is a friend. Now I must answer the door.' She hurried off, adding to the sense of bustle and busyness that filled the room.

Both men smiled in a friendly way and Rupert, in jeans and an old tweed jacket, got up and pulled out the chair for Laura. She sank on to it, wondering how soon she could go home. There was no way she could make a useful contribution at a meeting like this. She would just sit quietly and listen. Johnny, in black jeans and T-shirt with a cashmere scarf looped round his neck, poured her a glass of water and wrinkled his eyes at her in greeting. He was young and had an earring that looked to Laura very like a hearing aid. As almost everyone else apart from Fenella and Rupert, but including Laura, was wearing some sort of a suit, he seemed like welcome light relief.

'Is Hugo coming?' called Rupert as Fenella returned, followed by an attractive young woman carrying a bundle of files who apologised for being late, but oozed efficiency in spite of it.

'No. He's working.' The young woman took a seat and arranged her papers into neat piles in front of her, making eye contact with everyone.

She seemed to epitomise everything Laura was not; she was outgoing and utterly confident. She has a nice smile, Laura thought, and she can't be much older than me, but I'm still scared of her.

'Right,' said the man sitting at the head of the table, 'shall we start?'

Everyone shuffled and coughed in agreement.

'I suggest we go round the table introducing ourselves, and saying what our role is in all this,' he said. 'Fen, maybe we could have name badges?'

Fenella looked horrified for a moment until the woman who had arrived last said, 'I've got some!' She pulled out a packet. 'You will have to write on them yourselves, though,' she added. 'I couldn't do them beforehand because I wasn't sure who was coming.'

'We don't usually do meetings like this,' murmured Rupert. 'I prefer the kitchen table and a few bottles of wine.'

Johnny, to whom this aside was addressed, laughed. 'Mm. I know. I've been to a few like that.'

Rupert smiled at Laura to include her in this conversation but it didn't help much. The delay while people found pens and wrote their names postponed the moment when she'd have to introduce herself to a room full of strangers, and was very welcome. But she'd have to do it eventually, and to think up a role for herself, when she didn't think she had one.

She caught the eye of the girl who'd said hello and she made a face in solidarity. Laura raised her eyebrows back and wondered why she felt she recognised her.

'OK,' said the man at the top. 'I'm Bill Edwards, I'm going to keep us all in order. Let's go to the left.'

'Sarah Stratford,' said the woman who'd produced the badges. 'I'm here because Fen thought I'd be useful. Not sure if I will.'

'You've been useful already,' said Fenella. 'Producing name badges.'

'If we could press on,' said Bill Edwards, sitting down hard on any inclination to chat.

'Sorry,' muttered Fenella. Laura felt the man was being officious. It was Fenella's house, and her festival, she should be allowed to at least open her mouth.

'I'm Dylan Jones, representative of Alcan Industries.' He sounded as if giving presentations to hundreds of people was all in a day's work for him and he made Laura feel she should have heard of Alcan Industries, although she hadn't.

'Monica Playfair,' said the self-confessed 'girly'. 'Here to liven things up!' She made it sound as if her role was vital. She raised her eyebrows conspiratorially towards Laura who allowed herself to smile back.

'I'm Tricia Montgomery, I'm here on behalf of Eleanora Huckleby.' Tricia sounded confident and smiled at the table full of people. 'She couldn't come.'

Laura couldn't decide if she was glad Eleanora was involved or not. And why hadn't Eleanora mentioned her assistant was coming? Still, if she didn't have to work with her directly it might not be too bad. Tricia seemed a lot less daunting than her boss.

'I'm Fenella Gainsborough. Eleanora Huckleby is my aunt, and this festival was my mad idea to begin with.' Fenella said all this in a rush, as if confessing her sins at a self-help group.

'Jacob Stone,' said the man on Fenella's right. He just stated his name and didn't try and engage with his audience.

'I'm Rupert Gainsborough – also responsible for the mad idea.' Fenella smiled across at him, obviously grateful for his support.

It was her turn now. She cleared her throat and thought of Grant, egging her on. 'I'm Laura Horsley and I'm not sure why I'm here, really, but I was asked to come, so I did.' Although she knew that Grant would have been ashamed of her, she couldn't really say that Eleanora Huckleby had felt she could make a contribution.

'Johnny Animal. I'm in charge of the music side of it. Getting artists, stuff like that.'

'Stage name,' muttered Rupert.

Well, he may have a silly name and be very young but he had an air of huge confidence about him, thought Laura.

Now everyone had introduced themselves they began chatting again. Sarah dished out pads of paper; people who hadn't done so before wrote on their nametags. Bill Edwards looked around, fearing he'd lost control already, coughed and tapped his water glass.

'May I declare this meeting open?' he said.

'If you must,' muttered Johnny to Laura and she smiled.

'Now,' he said, 'we're all here?' He looked around eagerly. He obviously loved being in control of a room full of people.

Everyone nodded.

'So, can we have a report on the music side?'

Several people began to speak. Bill held up his pad and waved it until they stopped. 'Please, one at a time, and through the chair please!'

Johnny Animal looked confused for a moment and then said, 'Do you want me to tell you about the music side?'

'Yes please,' said Bill, writing hard.

Laura wondered what on earth he could be jotting down and noticed similar wonder on Sarah's face.

'Not sure how to speak through a chair, but we've got some quite big names booked – or nearly booked. It's always quite hard to get people to commit.'

'Isn't it just?' muttered Monica, who received a frown from the chairman in reply.

'So who have you got – Sorry . . .' Rupert looked at

the chairman. 'Mr Chairman, may I ask which bands have actually agreed to come?'

'The Caped Crusaders,' said Johnny. There was silence when he obviously felt there should have been applause, or at least approving murmurs. 'They appeared at Glastonbury last year?'

'Oh yes,' said a few people as their memories kicked in. Laura decided she was probably the only person there who had never been to Glastonbury. Well, her and Bill Edwards, anyway.

Johnny mentioned a few other bands and it transpired that the music side of the festival was beginning to take shape. Laura drew roses on her pad of paper, determined to apologise to Fenella as soon as possible, and say she couldn't run the literary side of the festival, not if it involved speaking through the chair at meetings like this.

'So,' said Bill Edwards when he'd filled two sides of A4 with notes and Laura had quite a pretty pergola going, 'what about the literary side?'

Fenella cleared her throat, looking anxiously at her blank pad and then at the chairman. Laura stopped doodling, feeling instantly nervous as if the question had been asked of her directly, even though she wasn't involved yet and probably wouldn't be.

'Shall I do this bit?' said Sarah, much to Laura's relief.

'Oh please do,' said Fenella, subsiding into her chair, also with obvious relief.

'As you all may or may not know, this was Fenella's idea and it's brilliant! So many people wouldn't go near a music festival but add big literary names and they'll come in droves. Think of Cheltenham, Edinburgh, Hay-on-Wye.'

'I'd rather think of Glastonbury,' muttered Johnny Animal, and received a dig in the ribs from Fenella.

'It's a huge potential market,' went on Sarah, 'but what

we need is a sponsor.' She looked round the room, smiling in a way that invited people to volunteer. 'Bill?' She looked expectantly at the chairman.

'I'm just here to keep order, as a local councillor,' he blustered. 'I'm not saying I won't get the council to sponsor an advert or a small event, but I can't spend the ratepayers' money, or at least not much of it.'

Something about Sarah's manner told Laura this didn't greatly surprise her. Sarah turned her attention to Tricia Montgomery. 'We need top-class authors, to attract a lot of people.'

Laura remained silent, taking it all in. If they had Tricia's expertise and Fenella in charge surely they wouldn't need her, she reasoned.

'I'll do my best, of course,' said Tricia. 'As a top-class agent' – she made a face – 'Eleanora does have all the right contacts. She could probably get Damien Stubbs to come and Amanda Jaegar—'

'Who?' asked the chairman, speaking on behalf of many.

'Shortlisted for the Orange,' said Laura automatically, forgetting she didn't want to draw attention to herself but she just couldn't help it. They were on her territory after all. 'Should have won it last year, lots of people felt.'

Tricia smiled at her. 'And Eleanora felt . . . we were rather hoping that Laura here would be able to get us authors we can't lean on.'

Laura dropped her pencil in panic when she realised everyone was looking at her and cursed herself for piping up about Amanda Jaegar. That was what happened if you were a know-all. 'I'm really not sure . . .' she said. 'I mean . . . I have no experience—'

Sarah interrupted her smoothly. 'Shall we just discuss what we'd like, who we'd like, give ourselves a dream scenario and then see how near we can get to that?'

'She's a wedding planner in her day job,' muttered Rupert.

'She seems very efficient,' said Laura, thinking with relief that with Sarah on board, she really wasn't really necessary. She could make her excuses and leave. They'd manage just fine without her.

The discussion went on, not really achieving anything until Fenella got to her feet. 'Right! Teatime! Down to the kitchen everyone. I've got sandwiches and cake and scones and it's all got to be eaten.'

There was a moment's 'politesse' and 'this meeting is adjourned' from Bill and then a stampede. Laura found herself next to Monica on the stairs.

'Boring or what!' Monica said. 'I think it'll be great when it actually happens but until then – God!'

'It's weird, but I really think I recognise you,' said Laura. 'Are you on telly?'

'Not often. I'm in a band.'

'Oh!' squeaked Laura. 'Now I know why I recognise you, only you haven't got pink hair! I've seen you on stage! You were brilliant!'

'Where did you see us?'

Laura told her about the venue. 'Just a couple of nights ago. I loved it!'

'Oh great! Nice to meet a fan. We're appearing at this festival. Johnny got me in. Something a bit different for the punters. And I said I'd help out too if they needed me.'

'Maybe you could do something in the literary bit as well. You know, someone – an actor – reading a bit of a book and your band singing an appropriate song.' Then Laura remembered she wasn't going to have anything to do with the festival and therefore shouldn't have ideas. Although she had to admit she was beginning to feel getting involved might not be such an impossible thought after all.

'Great!' said Monica. 'That sounds cool! Something like Philip Marlowe would be fab! We could do a really sleazy, smoky number to go with it. We could have fake smoke to get the nightclub atmosphere.'

It did sound rather good, but as they had reached the ground floor and the stairs to the kitchen were too narrow to chat on, Laura didn't feel obliged to explain she wasn't the one to talk to about it.

Fenella, or someone, had put on a wonderful old-fashioned spread, in the best traditions of cricket clubs, the WI – in fact, anywhere where sandwiches and cake might be comforting. There was an urn providing tea and a big jug of coffee.

'This is amazing!' said Laura when she found herself next to Fenella. 'I thought I might get a stale Rich Tea if I was lucky.'

'When I've got lots of people coming, I like to barricade myself in with food. I didn't make all this, though, only a few of the cakes. The dogs will eat anything that's left over. I've shut them all away, because of the meeting.'

Johnny spoke with his mouth full, holding a laden plate. 'If I have my way, the dogs won't get anything. If you weren't married already—'

'I wouldn't marry you, but thank you for the offer,' said Fenella, laughing.

Tricia Montgomery joined the little group that was forming next to the Aga, away from the table. 'Eleanora tells me you've read everything, and that you put on a fantastic reading for Damien,' she said to Laura. 'I wonder if he would come? He likes literary festivals.'

'That would be brilliant,' said Fenella, scribbling on a napkin. 'What's his surname?'

'Stubbs,' supplied Tricia. 'But Eleanora was really impressed with you, Laura. She said she'd never met anyone so well read, so young.'

'Oh well . . .'

Her self-deprecation was ignored. 'It's not often someone who works in a bookshop has such a wide knowledge of contemporary literature,' went on Tricia, to Laura's huge embarrassment.

'Oh,' said Fenella, 'I don't get nearly enough time to read but what do you think of Anita Dubrovnik? I know she's the novelist of the moment – like every other book group in the country, we're reading her latest.' She paused. 'And I know I won't have time to finish it.'

Laura laughed. 'I run a book group at the shop and I always tell people they should come even if they haven't read it. They can often ask questions that really get the discussion going.'

'I don't think I can trade on that for ever,' said Fenella. 'So? Could I have a cheat's guide?'

Laura found herself giving potted reviews of all the latest bestsellers and, unusually for her, content to be the centre of attention. It must be the relaxed atmosphere of the kitchen, she thought, away from all that forced formality upstairs.

Jacob Stone, who hadn't really opened his mouth up to this point, came over to their group. He was short and stocky but had presence. People seemed to listen when he spoke, and as he didn't, often, it made an impact when he did. Now, holding his mug of tea and with a piece of cake in his other hand, he said, 'Do you know Dermot Flynn?'

'Oh yes!' said Laura, genuinely keen. 'He's brilliant. He was—'

'Get him to the festival and I'll sponsor it – however much money you'll need,' said Jacob Stone, cutting through her rush of enthusiasm.

Laura swallowed, her mouth suddenly dry. This man thought she actually knew him. He was possibly her favourite writer, ever, but she didn't actually know him, any more than she actually knew Shakespeare, however many essays she'd written about him. She had to explain. 'Um—'

'Oh, that would be marvellous!' said Fenella, not noticing this small interjection. 'I can't tell you how grateful we'd be. Basically we can't do this without a sponsor and – well, it's hard to get them,' she added, suddenly looking a little sheepish.

'And I was the only millionaire you knew?' said Jacob Stone.

'Yes, frankly, but we'd be terribly thrilled—'

'If Dermot Flynn is there, I'll be proud to support it.'

'But—' Laura tried to break in. Now everyone seemed to think she knew him. She had to put a stop to this. 'I don't—'

'He's one of Eleanora's. Utterly charming but almost impossible to manage.' Tricia Montgomery had the look of someone who really wanted to be outside smoking a cigarette. 'You won't get him to the festival unless he really wants to come.'

'I didn't mean I knew him as a person,' said Laura, getting her word in at last. 'I meant I know his work. I studied him at university and think he's utterly brilliant.'

'Oh he is!' agreed Tricia. 'But he's an *enfant terrible*. As I said, can't be managed and we think he's setting a record for lateness on his latest book. It's *years* past its deadline.'

'As I said, I want him here,' said Jacob Stone, his tone brooking no argument. 'And without being mean, if he's not, you'll have to find another sponsor.' Then he turned and walked away.

Everyone inhaled at once and then they all started talking at Laura who wanted to put her hands up to her face and hide. She managed to keep from doing so by sheer effort of will.

'If you could get him, it would be such a coup,' said Tricia. 'Every opinion-former in the literary world will come. I know there will be lots of other writers but no one's seen him for years. It would be amazing.'

'Oh please, Laura! I beg you! Do try and get him! We need the money. God knows who we'll get to be a sponsor if Jacob Stone doesn't cough up!' said Fenella. 'We wouldn't have approached him if we'd had a choice, he's so eccentric.' She turned to Laura, slightly accusing. 'You said you know him!'

Had no one been listening to her? she thought with frustration. 'I know his work! Like Shakespeare!' she squeaked.

'Now that really would be a coup,' said Rupert, winking at Laura, 'getting Shakespeare along.' He put a fairy cake into her hand.

'Isn't he supposed to be rather gorgeous?' said Monica.

'Who, Shakespeare?' asked Fenella.

'No! Dermot Flynn!' said Monica.

They all regarded Laura, as the official Dermot Flynn expert. 'He was when he was young, going by the pictures,' Laura admitted, wondering if people would stop expecting things from her if she stuffed the cake into her mouth whole.

'And Eleanora told me he's doing a little festival in Ireland at a place called Ballyfitzpatrick,' said Tricia, taking a fairy cake from Rupert and unpeeling the paper.

'Oh,' said Monica, sounding surprised.

'I think he lives there,' Tricia explained. 'And I don't think it's really literary, just some people who are friends who've got together to put something on,' she went on and then bit into her cake.

Laura saw her way out. 'Oh well then, you just need to get Eleanora to ask him to come to this one. It'll be small and friendly, he's bound to say yes.' She passed the buck with both hands.

Tricia gave a hollow laugh. 'But how to get in touch with the man? He doesn't open letters, or email, or answer

43

his phone, or ring back. I told you, he's an absolute nightmare!'

'So how did you find out he was doing this festival?' asked Monica. 'If he doesn't communicate?'

'Eleanora was looking for something else and it came up on the Internet. It's Irish music, poetry, food, stuff like that.'

'It sounds great!' said Monica, full of enthusiasm. 'But who has a literary festival in winter?'

Fenella ignored her protest as she addressed Laura. 'You'll just have to go there and ask him to come here,' she said. 'If that's the only way we'll get him.'

'Fab idea!' said Monica. 'I'll come with you. We'll have a great time!'

Just for a second, Laura was tempted. Monica was such fun, her confidence and zest for life were infectious. And it was her singing that had made Laura do some serious thinking. For whatever reason, she felt a bond. Then she got a grip on reality. 'You don't seem to under-stand—'

'But you've arranged loads of literary events at your bookshop?' said Fenella, sounding indignant.

'Yes,' Laura tried to explain, 'but when I did that, I wrote polite letters via the publisher or agent. It was the publicity department who decided whether or not they came and when they came. It was all down to them. I didn't have to visit the writers in person!' She turned to Tricia for support, feeling things rapidly sliding out of her control again. 'Who are his publishers? Get them to ask him.'

'He's been out of contract for years, and if he doesn't respond to Eleanora, who's a tough cookie, believe me, he wouldn't take any notice of the publicity department.'

'That's my aunt you're talking about,' said Fenella, 'but you're right, she's very tough.'

'So you need to go to Ireland and bring him back,'

said Monica. 'Like a Canadian Mountie who always gets his man.'

The ridiculousness of the situation got to Laura and she started to giggle. 'I'm not a Mountie, or even a Labrador. I don't do fetching.'

'But it would be such fun!' went on Monica, laughing too. 'I'll come with you! It'll be a riot!'

Fenella seemed to sense Laura teetering; going anywhere with Monica would definitely be different. 'Oh God, thank you so much!' Shamelessly, she played the guilt card. 'I can't tell you how much this means to me. And we'll obviously pay for you to get there . . .'

'But supposing I go and he refuses to come?' Although still chuckling, Laura was feeling the pressure badly.

'At least you'll have done your best,' said Tricia.

Monica struck an attitude. 'Good God, girl! Do you think he'll be able to resist? Irish men are all awful womanisers. He'll be made up to do anything for us!'

'Just say you'll give it a go,' said Tricia. 'Maybe Jacob Stone would still sponsor the festival if you've done your absolute best.'

Fenella shook her head. 'Don't think so. He's a man who means what he says.'

'How did he get to be a millionaire?' asked Tricia, which pleased Laura because she didn't like to ask herself but really wanted to know. She was glad, too, that the conversation had finally veered away from her.

'Industrial diamonds,' said Fenella. 'And he's just as hard.'

'So how did you get him to come to the meeting?' Tricia was obviously intrigued.

'Well, he's connected to Rupert's family in some way and although he didn't go to university himself or anything, he's a great fan of literature. Reads the entire Man Booker shortlist every year, stuff like that. He was the natural choice when we were looking for a sponsor.'

45

She turned her gaze on Laura. 'Which is why it's so important you get Daniel O'Flaherty or whoever it was.'

'Dermot Flynn,' said Laura and sighed.

Monica had decided. 'We'll go to Ireland and get him.' She paused, looking at Laura. 'I'll give you free tickets to our next gig if you agree.'

Laura regarded Monica thoughtfully. The tickets would be a good present for Grant, and she owed him something for lending her his car. 'So why are you so keen?'

'I really want to go.' She paused. 'I've got a bit of unfinished business over there.' She hooked her arm into Laura's in a friendly way. 'And it'll be fun, for feck's sake!'

Everyone laughed as she broke into an Irish accent.

Laura felt she'd fought her hardest and could fight no more. She put her hands up in surrender. 'OK, I'll do my best. But I'm not making any promises.'

Fenella leant forward and hugged her. 'You're a star! Thank you so much! I'll get Jacob Stone to pay for your fares.'

'A free holiday in January,' said Laura. 'In Ireland. How can I resist?'

Chapter Four

'It's awfully kind of you to come with me,' said Laura
to Monica as they waited in her Volkswagen Beetle – a
car she declared suited her image as a singer in a forties
band – to get on the ferry. 'Especially at this godforsaken
hour.'

It was half past two in the morning and they were
very tired.

'It means we can drive in daylight the other side,' said
Monica. 'And I wanted to come. You'd never have gone
on your own even if you could have got there and I told
you, I have my own reasons for going. Besides . . .'
Monica paused. She frowned a little as if thinking how
best to express her thoughts. 'There's something about
you I like. I think if you came out of your shell a bit you
could be jolly good fun.'

Laura laughed. 'Some people think I'm quite fun in my
shell.' Grant was probably the only one who qualified,
even if he was also trying to get her out of it, but she felt
she ought to protest a bit about Monica's backhanded
compliment.

'I'm sure, but I think you'd be a lot more fun if
you mentally came out from behind the counter of a
bookshop.'

'Have you been talking to my friend Grant?' she asked
suspiciously.

Monica laughed. 'No. I haven't met him yet.' A man
came out of the shadows and beckoned them forward.
'Thank goodness, it's our turn now. I hope they don't

put us on a shelf somewhere. Technically called the swing decks.' She moved the car gently forward.

'How do you know so much about ferries?' asked Laura, glad she didn't have to plunge the car into Stygian gloom and interpret the hand signals of men wearing fluorescent jackets walking backwards at speed.

'I used to drive the band round in an old van,' said Monica, coming to halt at the end of a chain of vehicles. 'Ferries are no problem.'

Fenella had insisted that they booked a cabin, even if only for a very short time. Jacob Stone was paying, after all, and he could afford it. Whether or not he would demand his money back if they returned empty-handed, so to speak, had yet to be discovered.

'We'll think of something to tell him when we meet up for our first proper meeting,' Fenella had said casually. 'As long as you try your best, it won't be a problem.' Then her insouciance had left her. 'You do realise we have to get Dermot Flynn to confirm as soon as possible? Otherwise we'll have to find not only another literary superstar but another sponsor, and God knows where we'll find one of those.'

Laura had nodded. 'We can only do our best but we will do that, I promise. But if I can't get time off work, Monica will have to go on her own.'

However, she was not going to get out of it that easily. Henry practically pushed her out of the door.

'It's a quiet time after Christmas and I can always give Brenda a few more hours if we're busy.'

With that excuse not to go denied her, she went to see her parents, feeling it was time they knew about her imminent redundancy. She and Grant discussed the visit before she set off. This was one of the things that bonded them: Grant's aunt had never heard of homosexuals and Laura's parents still berated her for going to university, getting a good degree and ending up working in a shop. The fact that it was a bookshop made no difference.

'Still, we've got our night out to look forward to,' said Grant, who had once brought Laura home to meet his aunt so he could appear to have a girlfriend.

'Yes, and my mother will send me home with a fruit cake because in her heart she thinks I'm still a student.'

'Hmm. I might have overdosed on fruit cake over Christmas, but bring it anyway.'

Her parents greeted her in their usual understated way. They were pleased to see her, but her monthly visits did disrupt their routine rather.

'Hello, dear,' said her mother, kissing her. 'Supper won't be long. You go and watch the news with your father and I'll call you when it's ready.'

'I'll set the table for you, Mum,' said Laura, feeling a wave of love for her mother. She might often feel like a cuckoo in the nest, but she knew her mother had done her absolute best for her. It wasn't anyone's fault that Laura had always been so different from her parents.

'You don't mind eating in the kitchen, do you?'

As she filled a glass jug with water Laura wondered why on earth her mother might think she'd mind. It was a 'kitchen-diner' and they always ate there.

'I hope I'm not so much a guest as you feel we should eat in the dining room.' Laura found the place mats in the drawer and distributed them.

'Well, we don't see you all that often.'

'I know and I'm sorry, but it's not always easy for me to get here.'

Her mother pursed her lips. 'I'm sure you could get a job in a bookshop a bit nearer home.'

'Well, yes. Actually I've got a bit of news. But I think I'll wait until Dad's here – save me going over it all twice.'

'I can't believe you're gallivanting off to Ireland when

49

you should be looking for another job!' her father had declared a little later, putting down his knife and fork to lend emphasis to his words.

'This literary festival could be a great opportunity,' Laura said quietly. 'You've always said I was wasted working in a bookshop. They were impressed by my knowledge of contemporary literature.'

This only set her father off on a familiar rant about English degrees and a 'knowledge of contemporary literature' being a complete waste of time. Her mother hadn't been too thrilled by it all either. Laura had left as soon as she possibly could, glad she'd arranged to meet up with Grant later.

Grant loyally took the opportunity to reiterate what a chance this was for her.

'You need to spread your wings, have new experiences! I know you think you just want to find another bookshop, just like Henry's, and bury yourself in it for ever, but you mustn't! You must follow your dreams! Which are?' he added, to check she actually had some.

Laura took a breath. 'Well, I've always wanted to work for a publisher really, as an editor. I don't suppose this festival is going lead to anything like that, but it has opened my eyes to other book-related opportunities.'

'Fantastic! Let's have another Baileys to celebrate.'

Thus, just over a week later, Laura and Monica found themselves on a ferry to Ireland.

Monica and Laura were now sitting in a café in the little fishing village on the west coast of Ireland that was the venue for the 'Festival of Culture' they had come to see. They'd been travelling, give or take a few stops, some hours in a ferry and a catnap in a lay-by, for approximately nineteen hours.

'I don't think I'll ever eat again,' said Monica, looking at her empty plate with disbelief.

'Well, we won't need to eat this evening, that's for sure,' said Laura. 'Now I know what the difference between an English breakfast – high tea, whatever – and an Irish one is: size.'

'And those scrummy potato pancakes.'

'And the black and white pudding.'

They both leant back in their chairs and drained their mugs of strong tea, sighing with pleasure and feeling a little more human again.

'I never thought we'd get here,' said Laura. 'It feels as if we've been travelling for days.' She yawned. 'I'd only just got off to sleep when it was time to get up again.'

Monica was dismissive. 'At least it wasn't rough, and I think the time in the bar got me in the mood for Ireland, all that singing, fiddle-playing and the drum thing. And sleeping together has made us practically best friends.'

Laura laughed sleepily. 'Mm.'

'Being on the road together really does bond you.'

Laura nodded agreement. 'We could make a movie.'

Monica was right, they had got to know each other very well, and luckily, the more they discovered, the more they bonded. They'd been up half the night chatting too. She yawned widely. 'I think we should check into the bed and breakfast and have a nap.'

'Then we'll fall asleep for hours, wake up at midnight and not be able to get off again. I know, I've done that. No fun at all.'

'OK, let's check in, then go for a walk or something.'

'Actually,' said Monica. 'I wouldn't mind getting the car checked out. Its steering has gone a bit funny. It probably would be all right, but if there is a garage it would be silly not to have it looked at.'

'Oh goodness! Of course you must get it checked out. Will there be a garage here that can deal with antique cars, though?'

'Of course. It's not that old. I'm sure there's nothing

much wrong with it. I'm just a bit nervous about breaking down far from home. We had some grisly times in the van, I can tell you.'

'I can imagine,' said Laura, slightly relieved that Monica, who seemed so well travelled and super-calm, had some normal neuroses.

'The bed-and-breakfast people will know,' said Monica.

'I hope it won't take us too long to find it,' said Laura.

'Oh come on,' said Monica. 'How hard will it be to find in a place this size? It's tiny!'

'I know. I can't make out why they're having the festival based here, and not in the town five miles up the road. And why is it so popular we could hardly find a place to rest our heads?' Resting her head was a high priority at the moment.

'Perhaps it's that writer the sponsor is so keen on. Maybe he's bringing them in in busloads.'

Laura shrugged. 'Well, we certainly travelled quite a way to come and see him, although we do have an ulterior motive. But it is a charming place, isn't it?'

They looked around at the brightly painted houses, the cars parked all higgledy-piggledy and the fishing boats tied up in the harbour. It wasn't conventionally pretty, but it had great character.

'Mm,' agreed Monica, 'and if it has a garage I'll think it's even more charming. Let's get going!'

As Monica predicted, the bed and breakfast was not hard to find. It was a bungalow, tucked behind a hedge to shield it from the road, not that there was any traffic of note. The landlady was one of those useful people who imparted information without you having to ask for it.

'Good afternoon girls, I'm Marion,' she said cheerily. 'Come in, come in. Would you like a cup of tea now? Come into the kitchen. You're here for the festival? I expect you're wondering why we have it in January.'

She paused for breath. 'Fact is, the place is heaving in summer. It's a real tourist spot, but there's nothing going on in the winter, so they thought they'd have a festival of some kind in Patricktown – you know? Up the road?'

Laura and Monica nodded and took seats at the big wooden table.

'Well – is it builders' tea you like? Or I've got Earl Grey, Lady Grey, any amount of herbals, White tipped China—'

'Builders' tea please,' they said in unison.

'But Himself said – that's your great writer man, Dermot Flynn – he said he wouldn't go to a festival he had to travel five miles to, and so they have it here. It's grand for business. Now, have you had tea – I mean proper tea, not just a cup of tea in your hand?'

'Yes, we had an all-day breakfast at the café.'

'He would have given you a grand big Full Irish, didn't he?'

'He did, only we saw a girl.'

'Oh yes. She's my niece. A lovely girl.'

Accompanied by constant, amiable chat, the girls were escorted to their room. It was, Monica declared, a picture.

'I've never seen anything so fantastically kitsch in my life! It's a fairy palace!' she said once their landlady was safely out of earshot.

'And all in mauve,' agreed Laura, slightly less enthralled. 'I don't think there's anything that could take another purple frill if its life depended on it.'

Monica bounced on one of the single beds. 'Comfy. What's the bathroom like?'

'Mauve,' said Laura, peering into a little room adjacent to theirs. 'Even the loo paper is mauve. But it seems to have everything, including a bath.'

Her yearning for one must have been audible because Monica said, 'Why don't you sink into it while I sort the car out? Then we can either go out or just stay in and watch television.'

By the time Monica came back the television was watching itself with Laura lying on top of one of the twin beds in a mauve towelling robe, fast asleep.

'There's nothing like an early night for making you feel like exercise!' said Monica, sounding uncharacteristically Brown Owl-ish.

Laura sipped the tea Monica had brought to her bed. 'So you didn't wake up at one in the morning then?'

'Nope. And the sun is shining, and as the days are so short, we should get out there and enjoy it!'

'Did you manage to get your car sorted?'

'Yup! A sweet man is going to sort it out today. It won't be ready until tomorrow but I've had a brilliant idea how to spend our time.'

Laura hadn't known Monica particularly long but she saw Ulterior Motive written all over her. 'How?'

'While I was finding the garage I passed a bike-hire place. They don't get much custom in the winter so they've let me have two at a bargain rate.'

'Bicycles.'

'Yes!'

'Did you notice that we came down a long hill to the village? Wherever we went would involve a long hill up.'

'It's good exercise.'

Laura hid her smile behind another sip of tea. She'd find out what the ulterior motive was soon enough. 'OK then.' Knowing Monica as she felt she now did, Laura suspected it was a man.

'Anywhere particular you want to go on your bike, Mon?' she said a couple of hours later, when, full of Irish breakfast, including several pints of tea, they pushed their bikes up the hill, out of the village.

The bike-hire place had given them a map, helmets and reflective clothing, none of which were particularly attractive but though all very practical. The map was rather creased but Monica had inspected it closely before they set off.

Monica didn't answer. 'The trick when you're cycling is to calculate the distance at about two miles an hour and then multiply by three. It usually works out about right if you add half an hour.'

'I haven't ridden a bike for years.'

'That's fine. You never forget how to ride a bicycle,' said Monica. 'It's just like—'

'Don't tell me,' grumbled Laura as she clambered on to the saddle, 'riding a bicycle.' She pushed on the pedals and moved forward a few feet, wobbling slightly. 'I'm not sure I'm going to be able to cope with the hills.'

'You'll be fine.'

'I will be if you tell me what you're up to. I'm not expiring with a heart attack without knowing why.'

Monica allowed herself to pant for a few seconds. 'One of the reasons I was so keen that we should come to this little hole in the hedge was because it's bang next door – well, a bike ride away – to another little hole in the hedge I really want to visit.'

'Because of a man,' Laura stated.

'Did I tell you that or did you just guess?'

'We may only have been best friends for quite a short time but I think I know you well enough to work that one out.'

Monica tried to look offended, but not very hard.

They stopped talking while they climbed a few more yards. When it flattened out a bit and Laura had more breath to spare she said, 'You did give me a bit of a clue. You said you had unfinished business at the meeting.'

'Did I? Well, yes, and he's called Seamus. He's a real doll. I met him at a gig last year. We exchanged emails and postcards for a while and then I just stopped hearing. I want to find out what's happened to him.'

For all her efficiency and practical nature, Laura had a strongly romantic streak. She may not have had much of a love life herself but she'd read a lot of romantic fiction at an impressionable age. 'So were you really in love with him?'

'No, not that. Obsessed, probably. He was tall and dark with blue eyes.' Monica's halted her bicycle for a minute so she could think better. 'Let's just say he's on my To Do list.'

'How do you mean?' Laura was confused. She was beginning to perspire and she wondered if it was affecting her brain.

Monica shrugged. 'Well, you know.' She paused and checked out her friend who was a few feet behind her. 'Haven't you a To Do list?'

'Frequently, but it doesn't have men on it.'

'Doesn't it? Mine's only got men on it.'

Laura felt suddenly envious. Not for Monica the mundane 'washing', 'ring home', 'buy loo cleaner' type of list that kept her life on track. Hers probably started with George Clooney and worked its way down through Harrison Ford to Jeremy Clarkson. 'But you're not in love?'

The idea was obviously ridiculous. Monica laughed. 'What is it with you and love? No! I want to find out if he's as good in bed as he looks. Laura, why are you looking at me like that? Have you never fancied the pants off anyone?'

'No,' she panted. 'Not really.' She took a little run up the hill, trying to catch up with Monica who was taller and obviously a lot fitter.

'What, never? I just couldn't sleep with anyone I didn't really lust after.'

There was a tiny pause before Laura said, 'Nor could I.'

Monica pressed on cheerfully. 'That's all right then. But I don't think it's right to sleep with someone just because they're there, or you need a lift home or something.'

'I wouldn't know,' Laura muttered. 'I'm a . . .'

'Hang on.' Monica stopped suddenly and turned round. 'Are you telling me what I think you are?'

'I don't know. I hope not.' Laura was panting when she came level with her friend and regretting her momentary need to confess something she wasn't exactly ashamed of, but did make her a bit unusual and possibly strange. Monica was looking at her curiously.

'When you say you wouldn't know, does that . . . Are you – a virgin? I mean – have you never gone to bed with a man?'

'I do know what being a virgin means.'

'And are you one?'

Monica didn't seem to be judging her. 'Yes,' Laura admitted, embarrassed. It wasn't so much that it was wrong to be a virgin but it was odd. She wiped her brow, so she didn't have to see Monica staring at her.

'How old are you?' Monica wasn't staring but she did seem curious.

'Twenty-six.'

'Wow!' said Monica, impressed. 'And you've waited this long!'

'I wasn't waiting, it just didn't happen.'

'Well, I think it's sweet,' said Monica after a pause. 'Weird but sweet.'

She set off up the hill again and Laura fell in beside her. 'It's no big deal,' said Laura. 'But I do think it would have to be the right person for me.'

'Of course,' said Monica uncertainly. 'I think it's lovely that you don't just sleep around like I do.'

'Do you?' Monica was obviously what her father would

57

describe as a 'goer' but she didn't appear to lack the normal morals, either.

Monica shrugged. 'Well, not really, but I don't hold back, if you know what I mean. I'm always very careful, always use a condom, make sure I like the guy a bit, and it's not only that I want to get into his pants.' She paused. 'But your way is better, I'm sure.'

'It wasn't a deliberate policy.'

Monica was thoughtful. 'Or maybe you could do a lot worse than sleep with a friend, sort of get it over with.'

Laura shook her head. 'I'm not being precious about it, but being a virgin doesn't really interfere with my life. Besides, my best friend is gay.'

'Oh, Grant? Well, maybe you'll meet some other nice man who'd be nice and safe to do it with.'

'Maybe,' said Laura. But however weird still being a virgin made her feel she didn't think she'd want to deal with the matter so pragmatically. It had just sort of happened that way and she'd never felt the need to get rid of it just for the sake of it, like a outmoded piece of furniture.

Laura walked most of the three miles to the little village they were heading for, but she was looking forward to being able to coast all the way back down to Ballyfitzpatrick. It had been a long time since she'd taken so much exercise but in spite of being aware of her unfit state she was enjoying the sensation of all her muscles working and felt exhilarated and energised.

'You must admit, the views are absolutely stunning!' said Monica, who was used to cycling and, unlike Laura, panting only slightly.

'Oh yes, it's amazing.'

They were standing on a cliff, gazing out to sea, re-gathering their energy before going to hunt out Monica's Lust Object. The sun sparkled like diamonds on the little waves. The sky was pale blue and seemed to glint with potential frost. The grass on the clifftop was close-cropped, green still, although it was winter. Behind them was a row of whitewashed cottages. When Monica had stopped sweating, the plan was that they were going to knock on the door of her potential lover. Laura was planning to stay and enjoy the view but she hadn't told Monica that yet. She wasn't sure how'd she'd take it.

'Actually,' said Laura. 'I might lie down.'

She did and it was wonderful. Her long walk uphill had made her warm and the sun on her cold face made her think of summer. Maybe this trip wasn't a wild-goose chase, and if it was, maybe it was fine just to have fun. Grant was always saying she took life too seriously. Well, maybe she'd stop doing that and just go along for the ride. Although maybe he wouldn't appreciate arranging cover for her absence from the bookshop just for her to have a little winter sun.

Monica lay down next to her. 'Oh, this is rather blissful, isn't it? If I told the girls in the band that I'd spent half a week lying on a clifftop in Ireland, in January, they'd think I was mad.'

Laura chuckled, watching a bird cross the sky through half-closed lids. 'Don't you think they know that already?'

'Mm, probably.'

'It's funny, all the people I know think I'm incredibly sensible, except for my parents, of course,' said Laura sleepily. 'You should have heard my father when I told him I was coming to Ireland. He thought I should spend any time off I had looking for another job.'

'Well, you are in a way. The festival is another job.'

'Hm. Not exactly well paid.'

'I'm not being paid at all. Although I don't mind. They're giving the Sisters of Swing a really good spot at the music festival and this –' she indicated the crisp winter day around them '– is just a jolly.'

59

'I don't think my parents would ever understand the concept of "a jolly".'

'Jaysus, they should be grateful you've got a job and aren't living off "the burroo".'

'You've got very Irish all of sudden. What the hell are you talking about?'

'It's what they used to call benefits over here. A man on the ferry told me. And I'm practising. I may go home with a leprechaun.'

Laura chuckled. 'Personally I prefer my men a little taller.'

'Huh! I didn't think beggars could be choosers!'

'I'm not a beggar, I'm just looking for Mr Right.'

'Big mistake. Mr Right Now is far better. Take it from one who knows.'

Laura laughed. There was something about lying on one's back in the sunshine that made one inclined to laughter, she discovered. When Monica finally decided she no longer looked like a scarlet woman in all the wrong ways, she ordered them both to their feet. Laura had forgotten about leaving Monica to her embarrassing errand, and got up. They brushed bits of grass off each other's backs, picked up their bikes, and headed on into the village.

The village was postcard pretty, with its whitewashed cottages around the cove. Not for this village the garish colours of Ballyfitzpatrick – here there must have been rules, but the effect was delightful. Even in January it looked like the perfect holiday destination. The cottages were no longer thatched and the boats in the harbour were all modern but there was a man sitting mending nets in the sunshine.

'They pay him to look picturesque,' said Monica.

'He does his job very well,' said Laura. 'He looks perfect.'

'And if we can't find Cove Road, we can ask him, but

I think it's all Cove Road, so it's just a case of finding the right house.'

It was surprisingly straightforward, only, on the doorstep, the ridiculousness of the whole thing hit Laura and she got the giggles. 'Oh God, Monica, I'm so sorry, I can't do this. You'll have to do it on your own.' She could hardly speak. 'It's just so silly! We've ridden bikes, for goodness' sake, to meet a man who may not even live here. We're grown women, not thirteen-year-olds!' She went off into another fit of laughter and crossed her legs, just in case.

'Really, Laura, I thought you were the sensible one of us! I'm flighty, you're sensible: those are our roles. We must stick to them.'

'I'm sorry,' Laura spluttered. 'I just can't knock on the door and say, "Can Seamus come out to play?" I just can't! And I can't stand behind you while you do it.' She swallowed, took a deep breath and got a grip at last. 'Tell you what, we'll get the bikes out of sight at least. I'll look after them, and you can do this on your own.'

'Don't be silly!' Monica was indignant. 'How sad will that make me look?'

'Not much sadder than if we're both here, me giggling and both of us holding bicycles as if we're kids from school. What are you going to say anyway? "We were passing so we thought we'd drop by?"'

Monica humphed in irritation. 'Well, why not? It's true!'

'No it's not. We cycled bloody miles, we were not "just passing".' She sniffed, found a bit of old tissue, blew her nose and then said, 'But I've stopped giggling now, so go ahead, look a fool. I'll look one with you.'

'Thanks, Laura, you're a good girl.'

Monica lifted the knocker and banged hard. There was no answer. 'Well, now what do we do?' she said after a minute and another knock.

'Write your mobile number on a bit of paper and post it through the letterbox. Although you may have to write a short essay reminding him who you are,' said Laura.

'Not at all! He'll remember exactly who I am, but the mobile number's a good idea. Oh, do you think it'll work in Ireland?'

'Mine did. I phoned the shop while you were in the Ladies.'

'Don't you mean *Mna*?'

'Oh, shut up and write your note. I want to get back to the b. and b. I may need a bit of a lie-down before tonight.'

She was briefly aware of a flutter of anxiety and then dismissed it. She was enjoying herself and didn't want any nerves about the coming evening to spoil this delicious feeling of freedom.

'Lightweight,' muttered Monica, writing.

Laura's giggliness continued for the journey home even though she was now exhausted.

'I'll never ride a bike again,' she said as they finally made it back to the b. and b. 'In fact, I don't suppose I'll ever sit down again comfortably.'

'Shut up moaning. It was downhill all the way.'

Their landlady provided a huge plate of sandwiches with a monster teapot full of strong tea. They ate every scrap and drained the pot. The sandwiches were followed by two sorts of cake, both home-made, both utterly delicious.

'I can't believe we ate all that!' said Laura as they tottered from the dining room back to their room. 'I'm going to need some indigestion tablets or something.'

'Good idea,' said Monica. 'Top tip: before a big night out, take a Zantac, stops you throwing up afterwards.'

Laura paused, her hand on the bedroom door. 'We're not having a big night out, Monica,' she said. 'We're going to worship at the feet of a great writer and persuade him to come to our literary festival. Throwing up is not on the To Do list.'

Monica laughed, obviously not convinced. But now it was nearly upon her, Laura suddenly felt the weight of responsibility for securing Dermot Flynn. It was her mission. She so wanted to make a success of this project. Helping with the literature festival was her first foray outside the bookshop since she'd left university. If she failed she'd feel less able to attempt any other new challenges. And she had personal reasons for wanting to meet Dermot Flynn and get him to the festival: he was her favourite living writer. How would she feel if he was a complete show-off, happy to rest on his early laurels? Seeing a man in the flesh you'd worshipped through his writing for years was a risky business!

After much discussion, the girls had decided to dress down, in jeans and sweaters. Monica added a cashmere pashmina for warmth for the walk to the venue, Laura a cheery but unstylish scarf an aunt had given her for Christmas one year.

The event, as Laura called it, or the gig, as Monica referred to it, was in the only large building in the village and any doubt they might have had about finding it was dispersed by the streams of people making their way to it, many of them clearly coming from the pub.

'I can't believe how many people are going!' said Laura, daunted. 'It would be amazing if we could get a crowd like this for him in England. If so many people come this far to see him, imagine how many might come if he was on the mainland.'

'Absolutely! Not all these people can be locals.'

But then pessimism descended. 'But if he won't do an event practically next door, he's not going to come to our festival, is he? Even if I can get near enough to ask him.'

'Don't give up! And you want to see him anyway, don't you?'

Laura agreed that she did. She had butterflies in her stomach at the prospect although they weren't all good ones. She had so loved his books – there were only two of them – at university that she had practically learnt them by heart. And the author photograph in the back was stunning: a mean and moody young man in a black T-shirt. While her contemporaries were in love with band members, Laura used to gaze at the photo of Dermot Flynn.

The trouble was, that was years ago, and the photo hadn't been new then. She still loved the books and felt that in them was some of the tenderest, most erotic writing she had ever read, before or since. What she was dreading was that her hero had turned into a fat and balding has-been, trading on the bright young talent he once had.

Still, she thought as she and Monica joined the throng, if this had happened, it would be sad, but not heart-breaking. What was slightly more desperate was the fact that he wouldn't move out of his home village; she'd have to go back to England empty-handed, so to speak.

Their tickets were unnumbered, and Laura was resigned to standing at the back behind umpteen other people, but Monica was an old hand at gigs with standing room only, and wriggled and wheedled her way to the front, Laura following, embarrassed and apologising as she went.

They found a spot near the stage and although they had to stand, they could at least lean against the book table that had been set up.

'What time is he due on?' asked Monica.

'About ten minutes ago,' said Laura. 'He's late.'

'Oh, don't be saying your man is late,' said a friendly

man who was leaning on the same table. 'I'll get us all a drink to pass the time with.'

'Oh no—'

'Yes please,' said Monica firmly. 'That would be lovely.'

'And what will you have?'

'Better stick to shorts,' advised Monica. 'We'll never get to the loos.'

'I'll be right back,' said the man, and began shouldering his way against the tide of people to the bar.

'We don't know what we're getting,' said Laura.

'That's the joy of travel,' said Monica. 'Surprises.'

'I think I'm getting the hang of it at last,' said Laura ruefully. 'I've led such a sheltered life.'

The man handed each girl a glass of brown liquid. Laura took hers wondering if they sold sherry by the tumbler everywhere, or if it was only in this particular venue. Only it wasn't sherry, it was whiskey, and it was neat.

After watching Laura's range of expressions from horrified realisation of what she was drinking to appreciation as the fiery liquid warmed her, Monica said, 'We may as well be drunk as the way we are.'

Laura wondered how much longer it would be before Monica started saying, 'top o' the morning' and 'begorrah'.

'Well now, girls,' said the man who'd bought them drinks. 'What are you doing in these parts in January? Have you just come to see Himself?' He nodded to an old publicity photograph mounted on a battered showcard.

'We have,' Laura admitted, sipping her drink, beginning to feel its effect.

'He's great now, isn't he? He's a lovely man but I warn you, he's often late to things if he doesn't really want to do them.'

'Oh.'

'But it's OK, the crack will keep you entertained until he turns up.'

Laura was surprised to discover it did. The air was buzzing with chat, with laughter, people squashing past with drinks. The sheer numbers of people helped boost the limited warmth coming out of a couple of ancient heaters and added to the cosy atmosphere.

Laura had pressed euros into the hand of their self-appointed escort and bought more drinks, and the time passed quickly enough.

An hour after the appointed time, a roar started at the back of the room and gathered momentum. It was in the wake of a tall man in a tattered sweater, black jeans and boots. Dermot Flynn had arrived. For a second Laura wondered if he was in the same clothes he'd been wearing in his author photo but concluded he just wore a lot of black. He leapt up on stage without using the rickety steps and turned round and greeted his audience. He raised his hands for silence and then smiled.

Laura felt as well as saw the smile. It was like a zillion-watt lightbulb. The whiskey probably had something to do with it, she realised – she was now on her third – but it was truly dazzling.

'Ladies and gentlemen!' Dermot Flynn had to shout over the applause and the whooping that had greeted him. Eventually, the crowed quietened apart from the odd stray whistle.

'Ladies and gentlemen,' he repeated. 'Will you ever shut up?'

He certainly had a brogue, thought Laura, but it wasn't really an accent.

There was laughter.

'Now I'm going to read to you, but I'm not taking questions.'

Laura felt a moment of panic. This was awful news.

How was she going to ask him to come to England if he wasn't taking questions?

'I'll take questions tomorrow when the drunks aren't in.'

Huge relief swept over Laura and then she realised she was probably one of the drunks. She resolved not to drink any more. Monica was now holding a pint glass containing a neon-orange liquid she said was lemonade. Laura accepted she was naïve but felt this was unlikely. She herself had decided to stick to what she knew: namely whiskey.

His voice was like tweed made of silk, rough-smooth, dark brown and the sexiest thing Laura had ever heard in her life.

'Good evening, everyone.'

'Good evening!' the crowd roared back. This was unlike any event Laura had ever been to.

'It's nice of you to show up,' went on Dermot. 'People have been asking me why I showed up myself, but you asked me, so I came. I wrote these books a long time ago and I'm going to read you some out of both of them. Afterwards I'll talk a bit about how they came to be written.' He paused, cleared his throat and began to read.

She knew the words by heart – the opening passage of his first book – the bestseller that shocked the literary world. Dermot Flynn had been only twenty when out came this masterpiece. It won every literary prize it was eligible for.

She had studied his books – there were only two – at university, and of all the books she had read since, and there'd been many, these were the two she loved best.

Laura was not the only person entranced. He had such a beautiful voice. Listening to it was like hearing a musical instrument playing the most beautiful piece. The applause when he'd finished was deafening. And then he spoke about how he'd come to write them, how when he lived abroad for a while he was so homesick for his home, his land, its culture and its geography, the only way he could ease his pain was to write.

Laura clapped until her hands were sore. She drummed her feet and she may have even whooped a bit. The audience was treating him more like a rock star than a writer; the event was the most exhilarating thing she'd ever experienced. She was flying and didn't want to stop. He was every bit as wonderful as she had always dreamt he would be. When he jumped off the stage she felt as if a magic spell had suddenly been broken.

Chapter Five

'Come on,' said Laura. 'We're going to the pub.'

Monica looked at her quizzically. 'Are we? Are you sure?'

Aware she was behaving out of character, and that this was probably caused by alcohol as much as anything, Laura made her case. 'I know we've had more than enough to drink and I'm worn out and should probably go home but I'm not ready for the evening to end just yet.'

'But, Laura!' Monica was amused as well as surprised. 'We've had a long day. He's doing another gig tomorrow.'

Laura shook her head. 'It's hard to explain but I need to ask him my big favour now, before I lose my nerve.' She paused, wondering how to express her feelings about Dermot without sounding completely deranged. 'I sort of feel fired up for it and I know the feeling won't last.'

'Fair enough,' said Monica. 'Although it'll be hard to get near him.'

'I know.' She just stopped herself telling Monica that even watching him drink pints with several dozen people between her and him would be good. Being sensible could wait until she was back in England. Here, she didn't want to miss a minute of him, even if she could only look at him across a crowded room. Seduced by the romance of the place, the beauty of his writing, the charm of his voice, she felt as if she was in another world, one sprinkled with fairy dust, she didn't want that feeling to end. An enchanted evening, very different from the one in the song, had already begun.

Not all the audience went to the pub afterwards, in fact Laura saw several dozen of them scattering into the darkness, but there was still a stream of people to follow through the narrow streets to the village local. It was a long, low building that seemed to occupy the width of several shopfronts. It was still going to be a crush.

The smell of the turf fire was the first thing that hit them as they fought their way in. The bar was just visible and behind it could be seen at least three young men, pulling pints, pouring whiskey and handing over change with astonishing speed and accuracy.

Laura kept her quarry in her sights, wondering if this made her a stalker, or just a fan. Because he was so tall, she could follow him as he wove through the crowd in the main bar to where someone was gesturing to a pint glass of black fluid that had been ordered for him. The pub seemed to consist of several small wooden rooms; the now illegal nicotine had stained the walls to a warm brown. Her moment had come. It would have been easier to have ducked out of the way into one of the side rooms, but she was determined not to lose sight of him now.

Laura watched him dispose of most of what she assumed was porter in one draught. She leant in to Monica to ask if she thought 'a pint of plain' meant porter.

Monica, who had no literary references to worry about, shrugged, struggling to make herself heard over the noise. She said, 'We've got to get nearer to him. You can't ask him to come to the festival from here.'

Dermot was obviously in full flow, talking, laughing, gesturing with his glass that had somehow got refilled.

Laura's habitual reticence returned with a vengeance. The thought of actually talking to her hero was suddenly too daunting. 'Well, he's not going to say yes, is he?' Laura shouted. 'There's no point! Let's just have a quick orange juice or something and then go back.'

Monica was not having this. 'You've got us to the pub, you must complete your mission. You can't travel all this way and not. Follow me.'

With the skill Laura had admired before – a smile here, an 'excuse me' here, and a couple of times, a very suggestive wink – Monica got through the throng and to her destination.

Laura hurried after her, smiling and 'excuse me-ing' in her wake, not daring to hang back in case she got separated from Monica for ever.

'Hello, Dermot!' shouted Monica. 'I've got someone here very anxious to meet you.'

Laura cringed. 'Hello!' she said, trying to smile. Now she was up close, she could clearly she that Dermot was even more attractive than he had been in his author photo of fifteen years ago. His hair and eyelashes were just as curly but there was a definition about his features now, lines and shadows that proclaimed him a man and not a boy.

'Hello,' Dermot said back and then crinkled his eyes slightly in thought. 'Weren't you at the gig? I think I noticed you there in the corner.'

'Really?' This time her smile was spontaneous and completely incredulous. She chuckled, pleased her anti-Blarney device worked as well as any girl's although she thought so highly of him. There was no way he could have spotted her in that crowd.

'No, I did. I saw you with your tangled curls and your slightly red nose.'

Her hand went up to it. 'Is it red?' She knew about the tangled curls. She hadn't packed her straighteners and her hair had responded to the sea air in its usual exuberant fashion.

'A little, but to be truthful, I didn't see that until just now.'

She felt herself blush, hoping the heat of the room would justify it. It was hot, and there were a lot of Aran sweaters about – they probably raised the temperature as much as the fire did. 'I don't know how you could have seen me in all that crowd of people . . .'

'I did spot you, however,' he said, possibly sensing that she didn't know how to finish her sentence.

Now Laura worried that he would have seen her adoring expression, too. 'Well done you,' she said lamely, silently admonishing herself for losing the art of conversation now she'd got him to herself.

She rather expected him to turn away and speak to some of the other people who were standing around, all wanting a piece of the great man. He seemed to know everyone. He didn't. 'So, you've read my books?'

'Yes. Both of them,' she said.

To her consternation, he flinched, although it was the last thing she'd wanted him to do. 'If you're going to talk like that,' he said, 'I'll find someone else to make conversation with.'

As he didn't move she had the courage to say, 'I only said—'

'I know what you said.' His words were a full stop on that topic of conversation. 'Why haven't you two got a drink?' Before either of them could respond he'd said, 'Charles, will you do the decent thing?'

Charles nodded and smiled. 'Coming up.'

He'd set off for the bar before either of them could ask for orange juice. If it was alcohol, and Laura accepted it would be, she'd just sip it.

'It's very kind of your friend to get us drinks,' said Laura. 'Obviously—' she'd been going to say that they would pay him back, but Dermot made one of his sweeping gestures.

'I have a tab behind the bar tonight,' he said.

'Oh. Thank you.'

The ensuing silence seemed to amuse Dermot. It was killing Laura. Monica decided to put her out of her misery.

'Laura's got a favour to ask you,' she said.

'Laura? That's a pretty name. What does it mean?'

'To do with laurels. Shall we move on?'

Dermot Flynn laughed. His laugh was as sexy as his voice, Laura observed with a sort of detachment. It was like being up close to a tiger or something. It was really fascinating but somehow nothing to do with her.

'So what's this favour?' asked Dermot, sipping the drink that looked like black treacle.

Laura wished Monica hadn't said anything. 'I'm not going to ask it because I know you'll say no. There's no point.'

'I might not. You don't know for sure.' He seemed amused.

'I do so know for sure,' said Laura, falling unconsciously into the local speech pattern and swaying slightly. She steadied herself on a wooden bench.

'Why are you so sure?'

Laura was frustrated. This was embarrassing and stupid; she wished she could magic herself back to the bed and breakfast. 'I just am.' She didn't want to go into what their hostess had said about him not being willing to attend a literary festival in the town five miles away. He must already think she was an idiot.

'Ask me anyway.'

'You might as well,' said Monica, her frustration obvious. 'We've come a long enough way.'

At that moment two tumblers of whiskey appeared and were handed to the girls. Laura had resolved not to drink any more – she was already feeling the effects – but she was so grateful for the diversion she said, 'Thank you very much,' and took a large draught.

'Steady,' murmured Monica. 'It's strong stuff.' Like a contrary teenager, Laura just laughed and took another gulp.

'So, what were you going to ask me?' Dermot seemed very insistent that her favour be asked.

It's a funny thing about alcohol, thought Laura, feeling far removed from reality. You're perfectly fine, not drunk at all, and then one more sip and you are completely out of your head. Although she knew intellectually it was a bad thing, a very bad thing, just at that moment, it felt really good. It seemed to make her perception extra clear. She felt bold and confident.

'OK, here goes nothing.' Laura smiled, suddenly loving the world. 'Will you come to a literary festival I'm organising in England?' Then, before he could answer she quickly added, 'No? Well, I told you you'd say no.' She may have suddenly taken the possession of the meaning of life but she wasn't silly. She knew when she was beaten.

'But I haven't said no.' Dermot stared at her. His gaze was direct and very unsettling.

'But you will.' Laura was sure of her ground even if physically it wobbled a little beneath her feet. Another sip of whiskey and suddenly she knew everything.

'No I won't,' he said, his eyes narrow, his mouth slightly lifted in one corner.

'Told you!' said Laura, and then turned to Monica. 'We can go back now. In fact, maybe we should.'

Monica was looking at her anxiously. She seemed miles away. Laura smiled lopsidedly at her and raised a glass. 'Can we have some water, please?' Monica turned to Charles, who was hovering in a helpful way.

'Two waters coming up,' he said.

Laura's head had begun to swim. It was pleasant,

if strange. She smiled at Dermot. He was so utterly lovely! And he was talking to her! Why was that? She did find it a little difficult to work out what he was saying, though. She leant closer and concentrated very hard on his mouth.

'I didn't say I wouldn't go to the literary festival,' Dermot said slowly. 'I said I wouldn't say no.'

Laura's uncanny clarity left her. She was now very confused. 'What?'

At that moment Charles arrived with two glasses of water. 'Drink up,' said Monica, thrusting one of them at Laura. 'Or you'll want to die in the morning.'

'She's right,' said Charles.

Laura obediently sipped her water. It seemed to make her drunker than ever, but she felt it was a good thing that she realised she was drunk. Before she'd just thought she knew everything. Dermot was speaking again so she focused on his mouth.

'I will go to the festival you're arranging in England,' he said. 'On one condition.'

She was concentrating very hard, trying to gather her scattered brain cells. She was here to get Dermot to the festival. He was asking for something. OK. He could have it. Enunciating carefully she said, 'I'm sure anything that we can do to make—'

He was doing that unnerving starey thing again. He really did have the most amazing eyes, and lips and . . .

'I'll go on one condition – if you'll sleep with me.' He smiled his challenge.

Laura blinked. He couldn't really have said that, could he? She must have misheard. There was something wrong with her hearing as well as her balance. She looked for Monica for confirmation but she saw that she and Charles had gone into one of the other rooms. She was alone with Dermot – if you discounted about thirty other people. She'd have to work this out for herself; she hadn't misheard, of course, Dermot had said she had to sleep

75

with him and then he'd go to the festival. She worked on it in her mind. Did she want to sleep with Dermot Flynn? She smiled. This was what they called a 'no-brainer', which was quite funny because she no longer had a brain. She did want to sleep with him.

'OK.' She nodded. Why not.

Dermot looked down into her eyes once more and something in her flipped. What was this feeling? The poetry-loving romantic in her wanted it to be love, but she had just enough grip left on reality to realise it was lust that stirred her. Both emotions were practically unknown to her.

She was vaguely aware of a tiny voice buried deep inside her telling her she would probably regret what she'd just said, but she drowned it out with another sip of whiskey. She knew there was nothing else in the world at that moment that she wanted to do more.

'Well, isn't that nice?' he said slowly, raising an eyebrow.

Another drink was put into her hand and she sipped it. Monica appeared and murmured to her that she'd been asked to play something and then she disappeared once more into another of the rooms. Laura wasn't quite sure how Monica's sassy American swing would fit into the traditional Irish instruments she heard playing, but that wasn't her problem.

'So tell me,' said Dermot. 'How do you come to be organising a literary festival at your tender age?'

'I'm twenty-six. You'd written two bestselling novels before you were my age.'

'True, but you haven't answered my question.'

'I'm not really sure, to be honest. I sort of got roped in. I'm a bookseller by trade.'

'Go on.'

'Well, I met an agent—' She suddenly remembered that Eleanora Huckleby was his agent, too, and made a split-second decision not to mention this. She heard herself answering in a confident manner. Well, tonight she did feel confident: confident, intelligent Laura. 'She and I got talking and she discovered I was better read than some people. Of course, working in a bookshop, I had access to everything that came out, before it was out truly. I didn't have to pay for my reading habit.'

He chuckled. 'It sounds to me as if you did have to pay for it, by running a literary festival.'

Laura smiled back. 'It's not that bad. Why don't you like literary festivals?'

'How do you know I don't like them?'

'Our landlady told us. She said you wouldn't go to one five miles down the road which is why the Festival of Culture is in Ballyfitzpatrick and not Patricktown.' She'd admitted everything now. 'So why?' She wanted and needed to know and she didn't want him going off on a tangent about landladies or gossip.

'I had my fill of them years ago when my books came out. I don't want to go to them now.'

Laura forced herself to consider how she'd feel if she slept with him and then he refused to come to the festival and was relieved to discover that getting him to England, so they would have a sponsor, was not at all the reason she wanted to sleep with him – if he really meant it, of course, which she doubted – he was knee-tremblingly attractive. 'But you did this one?' She was trying very hard to enunciate and was pleased how sober she sounded.

'The place is dead in winter. It's where I live and it would be churlish not to put on a show that will fill the pubs and all the accommodation if I can, without much – any, frankly – effort.'

Laura sipped at her drink. 'I think I'm drinking neat whiskey.'

'It won't do you a bit of harm.'

Laura laughed ruefully, aware that it may have already

got her into a lot of trouble if not actually done her harm. She couldn't decide what was to blame for what she was about to do: the whiskey or her wanton lust.

'So what have you read lately that you've got really excited about?'

'Well . . .' She went on to enthuse about a recent prizewinner, and a new women's fiction writer, and several other books that she'd enjoyed. She was proud of how lucid she sounded – to her ears at least.

He countered with books and films he'd liked, only of course he was far more critical than even Laura was, and she always thought she was picky. As she talked she saw his attention wander. No male writer could resist talking about their work, she remembered – something Henry from the bookshop had told her when she'd first started organising events. 'Of course,' she said, 'what we're all waiting for is another book from you.'

There was a pause and then he took the glass out of her hand and put it down. 'I think it's time I took you home to bed.'

Her reactions were slowed by strong drink and it took Laura a moment or two to realise what he'd said. She forced her brain to pay attention and tell her to politely decline. It wouldn't. She wanted to go home to bed with him and that was that. She realised she hadn't really believed he meant it, she'd just enjoyed flirting with him. It had felt good. But she liked the idea of sleeping with him even better. She pushed aside any lingering sensibility and nodded her assent.

She retained enough sanity to text Monica to say, if not where she was going, whom she was going with, confident that someone would give Monica the address should she need it. She also added 'I really want this' to stop Monica rushing to the rescue. She knew that Monica would really like an in-depth discussion about what Laura was about to do, her motivation, and what she felt the outcome might be. But Monica even saying, 'Are you sure?' might make her change her mind, and Laura really wanted her virginity to go to her favourite writer in all the world (who also happened to be the most attractive man on the planet). She may never have another opportunity to really live and she didn't want to be talked out of taking it.

It took them a little while to get out of the pub, Dermot had to say goodbye in various ways to so many people. But no one seemed at all surprised that Laura was going with him. She realised he could probably have had any woman he wanted in that pub at that moment; while they might have wondered at his choice, the fact that he was going home with a woman was to be expected.

'I'm just one in a long line of women,' she told herself during the last 'goodbye' conversation. 'But that's all right. Poets are all womanisers. At least it means he'll know what he's doing.' Anticipation and fear heightened her desire. She remembered reading that they did and her addled brain tried to think where. 'It's going to be fine,' she told herself, 'and if it isn't, it's something to tell my grandchildren.' Then she giggled as she imagined the unlikely scenario of her own grandmother telling her about her first sexual encounter.

Eventually they were out into the cold air. She stumbled slightly and he took her arm. Should I tell him I'm a virgin, she wondered, and then decided not to. It might stop him. It would make it far too big a deal. I want to have sex with him for all the right and all the wrong reasons, she reminded herself. I don't want to make him feel bad about it.

She was barely aware of the short journey to his house. He strode purposefully up the path, opened the front door and pushed her gently inside. Before she had time to take anything in he'd pulled her into his arms and kissed her. He was an expert, she decided, her knees almost buckling as whiskey and desire hit them at the same time. I have made exactly the right decision, she thought: my virginity is safe in this man's hands! Is that what I mean? Her brain seemed to be twirling away on its own, disconnected from anything that made sense. She decided to put all thinking on hold until later; just now, she wanted to relish every moment.

Without letting go he manoeuvred her into a bedroom and carried on kissing her. He held her very tightly, pressing her to him. His hand moved from the back of her waist to her bottom and she realised she had never wanted any body else's hand to go there – how strange it was that an intimate touch could be so horrible from the wrong person and so wonderful from the right one.

'Do you need to use the bathroom?' he murmured into her hair that he was now curling his fingers into.

'No thank you,' she murmured back, knowing that if she stopped she might lose her nerve. It wasn't her nerve she was intent on losing. Tenderly he undid the buttons of her jacket and took it off. Underneath she was wearing one of her collection of black V-neck sweaters. This was lifted and pulled over her head. Now she stood before him in a strappy top and a pair of black trousers. A part of her registered that they were the same clothes she wore for work and felt that was a bit odd. But Dermot didn't seem to care what she was wearing; he was only intent on getting it off. He found the hook at the waistband of her trousers, and the zip and then they fell off her hips. He pushed her gently back on to the bed and laughed.

'You're wearing socks!'

'Of course I am,' she said hazily. 'What's wrong with wearing socks? I expect you're wearing them too.'

He unzipped her short boots and they joined her other clothes on the floor. It ought to have felt odd being with a man she didn't know in just her underwear, but it felt right, nice. Sexy.

He stood looking down at her as she lay there in her bra and pants. He was still fully clothed.

'You're beautiful, you know that?'

Laura chuckled gently. He probably said that to everyone. She didn't mind. She wanted him to treat her just as he'd treat any of his previous girlfriends.

'Get under the duvet, you're shivering,' he said, tenderly amused as he started to strip off his own clothes.

From under the duvet, Laura watched him. His body was fit and well muscled. He may have been a writer but he obviously didn't spend all day sitting at a desk. As his boxer shorts dropped she closed her eyes. The room swung round as if she was on a carousel and she quickly opened them again.

He switched off the main light and replaced it with the bedside one. Then he took Laura into his arms.

The feeling of his skin against hers was like silk. She closed her eyes again, in spite of the spinning room, and let herself enjoy the sensation of lying in his arms as he got rid of her bra and pants. Miraculously any nerves she might have felt seemed to have fled with her inhibitions. He pulled her towards him and began to stroke her back. And all the time he breathed endearments in his deep, sexy voice. He raised himself on his elbow and kissed her face, lightly, more a breath than a kiss, all over her eyes, her lips, her cheeks and then he moved down to her neck, just under her ear.

She sighed deeply and snuggled closer. Only then did he touch her breasts and kiss her chest. Now his hand moved over her body, featherlight caresses, tantalising in their tenderness. He had just discovered that the backs

81

of her knees were particularly sensitive when he said, 'Excuse me. I'll be back in a minute.'

She sighed ecstatically and passed out.

She awoke to find him snoring beside her. She felt terrible: thirsty and a head that felt as if it was about to split. Panic filled her. What had she done? How on earth had she ended up naked in bed with a naked man? She flew out of bed and hunted for her clothes. She was dizzy and couldn't tell if she was still drunk or if the dizziness was part of the hangover.

She found her knickers and socks in separate parts of the corner of the room. Waves of panic came over as she tried to navigate her limbs into them. What had she done?

Terrified Dermot would wake up she tried to assemble what she could remember of the night before as she pulled on her trousers and top. Dermot's event was clear in her mind. Then she remembered dragging Monica to the pub and some of what had gone on there was clear, but how in merry hell had she ended up in Dermot Flynn's bedroom, naked, with him in the bed next to her?

Terrible flashbacks came to her as she pulled on her coat – some dim recollection of him saying he'd come to the festival if she went to bed with him. Had she really said yes? Surely not! However much she admired and fancied him, surely she wouldn't have agreed to sleep with him? Would she? It would make her little better than a prostitute! She didn't dare look at the sleeping form in the bed. If she couldn't see him perhaps he didn't really exist: it was all a figment of her over-active imagination. But she knew he was very real. Oh, why had she drunk so much? Her mother was right about the demon drink. This thought brought a fleeting smile to her lips until the reality of the situation came flooding back. She had to remember what happened last night.

She did remember fancying him. She remembered him taking her clothes off, and her liking it very much. As she did up her trousers she wondered if she'd ever feel the same about that particular pair again.

She looked at her watch but it was too dark to see the time. She'd have to get back to the bed and breakfast and hope she could wake Monica to let her in. Thank goodness it was a bungalow and their bedroom window was round the back. If she was attacked and dragged into the bushes by a passing rapist on her way there, she had only herself to blame.

The Patron Saint of Stupid Women guided her back down the road and along the lane to where the bed and breakfast was. Laura had a terrible sense of direction and knew it was only the intervention of this divine being that got her there. By now her head was clearing a little; she studied the outside of the building and worked out where their room was. She tiptoed round and knocked on the window.

Fortunately Monica was a light sleeper. A tousled head appeared behind the curtains. 'Laura! What the hell are you doing here?'

'Oh, just let me in, Monica, please!'

'OK. Go to the front door and I'll see what I can do.

'You're bloody lucky they don't go in for burglar alarms round here,' whispered Monica a few minutes later.

'I feel like a burglar. Worse.'

'What happened?'

'I don't know. Nothing. I don't think. Can we talk about it in the morning?'

'Fair enough. Get into my bed, it's warm and you're shivering like a jelly. I demand a blow-by-blow account in the morning though.'

Laura just wanted to get into bed and search for oblivion but Monica was firm. 'Here,' she said, holding a glass. 'It's got something in it to restore your salts. You'll feel less awful in the morning if you drink it.'

Laura drank it but as more and more memory came back to her in Technicolor detail she felt that it wasn't going to be a hangover that made her feel as if death was an attractive option.

'Tea's up!' said Monica, cruelly loud, the following morning. She was fully dressed and made up and seemed on top form.

'Oh God!' Laura moaned, yawned, moaned again and then sat up and took the tea.

'How are you feeling?'

Laura considered. 'Better than I should, probably. Physically, anyway.'

'I want to hear every detail later, but now we should have breakfast.'

Laura, who hadn't felt like eating anything, did feel a bit better after a pint of orange juice, a huge Irish breakfast and several mugs of tea, and two strong painkillers. Monica hustled her into her warmest clothes, put on her own, and dragged them both off for a walk.

'OK, so tell me everything. Was it wonderful? First times can be dodgy, but at least with a man like that he'll know what he's doing.'

Laura remembered this thought making its appearance in her own head sometime the previous evening.

'Well?' Monica was insistent. 'You have to tell me everything. That's the first rule of Girlfriend Law.'

'I've never heard of the Girlfriend Law,' said Laura.

'I've just made it up, but you've still got to tell me. Don't hold out on me.'

'I'm not holding out. I'm just trying to remember.'

'What? Surely you weren't that off your face?'

'I had had a fair bit to drink, I know that. I must have or I would never have gone back to his house. Although . . .'

'Confession time,' said Monica, accurately interpreting

her sudden pause. 'You fancied him rotten. I'd have gone back to his place after a glass of Ribena. He's a ride.'

'What?'

'Local expression. Self-explanatory. Shall we go and sit down on that bench over there? I've had a broken night.'

'Oh, me too.' Shivers were convulsing Laura's body and she didn't know whether they were caused by the cold, her hangover or by what had happened the night before. She remembered now exactly how much she had wanted to sleep with Dermot Flynn. She remembered how she'd decided that of all the men in the entire world he was the one who should have her virginity. And although the light of day was horribly cold and she felt iller than she could ever remember feeling, she hadn't changed her mind. Not really.

'So, did you have fun?' asked Monica. 'I won't ask if you had an orgasm, because you probably didn't.'

'No . . . I don't think I did.'

'What? Have fun or the orgasm?'

'Monica, I know this sounds really mad but I'm not sure if we had sex or not.'

Monica didn't answer immediately. 'Do you think it's possible that you had sex and can't remember?'

They reached the bench and as they sat on it, Laura winced.

'You're tender – down there?'

Laura acknowledged that she was. 'But we went on that bike ride to see your boyfriend.'

'But I'm fine! I know I'm more used to cycling than you, but you're young and fit. I wouldn't have thought you'd be that uncomfortable. You walked most of the way, after all.'

'There were some very bumpy bits on the way home.' Laura turned to her friend. 'I do need to find out, Mon. I have to know if I had sex or not. I feel it's important.'

85

Monica laughed gently. 'Well, of course it is important, but—'

'No, really. I have to find out. I can't go back to England not knowing. I just can't.'

Monica became practical. 'OK, let's try and work it out. Were you alone when you woke up?'

Laura shook her head. 'No. He was asleep beside me. Snoring. And naked.'

'Hmm . . . Well, did you notice anything, er, discarded on the floor? You know, like a condom?'

Laura pulled a face. 'No, but then I was too busy finding my clothes and wanting to leave as quickly as possible.'

Monica sighed and shook her head. 'It's not looking good, Laura, if you don't want to have had sex with him. A man like that, naked in bed with a girl, who was also naked, I presume?' Laura nodded. 'The chances of him not having had his evil way with you are slim. And no sign of a condom – very irresponsible.'

'But surely I'd remember if we had?' Laura asked quietly, looking down the lane towards the pub where this whole sorry situation had started. She sighed and pulled her coat round her more tightly.

'Not if he put Rohypnol in your drink,' said Monica matter-of-factly.

'He wouldn't do that. He wouldn't need to.' Of this Laura was absolutely sure.

'You don't know that, sweetie, you know very little about him,' Monica reminded her, albeit gently.

'I wrote my bloody dissertation about him! I know everything there is to know. And besides, where would he get Rohypnol in Ballyfitzpatrick?' She doubted they'd even heard of it here.

Monica chuckled again. 'You have a point, and you may be able to quote his books by heart, but you don't know about his sex life, now do you? I got the impression from

Charles that he's quite a ladies' man. You can never be too careful, you know.'

'It wasn't mentioned in the author biog in the back of the books, no,' said Laura. 'You do have a point.'

'You're really worried about this, aren't you?' said Monica, touching Laura's arm, serious now.

'Well, yes! I, the last virgin in the Northern Hemisphere over twenty-one, may or may not have had sex. I would kind of like to know.'

'Do you want to go home? We could leave early . . .'

Laura shook her head. 'Oh no. We can't go before his other session – and I've got to get him to say definitely that he'll come to the festival. There's more than just my virginity at stake here! Besides,' she went on in a small voice, 'I can't pass up a chance to see him again.'

Monica patted her hand. 'Of course.'

'But I also need to know what happened last night. Otherwise how can I speak to him about the festival, make arrangements, stuff like that?'

'I see your point. We need to find out.' She stood up, putting out a hand to pull Laura up. 'Come on, it's freezing out here, let's go to the café and warm ourselves up.'

'But, Monica, how? I'm certainly not asking him,' said Laura as they walked towards the café where they'd had their first Irish breakfast what seemed like days ago now.

'OK, then I will,' said Monica.

'Mon! You can't ask him. You cannot go up to Dermot Flynn and say, "Did you have sex with my friend?" You've got to promise me you won't. It's too embarrassing.' She thought for moment and then flourished, 'It's Girlfriend Law.'

'I invented Girlfriend Law,' said Monica firmly, 'but I admit it is the sort of thing that would be on it. Tell you what, I will ask him, but he won't know I'm asking him, so it'll be all right.'

'I may not be at my intellectual best – my head is

aching so much I think my brain has atrophied – but how on earth are you going to do that?'

'I'll think of something.' Monica flashed her irrepressible grin, but Laura wasn't convinced.

Chapter Six

The second event, although in the afternoon, was just as crowded. If this was an indication of how many people he would attract to the Somerby festival, Laura could see why everyone was so keen to have him. Maybe, she said to herself, it's just because he's local. But although lots of the voices around her were Irish, there was a substantial smattering of English and American accents too.

This time Laura hid at the back. Her hangover was mercifully a distant echo but whatever had – or hadn't – happened the night before, seeing Dermot again was going to be acutely embarrassing. Although, if it tran-spired that they had made love (even in her imagination, Laura didn't think this was really the right expression) she would hold him to his promise. But how terribly sad – tragic, really – that she'd been so drunk she couldn't be sure if it had happened or not! Supposing she had given her virginity to the man she wanted to have it more than anyone and not been aware of it? She knew what she felt for him wasn't love in any real sense, but it was the sort of adulation young women usually reserved for singers or film stars. Being unconscious through the process was unforgivable.

Monica had agreed that she would go nearer the front so she could grab him and ask her question before everyone went to the pub. Laura needed to know as soon as possible, and while she and Monica agreed that several pints or shots down the line it would be easier to ask, the answer might not be coherent, or lead to other things. Both women agreed that for their livers' sakes, they shouldn't spend longer in the pub than they had to.

The 'what on earth are you going to say?' conversation had gone on some time.

'How about "Have you ever had sex with a virgin and if so, when was it?"' suggested Monica.

Laura had spent several seconds in shock before she picked up that Monica was joking. 'Why beat around the bush, Mon? Why not just come out with it?' Laura was giggling now, as Monica had intended she should. But there was an edge of hysteria to it.

She tried again. 'What about: "Have you ever acted out the sex scenes in your books and if so when?"'

Laura stopped giggling and became indignant. 'No! There are no sex scenes in his books that would give us the remotest clue!'

Monica shrugged. 'Sorry, haven't read them.'

'That's blindingly obvious!'

'Hang on! I'm doing you a favour, don't forget!'

Laura was apologetic. 'I'm sorry! I'm being a bitch. I got myself into this, I should get myself out of it really. Why should you embarrass yourself for me? If only I wasn't such an idiot!'

'Look, it's OK. You don't need to beat yourself up more than you already have done. Hair shirts are so last century, or even several centuries before. I'll think of something at the time, so it sounds more natural.'

Laura was not reassured. 'I've set up a lot of signings, readings, Q and As, and been to a few I haven't arranged, and no one ever, ever, asked about the author's sex life.'

Monica was dismissive. 'But I'm a scary rock chick. I can ask stuff you literary types wouldn't.' Monica put on an expression of insouciance that might have convinced Laura when she first met her, a couple of weeks before, but by now she realised that the 'scary rock chick' or in her case a 'scary swing band chick' was an image that went on with the pink wig and false eyelashes.

'I should do this myself. I'm sure if I got drunk enough – hell, when I got drunk before I was ready to have sex with him!'

'Yes, and you were so drunk you can't remember if you had sex with him or not,' Monica reminded her kindly, in case this had slipped Laura's mind. 'Much good it'll do us if you tank yourself up so you can ask him, and then can't make sense of the answer, or forget what the answer was. No, I'll do it.'

Shamed by the truth of this, Laura shut up.

While Dermot had said he'd do a question-and-answer-session, 'Did you have sex with my friend?' was probably not one he'd be expecting. Laura had no idea if Monica was going to manage to ask it, and was frantically thinking about a plan B. Could she get an email address for him and send him a quick, 'You may not remember me, but I came and saw you at the Ballyfitzpatrick literary festival and we might have had sex. Ring any bells? Did we do it, or didn't we? I feel I ought to know . . .'

No, probably not. She had to put her trust in Monica.

Dermot Flynn leapt up on the stage in the same rock-star way he had the night before. Laura sighed. She felt a mixture of huge relief that he was possibly even more attractive than she'd remembered him, which meant she hadn't had beer glasses (or whatever the expression was) on last night, and a huge sweep of longing. She really, really hoped she hadn't wasted what should have been one of the most wonderful experiences of her life because she was drunk.

Her knees weakened as she thought of what they had shared that she *could* remember. He couldn't have done anything she hadn't liked or surely her body wouldn't go weak at the sight of him – or at least not weak in the gooey, chest-heaving way she was feeling now. There'd have been some sort of psychic wound, surely? Something her brain might have suppressed but her body remembered? That's what happened in crime novels.

There was no one with him to introduce him or chair the event. Everyone knew who he was and he didn't need a minder – she could almost hear him say it. He had two books under his arm and Laura could see bookmarks in them. Someone near her muttered, 'He might read from both of them. Brilliant!'

'I've come from Canada to hear him,' said another. 'I'd go anywhere, pay anything.'

'If only he'd bring out another book! I know both of his by heart!' said the first mutterer.

Agreeing silently but wholeheartedly, Laura shifted slightly behind her neighbour as she saw Dermot rake the audience with his gaze. She hoped this time he wouldn't be able to see her at the back. She'd made such an utter fool of herself.

She wasn't entirely sure but she had a feeling he paused as he got to her section of the crowd. She closed her eyes – that way he'd never spot her. Or, more importantly, she'd never know he had.

She recognised the reading straightaway, but then, she reasoned privately, she would. Like the person now crushed to her left arm, she knew every word almost by heart. It was a scene where the protagonist is describing the woman he loves to his best friend. The hero is saying one thing, but thinking another. There was nothing explicit or lewd or remotely pornographic, but the young man's passion and desire for the woman was absolutely clear. Just hearing his beautiful voice saying those beautiful things was enough to make her want to promise to be his sex-slave for ever, and never ask him to go near a literary festival.

When he stopped reading she had to remind herself to

breathe. She wasn't the only one affected; women were near to swooning all around her. Group lust, she concluded, like group hysteria, only (happily) more private. It would only take one of them to start screaming, or throw their knickers on to the stage, for them all to follow suit – or at least all those who didn't have to struggle out of their jeans, hopping on one leg, fighting with thick socks. Laura felt grateful the venue wasn't well heated and that the punters had dressed up warmly.

'Right, any questions?' he asked.

After a round of questions which Dermot handled expertly with charm and candour, he looked at his watch.

Laura was beginning to wonder if Monica had lost her chance. Her hand had been waving for quite a while.

'Just time for a few more . . .'

'Here! Me!' Monica's voice sang out from the front of the room. Laura could tell she either didn't share the feelings of almost all the other women in the room or she was rising above them. But what on earth could she say in front of a large audience to get the required information?

Monica cleared her throat. 'They say that all first novels are autobiographical. Was this true for you?'

How, Laura wondered, feeling frantic, could Monica get from this pretty bog-standard question, to 'Is my friend still a virgin?' It was absurd! Then she chided herself – Monica was a friend doing her a favour, not an expert interrogator. She knew she should ask Dermot herself – but the mere thought made every nerve ending go into spasm. Perhaps it didn't really matter if she never knew.

Dermot Flynn had of course fielded this question a trillion times. He gave his lazy, charming smile. 'Well, you have to remember that I wrote this book when I was very young. I didn't have much to be autobiographical about.'

Monica was obviously not satisfied with this answer. 'Well, did you go round shag— um – sleeping with every woman you laid eyes on?'

Laura cringed.

Dermot was clearly amused. 'Let's just say there's more imagination in that book than experience.'

'I'm just wondering,' Monica asked, 'if you practise safe sex—' She seemed to be off on another tack now.

Laura gulped. Dermot looked confused, as did most of the audience.

'I mean,' Monica went on, 'a lot of young people read your books . . .'

Where did Monica get that from? Maybe she had read the book herself, after all.

'I don't quite see—' broke in Dermot, but Monica was set on her course and wouldn't be diverted or stopped.

'Don't you think it's important that you set a good example?'

'Of course—'

Monica interrupted before his audience could find out if Dermot was agreeing with her on the subject of good examples or was just going to say something else entirely. 'When did you last use a condom?'

It all came out in a rush and Laura wanted to die.

Silence fell over the audience as everyone tingled in expectation. It was a very rude question, and if Laura hadn't known her friend had asked it only for her, she would have thought it unforgivable. Supposing the crowd turned on Monica? Would she be able to save her?

'I have to say,' said Dermot, not at all put out, 'that that is a question possibly better suited to a more intimate setting, but since you ask, it was about four months ago. Next question?'

Laura edged her way out of the crowd to the door and escaped. It was a freezing night, her friend had humiliated herself and she still didn't know how far things had gone between her and Dermot the night before. Monica soon joined her.

'Thanks for trying, Mon,' said Laura before her friend could apologise. 'I know you did your best. I don't think we'll ever know. Let's just assume nothing much happened, shall we?' A recollection of what had gone on came back to her suddenly. It didn't seem like 'nothing much' really, it had been fantastic – with or without full-on sex.

'I'm not giving up until I know for a fact,' said Monica. 'You'll never have any peace of mind if you don't know. We'll go to the pub now, get the drinks in before the rush, and I'll ask him a supplementary question. That is what they're called, isn't it?'

'Maybe,' said Laura dolefully, 'but you might get us both thrown out for harassing the star! You were quite – er – upfront in there.'

Monica bit her lip, possibly in remorse. 'I know. But I had to be.'

'I feel such a total idiot for not noticing –'

Monica stifled a giggle. 'For not noticing if you had sex with one of the sexiest men on the planet? There's such a thing as being too unworldly, you know.'

Laura groaned in frustration at herself.

Monica patted her soothingly. 'Now let's go and get some Dutch courage – we're going to need it!'

'I thought we said—'

'Do you want to know if you're still a virgin or not?'

Laura nodded and followed her friend obediently down the road to the pub.

The fact that she had a big black pint waiting for him seemed to endear Monica to Dermot – enough for him to go near enough to her to pick it up, at least. Laura had taken refuge in one of the other small rooms and was listening from behind a panel. They'd decided it would be easier if Monica confronted him by herself.

95

'You gave me a hard time in there,' he said. Laura heard the glass land on the table after several long seconds. She could imagine the movement of his Adam's apple as he swallowed. Then she remembered it was a secondary sexual characteristic and stopped herself.

'I just thought you were completely irresponsible,' said Monica.

Laura winced. Here she goes again. How could Monica be so rude? She couldn't tell if Monica was genuinely cross on her behalf or trying to provoke a reaction.

'Why, for feck's sake?'

Laura could imagine his indignation and didn't blame him for it – or the language.

'Because you should always use a condom,' said Monica. 'Not just when you're asked to.'

You had to admire her persistence, thought Laura, even if it was making her personally want to tie herself in knots to suppress her embarrassment. She didn't dare actually cross her legs, or hunch over; she was getting the odd funny look as it was.

'I quite agree,' said Dermot, sounding quite affable. 'I always do.'

There was silence. Laura could almost hear Monica narrowing her eyes.

'So when was the last time?'

Laura wiped away the film of sweat this question created and stuffed her knuckles in her mouth. She no longer cared what the people around her thought about her behaviour.

'What, that I used a condom? Or had sex?'

Laura let out a little moan.

'Either. Presumably the answer's the same.'

Monica was a terrier when it came to getting information, Laura realised, and really wished she could have emulated some less tenacious breed. But would a cocker spaniel really do the job? She was dimly aware that a combination of embarrassment, terror, remorse and a whole lot of other emotions too complex to be named was making her train of thought spin off the rails.

'As I said before, about four months ago,' said Dermot and then added, 'Ah, I think I've worked out what this is all about.'

Laura, suddenly terrified she was about to hear herself talked about behind her back, squeezed past several people and appeared in front of them. She couldn't rely on Monica any longer – she had to confront Dermot herself.

'It's me,' she said from the door of the snug, trying to look as natural as possible and as if she hadn't been hiding nearby all along.

'Ah ha!' said Dermot – cruelly, in Laura's opinion.

Laura pushed aside some innocent bystanders in order to get nearer to Dermot and Monica. 'I needed to know if we had sex last night or not,' she said breathlessly, grateful that Monica had insisted on a hair of the dog and that she'd consumed at least some whiskey.

Dermot's smile was devastating. 'And you couldn't have just asked me?'

Laura swallowed and shook her head. 'Too embarrassed,' she explained. 'I felt I should have known.'

'If you didn't know,' said Dermot softly, 'the fault would have been mine, not yours. But you fell asleep and then you disappeared, obviously thinking better of it. I'm trying not to feel hurt,' he teased.

'It wasn't really that—'

'I'm going to find Charles and some music,' said Monica, relieved that she'd done her duty. 'You two can sort yourselves out now.' She wriggled through the crowd with Laura looking plaintively after her.

'That woman is a piece of work,' said Dermot admiringly.

'She's a good friend,' said Laura. 'She put herself through hell for me. Or at least a lot of embarrassment.'

Dermot was not impressed. 'Quite unnecessary. She, or you, could just have asked.'

Laura lost some of her numbness and began to giggle. 'How would that conversation have gone, I wonder. I could have said, "Excuse me, Mr Flynn, can you just remind me, did we or did we not have sex last night?"'

'You would have used my Christian name. I wouldn't have thought you forward. After all, I have seen you naked.'

Laura tried to take a sip from her glass but found it was empty. The thought of him seeing her naked, of being naked in his presence was intensely erotic and excruciatingly embarrassing at the same time.

'You need another drink,' said Dermot and lifted his hand. 'Whiskey for the lady.'

Magically a glass appeared. When she'd taken a good gulp and feeling she'd been through the worst embarrassment a woman could experience and survive, she said, 'So, will you come to my literary festival?'

Dermot's smile made Laura's stomach turn with desire but her brain told she was probably not going like what he had to say. 'All original terms and conditions apply.'

Helplessly, Laura looked up into his eyes. They were smiling, but resolute. She looked away again quickly, spent some moments biting her lip and generally trying to make the floor open up and swallow her. When she finally accepted that it wasn't going to she said, 'Oh well. No one could accuse me of not doing my best.' She had agreed to his terms once, while very drunk, but with sobriety had come sanity, and she was not going to let herself do anything quite so foolish now. She turned, preparing to fight her way through the people to find Monica.

She felt a hand on her arm.

'Hang on now, I didn't mean there was no room for negotiation!'

Laura turned. She hadn't meant to be clever, and bluff him into changing his mind, but by some fluke that had been the effect of her reaction.

'You mean, as we've gone some little way towards having sex, you'll take that part into consideration?' She smiled, aware that she was flirting again and enjoying the sensation. She hadn't done much of it herself, but had read enough about how it was done to realise what was happening. She felt on surer ground now that he hadn't dismissed coming to the festival outright.

'I don't mean I'll cross the Irish Sea and reach England but not actually go all the way to the venue, which is more or less what happened last night.' His eyes twinkled with wickedness and sex appeal.

'Oh good,' she quipped, feeling her confidence grow. 'I don't think that would help me convince the sponsors that as you'd come that far, they should still give us money. Not as much as they would have done though, obviously.'

'Oh, so it was to get sponsorship you were so keen to get me to your festival. I thought you "really admired my work".' He put on an irritating imitation of a female voice that didn't sound a bit like her. He wasn't flirting any more.

'I do – did – admire your work,' snapped Laura, no longer wanting to flirt back. 'That bit is absolutely genuine. But there hasn't been much of it lately, has there?'

The twinkle was more speculative now. For a moment she wondered if she'd overstepped the mark. 'You are very cruel,' he said, fortunately still amused, 'but perhaps I deserved it.'

Laura was aware that a woman who'd had more practice with real men rather than literary heroes would have had something clever to say now. Jane Austen, Georgette

Heyer, or one of the younger writers of chick lit would have had this man begging to come to her literary festival in a few terse lines. She said nothing.

'Tell you what,' he went on, obviously having come to some kind of decision, 'let me show you a bit of the countryside. Come for a walk with me tomorrow morning. Then perhaps you'll understand why I'm not eager to leave, even for a short time.'

Laura thought about it. There'd be time: they weren't due to go back to England until tomorrow evening. Monica wouldn't mind. 'Actually, Monica and I went cycling yesterday. I've seen the countryside.' Why did she say that? she admonished herself. He was offering her an olive branch.

'It'll look quite different through my eyes, I'm telling you,' he persisted.

'I'm sure.' She still didn't feel quite ready to give in yet. She was enjoying not agreeing too readily to any suggestion from a man who was obviously used to women jumping at his every word.

'But you and Monica. You're not joined at the hip, are you?'

Laura put on a good impression of wide-eyed innocence. 'Do you not want to show the countryside to a woman who asks such pertinent questions?'

He laughed. 'You may not think much of my morals, but I can assure you I only ever court one woman at a time.'

'If they know about each other,' Laura said, as if to confirm it.

He grinned. 'That's right. So, will you come with me?' He studied her earnestly.

She felt herself being drawn in by his magnetic gaze, despite her intention to remain calm and collected.

'For a walk?' Again, she appeared to be seeking confirmation that nothing too much was being asked of her when she knew perfectly well if he'd asked her to row the Atlantic with him she'd probably have agreed to it.

'That's all I'm asking you to do – on this occasion. I'll bring lunch,' he added as if this would clinch it.

She gave him a prim little smile. 'Then yes, that would be very nice.'

'Very nice?' Her choice of words obviously offended him. 'Hmph!'

'Will it not be nice, then?' she asked, still prim, hoping her amusement was well hidden.

He narrowed his gaze so that his eyes almost disappeared. 'It will be spectacular.'

Laura swallowed. His voice was so sexy she pressed her knees together to stop them wobbling.

He paused. 'I'll get you back in plenty of time to set off for the ferry.'

'You are keen to get exercise, aren't you?' Laura struggled to be brisk. 'If it's that difficult for you normally, I'm sure you could find a personal trainer.'

'Listen, Miss . . .'

'Horsley.'

'You're getting the chance to see one of the most beautiful spots in Ireland through the eyes of—'

She broke in, smiling, pretending to be teasing but in reality being perfectly serious: 'One of the most gifted writers to have come out of Ireland for a long time?'

His slow, crooked smile could have been ironic, or could have been completely accepting of this description. 'Well, you said it.'

Laura pretended to be appalled. 'You're not supposed to agree with me! How conceited are you?'

'Some would say: very.'

She held up her hand. 'Count me as one of that group.'

His eyebrow acknowledged her challenge. 'Others would say a craftsman should know his own worth.'

She shook her head. 'Only those very keen to suck up to you.'

'Yesterday you'd have been the founder member of that group. Good God, woman, you were willing to sleep with me!'

She had to acknowledge that this was true, however much it would boost his over-inflated ego. 'Fortunately I was saved from myself.'

He laughed. 'And maybe you can save me from myself.'

Laura laughed back at him. 'Where shall we meet tomorrow morning?'

'On the corner, by the shop. We'll drive a little way first.'

Monica allowed Laura to walk back from the pub on her own after she was convinced nothing bad would happen to her. Laura wanted to be fresh tomorrow and not hungover. Although she'd already drunk far more than was compatible with healthy living, if she drank enough water and took an aspirin, she should be OK in the morning. She'd drunk more in the last couple of evenings than she'd ever drunk in her entire life, even as a student.

It was Monica's turn to sneak in during the early hours and Laura's to be self-righteous, although Monica was fit enough to get up for the massive breakfast they no longer just expected, but looked forward to with worrying eagerness.

'I've got a horrible feeling,' said Monica, loading a piece of soda bread with butter and Old Thyme Irish Marmalade, 'that a bit of toast and a banana isn't going to be enough for me any more. I'll need the Full Irish every day.'

'Well, I need a big breakfast because I'm going to be taking exercise,' said Laura.

'Mm, so you are. Do you care to be specific about what exercise exactly you had in mind?'

102

Laura laughed. 'To be brutally honest, I don't think the sort of exercise I have in mind is the kind of exercise I'll be having but I'm sure I'll be burning up plenty of calories either way.'

'So you really like him?' Monica was studying her closely.

'God yes,' said Laura, too late realising she should have been less vehement. She knew full well that she was deeply infatuated, and equally well that it could go nowhere and she'd better start getting over it as soon as she could – immediately after they'd had their walk together. Until then she could have her few hours of joy, even if having them was likely to make the getting-over part far, far worse.

'Well, I wish you luck with him. He's a stunner, I'll give you that but not a novice ride, if I can make an equestrian pun.'

Laura raised her cup in congratulation. 'It's a very good pun. With Irish connections too. Excellent.'

'But it's too late, isn't it? All my good advice, too late, no use.'

'Good advice almost always is, isn't it?'

'I expect so, but do me one, big, massive favour; if you sleep with him, remember it this time – and take precautions!'

'Monica, it's January, in Ireland. We're going for a walk. I think that'll provide all the precautions we need.'

Chapter Seven

Well wrapped up in all the sensible clothing they had between them and with a bag of toffees in her pocket for emergencies, Laura waited for Dermot on the corner, as arranged. Just as she had convinced herself that he'd overslept and wasn't going to come, a rackety old Citroen appeared and drew up next to her.

'Get in, we've a way to go.'

She got in, reminding herself that she was sharing a car with one of the great names of modern Irish fiction – modern anything fiction, in fact. She made a decision to start keeping a diary, simply so she could record this moment.

The car got them up the hill a great deal quicker than the bikes had. At the top, they took the other road along the coast, in the opposite direction to where she and Monica had cycled a lifetime and several dramatic experiences ago. As they passed the sign to the village they had cycled to, Laura wondered if Monica would use the car and her free day to go and see the boy she'd been so keen to catch up with. Although she'd asked her, Monica had been non-committal but cheerful. Laura didn't know if Monica had had a reply to the note she had stuffed through his letterbox but her new friend wasn't one to let things lie. She would make the most of her opportunity.

Laura, on the other hand, wondered if her attempts to get Dermot Flynn to come the literary festival would come to anything. Would he just string her along?

Monica would get him to sign something, possibly in blood. If only she could make herself more like her feisty companion, all would be well. The trouble was, she couldn't.

Laura realised these mental ramblings about Monica were a distraction from her own situation. What was happening to her was almost too wonderful, and she wasn't sure she could cope. She just had to hope her 'in-love state' or whatever it might be, didn't make her do anything stupid again. Although before, when she had so blithely agreed to sleep with him, she had probably just been in lust (and, of course, very drunk). Now she was in a position to spend a day with a writer she'd admired all her adult life – she mustn't let anything interfere with that.

Conversation, however, didn't seem possible. She tried to think of some casual remark – about the scenery, for example. But there didn't seem to be any way of describing it other than as 'beautiful' or 'lovely' or, worse, 'very pretty', and clichés would simply not do. Besides, the scenery was so beautiful, conversation seemed superfluous, intrusive, even. And she wasn't going to talk about his work. Or hers. So she stayed silent.

Eventually, he turned the car down a narrow lane. The hedges either side were in desperate need of attention and there was a good solid strip of grass growing up the middle. It went downhill and seemed to lead towards the sea. It got even narrower and the hedges higher as they progressed.

'Are you sure this is a road, and doesn't just lead to a farm or something?' said Laura, anxiety breaking her self-imposed silence. 'It's hardly wide enough for the car.'

'It does lead to a farm. We'll leave the car there and then walk. I hope you've got the right sort of shoes on.' He glanced down at her feet.

'Of course I have,' she said, glad of her sturdy, flat-heeled boots, aware that he might think she was a complete airhead now. Just because she had got very drunk and had nearly done something very silly, had he got her pegged for a fool? If so, it was very unfair. She was intelligent and efficient in her real life. If only he could see her in the shop, discussing the latest literary phenomenon, running an event, then he'd be impressed.

Even before he parked the car, several farm dogs came leaping up to it, barking furiously. Laura thought of herself as an animal-lover, and any pet dog she met was greeted with a pat and a warm 'hello' but she suddenly felt unwilling to open the door. They looked positively feral.

Dermot seemed not to notice the ravening swarm and got out and walked round to the boot of the car. The dogs surrounded him. Laura turned anxiously from the front seat, wondering how she'd get help if they attacked him. They didn't seem to be savaging him, however, or if they were, Dermot was saying very little about it. But why did no one appear to call them off? Or if they were guard dogs – the farmyard wasn't far away – why didn't anyone appear with a shotgun to order her and Dermot off their land? Surely someone must have heard the noise. Presumably Dermot actually knew the people and they wouldn't mind him parking here. She'd spent most of her life in small towns and wasn't sure of the ways of the countryside. And Ireland, by all accounts, was not just the countryside, but somewhere else altogether.

Dermot came round to her door and opened it. 'Come on, time to stretch our legs.' He had a rucksack with him, which clanked rather.

She hesitated, but before she could force a leg out of the safety of the car he said, 'Are you nervous of the dogs?'

'A bit. I was once bitten by a collie, who had no excuse at all to bite me.'

'You mean you weren't threatening its young, or eating its food?'

'No.'

Dermot shrugged, obviously unable to explain this freak of nature. 'This lot may be noisy devils but there's no harm in them.'

Gingerly, she got out. The dogs surged up to her, still barking their heads off.

'You see? They're fine.'

Laura didn't think they were fine at all. They had wall eyes and looked thin and hungry. They jumped up to smell her better. Although she tried hard not to, she whimpered.

'To hell with this,' he muttered and without warning, swung her off her feet and over his shoulder and carried her in a fireman's lift across the muddy distance towards a gate. The dogs, even more excited now their titbit was tantalisingly out of reach, jumped and barked higher and louder. Laura shut her eyes, bracing herself for a bite on the bottom at any minute. She knew she wasn't enormous but also that she must have felt quite heavy. Dermot was definitely panting.

At last he set her down and she opened her eyes.

'You stay there while I get this open.' He indicated a rusty gate made out of scaffold poles. 'It'll take a while; it hasn't been opened in years. I always climb over.'

'I'll climb over!' she offered, feeling pathetic enough already. 'Just don't let – oh!'

One collie jumped up and left saliva on her arm.

Dermot turned on it. 'What do you think you're doing, you miserable hound of hell! Frightening the poor girl out of wits like that! You'll have her thinking we have no manners in Ireland – if she doesn't think that already!'

'I don't think that,' she said. 'At least, only about the dogs,' she added in a small voice, feeling very pathetic.

Dermot ignored this squeak. 'Are you sure you can climb over OK? I'll open it if you'd rather.' He paused. 'Although the ruts mean I'd have to lift it quite high—'

Before he could finish, she put her foot on the second scaffold pole. Sadly, her legs were just a little bit too short to make the process of climbing the gate easy. What would have been for a taller person a simple matter of swinging one leg over and then the other, for her meant an uncomfortable few moments stranded on the top, unable to progress. Dermot held her arm.

'Bring your leg back over. That's right. Now, climb up to the next bar so you're higher. There. I've got you.'

Somehow she scrambled over, ending in a heap on the other side. Was there no end to her humiliation? He'll hate me now, she thought. I'm such a townie I can't even be taken for a country walk because I can't climb over the gates without help.

'Are you all right now?' he asked when, after an athletic leap, he was over the gate and by her side in one elegant move.

'Fine, thank you. I'm just a bit out of practice.'

'When did you last climb over a gate?' He sounded amused, as if he expected her to have never climbed one before.

'A while ago,' she said, trying frantically to remember.

'I bet you were about six,' he said.

Although she fought it, a smile appeared at the corner of her mouth as she recalled a family holiday in Cornwall. 'That would be about right.'

'We've a couple more to climb later. I expect you'll get the hang of it.'

'I'm sure I will,' she said seriously, but smiling inside, and they set off, Dermot setting a cracking pace.

They went uphill. It was a bright, clear day, cold but

sunny. Currently the sea was on their left but quite far away. The sun bounced off the little waves as it had done before, twinkling like fairy lights in the distance. The land was covered in short, springy grass. Here and there a sheep looked at them curiously, wondering who on earth was mad enough to be out here if they had a choice. Laura, though, was warm as toast. It was hard work keeping up with Dermot, although she sensed he was going slowly for her benefit. Soon her calves were burning and she had to stop for a breather. The blood pulsed through her muscles like mild electric shocks. Although she was tired she felt totally in touch with her body and utterly exhilarated.

'Not much further now. I want us to have lunch in the most perfect spot.'

Laura nodded agreement. She couldn't spare her breath for idle chat.

On and up they went. Laura took off her jacket and tied it round her waist with the sleeves. Even then she was sweating under her clothes. She was elated though, and although she was pleased when he called a halt, she'd have happily gone on for much longer.

'Right now,' he said, swinging his pack down from his back and rummaging inside it. 'What have we got here? A bit of something waterproof to sit on.' He spread out an old plastic mac.

Eager to oblige she sat down, aware as she did so that is was a rather small bit of plastic and they would have to sit hip to hip on it. Then ruefully she remembered that other things they had done together made sitting side by side while fully clothed, even if touching, completely respectable.

'Right now.' He produced a brown paper bag and stared into it. 'We have hard-boiled eggs, but they need peeling, I'm afraid, some rolls, cheese, ham, and a couple of cans of lager. Are you OK drinking it from the can?'

'Of course.'

'Chocolate for afters,' he said.

'My favourite. And I've got toffees in my pocket. I forgot about them earlier. They were to make the journey go quicker but it seemed to go quite quickly anyway.'

She realised she was twittering and tried to calm down. He was just a man, after all. But she realised that to her, he wasn't just a man, he was the equivalent of Seamus Heaney and how many young women who'd studied him at university would feel perfectly relaxed in his presence? Lots, probably, she concluded dolefully, but not her. When they'd been walking she'd felt comfortable in his presence but now they'd stopped she suddenly felt shy and self-conscious again.

He handed her a roll and produced a bit of kitchen foil that had butter in it. 'I've tomatoes and cucumber, but no lettuce. I'll cut it up.' He produced a Swiss Army knife from his pocket and divided the cucumber into chunks. The tomato followed. He seemed anxious to please her, which was touching. 'How are you doing? If you pile it all into your roll you can add your ham and cheese. I've mayonnaise as well.'

'Yummy!'

'I should have brought plates, really,' he said. 'Or one of those nifty little sets.'

'I read somewhere that you should never trust a man who had his own picnic set,' she said, relaxing a little and then suddenly realising she'd strayed into territory she'd rather have avoided. You should never trust a man with a voice like molten gold, eyes as blue as the sea either, but reading that it was a bad idea didn't stop you doing it.

'Well, you'll be perfectly safe with me then.' He looked at her quizzically.

She forced herself to meet his teasing gaze. 'That's all right then.'

'So, tell me about yourself, Laura,' he said after a fair amount of munching.

In spite of her huge breakfast, Laura found herself eating with enthusiasm. When it was all gone she lay back and stretched. The sun was shining in her eyes and she closed them. She heard him lie down next to her.

'Not much to tell. Only child, good girl at school, went to university, got a good degree and ended up working in a bookshop. What about you?'

'I was the youngest of a large family. Bad boy but bright enough to escape being found out. Wrote a couple of novels and ended up being a writer.'

'But you also went travelling, didn't you? I do regret not doing anything like that before I settled down.'

He chuckled. 'You're only twenty-six. I don't think you can describe yourself as "settled down". You've got your whole life ahead of you to go travelling.'

She shook her head. 'I'm too timid to go backpacking on my own. At least,' she added as she thought more about what she'd said, 'I have been up to now.'

'You don't have to go backpacking on your own. There's lots of ways to see a bit of the world that doesn't involved hefting huge weights about.'

She chuckled and sat up, eyeing the components of the picnic. 'I suppose so. I've done my travelling via books so far, but as you say, there's time to change.'

He leant up on one elbow and studied her. She sensed the warmth of his body next to hers and felt a glow of contentment. She was conversing with her all-time favourite writer, against the backdrop of a magnificent Irish landscape.

'The best writer in the world can't be a substitute for your own experience,' he said.

'No, not a substitute, but it can be something better, can't it?'

'How do you mean?'

She made a gesture towards the view. 'Well, take this, for example. It's brilliant to be here because it's stunning, really lovely. But if you were describing it in a book, you could give it layers of meaning that a mere picture, or just looking at it, couldn't.'

He made a sound somewhere between a sigh and a chuckle. 'Are you talking about me in particular or writers in general?'

She shrugged. 'Either. Whichever you like.'

'I think I'll take the general option. The responsibility is too great otherwise.'

'Do you feel your responsibility as a writer?' This was something Laura had always wondered about.

'A bit.' He seemed not to want to carry on with the conversation. 'Would you like to walk a bit further? We can leave the things here and then come back and have tea.'

'Oh yes.' She got to her feet, 'Maybe I'll take the opportunity to go travelling but keep it on a very small scale.'

He laughed. 'Come on then.'

They walked to the top of the hill from where they could see a slightly different view. Still the sun shone and the sea sparkled. Because she was staring out to sea, trying to spot an island Dermot had said was sometimes visible, she stumbled. He caught her arm.

'Are you OK? You didn't twist your ankle did you?'

'No, I'm fine.' Unnerved by his closeness she moved away from him. 'Race you back down to the picnic things!'

As she ran, making very sure of her footing, she wondered why she had run away from him. Was it him or herself she didn't trust? As she collapsed in a heap by their belongings she knew it was her. She might do anything. If he asked her to go with him to a sheltered spot and suggested they made love, she might not say no.

And she couldn't. She had to leave soon and she already liked him too much to want to risk doing something she might later regret. She knew herself too well.

'Well now,' he said as he joined her. 'Are you ready for tea? There's fruit cake to have with it.'

'Let's wait, I couldn't eat a thing now.' Suddenly tired she lay on her back, listening to the sea and the sounds of the countryside: the occasional baa from a sheep; a distant tractor; seagulls. As she closed her eyes she realised she very rarely just enjoyed nature. Usually she'd have brought a book with her and while she would have appreciated her surroundings, she wouldn't have given herself up to them in the same way.

A little later she opened her eyes and became aware of him next to her. Although she didn't stir he must have sensed she was awake because he said, 'You wouldn't think you could take a nap in the outdoors in January, would you?'

She chuckled sleepily. 'No, although of course we are very well wrapped up.'

'And a good thing too, in my opinion. Although I can't believe you fell asleep on me again!'

She swiftly changed the subject. 'I must say this spot is very heaven. I can understand why you don't want to leave it, although . . .' she went on, 'my literary festival would only mean you being away for a few days.' She closed her eyes again against the sun.

He laughed. 'To be honest, that's not the reason I don't like doing literary festivals any more.'

Knowing that he must have done hundreds of them when he was first published she didn't need to ask for his reasons; he'd be bored stiff with them.

'So,' he went on, 'why are you so eager to get me to come to yours?'

She would have liked to deny being eager – she hated to sound needy – but she couldn't. Besides, it was surprisingly easy to talk while lying on your back with your eyes closed, knowing your companion was doing the same. 'Well, we'll get sponsorship if you come, that's all. I was sent here on a mission to get you to come at all costs.'

'Hm. I don't like to be indelicate . . .'

She chuckled, 'Well, I'll pretend to believe you.'

'But would you have shown quite so much dedication to duty if I'd been eighty, with no hair and false teeth?'

'No. But if you'd been eighty, with no hair and false teeth, would you have said you'd come if I went to bed with you?' She paused. 'No, don't answer, I don't want to hear it.'

He was chuckling now. 'You're quite right. I've been in training to be a dirty old man since I was seventeen.'

'I thought you were in training to be a writer when you were seventeen.'

'The two activities go together.'

Lying supine was making her prone to giggling. 'I don't want to hear that. I'm a serious student of literature. I am a big fan of your work, and I was very drunk. And I'm also a virgin – I thought—'

All desire to giggle left her. Why had she said that? Why had she let the words escape? Her train of thought was perfectly logical: she'd been going to tell him that she thought she would like him to have her virginity because of who he was, how he wrote. But that wasn't the sort of thing you told people, unless they were very close friends, like Monica.

He didn't speak for some seconds. 'Oh. So when you agreed to go to bed with me, it would have been your first time?'

'Uh-huh.'

He laughed gently. 'No wonder you ran away.'

'I said, I was very drunk, and I wouldn't have run away if I hadn't fallen asleep.'

'So what was so frightening? The sight of me snoring my head off or the thought that you might have given your virginity to a wild Irish writer?'

Although she wanted to be entirely truthful, she didn't then tell him that there was no one else in the world she'd rather give her virginity to. His tone was teasing and she wasn't sure if it was just a game – albeit a very pleasant one – to him or not. She would keep her answers as light as possible. 'The realisation that I'd been so drunk I didn't know if we'd made love or not. I was appalled at myself.'

'But not at me?'

'No. You're a man. You'd made a casual suggestion; you didn't expect me to take you up on it. Did you?'

He paused for a long time. 'As we're being totally honest with each other, I'll tell you: I don't get turned down all that often.'

She put her hand over her eyes, although he wasn't looking at her. 'Oh God! Now I feel like I'm in a long line—'

'If it's any consolation to you, I don't ask anything like as often as I used to. I'm quietening right down. And I always use a condom, you can tell Monica.'

She chuckled softly. 'I'm glad to hear it. And I think you convinced Monica about the condoms. I'm so sorry she harassed you like that. She was only looking after me, but it must have been desperately embarrassing.'

'Not at all,' he said softly. Laura could hear the smile in his voice. 'I've been asked worse things, I can tell you.'

'Really? You didn't look embarrassed, I must say.'

'So you could see, could you? From your spot at the back there.'

'Yes. It was quite a small hall.' So her trying to hide at the back again hadn't worked.

'And I filled it. You don't need to say anything else about me being a big fish in a small pond.'

'I wouldn't dream of it! I've no doubt you could fill the Albert Hall if you'd agree to go.'

'I don't know about that,' he said dismissively, and then went on, 'And another thing. I promise you that if we had made love you would have known about it, drunk or not.' He paused. 'Were you really that far gone? You didn't seem it.'

She sighed. Being drunk seemed a better excuse for her behaviour than being in love – thrall – lust – she still couldn't decide quite how to define her feelings for him. That would be really outrageous. 'I'm not used to drinking whiskey by the tumbler full.'

'No, I suppose not.'

'And the fact that I'm a virgin is not something I usually tell people.'

'Well, it's nothing to be ashamed of.'

'No, but at my age it's a bit – well, odd, really.'

'Is there a reason for it?'

'Nope. Only I never found a man I fancied enough.' She blushed, praying his eyes were still shut and he wouldn't see. She'd virtually told him that in him she had found a man she fancied enough.

'Well, I have a confession to make too.'

'What?'

'I've had writer's block for nearly fifteen years.'

'Oh my goodness.' Laura didn't know what else to say. It was quite a revelation.

'And the reason I'm telling you is there's something about confession being sort of mutual. Not that I expect Catholic priests hearing the peccadilloes of their parishioners necessarily say, "Don't go worrying about that now, I often have a wee peep at that sort of magazine myself," but you shared something with me, and there's been no one else I can tell.'

She felt incredibly privileged, although she also thought that maybe people would have guessed.

'Well, you can understand it.' He seemed eager to justify himself. 'Two books straight off the blocks on to the best-seller lists and the literary prize shortlists.'

'And you won most of the prizes.'

'I did.' He sounded embarrassed. 'They're all waiting for me to fail now.'

She wanted to deny it but she knew how cruel the literary world could be. Cutting down tall poppies was what it liked to do best. 'Does your agent know?'

'Nope, and she mustn't. I fob her off every time she rings me, tell her I'm working on a huge book that'll take years – is taking years.'

'Does she buy that?' She was pretty sure Eleanora didn't for one moment.

His laugh was rueful now. 'Never mind buying it – she'd much rather have something to sell.'

She joined in his laughter. 'There isn't a publisher out there who wouldn't pay millions or at least hundreds of thousands for it.'

'I know. And I could do with the cash.'

'You couldn't offer them three chapters – they wouldn't have to be all that good after all – and get them to cough up an advance?'

'That, young lady,' he said, sounding stern, 'would not be ethical.'

She sighed. 'I suppose not. Plenty of writers would do it, though.'

'I feel if I did that, my block would be permanent. The guilt would make it even harder for me. The Irish are cursed by guilt, you know.'

'Really?' She didn't mean to sound disbelieving, but she did. To gloss over it, she said, 'Or you could teach creative writing. They run courses in wonderfully exotic locations. I don't suppose they pay that much but they might be fun.' She hesitated. 'All those eager young women writers. You could have your pick.' It cost her something to go on in this lighthearted manner. He could have his pick of any group of women, she was certain. Knowing it didn't make it easier for her. Now that she'd actually met him and talked to him properly, she knew her feelings for him were no longer just infatuation, but were in danger of becoming the foundation for something much stronger.

'I do give the odd lecture, but I always felt those writing courses were for writers who didn't write any more.'

'Not at all. Some very busy writers do them because they want to give something back, and like encouraging new talent.'

'Ah, you wouldn't be muddling me up with one of them, would you?'

She giggled again. 'Not at all, at all.'

'Don't mock me.'

'I wouldn't dream of it.'

'I'd love to know what you do dream of,' he said.

Laura swallowed. 'I've confided in you quite enough,' she managed, sounding suitably prim. She felt she would literally die rather than let him know what she was dreaming of right now.

He laughed softly and they fell into a comfortable silence. She felt a contentment she had rarely felt before, even at the bookshop where she'd always been so happy. Now it seemed far away and no longer so desirable.

But would she have felt like this, about this headland, this wildness, if the bookshop hadn't been about to close? She didn't know. Nothing was certain any more. But she did know that even though it was January, she felt she was in the most beautiful spot on earth. And it wasn't just being with Dermot, it was something more.

A while later he said, 'I could help you out with your problem, you know. Not here and now, obviously, but in more comfortable surroundings.'

The thought of this was somehow a bit heartbreaking. He obviously didn't feel the same way about her as she did him – how could he? She felt she'd known him all her life, but he'd only just met her. She didn't know how he really felt about her, if this really was only a bit of fun for him, and she couldn't ask. It would sound so serious. But she just couldn't let go and call his bluff. Whether it was bluff or not, she couldn't do it. And if he was just being kind that would somehow be worse.

'No thank you, I'll be all right,' she said and then paused, struggling to think of something suitably light and flirtatious, to give the impression that she wasn't really bothered. 'I've got used to being a virgin, after all these years.'

He chuckled. 'The status quo has something to be said for it.'

Thinking the status quo wasn't as easy to live with for him, she said, 'I don't suppose I could help you with your problem?'

He shot her a glance filled with mischief. 'If I was really wicked, I'd tell you that the virginity of a young girl was a well-known cure for writer's block.'

She twinkled back at him. 'But you're only partly wicked?'

'Most of the time, yes.'

She considered for a moment whether, if he did really think her virginity would cure him, she'd give it to him. The answer was probably. And not just so the literary world would be so grateful (it was not a favour she could call in, after all), but because underneath all her reservations, she really wanted to sleep with him, almost as much as she wanted to help him. But the moment was lost.

'It's a shame really,' she said, thinking aloud.

'What? That I'm not exploitative enough to demand the sacrifice of your maidenhood?'

She laughed, to deny it, but in her heart she was saying, 'Yes!' 'No, I meant it's a shame that things aren't so easily solved. Things like not being able to write any more when really, in your heart, you know you can write like an angel. You may have your problems with the people who give literary prizes but they don't give them to people who can't write.'

'Oh they do, you know, but let's not argue about it. It's time for tea. You English must have your tea, isn't that so? But don't worry, you don't have to move. I have all the makings.'

'The thermos is a wonderful invention,' she murmured.

'Indeed, but we're not having any truck with them. I have my Volcano kettle with me.'

She sat up. 'Your what?'

'Do you not have them in England? Sure you're terribly behind the times over there.'

She watched as he took out of his rucksack a copy of the *Irish Times* and a large cylindrical object in a drawstring bag. He took this out and then started to tear up sheets of newspaper and stuff them down the column in the middle. When all the newspaper was used up, he took the cork from the top. 'Right now, I'm off to find some water.'

He took a small can from the rucksack. 'You can go back to sleep if you like. I may have to go a little way away to find it.'

She closed her eyes. This was so blissful. The thought of catching the ferry and going back to England intruded on her joy and she batted it away. Live in the moment, she told herself, using a saying that was printed on uplifting postcards they sold in the bookshop. Just enjoy what you have right now, she added, quoting another of them.

Dermot came back a few minutes later. He poured the

water into a little spout at the top of the kettle, and then set light to the paper.

'How does it work?' she asked, fascinated and amused.

'The paper burning in the central column heats the water in the jacket outside. One copy of *The Times*, or the *Irish Times*, is just enough to boil the water. Madam will have her tea in but a moment.'

'I don't remember Madam asking for tea, she was offered it.'

'Don't split hairs.'

'Well no, that would be cruel,' she agreed.

'You're a mad girl, so you are.'

The sun, which had burned so enthusiastically, was fading. She lay back on the heather, although she was getting cold now. She loved him thinking she was a mad girl, when really, back on the mainland, she was almost boringly efficient and predictable.

He put tea bags into mugs and then poured on the boiling water from the little spout in the water-jacket. Milk came from a jam jar.

They sat together companionably, clutching the mugs of tea and looking at the sea. A few clouds were gathering now, and a chilly wind was getting up.

'Thank you so much for bringing me here,' she said, aware that their final parting would be hard for her. 'It's been a lovely day.'

'For me too,' he said. 'You're great company.'

She sipped her tea.

'Damn, I forgot the cake. Here.' He handed her a plastic container that was full of wedges of fruit cake. 'What time is your ferry again?' he asked as she took one, and she knew her perfect day was over.

She told him.

'I'll get you back in plenty of time to leave. And I will come to your literary festival, without your sacrifice, if you don't tell anyone about it – any press, I mean. Not until the last minute, anyway. I don't want to have to battle with all the publicity.'

Laura found herself close to tears. 'Thank you,' she said huskily, hoping he would think it was the cold wind that was making her eyes water.

Chapter Eight

'Don't mind the hounds, they get out of the way eventually,' said Fenella, opening the door to Somerby wide.

'Hello, hounds,' said Laura, wondering why she was coping with Fen's pack perfectly well, although they were completely blocking her way, when those on a certain farm in Ireland had seemed so threatening. (Possibly because none of this lot were snarling and curling their upper lips.) 'Are there some new ones, or did I just not notice them when you let them out as I left last time?'

'I'm looking after my sister's two little Tibetan terriers while she's on hols. Treacle and Toffee. I'm not going to want to give them back.'

'They are very sweet,' said Laura, putting out a hand to be sniffed and finding six noses eagerly searching for food traces. She stifled a sigh, remembering how Dermot had rescued her in Ireland. Ballyfitzpatrick seemed a world away. She had half hoped she might have heard from him – a friendly text at least – but then admonished herself. Why should he? And somehow she felt too shy to be the one to make contact first.

'It wasn't too hard getting the time off?' asked Fenella, kissing Laura on the cheek and stirring the dogs away with her foot.

'No, Henry's been very understanding. So's Grant. But Henry wants to supply the books and Grant wants to do something glamorous for the festival.'

'We'll be glad of all the help we can get.'

Laura indicated a cloth bag filled with files. 'I've been quite busy since I got back from Ireland.'

'Brilliant!' Then Fenella gave a little jump and clapped her hands. 'I can't believe you got Dermot Flynn! Jacob Stone is thrilled. He's going to give us lots of money and I've insisted we increase your fee. Five hundred pounds.'

'Brilliant. Thank you.' She had phoned Fenella the moment she got back from Ireland with the good news. She had followed it up with the bad – that Dermot didn't want anyone to know he was appearing until the last moment – almost immediately. Fenella hadn't seemed to take in what a drawback this might be.

Now Fenella hugged her tightly. 'Sorry, I was so excited about Dermot that I forgot my manners. Come in properly, dump your bags and come on down to the kitchen. I'll show you your room when the fan heater's had time to warm it up a bit.'

Laura put her case down and separated the carrier bag with a box of chocolates and a plant in it. She had come for a serious planning weekend. 'So Jacob Stone didn't mind that Dermot wanted to keep it all under wraps for as long as possible?'

Fenella shook her head. 'I don't think he cares that much about the festival, he just wanted to hear Dermot Flynn.' She paused. 'Well, come on. Let's go down to the kitchen and have a drink. Rupert's cooking supper. It smells heavenly. I'm doing pudding, which is the very exotic ice cream with Marsala poured over it.'

'Unusual,' said Laura, following her hostess down the stairs, holding her carrier.

'Actually it's delish, but not exactly labour-intensive, which is why I serve it so often.'

'You don't think we should start work before we eat? I've come to work, after all.'

'I know and you will but tomorrow will do. My brain

doesn't function after five o'clock anyway. Just be a guest and relax tonight.'

Within minutes the present was delivered and exclaimed over and Laura was seated at the kitchen table with a big glass of wine and a bowl of pistachios in front of her. Rupert had delivered these shortly after he had embraced her warmly. 'Oh that's delicious!' she said, having taken a sip. Although superficially she was talking about the wine, privately she was commenting on the welcome. Her own family didn't do hugs and wine, more 'Oh, hello dear' and 'I suppose I'd better put the kettle on'. She had yet to tell them how she'd got on in Ireland, but as they hadn't asked either, she didn't feel too guilty. And she'd been too busy to visit them since she'd got back.

Fenella took the seat opposite her, having been assured by her husband that there was nothing she could do to help with the meal until later. 'So,' she said eagerly, anxious to prise all the details out of Laura. 'Tell all. Did you have to offer Dermot Flynn your body to get him to agree to come?'

For a stunned moment, Laura wondered how on earth Fenella could have known this, but then realised she was joking. Monica, the only other person apart from Dermot who knew, wouldn't have told her.

She decided the truth would be a good disguise. 'Practically, but you'll be glad to hear he didn't take me up on it.'

'Oh?' said Rupert, stirring thoughtfully. 'That's not his reputation. I heard he was a bit of a womaniser.' He lifted his spoon to his lips. 'Ah yes. The gravy is coming along nicely.'

'Going by his photo he wouldn't have to work too hard at it,' said Fenella. 'Is he as gorgeous in real life?'

'Mm, but older,' said Laura carefully.

'I think men improve with age, like fine wine. Isn't that right, Rupert?'

'Whatever you say, honey.'

'So,' Fenella turned her full attention on Laura again. 'What did you have to do to persuade him to come? Eleanora said for years you couldn't drag him out of Ireland for love nor money, but now he's doing this course as well.'

'What course?' Laura put down the nut she had just prised open and looked at Fen.

'Oh, haven't you heard? No, I suppose you wouldn't have, it's only just been settled. It's a writing course – a competition – at Bath Spa University. People have to send in their novels and the best ten or so get to go on the course. One of Eleanora's other clients – can't remember who – was supposed to be doing it but they had to pull out for some reason. Anyway, she's got Dermot to do it.' She frowned. 'In fact, I think he might have actually offered. She mentioned the problem with the other author while she was talking to Dermot about something else, the festival probably, when he suggested he did it. She was quite taken aback – especially as she's hardly spoken to him in ages and he usually avoids her calls.'

Laura found herself oddly put out. It was nothing to do with her, but somehow, after the enormous lengths she had gone to just to get Dermot to give a talk at a literary festival, let alone the lengths she had been willing to go to, she felt affronted that he had actually offered to teach a writing course, which would be a far bigger deal. 'I must say, I am a bit surprised. I had to go all the way to Ireland to get him to do an hour sitting on a stage being asked questions by a sycophantic interviewer. Piece of cake compared to actually setting exercises, thinking up a course, all that stuff. And he offered to do it? It doesn't make sense.' She really wanted to say that it didn't seem fair but didn't want to appear churlish.

'Maybe he felt once he'd decided actually to leave his native land for one thing, it wouldn't be so hard to do it for two.' Fenella frowned for a second, 'Although the course thing is first, come to think of it. Maybe he'll be moving straight here after the course. Anyway,' she went on enthusiastically, 'do you suppose having done the course he'd let us advertise him for the festival?'

'I don't know, but if he's actually had students, who couldn't all be sworn to secrecy, he should do by then.' Laura was still miffed and tried to shake herself out of it. Another sip of wine helped. 'How's the music festival going?'

'OK, I think. We've got one or two quite famous bands who have almost definitely confirmed. And Monica, of course. Did you and she have fun in Ireland?'

'Gosh yes. She's a real laugh. She made me hire a bicycle with her to go and track down an old boyfriend.'

'Did she find him?'

'He wasn't in when we first arrived on our bicycles, thank goodness, considering I was giggling so much I was nearly wetting myself. And afterwards, when she had a another chance to visit him, she got no reply either.' Finding she didn't want to explain now about why Monica was on her own for a day, she moved on. 'But she was a great travelling companion. Made me go to the pub and things.'

'Was it a real Irish pub with music and lots of crack?' asked Rupert, still stirring his gravy.

'I don't think anyone was taking drugs,' said Laura, pretending to misunderstand.

Fenella laughed. 'It sounds fun. And is Dermot Flynn really "Oirish"?'

'He has a definite lilt but he doesn't sound like someone out of *Father Ted*.'

'Oh! *Father Ted*! How wonderful was that?' Fenella sighed.

'Are you two planning on doing any work tonight?' said Rupert. 'Do you want more wine or not?'

'Yes please,' said Fenella. 'We decided we're going to start early tomorrow. Tonight we can just toss around ideas.'

'Alcohol always helps with that,' said Rupert, pouring. 'And we're just about ready to eat.'

'I'll set the table.' Fenella reached into a drawer and pulled out a random selection of knives and forks. Then she cleared one end of the table with her elbow, sending a miscellany of papers, a fruit bowl, a pile of clean underwear that had presumably been drying over the Aga and a screwdriver up the other end. Fortunately it was a long table.

'I should really have tidied up a bit more for your visit,' Fenella went on apologetically, setting places. 'But I never seem to unless we've got a huge event on. We don't do weddings much in the winter so we never see the whole table cleared until spring. Maybe we should just force the family to come to us for Christmas. Then I'd do it.'

'I don't think I've ever seen such a huge joint of beef,' said Laura, watching Rupert carve.

'It's locally produced,' said Fenella, 'and we'll eat it cold for ages now, with soup and baked potatoes. I'm always a bit vague when it comes to ordering meat. I seem to buy it by the haunch rather than the pound.'

'As long as you're not vague when it comes to organising literary festivals,' said Laura. She was teasing but there was a thread of anxiety in the back of her mind.

'Oh no, work wise, I'm spot on. It's just domestically I'm a bit of a dilly.'

'Here you are, Dilly,' said her husband fondly, 'and make sure Laura has plenty of gravy.'

When at last they were all eating, and no one had to jump up and get anything else, Laura said, 'I've had quite a lot of ideas about things we could do in the run-up for the festival. A reading group for instance.'

'Oh, that's a good idea. As you know, I'm in a reading group,' said Fenella. 'And there are another couple around, including one in the library.'

Laura nodded while she finished her mouthful. 'I've been in touch with the local librarian. She's very keen. We just need to get the authors sorted out as quickly as possible.'

'Then we'll sell lots of books and they'll be inspired to come to the events.' Fenella speared a piece of roast potato. 'It'll stir up interest.' She chewed thoughtfully. 'Although the library's group always get their books ordered specially. Not everyone can afford to buy a new book every month.'

Laura's bookseller's mantle fell away for a moment. 'Of course not. I couldn't myself if I didn't get proofs from the shop. But it's great to have the library on side.'

'We could get the local paper to sponsor something,' suggested Rupert. 'All the local institutions should have a stake in it.'

'What about a writing competition?' suggested Fenella, her mouth full of carrot.

'But who would we get to judge it?' said Rupert. 'We're going to have our work cut out setting this thing up, and we're not qualified, really.'

'Dermot,' muttered Laura, who was still faintly resentful about him offering to do that course and cross with herself because of it. She sipped her wine, wondering why she was feeling so resentful. He wasn't her exclusive property and he hadn't actually taken her virginity, after all.

'We'll find someone,' said Fenella. 'I've got a huge wish list of authors I want. One of them will be willing to pick a winner, if we didn't offer them more than about five to read.'

'Damien Stubbs might,' said Laura. 'We should definitely ask him to the festival. He's really good and very attractive. Eleanora could make him come. He's one of hers.'

'I hope we don't forget all this. Here, Rupes, chuck us that bit of paper and a pencil.' Fenella made a note.

'Oh,' said Laura, 'and a children's writing competition would be good. The best ones could be read out at an event and printed in the local paper.' Laura considered for a moment. 'Although would the parents come to the event if they could see their child's work in print anyway?'

'I should think so,' said Fenella. 'Hard to tell. But children's events would make the locals keen. It would be their festival too, not just something that's inflicted on them.' She chewed reflectively. 'I've no idea how to get in touch with my wish list of writers.'

'That's what I'm here for. We contact them through their agents or publishers,' said Laura. 'We find out who's in charge of their publicity and ask them. The only trouble is that it can take a while, if you don't get a named person to deal with.'

'Oh it's so good having you,' said Fenella. 'You know all the wrinkles.'

'And I'll probably get a few too,' Laura murmured.

Fenella ignored this. 'I want to involve the local schools, get them to all come to something.'

'Or it might be easier to get the authors to go to the schools,' suggested Laura, flinching at the vision of marshalling fifty or so children into a hall.

'Or both,' suggested Rupert. 'The authors go into the schools, give the children such a good time that they pester their parents to take them to the main event.'

'Good thinking. You're not just a pretty face, after all.' Fenella smiled at her husband affectionately.

'Where are we actually going to hold the events?' asked Laura, feeling gently envious of their relationship. 'Obviously you won't be doing everything here. Festivals always scatter themselves over a town, of course, but yours is a pretty small one.'

'Big enough though,' said Fenella, defending her home territory. 'There'll be some here, of course, but for Dermot or any other really big names, we can hire the cinema. Don't look at me like that! Apparently it's lovely! And there's a huge car park just next door. And I've had a word with the vicar and there's a chapel that's not used much that we can have. That has parking too,' added Fenella, looking at Rupert, who'd obviously been a bit obsessed by this issue.

'So the vicar's keen on the festival, is he?' said Laura. 'I'm sure that'll be helpful.'

'Not he, she, and she's in my book group.'

'Excellent!'

'So we'll need to sort out the venues, but Sarah – remember? She was at the meeting – is going to help decide who should go where. I'm hopeless about guessing numbers and how much space they'll take up.'

'Wouldn't a marquee here be better for Dermot than a cinema?' suggested Laura.

'You don't like my cinema idea, do you? Well, we can go and look at it and decide later.'

'Where are you going to put everyone up?' asked Laura.

'Here, as far as we can. We can sleep about eight, comfortably, and of course not everyone will be here at the same time. The authors will stay in the house on a rolling basis unless they're sharing, in which case they might have one of the cottages. There are also lots of b. and b's. locally, but we hope we don't have to put writers in them, unless they prefer it for some reason.'

'We must mention the b. and b.s when we do the flyers, so people know they can stay. It'll be part of the rural image: "Enjoy literature in the undiscovered beauties of wherever . . ."'

'We're not exactly undiscovered,' complained Rupert. 'We did have a lot of publicity for a celebrity wedding not long ago.'

'I meant the area in general,' said Laura. 'If people think the area is attractive, they're more likely to come. Think of Hay-on-Wye!'

'Are we going to have a theme?' asked Fenella. 'I mean, we've got the music stuff going on too.'

'At exactly the same time?' asked Laura anxiously.

'We thought alternate days,' said Rupert, 'or a few musical events, a few literary ones, and then a music one at the end. Or vice versa. We've got permission to use a couple of the fields.'

'That took a lot of tact and persuasion,' said Fenella. 'It's only because farming isn't doing brilliantly at the moment that I managed to swing it. I think they all imagined Glastonbury was moving up here.'

'But the farms should get something out of it,' said Rupert. 'Lots of them said they could rent out space for camping.'

'And we've got some really big names for the music side of it,' said Laura.

Fenella winced slightly. 'Not confirmed,' she said. 'That's why I wanted some biggies for the lit. bit. Monica is on the case though. She's pulled in all the favours she can manage and has used blackmail if that failed.'

'Well, I wouldn't refuse her anything,' declared Laura.

'And I hope you won't refuse another roast spud from me,' said Rupert.

'Of course not.'

'So, theme or no theme?' asked Fenella. 'I think not, on the whole.'

'The Cheltenham lit. fest. always has one,' said Laura.

'I know but they've got the pick of the bunch. We're brand new. Authors might not be so keen to come to us.'

'I think they will,' said Laura, pushing her plate away

from her so she could really make her point. 'Having Dermot will make it a big literary event, they'll want to be there. Amazing publicity for them. Besides, most of them will get to stay in a lovely country house and there's something special about the first year of a festival.' Laura felt herself getting excited. She realised she was going to enjoy working on the festival with Fen, however much work it might involve.

'It might be the first and last,' said Rupert.

'We might have to tell them he's going to appear and they'll get a chance to meet him. I wonder if he'd mind us doing that?' said Laura, ignoring Rupert's uncharacteristic pessimism.

'Or would he hate that even more?' asked Fenella. 'You know him, Laura. What do you think?'

'I don't know! He may hate other authors. I've come across a few who do. It's probably professional jealousy or something.'

'Maybe we could arrange a discreet authors' dinner before his event. He can choose which ones and we'll make it really special.'

'But would that be cost-effective?' asked Laura. 'A special dinner could cost loads.'

'We don't need to worry about that,' said Rupert. 'We have contacts.'

'Breaking even is all we can hope to do this first year,' said Fenella. 'Although the bottom line is important, we have to speculate in order to accumulate.'

'That sounds very businesslike,' said Laura, impressed.

'I read it somewhere,' said Fenella, 'but more to the point, do you think Dermot would agree to all this?'

'If we'd cleared it with him first,' said Laura. 'He's not easy. And a bit unpredictable,' she added, thinking of him agreeing to do a course, apparently without even being asked, when everyone in Ireland had told her that he wouldn't stir out of his village. 'He may love the idea.'

'On the other hand,' put in Rupert, 'maybe we shouldn't give Dermot so much control? He may never be able to decide who he wants to come. I think we should just invite who we think we'd like.'

On Saturday morning their work began in earnest. Laura sat at the computer and, with Fenella's help, typed up all the ideas that had flowed as freely as the wine had the night before.

'OK, now we've got our definitive list of authors, we must check up on who their publishers are.'

'How are we going to do that?'

'I've bought some trade mags. That'll help,' said Laura. 'But to be honest, I know lots of them. Now we've pruned it down a bit, it shouldn't take long.'

They had agreed that in order to be invited the authors had to (*a*) be still alive (this when Rupert expressed a burning desire to meet Evelyn Waugh) and (*b*) live either in the UK or near enough so their travel expenses wouldn't use up the entire budget.

When letters had been dispatched, including inducements such as nights to be spent in 'country-house style with old-fashioned hospitality', they spent the rest of the morning writing to schools, inviting entrants to their children's short-story competition. Laura knew a lovely children's author who could be the final judge and Fenella knew a couple of teachers from her book group who could draw up a shortlist.

After lunch, they took all the dogs for a gallop over the fields, and Rupert advised Laura on what sort of car she should buy. She couldn't go on borrowing Grant's for much longer; twice was enough.

On Sunday afternoon they had all repaired to what Fenella and Rupert referred to as 'the small drawing room', which would have swallowed up Laura's bedsit twice over. Rupert had built a dazzling log fire and they were all beginning to doze off in front of it. Laura had had a tour of the local area so she could see some of the venues (from the outside at least) and they had ended up at the pub for lunch. Laura was seriously considering Fenella's suggestion that she should stay another night and go back early the next morning.

Rupert had picked up the paper and was working on the general knowledge crossword when the phone rang. He and Fenella exchanged glances and then Fen got up. 'I can't think who'd be ringing at this time of day.'

'It's only four o'clock,' said Rupert. 'And if you answer it you'll know who it is.'

'Hello,' said Fenella, sounding efficient. 'Somerby.'

Laura stole the crossword from Rupert while his attention was distracted. Then she stole his pencil and put in the answer to a clue.

'Yes, that's right,' Fenella was saying. 'Uh huh, that's me. What? Oh. Well yes, I have, actually, but I can do better than that. She's here. I'll put her on. Laura?' Fenella came across the room and offered her the handset. 'It's for you.'

'It can't be,' said Laura, not touching the phone but at least getting up. 'Who is it?'

'Dermot Flynn. He rang me to get your number.'

Laura's knees went weak and her mouth went dry. She tugged at her polo neck, swallowed and took a deep breath. 'Right. OK.' She took the phone as if it might explode and walked away from the others. Her heart started to race with nerves and excitement. 'Hello? Dermot?' This was the first time she'd spoken to him since Ireland.

'Hello, Laura,' said a voice that made her knees go weaker and her mouth become drier. She sank on to a little chair that was near a small desk.

'Hello,' she said again, wishing she had a glass of water.

'It's a great coincidence that you happened to be there, isn't it?'

'Maybe. Great for whom?' she asked warily, wondering what he meant.

'Great for me, anyway. The reason I need to speak to you is, I want you to do a job for me.'

'What sort of job?' Laura was a bit panicked. She was busy enough as it was with the festival and still working at the bookshop.

'Did you hear about the writing course I've agreed to do?'

She turned away a little but was aware of Rupert and Fenella poring over the crossword as if it were an exam paper, they were working so hard at not eavesdropping. 'Yes. I was a bit surprised. It was all I could do to get you to agree to speak at the festival, now here you are offering to run a writing course. I thought you weren't keen on them.' She tried to sound lighthearted, but she found speaking to him almost unbearably lovely.

He gave a short, dismissive laugh. 'I'm not running anything, I'll just teach.'

Laura tucked a strand of hair behind her ear to help her think. 'But I thought people sent in their manuscripts and you decided who got on the course on the strength of them?'

'Oh, so you know all about it, do you?' He sounded amused.

'Not at all. Just what Fenella told me. But that's right, isn't it?' Now she pulled the scrunchy off her ponytail and shook out her curls as if doing so would settle her jumbled thoughts.

'It is so, and that's where you come in.' He sounded a little triumphant as if he'd solved a problem.

'Where? Where do I come in?'

'My agent, Eleanora, the old dragon' – his chuckle revealed he was fond her, old dragon or not – 'told me that you have a very good eye when it comes to fiction. You didn't tell me you knew her.'

'Well, er, yes, I do. And yes, I suppose I have read a lot,' said Laura tentatively.

'So I want you to read all the scripts and pick out the ten best.'

She gulped. 'What? But how would I know? When would I have time to do it? I'm organising a literary festival!' A second later she remembered that literary festivals were often run by people with full-time jobs.

'Not single-handed. Eleanora told me there's a team, including her niece, or god-daughter, Fenella – whoever it was I spoke to.'

'That's true.' Laura struggled to sound calm.

'Well then, you can do my scripts for me. I'll pay you,' he added.

'How much?' Too late Laura realised this must have made her sound awfully mercenary. She hadn't really asked because she cared that much, although she did need money. She just wanted to give herself a bit of time to think.

'We'll work out a fee, but probably about ten pounds a script. I'd need you to pick, say, thirty, and we'll decide on the best ten together, over the phone probably, or by email.'

'All right then,' she said meekly. Then a thought struck her. 'There's just one thing. I only live in a small flat, just a bedsit with a bathroom, really. I'm not sure I've got the space to do all this.'

'I'm sure it'll be fine. Don't you worry about it.'

Laura could tell he was now bored with the subject of the course, and his 'Don't you worry about it' really meant 'I'm not going to worry about it'. Well, he didn't need to, now he'd got her to agree to help him.

'So, how have you been?' he said now. 'Have you recovered from your trip to the Emerald Isle?'

The laugh in his voice was not helping her current heart condition. 'Of course. What was there to recover from?'

'Drinking whiskey by the tumbler full for a start,' he said. 'Not to mention the men you had to beat off with a stick.' She could just imagine him, lying back in his chair, possibly doodling, enjoying his gentle teasing.

'I didn't need a stick.' She was smiling too and she wasn't sure if he would be able to hear this in her voice or not.

'Sure now, I was meek as a lamb when it came to it.' He paused. 'So, I'll tell Eleanora to get whoever's in charge of this course to send the scripts to you. We'll keep in touch about it.'

'Thank you. I think.'

He laughed. 'Sure you'll thank me. You may discover the next Dermot Flynn and then the world will be at your feet.'

'I think one Dermot Flynn is quite enough for the world, thank you,' she said.

He laughed again. 'You're a lovely girl, Laura Horsley, and I have my eye on you.' Then he disconnected.

Laura examined the handset and then switched it off. She got up and walked slowly to where Fenella had answered the phone and found the rest. She was horribly aware of Rupert and Fenella studying her, desperate to find out what was going on.

'He wants me to read the scripts for his course and help him select the final ten. Apparently Eleanora recommended me.'

'Huh!' said Rupert. 'Far more likely that Eleanora got him to agree to do the course by saying, "I've got a lovely girl who'll do all the hard work for you."'

Fenella looked at her husband, about to reproach him for slandering her aunt but then obviously decided that was probably exactly what had happened.

'It's kind of Eleanora really,' said Laura. 'She knows I need the money. I wonder if there'll be many scripts?'

'There could be a few,' said Fenella. 'I gathered from Eleanora that the competition has been very widely advertised.'

At the sound of this word Laura's eyes widened. 'Ergh! Advertising! We haven't thought about it at all!'

Work, even on a Sunday evening, was an excellent displacement activity, she decided, forcing a reluctant Fenella back down to her office for another hour before she headed back to her flat. Dermot Flynn was taking up far too much space in her brain and they had a festival to organise.

Chapter Nine

Three weeks later, Laura was tipping white wine into a glass at the bookshop for possibly the very last time. It was their farewell party for all their customers. 'Yes, it is terribly sad the shop is closing,' she said to the recipient of the wine, a woman whom she couldn't remember ever seeing in the shop, but who obviously supported it now there was free wine going. 'But I'm sure you'll manage.'

'Of course, I buy all my books from charity shops,' said the woman taking on a pious expression. 'I do like to support charity.'

Behind the woman Laura observed Henry's rueful eyebrow. 'But not bookshops?' said Laura.

'Oh well, they're businesses, aren't they?' The woman looked into her empty glass, willing Laura to magic some more wine into it as a reward for her virtue.

Laura held the bottle firmly upright. 'Yes, and they have to make money, like any other business. And how would the authors make money if no one bought their books new?'

The woman frowned. Taking pity on her, Laura tipped a small amount of wine into her glass.

'I never thought of that,' said the woman, and moved away.

'Laura, dear!' A much-loved customer, stalwart of the reading group, came up. 'What are we going to do without you all?'

It was customers like this woman who made book-selling such a joy, Laura felt, and hoped she wasn't going to get emotional. Now the time had finally come she felt as if she was losing a friend. It was the end of an era for her. She'd cut her literary teeth here; she felt more at home here than anywhere else; this was the place where she could really be herself. 'Oh, Fiona! Don't say that! It's sad enough as it is. You will keep the reading group going, won't you?'

'Of course. It won't be the same without you, though. You've read so much.' She sighed. 'But we'll manage.' She paused. 'And what about you? Have you got another job?'

'Sort of. A temporary one, anyway.' Laura produced a flyer from the table behind her. 'I'm helping to set up a literary festival. In the summer. I do hope you'll be able to come to some of the events?'

Fiona inspected the flyer.

'Of course, we can't promise all those authors will be able to attend but some of them will.' Laura sounded a little more confident than she felt, knowing as she did that authors were sometimes very late making up their minds and some were known to pull out at the last minute. She dismissed this negative thought and smiled at Fiona.

Fiona inspected the flyer. 'Oh, it's a bit far, isn't it?'

'Well, maybe you get up a group of you and arrange to stay over. It's a really beautiful area.' She felt like a travel agent selling a holiday destination, even if it was all true, and tried not to look so eager.

'Mm, that would be fun and lots of us could use a break from our families. Can I take this with me?'

'Of course! Here, take several.' Well, she did need to drum up trade, after all.

Grant came up. 'It's going well, isn't it? And I've given away lots of your flyers. I must say, people have been really sweet, saying how much they'll miss us.'

'Not that woman over there, helping herself to crisps

by the bowlful. I don't think she's ever been in before.' Laura tried not to sound resentful, but she was, a little.

Grant glanced across. 'Don't malign her. I sold her a birthday card once. She's one of those people who doesn't use us but likes us to be here.'

'She buys all her books from charity shops,' explained Laura to another regular customer who joined them. 'I think she believes it's faintly immoral to buy them new.'

'Now don't you go knocking charity bookshops,' the customer said. 'There's many a new author I've discovered by buying their books for virtually nothing. Then I've bought everything else they've written new!'

Laura rewarded this jolly woman by emptying her bottle into her glass. 'I know, you're a star, and I don't really mind people supporting charity shops, of course I don't. It's when they try to make out they're more virtuous than the rest of us who wantonly buy our books new-from-a-shop.'

The woman chuckled. 'So what are you both going to do now?' It was a question they were being asked frequently.

Grant said, 'Well I'm applying to a couple of big bookstores, but Laura here is running a literary festival. Flyer, please.' He held out his hand.

Laura produced one. 'Of course, not everyone on this flyer will be able to come but—'

'Oh, that looks huge fun!' said the woman. 'Good for you!'

And they chatted for a while about festivals and favourite authors and what a shame it was that another independent bookshop was closing down, even if it was out of choice.

As she topped up glasses, answered questions and circulated among the crowd – the shop was understandably packed; it was a huge favourite and had been there for years – Laura felt a sense of pride and sadness. Not an overwhelming sadness, because she had things to look forward to, but she was going to miss it. It was as if she was throwing off her old, safe self, like a treasured overcoat, outgrown.

It was after ten before Henry closed the door on the last straggler: an enthusiastic member of the local press who'd wanted to get all his angles (and help them finish the wine).

'Well, that was a great party,' said Henry as he, Grant and Laura cleared up. The part-time staff had been sent home because Laura insisted they'd covered for her so much recently, she didn't want them doing extra washing-up as well.

'Yes. It was a shame Monica couldn't come though,' Laura said to Grant as she gathered up a pile of paper plates. 'You'd really get on.'

'Well, we'll have to have another get-together some-time.' Grant sighed deeply. 'It's going to be really sad not being a team any more.'

Laura put her arms round him. 'I know! I've suddenly gone all weepy.' She'd managed to keep any threatening tears in check all evening but now it was just the three of them she felt them pricking behind her eyes.

'Oh, do brace up!' said Henry, who couldn't be doing with all this emotion. 'You'll both go on to greater things and soon forget about this little shop.'

'It's not that little,' said Grant, releasing himself from Laura and tying up yet another black bag.

'And I won't forget it,' said Laura. 'It – well, you, Henry, really – taught me all I know.'

'Well, don't get all maudlin!' said Henry, dropping empty bottles into a cardboard box. 'We'll keep in touch over Laura's festival, won't we? And I'll give you both splendid references.'

'And we're not actually closing until the end of the week,' Grant reminded them, 'and then we've got a few days packing up.'

When Laura got home from the shop after its last day of business she was very tired. If she'd had to say, yes, it was very sad the shop's closing, and no, she didn't really have another job yet, but there was going to be this literature and music festival and would they like a flyer? one more time, she felt she'd have had a nasty turn. She'd done so much of it at the party, she hadn't been prepared to do it for the rest of the week as well. And the bookshop had looked so forlorn with its depleted shelves and bare floorboards. Although she'd wanted to help, she was quite glad Henry had insisted he and Grant would do the final days of clearing and packing up. She wasn't sure she could have borne seeing it as a completely empty shell.

She got up the stairs to her little flat, opened the door and put the kettle on, even before she'd shut the door.

She had just taken her first, perfect sip of tea when her phone went. She cursed inwardly. She could never drink tea and talk on the phone unless she knew the person well enough to explain that was what she was doing. Praying it was one of those, she found her phone and answered it. It was Mrs Ironside, her downstairs neighbour, who generally preferred to phone than walk all the way up the stairs to Laura's flat 'at her age'.

'Laura?' Mrs Ironside was an irritable person who didn't have enough to do and so filled her time with the doings of others. 'There are a great many parcels for you. I took them in when I saw the postman about to take them all away. Then you'd have had to go to the sorting office for them.'

'Oh, thank you so much.' Laura was truly grateful although she didn't always get on with Mrs Ironside.

'So will you come and collect them? There are so many of them. What on earth are they?'

'I really don't know. I'll come down now.'

She took a gulp of tea, which was slightly too hot for gulping, and propping her door open, went downstairs. Her tea would be too cold before she got back to it, and she knew that if she made herself another cup, it would not be as nice. It was not her day.

There were fifteen large Jiffy bags piled neatly in Mrs Ironside's hall. She had a much larger flat than Laura but they still took up a lot of space.

'Oh my goodness,' said Laura, wondering how many she could carry at once, and thinking longingly of her tea. If Mrs Ironside had been anyone else, she could have explained about the tea. 'Right, I'll take as many as I can and pop back down for the rest.'

She managed five at a time. Three journeys, a sip of tea between each one. She cursed Dermot every step of the way. The moment she had seen them she'd realised what they were: manuscripts for his wretched course.

There was hardly enough floor space for her to get to the kettle by the time she'd brought the last lot up.

'Oh Lord! What am I to do with this lot?' she said out loud. 'I won't have room to breathe!'

The thought that someone might have written to her about them sent her back downstairs to pick up her post from her pigeon hole.

Yes, there was a letter, and it had a frank on it that indicated a London literary agency. She opened it there and then, not wanting to clutter her flat with any more post, even a single sheet. It was from Eleanora.

'Darling,' it read, 'you'll be getting the manuscripts any day now. I've had them redirected. Any more will come direct to you.'

Thanks a lot, Eleanora, thought Laura, and read on.

'Don't feel you need to read every word. If you're

not enjoying it, stop. The first few pages should tell you if they can write, less even. Then just check the synopsis to see if there's any sort of plot on offer. Make a pile of the possibles, and then weed and weed.' For a moment Laura wondered if Eleanora had meant to write 'read and read' but realised she meant she had to go through the possibles and find excuses to turn them down.

She climbed the stairs again. In spite of the logistics of dealing with all that paper she was quite excited. She might, as Dermot had suggested, discover the next big thing. Maybe it would give her a chance to work as an editor, something she'd always longed to do, but had always felt was beyond her grasp. But it was a big responsibility and she was worried she wouldn't be able to recognise good writing from bad. At least Eleanora had told her she didn't need to read the whole manuscript if she wasn't enjoying it, so it might not take her too long. She hastened up the last flight, eager to get started, all tiredness forgotten with the challenge ahead. If she couldn't do it, she'd have to let Eleanora know right away.

It was, she discovered, quite easy to tell good writing from bad. After all, she didn't have to decide if it was publishable in the current market, something she'd learnt quite a bit about from Henry. She just had to decide who could write and who couldn't. And two hours later she realised that none of these aspiring writers could.

Some had dialogue so stilted it could have been examples from a grammar textbook. Others had characters who were not even dislikeable, let alone engaging; they just didn't have enough substance to be anything. Not one of them had a plot. She was very depressed. She decided to ring Eleanora about it the next day and leave a message if necessary. She also needed to think about buying a laptop. She'd lost her Internet connection after today, where she had it at the shop, and she couldn't organise a literary festival without email.

Eleanora was out when she rang, but returned her call shortly afterwards. 'Laura? Sweetie? Are they God-awful?'

'They are dire,' said Laura. 'Honestly, to start with I thought I'd give each one fifty pages, just to be fair, as I'd heard the judge for a major award say that was what he does. But after a couple I just couldn't bear to.'

'Sweetie, don't sweat it. Most of them will be dire, but how many have you read so far?'

'Fifteen. They all arrived at the same time.'

'Only fifteen? Nothing to worry about. There'll be at least a hundred.'

'A hundred?' Laura took a sharp intake of breath. 'Have you any idea of how tiny my flat is – no, of course you haven't. Sorry.' She paused. 'I haven't got to send them back, have I?'

'Are you saying they haven't got return postage, self-addressed labels? All that?' Eleanora was outraged.

'Well, I think most of them have but—'

'Then just stick on the return labels and bung 'em off to the post office.'

'I haven't got a car and the post office is miles away.' Laura didn't want to sound grumbly but she thought it had been a while since Eleanora had 'bunged anything off to the post office' personally. Did she know that many small, queue-free post offices had been closed?

'Well, wait until you can get a lift or something. These people don't need to get their hopes and dreams thrown back at them too soon. Give them a few days' hope before you let 'em down.'

Shortly afterwards, Laura ended the call. She needed to get to bed. Tomorrow she would address the car and laptop situation which was becoming more and more urgent. Then she had a more uplifting thought: a hundred scripts at ten pounds a throw would come to a thousand pounds. Handy! Her redundancy money wouldn't last for long.

'Why don't you buy my car?' said Grant. They had arranged to meet for coffee a week or so later so they could co-counsel each other on their bookshop-withdrawal. 'Then I could upgrade.'

They were sitting in their favourite café just around the corner from the bookshop. Laura couldn't help but glance in as she went past. It was empty now and except for the many shelves it looked like any other retail space. It had felt strange not to be going into work but she hadn't really had time to feel too bereft. And now she and Grant had been catching up as well as reminiscing.

'Isn't it supposed to be a really bad idea to buy cars from friends? What if it goes horribly wrong? I might never speak to you again,' she said.

'I'll take the chance,' said Grant. 'I've got lots of friends, after all. I can afford to lose one. You're not so lucky, of course.'

'I've got loads of friends! You, and Monica. Fen's definitely a friend. All my uni friends—'

'Who are where, exactly? Not taking you out clubbing every weekend, are they?'

'They're not exactly local, I must admit.' Laura wondered if she could change the subject before she had to also admit that all her uni friends had high-powered jobs in London or were saving the planet in the Galapagos. 'Are you in close touch with all your uni chums?'

He shrugged. 'Only on Facebook, I suppose. But I really do think I'm the only normal person you know round here,' he said, sipping his coffee and preparing to dig into a slice of lemon cake.

'Monica's normal,' said Laura, wondering if someone who wore a pink wig for a living could truly be described as normal.

'I'd love to meet her.' He paused. 'Tell you what, I'll sell you the car for five hundred pounds and a night out with Monica. Can you manage that?'

'The night out with Monica, almost certainly, but as for the car, jot down its CV and I'll ask my car consultant.'

'Your who?'

'Rupert. He was advising me on what sort of car to get.'

'Well I should think mine ticks all the boxes and it's in good nick.'

'I know, and I like driving it, but I feel I should just run it by him as he was taking such an interest.'

'Give me a bit of paper then, and I'll write down the details.'

'Brilliant,' said Laura, taking the paper and putting it in her bag. 'Now do you think we should ask any sci-fi authors to the festival, or are they a bit specialist?'

'Depends who you have in mind.'

They discussed this for a while until Laura looked at her watch. 'Now I really must go back. I've got all those manuscripts to read and I must phone Rupert about the car. I'll ring you the moment I decide. OK?'

Back home, Laura decided to find out about the car before going back to her pile of manuscripts. Talking to Fenella was always cheering and there was some festival stuff they needed to talk about as well.

When they'd updated each other on who had confirmed and whom they'd need to chase, again, Laura said, 'Is Rupert there? Grant from work has suggested I buy his car. I borrowed it the first time I came to Somerby. Rupert said he'd help me get one and I want to ask his advice.'

'Well, I can't remember it, but I have no memory for cars. I'll put you on to Rupes.'

'Hi, Laura.' Rupert's deep voice sounded curious. 'What's all this about a car?'

Laura gave him the details. 'And he's anal about getting it serviced and things, so I think it should be all right,' she added, after they'd discussed it for a while. 'I just needed a second opinion really.'

'And you don't want me to come over and check it out for you?' Rupert said eventually.

'I really don't think it's necessary. I've driven it and I really like it.'

'Then it sounds just the job, and five hundred seems a good price. Go for it!'

'Brilliant, Rupert, thank you so much. Now all I need to do is get a laptop.' She spoke lightheartedly enough but she realised she was about to spend her entire fee for the festival on a car. Would a laptop take all her redundancy money? Suddenly Dermot and his writing course seemed like a life-saver.

'Would it have to be a new one?' asked Rupert.

'Oh no, I don't think so. I only really need something to write letters on and do emails.'

'They're not terribly expensive new, but don't buy anything without telling me. I may be able to get you one second-hand.'

'Oh Rupert! You are a star.'

'That's what they tell me,' he said with a laugh, and then rang off.

Having sorted out the issue of the car, she decided to call Monica. Today was turning into a catching up with friends day, after all. Monica was delighted to hear from Laura. 'I have such a lot to tell you! Yes, do let's go out, and any friend of yours can certainly come. As long as we get a chance to exchange girly chats.'

'Grant's good at girly chats,' said Laura, suddenly aware she didn't want Grant knowing too much about what had gone on in Ireland: it was still too raw. She wasn't fully aware of how she felt about it all herself. It was bad enough that Monica knew, she didn't want anyone else picking over the bones just yet. 'So when's good for you?'

Monica was silent, presumably flicking through her busy social calendar. 'I've been so frantic, trying to get bands to confirm for the festival,' she murmured.

'Me too,' said Laura. 'I must have spoken to every publicity department in every publisher there is, trying to get people to confirm. Then I've been on to the sales people to see if they can produce multiple copies for reading groups and put it all through Henry.' She paused. 'And I've got all these manuscripts to read as well.'

'Manuscripts? What the hell are you talking about?'

'Oh, it's all Dermot's fault,' said Laura and was about to explain when Monica interrupted her.

'You know something?' She sounded amused and happy. 'A lot of what's happened to you recently is Dermot's fault. You gotta love him.'

'No you haven't!' squeaked Laura, whose feelings for him were very confused. Did lust combined with huge liking and a touch of obsession equal love?

'I suppose I haven't, as long as you do.' Monica paused, to give this little barb time to find its mark. 'Anyway,' she went on, 'we can talk about all that when we meet. What about Friday?'

'Hang on, I'll just call him on my mobile. Friday?' Laura asked Grant when he answered.

Luckily he had read her mind, as he was so often able to do. 'Fine. Where and when?'

It was agreed to meet Monica in a wine bar in one of the better parts of Bristol. Grant said he'd drive home as it would be one of the last times he could. Once Laura had paid him the money, the car would be hers. Laura, however, had to drive there. She wasn't a very experienced town driver and the thought of the Bristol traffic terrified her. She wasn't going to let on to Grant though – he might decide not to sell her his car after all.

Meanwhile the manuscripts kept arriving. Mrs Ironside took them in if Laura was out and Laura took to calling at her flat before going upstairs to her own. Mrs Ironside had the kettle on and Laura had a cup of tea and a chat with her before going upstairs with her parcels. Relations had improved between them and Mrs Ironside was a lot less frosty these days. She told her about the festival and she became quite enthusiastic.

'I'd definitely come if Kathryn Elisabeth was going to appear,' she said, mentioning one of the most successful romantic novelists ever.

Laura dutifully wrote the name down, wondering if it would look rude to invite an author at this late stage. 'She's very popular,' she said warningly. 'She's probably booked up for years ahead, but I'll definitely ask her publishers.'

'She'd be a very big draw,' said Mrs Ironside.

'I know, and I'll try, but – well, we mustn't get our hopes up too much.'

Mrs Ironside folded her lips, making her disapproval at this feeble attitude plain.

Friday night arrived and Laura and Grant set off to meet Monica. It was amazing how much better you got at parking if you had to practise a lot, thought Laura as she finally straightened up and turned off the ignition. Not that she'd actually been able to fit in any of the five spaces she'd tried, but she did feel much more confident handling the car now: she knew the dimensions of the car precisely. They climbed out.

'God, I hope the car will be safe here!' said Grant,

checking that Laura had actually locked it, although he'd heard the clunk of her doing it just as well as she had.

'We're in Clifton,' said Laura. 'It's not going to get keyed, the hubcaps stolen or broken into. You're such an old woman sometimes!'

'You can talk! Now come on. Let's find this wine bar. I'm longing to meet Monica in the flesh.'

Monica was sitting at the bar, chatting to the barman. She jumped off her stool and hugged Laura. 'So lovely to see you, sweetie! And this must be Grant! Hi!'

Grant and Monica kissed each other. 'So,' said Monica. 'What are we having? Laura will have her usual pint of whiskey. Grant?'

'Pint of whiskey? That doesn't sound like the Laura I know and love!'

Monica laughed. 'You should see her when she's offshore. She's a madwoman.'

'I'll have a white wine spritzer,' said Laura, as if she'd never drunk whiskey out of tumblers, or lemonade the colour of highlighter pens, which is how it seemed to come in Ireland. Or, most importantly, offered her body to a famous writer so he'd attend her literary festival.

'I'll have grapefruit juice and lemonade,' said Grant.

'I'm buying Grant's car, but he's driving us home,' Laura explained to Monica as she and Grant sat either side of her at the bar.

'Buying a car? Haven't you got one already? No, I suppose not,' Monica said when she'd ordered the drinks.

'Bookshop pay, on the whole, is pants,' said Laura, sipping her spritzer. 'But I do – did – really love my job.'

'If you're buying Grant's car, how come he can afford to buy one in the first place if he worked in the book-shop too?' asked Monica, reasonably enough.

'I had a proper job in IT before I joined the book trade,' Grant explained. 'And a small inheritance. So that's my financial cards on the table.' He quickly closed the subject and turned to Monica. 'I want to tell you just how much I love your act,' he gushed. 'Just fabulous. Did Laura tell you how I dragged her along to see you?'

'I think I did,' muttered Laura to herself.

'And isn't she glad I did?' said Grant, looking at her.

Laura wondered if without Monica all the things that had happened to her lately would have happened and realised they wouldn't. While she did wonder if meeting Dermot was going to spoil her for all the normal men she would meet in the future, she wasn't sorry she'd met him. 'Oh yes!'

'Oh!' Monica sounded a bit surprised at her fervency. 'I love you too. Seriously, though, I'm really glad I met you because otherwise I wouldn't have gone to Ireland and met up with Seamus again. That's an old, turned new again, flame,' she explained to Grant.

'It's all back on then?' Laura sipped her spritzer. 'So that agonising bike ride was worth it? Tell all.'

'Well, a few days after we got home, he got in touch! He'd been thrilled to get my note apparently.'

'So how long ago was this?' asked Laura, trying hard not to be jealous. Dermot had called her but only to ask her a favour.

'A couple of days ago.'

'But you and Laura came back from Ireland ages ago,' said Grant. 'How keen is he?'

Monica flapped a scarlet-nailed hand at Grant. 'Very keen, he's just a bit laid-back. All Irishmen are. You just have to get used to it.'

'That's a bit of a sweeping generalisation,' said Laura, although Monica was quite right – as far as her personal experience went, anyway.

'He is laid-back but he's also mad keen to get his band to do a set at the festival.' Monica bit her lip. 'Supposing they're not good enough?'

'Haven't you heard them yet?'

'No,' said Monica, 'and to be honest, going on what Seamus says about them, they're a bit amateur.'

'Just because you're not paid for what you do, it doesn't mean you don't do it well,' said Grant, for some reason feeling the need to defend enthusiastic amateurs everywhere.

'That's very fair of you, Grant!' said Laura. 'Quite out of character if may say so.'

'Not at all. I'm always fair. After all, I did say I wanted to get involved in the festival too.'

'Oh, well, I'm sure we'll be able to find you a job,' said Laura, who was pleased as Grant didn't usually volunteer for anything. 'Remember, it's unlikely there's any money attached to it. My fee is nominal as it is.'

'I don't necessarily have to be paid,' said Grant. 'I'll have my redundancy money and my darling auntie, remember, and I've had some interest in the feelers I put out for bookshop jobs. Besides, apart from when it's actually on, I'd be doing it in my spare time. I just want to have some of the fun you two girls are having.'

'Mm, I wouldn't say it's that exactly – it mainly involves making endless phone calls – although the planning has been, and it has been lovely being in at the ground floor of something. Checking venues will be good, though, I should think.' She frowned. 'You'd probably be more use to Monica—'

'I wish you two would pay attention,' Monica cut in. 'What if Seamus's band is a pile of poo?'

'Then they can't come,' said Grant simply. 'Not only am I fair, I'm firm.'

'Well, lucky you,' said Monica, pushing him, as if they'd been friends for years.

'Seriously,' Grant went on, 'if it's a new festival you can't afford to have substandard acts.'

'What sort of music do they play?' asked Laura after she and Monica had taken in this basic truth.

'Irish, very traditional. I've asked him to send me a CD of something but he says there isn't one. They mostly just play in pubs.'

'Well, the musicians who played in the pub in Ballyfitzpatrick were brilliant,' said Laura. 'I've just had an idea,' she added, leaning in.

'Lie down until the feeling goes away,' suggested Grant.

'What?' said Monica.

'It's an idea I had before but then dismissed. Dermot has some poems, not many but very good. Supposing we ask him to read them, and have Seamus's band playing Irish music in between, or even very quietly in the background while he reads.'

Monica nodded, warming to the idea. 'Could be good.'

'The venue would have to be right though. It wouldn't work in an echoing great hall,' said Grant, ever the voice of reason, from his end of the bar.

'No, it would have to be in a pub,' said Monica.

'What, use the pub local to Somerby?' asked Laura.

'Is there one?' asked Grant.

'Yes. And it's lovely but I'd have to find out if they would be up for it.'

'Don't pubs have to have licences if they have music?' said Grant.

'I don't know,' said Laura impatiently. 'But couldn't they get one? It's such a good idea – even though it was mine. Although . . .' She paused. 'We may not be able to fit many people in.'

'That Sarah person would know,' said Monica. 'I'm just thinking how brilliant it would be, recreating that atmosphere in England.' She was really enthusiastic now, in part because she wouldn't have to face the possibility of telling Seamus he couldn't play at the festival.

'What atmosphere?' said Grant. 'If you're thinking smoke-filled rooms, fiddles and great crack, there's been a smoking ban for a while now.'

'Oh, you had to be there, Grant!' said Monica. 'There were times when the people enjoying themselves most were the ones outside flicking cigarette butts into the bin, but it was great, wasn't it, Laura?'

'Oh yes,' she replied, thinking back.

'There's just one problem,' said Monica, looking at Laura. 'You'll probably have to offer Dermot your body again to get him to do it.'

Laura's insides seemed to crumple away.

'I mean . . .' Monica hastened to make amends. 'I was talking in that way when you don't really mean it literally—'

Before Grant started asking awkward questions, Laura rushed in to cover her tracks. 'You were speaking metaphorically,' she said. 'That's what you meant. Me offering to sleep with Dermot is a metaphor for – well, saying I'd do anything to make him come to the festival. Because obviously, I wouldn't really offer to sleep with him, would I?' Fairly sure she'd protested far too much to uphold her status as a lady, Laura looked helplessly at Monica.

'No, of course you wouldn't,' Monica confirmed. 'No one would.' She laughed, sounding a bit artificial. 'Let's have another round!'

'Oh do let's,' said Laura. 'I'll pay.' She had jumped off her bar stool, twenty-pound note waving, before she realised she was already at the bar and could order from where she had been sitting. She could feel Grant's eyes on her and knew there'd have to be explanations on the way home. Had she enough money, she asked herself, to get so drunk she wouldn't be able to talk? But look where that had got her last time. No, she would just have to bluff her way through. Grant would never believe she actually had agreed to sleep with Dermot to get him to come to the festival. It was so out of character. Phew!

Fortunately for Laura's peace of mind, the subject changed and they went on to have a great night out. Grant and Monica got on as well as Laura had known they would and Monica had agreed to employ Grant – for free of course – as her second-in-command at the festival. He was delighted.

And suddenly it was midnight and time to go home.

They were barely in the car before Grant piped up, 'You didn't really offer Dermot Thing your body to get him to come to the festival, did you?' Grant was now as proprietorial about the festival as Monica and Laura were.

'Oh come on, Grant!' Laura felt that indignation was her best defence. She might have known nothing would get past him. 'Would I do a thing like that? How long have you known me?'

Grant drove in silence for a worryingly long time. 'No, I suppose not. In some ways you are a bit of a professional virgin.'

'Exactly,' said Laura, glad the dimness of the car would mean he wouldn't see how very near the truth he'd got. 'I wouldn't throw away my virginity on a one-night stand with a drunken Irishman, now would I? I mean, if I was a virgin, I wouldn't do that!' She paused, digging herself deeper. 'Or even if I wasn't! Oh, shut up and drive, Grant.'

Her friend glanced at her but didn't speak. Laura knew Grant wouldn't let the subject drop completely. He was just biding his time. But she was grateful to him for not mentioning it again as they made up the sofa for him and she crept up to her own bed. As she pulled the duvet round her she smiled. On the whole she was very lucky with her friends.

Chapter Ten

Laura sat in her car outside the school shaking with nerves. In a moment, when the minute hand landed at twenty past two, she would go in. She was about to tell a school full of children about the short-story competition. She had her notes; she had practised to herself in the mirror and had told herself it didn't really matter if the children all ran off screaming. Yet she was still terrified and she didn't think imagining her audience in their vests and knickers would help either.

After this, she was visiting the offices of the local paper, to talk to them about the festival. That would seem like a jolly social occasion after trial-by-small-children. Then, later, came the reward: her weekly chat with Dermot, ostensibly to discuss the entries for the writing course. In practice they talked about all sorts of things. It was Dermot's notes she had in her hand now, vibrating gently.

It was early afternoon and a beautiful spring day. The air shimmered with the promise of the summer ahead and the small, country primary school was of the type described in books by Laurie Lee and other such rural writers. It was picturesque, probably extremely inconvenient and the first of a few she would make similar visits to. The idea was to go to as many local schools as possible to foster interest in the festival in general and the writing competition in particular. Once she'd done it the first time, she knew she'd be fine and even enjoy it. After all, she used to do storytimes in the shop and had loved them. But although her confidence had grown so much over the last couple of months, her old shyness would occasionally reappear, as now. To say she was nervous didn't quite cover it.

A last peek in the driving mirror told her she looked OK, if about ten years old, and then she got out. An attractive middle-aged woman had obviously been on the lookout for her, and appeared the moment Laura set foot on school property.

'Hello! Laura? Hi! I'm Margaret Johns, head teacher. I'll just take you into assembly. The children are all very excited about you coming.'

During the walk to the hall, Laura wondered if she vomited in the playground they'd ring her mother and she'd be allowed to lie down in the staffroom and await collection. Then at last she accepted that she was a grown-up now and she had to just get on with it.

Rows of children sitting cross-legged on the floor confronted her. They were wearing royal blue sweat-shirts, and shorts, trousers or grey dresses.

'Quieten down, children! We have a visitor!' said Mrs Johns.

There was almost instant calm. Laura had hoped if they took a while to settle, it would use up her time. She had half an hour to fill when she'd have preferred ten minutes, or better, she could have just sent a letter and some forms to each school. But Fenella had pointed out a personal visit would really enthuse the schools and get the community inspired to support the festival.

'Miss Horsley is going to tell us about a very exciting competition.' Mrs Johns gestured Laura into centre stage. 'Miss Horsley!'

Don't be afraid of silence, Dermot had told her when he'd been coaching her for the visit. Let them just look at you for a couple of minutes. He'd been so helpful, really taking the time to pass on everything he'd learnt about talking to children – which was a surprising amount. Dermot apparently loved going into schools and talking to children. She wanted to be able to tell him it had gone well. She didn't want to let him down. She surveyed her audience.

'Hi, guys!' she said and instantly felt this sounded wrong and went on quickly. 'How many of you like stories?'

Lots of hands went up. 'We do!' they chorused. 'Me! And Me!'

She raised her own hands to quieten them, which seemed to do the trick. 'That's great! And do you know where stories come from?' Dermot had said he sometimes opened with this question.

'Books!' came the reply.

Laura nodded, getting into the spirit of it. 'Yes they do come from books, but how do the books get them?'

She had liked this image of books marching around on their own capturing stories when Dermot had suggested it and the children seemed to as well.

'They don't go around the place listening to stories and snapping them up between the pages like crocodiles, do they?' She didn't wait for them to answer this time. 'No! Well, someone put them there. Someone put the stories in the books. Who could have done that, do you think?' She looked expectantly at the sea of eager little faces. This time she did want their reaction.

'Mrs Johns!' called out a little boy from the front. 'She's got stories!'

'Yes, that's a good answer. And who else?' She looked at her audience carefully, to make sure she didn't overlook a shy child who might have a good idea.

'Writers?' This came from one of the older girls at the back.

'Writers, authors, yes, they make stories. But who else do you think can make them?'

Several rows of children looked at her, transfixed but bemused. 'You can!' said Laura triumphantly.

This caused a certain amount of uproar but Laura dampened it down quickly enough. She was beginning to get the hang of this. 'Yes, you can all make stories. And soon, when your teacher tells you it's time, you're all going to write a story. Now you could write a whole story each – that would be quite difficult – or you could make a story up as a class. Your teacher will decide which you should do. Now, have any of you written stories before?' A forest of hands shot up. 'Yes! All of you! That's brilliant! Well, when you've all written your stories, and drawn pictures to go with them – can you all draw pictures? Wonderful! So when you've written your story you must draw a picture of the people in the story. These are called "characters". So now, what sort of thing do you think you can write about? Where do stories come from? They come from ideas and ideas are everywhere!' She looked around to indicate the ubiquitous nature of ideas and the children did likewise, as if half expecting an idea to come popping out from behind a plant pot.

'But although ideas are everywhere, we have to look for them, to recognise them when we see them! Now . . .' Laura suddenly realised her mouth had dried up completely and she took a gulp of water from the paper cup Mrs Johns handed to her. At the same time she realised she was really enjoying herself.

'Has anything good happened to any of you today?' she asked her enraptured audience.

A little boy almost followed his hand skyward as he fought to get her attention. 'My dog had puppies!'

'Oh, that's a brilliant idea! You could write a story about a puppy. Or a fairy, or a cow. Or even a teacher!' This caused much amusement. 'Then, when you've written your stories and done lovely illustrations – that means pictures – your teachers are going to send them to me and if they're very good, they'll be read out loud to lots of people, including your parents. What about that?'

This notion was very well received.

'But before you start, a real-life writer, one whose stories are in books you have read, is going to come and talk to you some more about how stories get into books.'

A couple of minutes later she finished her talk to huge applause.

'That was really good,' said Mrs Johns. 'I thought you said you weren't used to dealing with children.'

'Well, not with so many children at a time, but I had a lot of help from a friend and then I just pretended it was a storytime, like we used to do at the bookshop, and it seemed to work.'

'Well done, dear! And you're making arrangements for a writer to visit? Would that come out of our budget or yours?'

'Yours if possible, the festival is operating on a shoe-string.'

'I'll see what we can do,' said Mrs Johns. 'The story competition is excellent and it's an excuse to read more stories in school.'

As she had known it would be, the interview with the local newspaper was easy. They were keen to support the festival and offered to fund an event and to print three of the winning stories in the paper. She found herself chatting away with ease, her answers flowing freely. Somehow it was so much easier when you were talking about something you felt committed to.

Just as she was leaving the journalist said, 'Could you let us have author biogs and photos as soon as poss? We'd like to do an "appearing at" feature.'

Laura stopped and turned round. 'Yes, of course. You do know our line-up isn't finalised? Supposing you did a feature on an author and then they couldn't come?'

'Oh dear, that wouldn't work!' The journalist, possibly perfectly reasonably, didn't want to spend a lot of time researching and writing an article about someone who wasn't going to come within a hundred miles of the county.

Laura considered. 'Tell you what, you give me a list of the authors you'd most like to feature and I'll chase them up. If they think there's a bit of guaranteed publicity it might help them decide to come.'

In the car she made some extra notes and then set off home, quietly excited at the prospect of talking to Dermot.

'So how did you get on with the kids?' was the first thing he said when he picked up the phone.

'Oh, it was great! I took all your ideas and once I'd got going I found I loved it. Perhaps there is a performer in me after all.'

'There's something about children though, isn't there? They don't let you get away with anything.'

Discovering that Dermot Flynn, who shunned his public, refused to have anything to do with the literary world and worked hard on his image of a hard-drinking, womanising has-been, actually went into his local school regularly as a helper had come as a shock.

'I don't tell many people,' he had explained. 'It doesn't go with the image.'

She had taken a moment to feel flattered that he had confided in her. 'Have you ever thought about writing for children?' It seemed an obvious thing for him to want to do.

'No way. Far too hard, and far too much responsibility. If I write a book and someone hates it, that's OK, they can just toss it aside and pick up another one. If a children's writer produces a duff book the child who reads it – or who tries to read it – may never read another one.' He obviously felt very strongly on the subject.

It was after this conversation that Laura had thought he'd be a good person to ask about how to pitch her short-story idea to the local schoolchildren.

Now, after she had received his congratulations and slightly smug 'I told you you could do it', she moved on to the competition itself. 'So all I've got to do is line up a suitably keen judge. I've got a couple of retired teachers to do the first cut.' She paused. 'It's all right, I'm not asking you. I've got a children's writer in mind. Right,' she went on briskly, 'how did you get on with the last batch of scripts I sent you? What about the one set in Greece?'

'A pile of crap,' said Dermot.

'How much did you read?' Laura was disappointed, it was important he trusted her judgement.

'Not very much. Why should I?'

'Read on. It gets better.' She was firm. Having selected her thirty manuscripts, had them copied, and sent to Dermot a few at a time, she now felt protective of them. They were her babies and she was going to fight for them, even though they had to be whittled down to ten.

Dermot was dismissive. 'It's no good it getting better. No one will read that far. I thought you were supposed to know about these things.'

She knew him well enough by now to know when she was being teased. 'I do. In the editing, we'll tell her to get rid of the first three chapters and start the book from there.'

'OK, I'll read a bit more and ring you back. But it had better improve.'

Laura put the phone down, smiling.

She had done the washing-up, written a few emails on the laptop Rupert had acquired for her courtesy of Jacob Stone, and was making a list of phone calls for the following day when he rang back. 'Ah,' he said without preamble. 'I see what you mean.'

'So shall I put her on the "maybe" pile?'

'OK, but if the "maybe" pile gets too huge, I'll send it back.'

'But we could do that with a few suggestions, don't you think? So these writers get help even if they don't get on the course?'

'You're all heart, Laura Horsley. I'm not sure that's a good thing.'

'It is a good thing. A few editorial notes could make the whole difference, and they've got this far, they deserve some reward. Have you had a look at Gareth Ainsley's one?' This was probably more up his street, she thought. It was science fiction, very edgy, but surprisingly readable, even to one to whom sci-fi was a bit of a turn-off.

'Yes, yes, I did. It's good, very good. But do you think he'd be a complete pain on the course?'

'I don't think you can ban him on those grounds,' said Laura.

'Mm. I don't know. I think he'll make it anyway. He doesn't need my help.'

Laura considered for a moment. 'Don't tell me you're jealous of the Young Turks snapping at your heels, Mr Bestselling Novelist?' She felt safe teasing him over the telephone. How she'd feel if they were face to face, she didn't know.

'Young Turks: is that a quaint English expression?'

'Hm, one I picked up from my old boss, Henry—'

Dermot cut her off. 'So which are your favourites out of those you've sent me?' Dermot didn't seem to want

to enlarge on the subject of Young Turks and his attitude to them.

'They all have merit,' she said carefully, 'which is why
I selected them. But we have to decide who'd benefit
most from the course. And you can't rule out the Young
Turks.'

'You'll just flirt with them,' he said.

'You're doing the course, not me,' said Laura.

'You're assisting. You're going to be there. I thought
you knew that.'

This came as a bit of a shock. 'I thought I was only
helping with this bit. I didn't know anything about you
needing me actually on the course!' She sounded quite
indignant but her heart was singing at the prospect of
spending so much time with Dermot. 'I don't know
anything about writing itself.'

'Oh yes you do.'

A shaft of doubt pierced her pleasure. 'But I've never
written more than a To Do list in my life!'

Dermot dismissed this. 'It doesn't mean you can't edit.
You've been doing it, and you've read loads more than
I have.'

As by this time she knew he read very little modern
fiction she had to agree. 'Oh. Well, I suppose I can do it.
Will the university mind?'

'Of course not. If they want me, they have to have you,
too. We're a team.'

Laura flushed, glad he couldn't see her. 'Oh. OK. Now,
what about the Samantha Pitville? I know it's not your
thing. It's chick lit, bubbly, funny, irreverent, but it's written
by a very pretty woman. I sent a photo. It's attached to
the back of the manuscript.'

She waited until he'd found the photo and examined
it. 'Mm. Not my usual type, but if she can write, I'll give
her a go. Why did you send the photo?'

'Eleanora said that being good-looking helped. It's such

a cut-throat industry that if two writers are of the same standard, it makes sense to take on the one who'll be good at publicity.'

'Well, I think that's extremely sexist—'

'No you don't, you don't care about sexism. Tell me, is she in or out?'

'I'll give her a go at the course. Nothing else,' he added firmly.

Laura was silent. She had sort of assumed that Dermot would be up for dallying with his students if they were attractive and willing. There was a fine old tradition of artists sleeping with their models – there were parallels.

'Are you surprised at my moral attitude?'

'A bit. You don't give the impression of someone who's led a life of purity and hard work.'

'No, well, you're right. But because I misspent my youth, it doesn't mean I'm keen for others to do it. What's next?'

'The one in the blue folder.'

'Oh yes, found it.'

'Dermot, don't you read any of them until we're on the telephone talking about them?'

'Of course I do.' He was obviously lying. 'Tell me about it.'

She sighed. 'It's worthy.'

'What do you mean?'

'I mean, it's a shortlist pick. It's literary, utterly gloomy and will be the book everyone buys and nobody reads.'

Possibly gauging her feelings about books like this, he frowned. 'Well, let's not have it then.'

'Oh no, we have to have it – her, I mean. It's good. I may hate it, but I have to admire it.' She ruffled through her file and produced another photograph. 'I should have sent you her photo, too. In fact I meant to, but forgot. She's beautiful.'

'You seem determined to fill the course with lovely young women.'

'Well, I know you're doing it against your will. I thought I should make sure you had some compensations.'

There was a silence. 'I hate to admit this, but I don't know if you're joking or not.'

Laura laughed.

Chapter Eleven

Fenella was firm. 'Laura dear, if you came and lived here, in this dear little holiday cottage that has no one in it, not only would be you be here when I needed you, you could give up your flat and save shedloads on rent.' She straightened a throw covering the sofa and twitched a curtain into place. 'I'd have offered it to you before if it'd been finished. All our other accommodation has been full. I won't throw you out afterwards until you've found somewhere else to live,' she added, anticipating Laura's objection.

Laura was extremely tempted by the converted cowshed. It was May, two weeks before the course, and summer was at its prettiest. Hawthorn blossom and cow parsley frothed in the hedgerows and verges around Somerby, the sun shone and the birds sang. Naturally a country lover, Laura's small flat in town had lost any charm it ever had for her, and living where she did meant she had to do a lot of driving. But she still protested politely.

'But you'll need it for a writer or something when the festival is on.'

Fenella ran her hand through her already tangled hair. 'None of the writers we've got booked so far, or even any of those who haven't got back to us, are as vital to us as you are! Do stop arguing and just move in!' She looked around. 'Although now I look at it, it is titchy. Fine for a weekend, or even a week, but otherwise . . . I don't know.'

'Oh no, it's plenty big enough,' said Laura instantly. Both women surveyed the room, wood-burning stove at one end with a sofabed and an armchair by it, little kitchen at the other, with a staircase to a gallery where the bed was. 'It's enchanting, you know it is.'

'I know it's a perfect jewel of a cottage, I'm just pointing out it's awfully small if you want to stay in it longer than a week. There's very little space for your clothes and things.'

'I haven't got a lot of stuff, to be honest. I could bundle up anything I don't need and take it to my parents. They have a huge attic. What I need around me mostly are books.'

'Well, there's plenty of space for them.' Fenella looked at the more or less empty bookcase. 'People will leave books behind when they come to stay.' She looked a little guilty. 'Last year, I took all the ones they'd left in the other cottages and read them. I'll have to put them back.'

'Don't worry. I've got actually got loads of books and should have a massive prune. I'll bring them and you can share them round your cottages. How many have you got?'

'Three, plus this one, but we're always looking to do up another old cowshed or something to put people in.'

Laura laughed. 'They're more than "old cowsheds" by the time you've finished with them.'

'I know. So . . .' Fenella was still thinking about books. 'If you were only allowed one shelf full, which books would you choose?'

Laura didn't have to think for long. 'Well, Dermot's first two, of course. Then there're a couple of authors I've followed for their whole careers. Poetry.'

'So is Dermot really as good as everyone says he is?' asked Fenella.

'Yes! He's amazing! I know he's driving everyone mad by not allowing his name to be used as part of the publicity, but he's really – nice.' 'Nice' was such a woefully inadequate way of describing him, she had to smile.

Seeing the smile, Fenella regarded her friend doubtfully. 'I know he's awfully attractive and all that, although of course I haven't met him. But are his books actually readable?'

Laura put her hand on Fenella's arm to emphasise the strength of her feelings. 'Do yourself a favour and read them. Really. They are truly wonderful.'

'I'd better anyway, if he's our star attraction.' Laura was disappointed Fenella wasn't enthusiastic about her task, but reading was so subjective, she reminded herself. 'And it's nice to be able to boast about difficult books you've read. Now, anything else you think you'll need?'

When Laura had insisted that there was nothing, several times, Fenella said, 'You do think Dermot will turn up, don't you?'

'Why? Why do you ask?' Laura was suddenly worried. Dermot had said he'd come; she assumed he would.

'It's just something Eleanora said. She was on the phone the other day and warned me not to have all my eggs in one basket, festival-wise. She seemed to think he might let us down.'

Laura considered. Dermot could be very kind and she didn't think he would say he'd come and then not turn up. But could she be sure? 'I'm sure it will be all right.'

But although she reassured Fenella, she had doubt in her own mind now.

Slowly the literary side of the festival began to take shape. Eventually writers confirmed they could appear, and pre-festival events began. A local writers' circle was writing short stories, the best to be read at the festival and put into a book. An art group was illustrating chosen works from some of the confirmed authors. There was going to be an exhibition and as many as possible would decorate the village hall that was going to host one of the events. A popular children's poet was hosting a poetry slam, so poetry workshops were going on in all schools as well as energetic story writing. Most of the local schools had already submitted theirs and Laura's retired teachers were making their first selection. The Knitters and Embroiderers' Collective was making a bedspread out of knitted or embroidered squares that was going to be raffled one evening. Fenella was already determined to win this, even if it meant buying all the tickets herself.

But the publicity was severely hampered. The fact that Dermot still wouldn't let it be announced that he was appearing meant that many people who might well have sponsored something weren't taking the festival seriously enough. They'd been promised a big name and, so far, no big name had been given to them.

Laura sent him regular emails explaining all this, begging for him to let his name be announced and, just as regularly, he emailed back saying no.

'We'll have a summit meeting,' announced Fenella, when one morning Laura had gone over to the big house and broken the bad news yet again.

'What? With Jacob Stone and Eleanora or Trisha, and that lot?' Laura was a bit startled. Although so much of the festival was going well, she was feeling a bit of a failure about this and didn't want to have to explain herself to all those people.

'Oh no.' Fenella made a dismissive gesture. 'No, I meant with useful, fun people, like Sarah and Hugo – he's Sarah's other half. Maybe Grant and Monica?'

Rupert came into the kitchen and moved the kettle across to the hotplate. 'Great if you want a party, otherwise better keep it small. Why don't you just ask Hugo and Sarah? We'll come up with something. When are you doing this course with Dermot, anyway?'

'Quite soon. End of the month.'

'That's only two weeks away!' said Fenella. 'Well, he must let us use his name by then, surely!'

'Even if he does, it's almost too late, publicity wise,' said Rupert. 'Bloody Irishmen! Always have to be so bloody mysterious.'

'Rupert! You're half-Irish yourself, don't forget, and Irishmen aren't always – oh my God!' Fenella paused, enlightenment dawning. 'I've cracked it! We don't need a summit meeting!'

'What?' asked Laura and Rupert simultaneously, watching as Fenella pushed her fingers into her hair, searched for a pen and generally became like an ant when its nest has been exposed.

'We'll make a thing of it!' she said, flourishing her pen and finding a pad to write on. 'We'll refer to our "mystery guest"! We'll prime all the literary press that the mystery guest will be announced at a certain time—'

'But will they think our mystery guest worth all that tra-la?' asked Rupert. 'Any mystery guest, come to that?'

'They would if they knew who he was,' said Fenella.

'But they don't!' said Laura. 'They mustn't! Until Dermot OKs it, anyway!' She was terrified that Fenella might ignore Dermot's desire for privacy for the sake of the festival. Truthfully, she wouldn't be able to blame her if she did, but Laura's loyalties were with Dermot.

'We'll leave heavy hints!' said Fenella. 'We'll get Eleanora to take all the relevant people out the lunch. The gossip columnists, the *Bookseller*, all the important mags. It'll be great!'

'It could work,' said Rupert.

'It will!' Fenella handed him a bundle of newspapers she'd just gathered up and carried on clearing one end of the table. 'Give Laura a cup of coffee while we make a list of everyone who needs to be convinced we've got the hottest literary date since – since – since some very big author did an event.'

Laura pulled out a chair, thinking rapidly. 'Eleanora will know lots of the names. I know a few. This could be a very good idea, Fen.' But secretly she was worried: Dermot would probably hate this, although he had rather forced them into it. Supposing it did make him back out, as Eleanora feared? 'Maybe we could imply we've got J. D. Salinger coming.'

'Isn't he dead?' objected Rupert, joining Fen in clearing the table.

'Not sure,' said Laura.

'Well, if you don't know, maybe they won't either,' said Fenella, 'and think he's coming.'

'They could just check on the Internet,' said Rupert. 'And better not to promise anything we can't deliver.'

'I only hope we can deliver Dermot!' Laura moaned, and then smiled to imply she was joking, although she wasn't. 'On a brighter note,' she went on, seeing Fenella's concerned glance, 'Monica's got a gig for Seamus. We should all go. Check him out for the festival. We did wonder about having his band playing, very softly, while Dermot reads.' Laura had seated herself at the table and was making notes in the notebook she had taken to carrying around with her everywhere. If she was ant-like too, her real anxieties about Dermot might not show. She felt she'd got to know him quite well over the phone, but Eleanora was his agent – surely she knew him better than Laura did?

'I think that sounds wonderful,' said Rupert. 'We want to try and do some things that involve the literary and the music festivals together.'

'Dermot will probably refuse to do it though,' said Laura, 'but I will ask him.'

'If it wasn't for the fact that Jacob Stone has been such a generous sponsor and it was because of Dermot that he came on board, I'd say to hell with Dermot!' said

Fenella. 'But I know you love him, Laura, so I'll shut up about it now.'

'It's not that I love him,' she lied determinedly, 'it's just that I really admire his work.'

'Yeah, yeah, yeah. So . . .' Fenella looked at her companions. 'Anyone else got any genius ideas?'

'I think if we're going to make the most of having a secret celebrity, we should offer a dinner with him, as a pre-festival treat, just for the important literary bods,' said Rupert. 'We'd make it really gourmet with decent wine.' He paused. 'Don't tell me, Laura, you don't think Dermot would agree.'

'Probably not, frankly. He hates literary bods. He thinks they're out to get him. And they probably are,' said Laura. 'Or at least, they will all pounce on whatever he writes next and want to tear it apart.'

'He hasn't produced anything for years, though, has he?' said Rupert.

'I think he's got something on the stocks,' said Laura, wondering if telling lies really made your nose grow longer. 'But I can't see him agreeing to it.'

'Maybe it wouldn't matter if he didn't turn up?' suggested Fenella. 'After all, we'd give them all a fabulous meal, a night in our "stately home". They'd have each other to talk to, after all. And we can't keep writing off ideas just because Dermot might refuse,' she went on. 'We'll have to work round him.'

'They'll probably hate each other,' said Laura, suddenly gloomy. 'They'll get drunk and pick fights.'

'Fabulous publicity!' said Fenella. 'It'll put my festival on the literary map!'

'Our festival, if you don't mind, darling,' said Rupert. 'More coffee, Laura?'

'No thanks, I'm jumpy enough already. I'll go and email Dermot with the next lot of stuff he's going to refuse to do.'

Dermot didn't refuse to attend a literary dinner at Somerby held in his honour, he just didn't mention it. After three emails asking him, Laura stopped bothering. She even said he could contact her by mobile if he preferred but to no avail.

Two weeks later, Laura parked in the university car park. It was late afternoon. In spite of their long chats on the telephone, she was nervous about actually seeing Dermot in person, especially since she hadn't heard from him for a while. However many times she reminded herself how well they'd got on before, she was sure that this time she would bore him and he would find some other young woman to go for walks with, to talk about and teach about writing, books, films and music. He'd have several to choose from, and four days to take his pick.

But despite her imagination throwing him into the arms of every woman on the course, she was determined to be more proactive herself about Dermot. She thought about Monica, going after Seamus all those months ago in Ireland. She knew she hugely admired Dermot, she liked him, and she fancied him desperately: she would make a move on him. She just hoped it wouldn't take a personality transplant to do it.

As she gathered her bags and made her way to the main entrance she asked herself why she had let so many attractive young women on to the course. Knowing his fondness for the female sex she could have arranged things a bit differently without compromising her position as an editor. The whole question of writing courses was fraught with controversy anyway. Many writers thought they were a complete waste of time, declaring that you could only learn to write by writing. Because of this, Laura didn't feel guilty about some of the young men who didn't get places on the course. She was confident they were well on their way already.

But the real reason she'd picked so many writers of women's fiction, women themselves, was because she felt this sort of fiction needed support in the literary world. Also, these writers were the most promising; they had given her the most fun while she was reading. And in a perverse way she wanted to test Dermot. If he succumbed to these women she'd know she shouldn't pursue him in a Monica-like way. No point in making a complete fool of herself, after all, or in allowing herself to fall in love with him – if she hadn't already – only to have her heart broken by his wandering eye.

Of course the photographs they'd sent in could all have been produced with a good dollop of Photoshop but Laura doubted it. Until you could apply Photoshop in those booths in the post office for taking passport photos, you got what you paid for. She was fairly sure in a couple of hours she and Dermot would be meeting someone her father would have referred to as 'crumpet'. And Laura had brought it on herself.

She had actually confessed all this to Monica, on the phone the previous evening. Her friend had been very brisk.

'For goodness' sake, Laura! You're mad! You don't believe he fancies you so you surround him with gorgeous women so he can prove you right. What sort of skewed thinking is that? Anyway, he does fancy you. He took one look at you and asked you to come to bed.'

'It wasn't quite like that and anyway, he was drunk. Probably.' This incident was still a matter of huge shame and even huger regret that she hadn't slept with him when all her normal defences were down. She'd rerun it in her head so many times she didn't trust her memory of it.

'You were drunk; I don't think he was.'

'Must have been, but even if he wasn't, he's probably

one of those men who'd go to bed with anything with a pulse.'

'I think to be fair, any female thing with a pulse, in his case.'

Laura laughed reluctantly. 'Well, whatever. What I'm trying to say is that I don't think he particularly fancied me, he just fancied sex, and I was there throwing myself at him.'

'No you weren't, you just said yes when you should have said no. He didn't ask me to sleep with him, after all, and I'm considered quite attractive in some circles.'

'No, I think if he'd really fancied me he'd have woken me up. He's not known for holding back. It could only mean "he's not that into me" to quote *Sex and the City*.'

Monica made a noise that indicated shock and awe. 'I didn't know you watched television, Laura! I thought you spent all your time reading improving books.'

'Oh shut up, Mon,' Laura whimpered. 'I'm just nervous.'

'Well, just go for it, that's my advice.'

'I'll do my best.' Laura sounded pathetic, even to her.

'Writers' course? Ah, now, well, is your case very heavy?' The man on reception was friendly and loquacious.

'No, it's on wheels,' said Laura.

The man looked over his desk as if to check this was true. 'Good. Your course is right at the corner of the campus. You could fetch your car and park it over there if you want to?'

'No, I'll be fine.' Laura continued to smile, trusting her key and directions to the building would transpire eventually. She felt she was less likely to get lost if she was on foot.

'That section is going to be demolished to make way for the new science block,' went on her informant.

'Ah!' said Laura. 'That's why the university offered to

host the course during termtime. They had spare accommodation. I did wonder.'

'Well, I wouldn't know about that,' said the porter. He produced a bit of paper with a map on it. 'You need to go along here, round the corner here, and there's the accommodation. The lecture halls – there are only a couple of them – are here.'

'Right.' Laura studied the map, hoping she wouldn't find it all as complicated as it looked. 'Has Dermot Flynn turned up yet?'

The porter looked down his list of names. 'Oh, him. He's in a staff flat, to keep him safe from all you students.'

Laura's smile was a little chilly, but she didn't explain she wasn't a student. 'But is he here yet?' They were going to meet up that evening and run through the course, find somewhere to eat and generally settle in before the students arrived.

The porter checked his register. 'No. Now, is there anything else you need to know?'

'I don't think so, thank you.'

Or at least, nothing you're likely to be able to help me with, such as: should I put on my sexiest dress (which wasn't, very) or should I wait until later on in the course to make my move on him? The thought of her making a move on anyone was so funny, so unlikely, she couldn't help smiling as she set off.

Once she found her room and was inside, she felt instantly thrown back to her own university days. There was the single bed, the noticeboard with remnants of posters and timetables still showing. There was a desk, witness to much struggle, boredom and despair, and the small shelf for books that meant that when she was at university, Laura's room had had neat piles of books ranged round the walls. There was a tiny shower room that smelt slightly of drains.

The whole place needed decorating and Laura hoped

that their students wouldn't feel disgruntled by having been put in this run-down block. Still, the teaching would be wonderful and they weren't actually paying to attend. It would be all right. She realised she was nervous about her part in it all, even if it was mainly administrative. She was to help with scheduling for private tuition, check everyone was happy and generally do anything that Dermot felt was not in his job description. But as she hadn't seen any of the correspondence regarding the course, she wasn't sure what this might involve. There was only so much you could cover over the phone.

Making sure her door wouldn't slam shut behind her, Laura went down the corridor and found the communal kitchen. This at least was clean and the fridge was on. She had better buy some tea bags, coffee and milk, she realised, but she could do that later.

As she went back to her room Laura wondered if she'd be invited to drink red wine out of paper cups and talk until the early hours? Or would she be considered to be a teacher, like Dermot? Worst would be to have governess status – neither one thing nor another.

She filled her kettle and made a cup of peppermint tea. She wasn't eighteen, leaving her parents for the first time; she was an adult. But actually she'd really loved university, getting away from home. She knew that if it weren't for her anxieties about Dermot, seeing him again, having to talk him into doing things for the festival that he was going to hate, she'd have loved going back to uni.

She was just wondering what she should do next when her phone rang.

'Laura? It's Dermot. What sort of a hole have they put me in?'

A smile spread across Laura's face, just at hearing his voice. 'Dermot! You've got a special staff flat. Don't tell me you're not happy with it?'

'It smells.'

Just for a second she allowed herself to feel pure joy that the planet contained both her and Dermot, and that very shortly she would see him again.

'Would you like me to come over and see if I can make you more comfortable?'

'And how would you be thinking of doing that?' His voice was teasing and full of laughter.

'With some lavatory cleaner and a stiff broom,' she said briskly, laughing too. 'What else?'

'If that's all you're offering I'd better have a shower instead. What time would you like to eat?'

'Well, I am quite hungry.' It had been quite a long drive from Somerby and although she had had a sandwich at lunchtime, it seemed ages ago.

'So am I. I passed a quite nice-looking pub on my way in. I thought we could have dinner there and discuss what's going on from tomorrow, check we're singing off the same hymn sheet.'

'That's sounds good.'

'Why are you laughing?' he demanded.

'How can you tell I am?' Laura had to fight to stop doing it out loud.

'I can hear it in your voice.'

He was stern now. This didn't make Laura any less inclined to smile. 'It's just the thought of you singing off any hymn sheet is quite funny.'

'I do have my spiritual side, I'll have you know,' he said, obviously trying to sound offended.

'I'm sure you have. It's just . . . never mind.'

'Well, can you find your way to my place and then we can go. In about an hour?'

'Fine. I'll find where you are on my map of the campus and come and meet you.'

'Brilliant.'

Laura held on to the phone for a few moments after

he had disconnected. In an hour she was going to see Dermot. Actually see him, not just talk to him on the phone. How lovely was that?

Then her elation faded just a little; what the hell should she wear?

Seeing him again made her smile and smile. He seemed pleased to see her too. Just for a moment, she wondered if there was just more than pleasure at seeing a friend in his look, of if she had imagined it. She had so little experience, and although she felt she knew Dermot quite a lot better now than when she'd last seen him, they had only met three times, and all those times were quite a long time ago.

He kissed her cheek. 'Well, hello!'

'Well, hello to you!' She had, she felt, achieved that hardest of images, the 'I just happened to be wearing this old thing, but bizarrely, it is one of my most flattering outfits, but no, of course I didn't put it on specially'. While she was changing for what felt like the ninth time she decided if a designer could create a line that captured this elusive look, they would clean up.

He stood looking down at her and grinning for a few long seconds and then said, 'Well, shall we find that pub then? It looked good and as we don't know what on earth the food is going to be like in the cafeteria, it might be the last decent meal we have for a few days.'

Unless we slip out and eat away from the students, Laura thought, and then felt instantly guilty.

'I feel we should eat with the students as much as possible. A lot of teaching and learning can go on in casual situations. They can feel more able to ask questions one to one, while you're jostling trays, than in a room full of other people.'

'You're displaying a very caring attitude,' she said as they walked along together, not touching apart from when she bumped into him by mistake from time to time. She felt ambivalent, wanting him to be caring on the one hand, but on the other, hoping he'd be keen to bunk off to the pub with her.

'You shouldn't be surprised. You know I go into schools regularly. I admit I prefer students to be under eleven, but I can cope with older ones.'

'You didn't seem quite so conscientious when we first started working together.' She frowned a little as she thought of his dismissive attitude to some of the manuscripts, how she'd had to nudge him into considering them seriously.

'I've turned over a new leaf,' he said, sounding a little smug. 'You should be proud of me.'

'Proud of you – why?'

'Oh, nothing in particular, just my general virtue. Now,' he went on, pushing open the pub door, 'what would you like? A pint of whiskey with a beer chaser?'

'A white wine spritzer please. We have to work tomorrow!'

Chapter Twelve

He walked her back to her accommodation, to her very door, after their meal out. 'There you are, sweetheart, safe and sound. We'll meet for breakfast, to make sure we're all sorted, and then expect the hordes to arrive at ten. Is that right?'

'It is.'

'Good. Nighty-night, then. See you at nine.' And he strode off to his rooms.

Laura was very happy, despite feeling slightly disappointed he hadn't even given her a goodnight peck on the cheek. The evening had been a wonderful combination of them just chatting – about everything – books mainly, but also films, music, politics, the state of the planet and the course, and there'd be other opportunities for a moment alone.

He had been delighted with the way she'd set things up to be easy for him. Each student had a brief CV, a résumé of their work and a photograph, plus the notes they had both discussed, neatly printed up. They both had full sets. He was going to study his now, he said, so he had half a chance of remembering people's names. What she hadn't got round to asking him was why he'd agreed to do the course, at short notice, in the first place. But there'd be plenty of time to do that later. And there'd be plenty of time to make her move on him, in the way Monica would. It would be easy. She got ready for bed with a smile on her face.

*   *   *

Laura, aware that the students might find the section of the university allocated for the course a little difficult to find, even if they had been sent maps of the campus, had printed out (courtesy of the office) some huge signs, and the following day, she and Dermot waited optimistically in the room allocated to them, smiles ready to pin on the moment anyone looked like arriving. They were both nervous.

'You do the opening bit and I'll take it from there,' said Dermot, walking up and down, reading old notices, opening and shutting cupboards and picking off bits of flaking paint.

'I've never done any public speaking of any kind—'

'Yes you have!' objected Dermot. 'You spoke to all those children. How many schools did you do in the end?'

'Only three, and I couldn't have done it at all if you hadn't coached me. You should do it.'

'I'm no teacher.'

'But you're a writer. That's why they're here!' Why didn't he understand the huge draw he was to the world? 'Besides, you liar, you've done loads of teaching!'

He chuckled. 'But not adults. I told you, I specialise in the under-elevens. And didn't you introduce the writers at all those signings you arranged when you were at the bookshop?'

As she'd told him she had, she couldn't very well deny it. 'All I had to say was what a wonderful writer the author was and how grateful the shop was to everyone for coming.'

'You could say that! I wouldn't mind at all!' He was laughing – at himself – at her – at the situation and looking at her in a slightly distracted way. Suddenly she found she couldn't meet his gaze without blushing, so she didn't. It was odd to see him so nervous. It was reassuring but at the same time she wasn't quite sure if it was just nerves about the course that were making him glance at her every couple of minutes. It certainly wasn't helping hers.

She busied herself with her register. 'All right. I'll just do a very brief hello, but then it's down to you.' Was this the moment to ask him why he'd agreed to run the course? Maybe not. It might have been complicated and someone could appear at any moment.

She looked at her watch and then at Dermot to see that he'd just done the same thing. It was still only ten to ten. They exchanged rueful smiles.

'Eleanora's coming on the last night,' said Laura to break the anxious silence. 'Which is good because she'll tell them what's what if we can't.'

Dermot nodded. 'She can be very scary. I always deal with Tricia, her assistant, if I can.'

'Oh, I've met Tricia.' Laura wondered if all this small talk was actually making them more nervous. 'So, have you got any ideas for exercises?'

'Mm. Some.' He smiled. 'I'll be fine once I've started, but I always get like this before a gig.'

'You would never have guessed it,' said Laura, recalling his prowl through his fans, his leap on to the stage, his rock-star confidence. He was wearing a rumpled linen suit which would have looked silly on anyone else but seemed to go well with his generally rumpled look. He was so staggeringly attractive he could pull on any old pair of jeans and manky sweatshirt and look sexy. She decided now was as good a time as any to find out why he was here. 'But if it terrifies you so much, why are you doing this course?'

He made a nonchalant gesture that didn't quite come off. 'The money.'

'Really?' She found this hard to believe. She didn't know anything about his finances, of course, but she doubted that the course would be well paid enough to tempt him if he didn't want something else out of it. Her own fee was welcome, but it wasn't huge.

'I'm doing it under sufferance. And under false pretences.'

'What do you mean? Are you saying that Eleanora made you?' If she had such power over him why hadn't she just ordered him to do the festival? Why had she been sent to persuade him?

He shrugged, sighed and came back to the desk. 'Let's just say that Eleanora told me – reminded me – that you learn what you teach. She thought it might get me writing again.'

'I thought she didn't know about your block?'

'She didn't actually say that, but I know it's what she felt. She must suspect. She's no fool.'

'Well, that makes perfect sense!' Laura smiled, happy that he was making a positive step towards getting over his writer's block.

'Does it?' His smile was incomprehensible. 'Then I'm glad.'

A bit confused, Laura went on. 'So what about the false pretences bit?'

He shrugged. 'I'm just not sure you can teach people to write.'

'I know what you mean, but there must be some tips you can pass on. I mean, what's the hardest part of learning to write?'

He shrugged again. 'I didn't ever learn to write. That's my problem. I just did it.'

Before Laura could react, the door opened and the first students arrived.

'Hi!' Dermot and Laura said brightly and simultaneously at the first couple. They exchanged glances and then Dermot went on.

'I'm Dermot Flynn and this is Laura Horsley. Laura's going to open proceedings officially when everyone is here. In the meantime, if you'd like to come up and collect your name badges.' He smiled. 'We want to start putting the faces to the work as soon as possible in case you don't look like your photos!'

Laura was pleased that any sign of nervousness from Dermot had gone and turned her attention to the group, which now numbered four, as they clustered round the table, looking for their names. They seemed so eager and pleased to be there. Would they still be so keen when she and Dermot started tearing their work to shreds? She felt personally that although she could criticise writing perfectly well when it was just her and the manuscript, she might feel different when the writer was actually present.

'Sit anywhere, but not too spread out,' she said as another clutch of potential writers arrived. 'There are going to be exercises and some of them might involve getting into groups. It's really important that we all feel comfortable with each other, so shyness is not acceptable.'

How she would have cringed if anyone had said this to her a few months ago. How her life had changed! This time last year she would never have dreamt she could pitch a short-story competition to schoolchildren, do interviews to local newspapers and all the other front-of-house-type things that had previously terrified her. She had discovered that when you were involved in a project, particularly one you felt passionately about, you just got on and did what was needed.

The ten writers carefully selected by Laura and approved by Dermot had arranged themselves among the chairs and were chatting to each other in low, excited voices. Getting on the course had obviously meant a lot to all of them. Laura couldn't decide if this keenness was a good thing or a bad thing.

She did a rough head-count and everyone seemed to

be there. She and Dermot exchanged glances and he nodded, indicating she should get things under way.

'OK, everyone, let me just check that you're all here.' She smiled. Having seen their photos and commented on their writing, in some ways she felt she knew these people already. 'Maybe when I've read your name and you've confirmed you're here, you could tell us a bit about yourself for the benefit of the group.'

'It would be quite hard to confirm we're here if we're not,' said one young man who Laura identified as the one Dermot hadn't wanted on the course, in case he was a pain. It looked as if Dermot had been right. She didn't look at him now but she knew he was looking at her knowingly.

'Very true,' she replied solemnly, and started reading the list. 'Gareth Ainsley?'

Rather to her annoyance, it was the young man who answered. 'That's me.'

'And what are you writing, Gareth?' Although she knew from his covering letter, and having read his work she wanted to hear him actually say it, for the others.

'I don't think that pigeonholing writers is very constructive. I'm not prepared to put my work into a slot decided by the publishers.'

Laura bit her lip to hide her emerging smile. Boy did this young man have a lot to learn! Then she realised he was about the same age as she was. 'OK, Gareth, but just to give us an idea, name a writer whose work you admire and who may have influenced you.'

Reluctantly he mumbled a few names of which Dermot's was one, and Laura made a note on her register.

'OK, Samantha Pitville?'

'I'm here. And I write chick lit!' The very pretty young blonde declared this with defiance as if she expected people to boo.

'There is nothing wrong with being commercial,' said

Laura. 'If you're keener on sales than critical acclaim it's best to know that as soon as possible.'

Samantha smiled, adding to her prettiness by about a hundred watts. 'Yes, but I'm writing chick lit because I can't write anything else. And I like it.'

'Good for you!' said Dermot.

Laura wondered if he could possibly resist such pulchritude. Her only hope was that Samantha didn't go for older men.

At last the register was taken and every one had nailed their colours to the mast in one way or another. The older women, Helen and Maggie, who declared they were writing cosy crime and 'thoughtful books for older women', did blush a bit as they did so, but Laura felt proud of them.

'Well that's all very interesting,' said Dermot. 'Now Laura's going to give you a bit of an introduction.'

'Well,' said Laura, 'I'm not going to say much, but firstly, well done for getting a place on this course. You probably know there were a lot of applicants and you were all picked because of your talent.' She smiled encouragingly. 'But now may be the only time you feel talented because I know this course is going to be fairly tough—'

'Can I just ask – er – Laura?' It was Gareth Ainsley and Laura stiffened. 'We all know who Dermot Flynn is, but who are you? I mean, what are your qualifications for assisting on this course?'

Dermot moved forward from where he'd been leaning against a desk but Laura put up a hand to stop him. She was going to deal with this herself. She felt she should. She didn't want them thinking she had no experience at all. 'I'm here to help Dermot. I used to work in a book-shop and because I've spent so much of my life reading, I'm now setting up a literary festival and I helped Dermot make the selection. So if any of you aren't up to it –' she glared at Gareth, trying to make him feel he might not be up to it '– it's my fault you're here. OK?'

Gareth glanced at Dermot and possibly sensed something protective and maybe threatening about his stance. 'Oh yes, fine.'

'Well then, I'll hand you over to Dermot.'

Sweating slightly in spite of her brave front, Laura withdrew to the second desk and sat behind it, arranging her pile of student notes and putting a secret mark on Gareth's.

'Hello,' said Dermot. 'Nice to see you're all here. As Laura said, there was very stiff competition to get on this course, but I'm afraid it's nothing to the competition of the real publishing world. Later in the week my agent is coming to talk to you. If I haven't managed to convince you of this, then she will. Now, I'd like to kick off with a question-and-answer session and general chat. Feel free to comment if you want to. We're not kids. And this will give us an idea of what you're expecting to gain from the course, and it'll give you lot a chance to find out more about each other. Who's first?'

A young man put up his hand. Dermot looked down at his pile of papers. 'John? You have a question?'

'OK,' said the young man who Laura remembered wrote literary, autobiographical, rather navel-gazing fiction. 'Obviously, I entered for the competition, but I started writing when I was a student. I mean, so much of the stuff we had to read was crap. I knew I was better than that.'

'Nice to have confidence,' said one of the older women dryly.

Laura glanced down at her notes. She had this Maggie Jones noted down as promising. The book she'd entered was a bit downbeat but Laura was confident she'd be able to put a bit of uplift into it, if she knew it was required.

'Well, if you're know you're good, there's no point in pretending you're not,' said John, although he flushed slightly.

'Confidence is a gender thing,' said Samantha, who didn't seem to be lacking in it herself.

'I think you're right,' said Tracy, a feisty young woman who had proudly announced she wrote short romance novels. According to Laura's notes, they were sparky and very sexy.

'And your point is?' Dermot said to John.

'I just wonder if there's any point in this course.'

John's words caused a frisson of anxiety around the room.

'Probably not,' said Dermot, his lazy delivery belying his critical gaze.

An anxious silence filled the room until Maggie spoke up. 'I'm sure we've all got a lot to learn. I know I have. After all, I presume we're going to be reading stuff out to each other. When you read it to yourself, it always seems amazing.'

Laura smiled fondly at her. She was going to contribute and co-operate, what a relief!

'I'd rather just work on my novel than do a lot of poxy exercises,' said John.

'In which case you shouldn't have entered the competition,' put in Laura. 'Exercises are extremely useful and we're going to be doing a lot of them.' Rather too late she remembered that she and Dermot hadn't discussed what they were going to do in detail. She shot him a look and he returned it with an amused eyebrow.

'Yes,' said Maggie. 'Lots of people would have given their eye teeth to be here. If you're lucky enough to be chosen, you should make the most of your opportunities.'

'Yes, but—'

'Writing is a strange, ephemeral thing,' said Dermot,

smoothing over potential troubled waters. 'You never know what's going to help and what's not. I don't intend to do exercises on punctuation. But writing for a given time on a given subject can really loosen you up.'

Dermot was cruel. They had five minutes to write about 'money'. Another five to cover 'death', but ten whole minutes to write about 'birth'.

As a concession, he allowed people to choose what they considered to be their best piece before making them read it out. He'd done the exercises himself and went first.

'It's to give you lot confidence,' he explained. 'When you see how crap I am, you'll feel a lot happier about exposing yourselves to the criticism of others.'

But of course, he wasn't crap. Laura was mildly surprised as she thought his writer's block implied he could barely write a shopping list, but then the workings of his literary mind were still a mystery to her. And reading out loud was still agony for most.

By lunchtime, everyone was settling down nicely and went off to the cafeteria talking away as if they really knew each other.

'God Almighty, what I have let myself in for?' declared Dermot the moment they were alone.

Laura laughed delightedly. 'You're brilliant at this! They love you! Although,' she added, less happily, 'I do think it was mean of you to make me do the exercises too.'

'Don't be silly – yours were just as good as anyone else's, but I do think there's some talent there, don't you?'

'Definitely. I just hope we can keep them entertained and happy for the entire time.'

'I've got a plan if things look like dragging,' said Dermot. 'I'll tell you later.'

* * *

194

The afternoon was taken up by students writing longer pieces. They were going to be read and discussed in the bar after supper. After lunch, Dermot said he'd see everyone later in the bar for a quick drink before supper. Trying not to feel disappointed, Laura went to her own room to work. She had quite a lot to do for the festival – inviting all the writers appearing to Rupert's pre-festival dinner for one – and she had promised to read one of Tracy's category romances. They had agreed between them that Dermot would be shown it only if Laura thought it was fantastic. Her afternoon flew by and she found she only had time for a mug of tea at her desk, although when she looked out of her window, she could see everyone else gathering on the lawn, lying around sunbathing, talking, no doubt, about writing.

She grabbed a quick shower and arrived at the bar late and a little damp.

'Hey, Laura! You're at least three drinks behind us,' said Samantha. 'What can I get you?'

'Oh, a white wine spritzer, please.'

'Oh, for goodness' sake! Have a proper drink!' Samantha made her opinion of Laura's choice very clear. 'Have the wine on its own, at least.'

Laura laughed. 'If I can have the water separately. I don't drink much as a rule.'

'That's not what I heard,' said Dermot, his eyes dangerously teasing.

'Isn't it?' she said blithely. 'Well, I can't imagine where you got your information.' Then she wondered if she'd been wrong to trust him not to tell everyone about her exploits in Ireland.

Someone touched her elbow. It was Tracy, the woman whose novel Laura had spent a lot of her afternoon reading. 'Oh, let's go and talk privately,' she said. 'I'll just get my drink.' She was relieved to have an excuse to change the subject.

'Well?'

Tracy was so diffident Laura hastened to reassure her. 'I couldn't put it down! I did my other work first and thought I'd just read a bit so I could tell you, one way or another, and I couldn't stop reading!'

Dermot was fantastic with the students in the bar. He bought drinks all evening and listened to everyone's comments with apparent respect and kindness, and even signed copies of his books a couple of the students shyly presented to him. He was particularly sweet to the older women who lacked the brashness of the young, beautiful high-flyers. It was a side of him Laura hadn't seen much of and she liked it.

'Finding time to write isn't easy,' said Tracy, feeling more confident since she and Laura had had their chat. 'Especially when you've got a young family. Writing seems very self-indulgent, sometimes.'

'If it's good for you, it's good for the family,' said Helen. 'I really believe that. You can't be a good wife and mother if you're stifling your creativity. Isn't that right, Dermot?'

He smiled and shook his head. 'Not having been a wife or a mother I'm not really in a position to comment but stifled creativity is a very bad thing.'

Everyone laughed. 'Not that you'd know about that either,' said John, who, having wanted to challenge Dermot to begin with, to establish his credentials, was now as admiring as everyone else. 'You obviously have no problem with it. What are you working on at the moment?'

It was natural that John should assume that Dermot was working on something, but Laura winced. She didn't want Dermot put on the spot like this.

'I never talk about my work-in-progress,' said Dermot, evading the question skilfully. 'But creativity is a wilful mistress,' he asked, 'she won't always do what you say.'

Everyone had had a couple of drinks by then and only Laura heard the tinge of pain in his words.

'Could I just have another word?' Tracy asked Laura. 'Not many people I know understand the genre as you seem to. Do you really think my book is publishable?'

'Well, obviously, I'm not an expert . . .'

Laura and Tracy discussed her book until they were summoned to dinner by the others. Several of them, including Dermot, were carrying bottles of wine and as Laura had already had two glasses, the second pressed on her by a grateful Tracy, she decided she wouldn't personally drink any more.

She didn't get to sit within easy reach of Dermot but she could see his students were lapping up every word he uttered. Still, that was fine. She was enjoying herself down her end of the table and she could talk to Dermot later, when they went back to the bar.

But by the time everyone had finished eating she felt too tired to carry on with the party. There would be other evenings, she told herself. She'd been working hard and it had been a long day.

'I think I'll just go to bed,' she told everyone, feeling sheepish and a party pooper. 'I seem terribly tired, for some reason.'

Dermot was so engrossed in a discussion about the merits of various genres he barely noticed her leave. She pushed down a feeling of disappointment. He was here for the students, she reminded herself.

'Well, I'm still up for it because I had a nap,' admitted Maggie, one of the older women.

'Me too,' said a couple of others. 'Learning stuff is so tiring!'

The next two days of the course followed the same pattern. Exercises in the morning, private writing or more exercises in the afternoon, long sessions in the bar, before and after dinner in the evening. Each student was to get a one-to-one session with Dermot. He had arranged this timetable himself although she'd been detailed to do it, so Laura didn't know when he would be closeted with a lovely young writer. This was probably a good thing. She had enough on her plate. A flurry of writers had confirmed for the festival and as Fenella was now totally tied up with weddings, it being summer and the wedding season, Laura was trying to work out a timetable. Her afternoons were spent on this, and on reading other people's work. Tracy had been so pleased with her criticism of her book, everyone else wanted Laura's opinion. As the time had passed it had become obvious how highly Dermot thought of her, and how much he valued what she had to say, so the students did likewise. Although she had twice managed to get to the bar after dinner, she could never stay up for more than one drink, however much she wanted to. And much as she'd planned to make a move on Dermot, there just hadn't been a moment. Nor had he suggested a quick, private coffee with her. He seemed to appreciate having her there but she just couldn't work out if there was – as she hoped – a bit more to it than that.

'OK, everyone, change of pace for today!' announced Dermot when the students had stopped talking and were paying attention. 'I've hired a small coach and we're going off to a stately home for the day. This is to give us all a bit of a break – we've been working really hard since we're been here.' Laura's sudden desire to yawn gave testament to this. 'So we're going to get right away. However, you're not just going to skulk around, you're going to work.' He paused for breath. 'In many ways writing is like painting. The artist looks at life and translates it into something else for the viewer. The writer does it with words, not paint. I want you to make written sketches of what you see. Some will be of physical things:

a wood, a statue, a vista. Some will be of people and how they relate to their surroundings. And for the more imaginative among you' – he glanced at the writers of commercial fiction – 'I'd like you to write a scene set in the period of the house we're going to see. It could even be about the real people who lived in the house. I want four pieces of the work by bar-time tonight! Oh, and the cafeteria has made up packed lunches for you all, if you'll just go along and collect them.'

Laura was thrilled. She felt she needed a day off from festival work and surely, during a day spent in a stately home, she'd have a chance for some private – intimate – time with Dermot. She felt sure she'd seen the same anticipation in the look he'd given her when he'd told them all.

'How did you get the cafeteria to make up packed lunches at such short notice?' Laura asked Dermot as they filed on to the bus.

He smiled down at her from the top step. 'It wasn't short notice. I booked them on the first morning. I knew we'd need a day away, to freshen us all up. It gives us a bit of time off too.'

Laura gave a little sigh of happiness and didn't mind at all that Helen had saved a place for her, and she couldn't sit by Dermot. There was bound to be an opportunity to be alone later; he obviously wanted it too.

Laura longed to doze on the bus trip, which was a little longer than she'd anticipated, but Helen wanted to talk about her work. Still, Laura felt she wouldn't need to stay up late in the bar, or try to, because she'd get Dermot on his own very soon. The thought made her very happy – and possibly more enthusiastic about Helen's book than perhaps it warranted.

The garden was attached to a great house that was not to be visited. Dermot had insisted.

'We'd have to pay more,' he said, 'and I want outdoor scenes. You can have people – today's people, people from the past, but use the garden! I want trees, flowers. In detail – remember "oak" not "tree". Off you go.'

Unrestricted by Dermot's orders, Laura did turn to the house. It was large and square and seemed to her to be Georgian. A huge magnolia climbed up one side and lace-cap hydrangeas the other. There was an avenue of lime trees leading to the front door, which, when you turned away from the house, framed the church spire of the nearest village. At the front, parkland stretched to the stone wall in the far distance. A green painted arrow indicated the formal gardens were round the back of the property. They were blessed with a beautiful day and everywhere looked at its best. It was impressive, but Laura found herself thinking that privately she preferred Somerby's more modest and wilder grandeur.

She stood and gazed for a few moments before turning to look for Dermot.

He'd vanished! How could he have disappeared so quickly? He must have gone with the first group of students who were all chattering away and not, Laura felt, taking in their surroundings.

She wandered slowly along the path, following the signs to the gardens. She'd come across Dermot shortly, she was sure.

The trouble was, there were paths to several different gardens: a cottage garden, a millennium garden, a stumpery – whatever that was – a walled garden and a rose garden as well as a vegetable garden and glasshouses. She suspected there was a more formal garden beyond all that – she could see tall clipped yews in the distance, and a copper beech covered with tiny roses.

She blinked in the sunshine, considering her options. His curiosity might lead him to the stumpery, or he might like glasshouses – she did herself – or would he be drawn to the yews and roses like stars against almost purple foliage? She couldn't guess, so, deciding simply to enjoy her surroundings, she set off towards the millennium garden. She was just about to reach it when she saw a group of students, including Dermot, right at the end of a wide mown path.

Feeling she couldn't really gallop down it without looking pathetically needy, like the friendless child on a school outing, she thought she'd try and find a way to meet them without them seeing her approach.

A convenient hedge described in green paint as 'tapestry' and consisting of several varieties of tree and quite a few climbing plants, including dog roses and honeysuckle, led, Laura assumed, to the more formal garden where the group was. Hoping she wouldn't meet anyone and feel obliged to explain why, she hared along it arriving at the other end to see the backs of the group heading along towards a woodland area.

Panting slightly and beginning to perspire she debated just running to join them, but still couldn't persuade herself that she wouldn't look pathetic. Why oh why didn't Dermot dispatch them on their separate ways to work on their pieces?

She decided running to join them would only work if she had something of vital importance to tell them. What could she say? She couldn't say there was a fire because there obviously wasn't, and anyway they were in the garden. Floods and swarms of locusts wouldn't work either. What about a particularly beautiful bit of garden, perhaps with a butterfly or, better, a dragonfly involved? She wiped her brow. No, she wouldn't just look keen like an ambitious Girl Guide but barking mad because if there was a dragonfly, there was no way it would still be there, even if everybody did troop off to look at it. And if it was a particularly fine bit of planting involving old roses and lavender, there would be no need for her to have run.

Sighing, she stumped off towards the stumpery – at least it sounded cool.

She spent the rest of the afternoon alternating between feeling like a very bad private detective, trying to stalk Dermot, and like a detective's quarry, trying to avoid being joined by any students, so if she did manage to get Dermot on his own, she would be on her own too.

When they finally met up in the tea room, she said to him casually, 'It's a lovely garden, isn't it? There must be acres and acres. I don't think I ever spotted you.' This was a lie but she didn't want to say she'd only spotted him from a distance because it would imply she'd been looking.

'Oh, I found a really hidden-away corner in the wood,' he said. 'I read my book.' Seeing her react he added, 'No, not written by me. If I told you it was poetry would you think I was impossibly pretentious?'

'Yes,' she nodded, smiling, lying again. 'But it's very writerly, so I'll forgive you.'

Back on the bus she sat at the back and soon fell into a reverie. Trying to get Dermot on his own was just too stressful. If he fancied her – and it was increasingly likely that he didn't – *he* could seek *her* out.

It was the last day of the course and everyone was anxious about Eleanora's impending visit. Although they had never met her, the students instinctively felt their work was going to be torn to shreds, even though Dermot had already taken it apart and put it together again. Dermot may well have been wondering if his agent would press him on his work-in-progress, although he didn't tell Laura this, there had to be some reason for his twitchiness. And Laura was convinced Eleanora would feel she should have got Dermot to announce his presence at the festival to the world. Although, when she thought more deeply, she realised this probably wasn't the case at all, and she was just picking up nerves from everyone else.

Eleanora arrived in style, driving herself in an old Ferrari that roared up to the building leaving an expensive trail of blue smoke behind it.

Dermot was there to greet her. He had put on his suit, which was now so creased it looked as if it had been run over several times by a steamroller. Laura had longed to tell him to brush his hair but had refrained, realising that Eleanora, who knew him quite well, wouldn't expect him to be smart. The rest of them had all got used to his scruffy, writerly appearance.

He kissed Eleanora warmly and said, 'I'm not sure you can leave your car there, Nellie, dear heart.'

Eleanora bridled and said, 'Don't call me Nellie, and I'm sure this nice young man will park it for me.'

The 'nice young man' in question was Gareth, whom Laura privately referred to as the Young Turk. He was only too delighted to catch the keys that Eleanora tossed to him. Grateful that she hadn't been asked to park it herself, Laura followed Dermot and Eleanora into the building and along the corridor to the lecture room.

Eleanora was ferocious! Laura thought that Dermot had been quite tough, but Eleanora was tougher. She'd suspected she'd tell it how it was but Eleanora went to town and what's more seemed to enjoy imparting every negative aspect of the writer's lot she could think of – and more. She told the students the chances of them getting published were hardly better than winning the lottery. She then went on to say that getting published wasn't half as hard as staying that way. If your first book didn't do well, your second wouldn't see the light of day, and if you weren't well published, you might as well burn your books in a corner of your garden because they might attract more attention that way.

No one actually burst into tears, but Laura felt it was only a matter of time.

Then Eleanora added the final can of petrol to the fire of despondency she had created. 'And if you're not good-looking, very old, very young, related to a football star or the managing director of a publishing company, forget it again. If you're not promotable, you're not publishable.'

Eleanora seemed faintly surprised that the room didn't erupt with applause. Dermot was struck dumb, a rare thing for him, and faint whimperings began to emanate from the students.

Laura got to her feet. She couldn't send them all home with their collective heart in its boots.

'Well, thank you, Eleanora, that was fascinating. And isn't it a good thing to hear the very worst-case scenario? Dermot and I know that there's a lot of talent in this room, and while I don't think any of you are best friends with a football star, or married to the head of a major publishing house . . .' She paused. 'But if you are and you didn't tell us, we'll kill you later . . . Dermot and I have seen the immense amount of work and dedication you're capable of, and I know – am sure –' she wasn't at all sure, but she said it anyway, aware that she was sounding rather like an over-enthusiastic headmistress '– that Eleanora would agree with us when we say that talent and perseverance are more important than any of the things she mentioned. Cream will rise to the top. Just you lot go and be cream! And meet us in the bar afterwards.'

The applause wasn't thunderous, but it was there. As her encouraging words sank in they came out of their state of shock and clapped gently.

'Darling, you're too soft on them!' said Eleanora the moment the three of them were alone. 'Tell it like it is!'

'Sure, I know every word you said is true –' Dermot ran his hand through his hair making it even more like a wind-damaged bird's nest – 'but they'd have all gone out and cut their throats if Laura hadn't rescued the situation.'

'Yes, Laura dear, you have done well! I knew you were the person to run Fenella's festival. You've done a splendid job with this course, too! Now I see why you wanted her on board, Dermot.'

Laura lost her breath suddenly. She'd assumed it was Eleanora who'd suggested she come. She couldn't work out how she felt about it. She was pleased he thought she'd be useful, of course. It was flattering that he thought so highly of her editing and organisational skills. But did this mean he really didn't fancy her at all, and just saw her as useful? Was that why he hadn't wanted to be alone with her? It was a devastating thought.

'Laura has been a complete star,' said Dermot. 'I couldn't have managed without her by my side.'

There was a moment's silence and then Eleanora patted Laura on the shoulder. 'Good for you! Now where's the bar?'

At first the students were wary of sitting near Eleanora, but gradually they crept nearer and found she didn't bite. By the end of the evening she'd bought them all drinks and, with a little prompting from Laura, offered to read anything they sent to her.

As Laura walked a rather intoxicated Eleanora back to the room where she was staying the night, she said to her, 'I don't know why I offered to do that. My slush pile is quite big enough already.'

'But these will be quality slush! I hand-picked them myself and their books will be a lot better when they've done more work.'

'All right, darling, I trust you. And Dermot trusts you too, which is very interesting.'

As Laura had always thought of herself as trustworthy, she didn't think it was that strange. But Eleanora, given her slightly drunken state, possibly wasn't thinking clearly.

The students all left immediately after breakfast, many of them saying they felt thoroughly inspired. Eleanora had left before breakfast, saying she was visiting an old friend on the way home, and so suddenly it was just Dermot and Laura.

'Well, I don't know what to say,' said Dermot.

'That must be a first!' Laura teased him, trying to sound lighthearted, although that was the last thing she felt. She remained puzzled by his behaviour over the course. He seemed to genuinely enjoy having her there, but apart from the odd almost brotherly look, she couldn't read him properly and felt completely confused by his attitude towards her. She was also sad because she hadn't managed to make the most their time together. She suddenly felt less confident – so much for her wanting to seduce him. A university car park wasn't the most romantic of settings. And he wasn't striking the pose of someone about to make a move on her as he stood there with his hands in his pockets looking anxious to get away. She told herself she'd see him again at the festival, but would they ever have a minute alone? She couldn't rely on it. And she had to face the possibility that he just didn't see her in that way, if he ever had. She was good old helpful Laura.

'Irishmen are famously loquacious,' she added brightly.

'Not this particular Irishman, at this particular time.' Then he put his hand on her cheek. 'You're a very sweet girl.'

She blinked to disperse her sudden tears. He was being very kind and gentle but it was only affection that she detected in his voice. 'Right then. See you in July at the festival.'

'Oh God, the bloody festival! I'd forgotten all about that.'

'Well, let me remind you!' she said, with feigned strictness.

'One of these days we'll meet under more auspicious circumstances,' he said. Then he kissed her cheek and walked off towards his car without looking back.

Laura stood and watched him go, her tears flowing freely now. She didn't care if anyone saw her.

Chapter Thirteen

❧

The drive back to Somerby gave Laura plenty of time to sort out in her mind her feelings for Dermot and, more importantly, his feelings for her. Although she couldn't really tell how he felt, Laura was now convinced she was really in love with Dermot. The course had given her an opportunity to see him as a man, and how he functioned in society. He could be cutting, sarcastic and rude but it was all tempered with humour, wit and extreme kindness. All of the students had been criticised, but all of them had received praise they would cherish for the rest of their writing careers.

He saw her as a helpmeet, that was it. Reliable, diligent, forgiving – none of the characteristics that made her a force to be reckoned with, unless they happened to be jointly reckoning the chances of a particular writer's success. His tenderness to her as they parted showed her how fond he was of her, but fondness was not enough. A part of her wished she'd never met him, that he'd remained the elusive figure she'd dreamt about. Now like all good heroines in the books she devoured as a teenager, she'd have to pick herself up and get over him as best she could.

She was soon thrown back into festival work with little time to dwell too much on the great Dermot Flynn and for that she was very grateful. She'd slipped the photograph one of the students had sent her of them all together into one of the books on her shelves after briefly tracing the outline of his face and then telling herself not to be so silly.

She'd been to stay with Grant for a few days, who was back from a holiday 'somewhere hot and expensive' and wanting to tell her all about it, with pictures. She was now returning to Somerby once more – and work.

Fenella greeted Laura as she drove round the back to park her car near her converted byre, calling through the open window. She seemed very over-excited.

'Have you heard? Dermot's gone public! Why didn't you tell me?'

'Let the poor girl get out of the car!' Even Rupert, following his wife, seemed less laid-back than usual.

Laura did this. 'Sorry, Fen,. what do you mean?'

'Jacob Stone phoned me. Apparently Dermot has gone public. He saw it on some news thing. He's thrilled, naturally.'

'But he hasn't!' Laura opened the back door to get her bag. 'I'm sure he'd have said something to me if he was going to do that.' She felt desperately betrayed. It was her festival! Surely she should have been the first to know, not some news agency and Jacob Stone! Anyway, on the course he'd said he'd forgotten all about it!

'We'll ring Eleanora,' said Fenella. 'She'll know.'

'Good idea. I think we need to check this story, I really do.'

Apparently it was true. They went on to an Internet news site on Rupert's computer. Some news agency had got hold of the story that *formerly reclusive writer Dermot Flynn has agreed to appear at the Somerby Literary Festival. There are rumours that he'll produce his first new work for many years and also that there's a bidding war for his next novel.*

'Oh fuck,' whispered Laura.

'Laura!' said Fenella.

'I know. I'm sorry, but that's the only word that will do. He'll be absolutely bloody furious!'

'Why? And anyway, the story probably came from him,' said Fenella. 'Who else would make up a story like this?'

'Eleanora, for one,' said Laura. 'She's got the most to gain.' She thought hard about the course, trying to remember if there was anything about Eleanora's behaviour that indicated she might have put this story about. 'But I don't think she did.'

'Well, we can ask her,' said Fenella.

Laura sighed. 'I hope to goodness it doesn't get on the main news.' She looked at Rupert and Fenella plaintively. 'After all, it's only literary news, not really of general interest.'

'It might not be like that in Ireland,' said Rupert. 'I mean, I don't really know, but I imagine if word got out that "the greatest living Irish writer" was producing a new book, it would be of huge interest.'

Laura buried her face in her hands. 'This is dreadful.'

'It's jolly good for the festival!' said Fenella. 'I'll be able to tell everyone that he's coming and then may be all those writers who haven't yet confirmed, will. And people will be queuing for tickets.'

Laura reappeared from behind her hands. 'I just don't know what Dermot will do when he hears about this.'

'Well, we can't do anything about it until he does hear,' said Rupert. 'I think we should all calm down. Let's go into the house and have a cup of coffee.'

Laura was plucking up courage to ring Eleanora when her phone went. Eleanora was phoning her. 'Laura?' she snapped. 'Did you put this story about?'

'No! Did you really think I had?'

Eleanora subsided. 'No.'

'In fact, I thought you might have released it,' said Laura.

'Me? Good God no! Why would I do that? If anything

was designed to give him writer's block for ever, it's something like this.'

'You knew about his writer's block?'

'Of course!'

'He was hoping you didn't know.'

'Who or what does he think I am? Stupid? I'm his agent, for God's sake. I know when my writers aren't writing, even when they're telling me they are! No, the poor boy's been blocked as hell for years. We just keep up the pretence that I don't know.' She paused. 'He told you?'

'Mm.' Laura didn't explain the circumstances, or that they'd exchanged deep secrets. Eleanora didn't need to know everything.

There was a long pause. 'I think you'd better come up to London right away. We need to make a plan.'

'But the festival—'

'The festival won't have it's star act unless we can think of something. This has to be a priority. Fenella will understand.'

Laura was explaining all this to Fenella and Rupert when her phone chimed to indicate she had a text message. It was from Dermot. 'Your festival can take a flying jump.'

It felt like a physical blow, not because the festival needed its star so badly, but because he might think that it was she who had betrayed him. Somehow, she had to tell him that she hadn't.

'I think we can take it as a no,' she said, fighting to sound calm, having shown her message to Rupert and Fenella. 'It's quite polite, really, for him.'

'Maybe he doesn't know you can text the "f" word,' said Rupert.

'You can?' said Fenella. 'I didn't know that!'

'We can be thankful for small mercies,' said Laura, proud of her lighthearted remark. In the circumstances it was a triumph.

'You'd better go to Eleanora's straightaway,' said Fenella. 'She's the one to get us out of this mess. If she says she needs you, go.'

'Maybe Laura would prefer to recover from the journey first?' suggested Rupert. 'She's only just got back. I know your family always do jump when Eleanora snaps her fingers, but there's no reason for Laura to do so too.'

'I think there is, actually, Ru,' Laura said. 'The sooner we can get this sorted out, the better. If we *can* get it sorted out.'

'If we could just find out who did it,' said Fenella. 'Then we could send them hate mail.'

'You'd have sent them fan mail when you first heard it,' said Laura, indignantly.

'That was before I knew what a disaster it was.'

A comforting bowl of soup and a lift to the station from Rupert did help Laura to calm down a bit. She read a light romantic novel on the train and by the time she reached London, she was feeling less desperate. After all, if the festival flopped it wasn't the end of the world. Then she remembered how much effort she and Fenella had put in to it, how much money had been spent, and decided it might not be the end of the world but it would be a terrible shame. And there was always the fear that Jacob Stone would withdraw as a sponsor. Supposing he asked for the money he'd already given to be returned?

She dismissed this idea as ridiculous as she walked to the taxi queue, trailing her case on wheels. She felt as if she'd been living out of a suitcase for weeks. She was more worried about Dermot than she was about the festival. And she knew Eleanora would be too.

'Darling, have a drink. God knows I need one,' said Eleanora before Laura had even negotiated the case into the flat. 'This is such a disaster.'

Laura abandoned the case and took off her coat, following Eleanora into what turned out to be an enchanting sitting room.

Eleanora went over to what seemed to be a Louis Quinze side table but probably wasn't, quite, even knowing Eleanora.

'Gin and tonic? Whisky? Anything you can think of?'

'Whisky please,' said Laura.

'Good plan. We need to be fortified.'

She handed Laura a glass filled to a level that would have fitted right in with the measures she'd had in Ireland. 'Sit!'

Laura sank on to the sofa. Eleanora took a chair opposite.

'Sorry to drag you up here,' Eleanora said, having taken a hearty sip, without any preliminary toast, 'but you're the only one who can get us out of this mess.'

'What do you mean? You're his agent.'

'Yes, and his opinion of me, currently, is not fit to print, not even in the grittiest East End crime novel.' Eleanora put down her glass. 'He told you about his block, he asked you to help him with the course – that means he likes you. You have to be the sacrificial virgin delivered to the dragon.'

Laura jumped.

'I was talking figuratively, darling.' One of Eleanora's pencilled eyebrows raised in surprise at her reaction.

Laura tried to gloss over the matter. 'Well, I suppose he does quite like—'

'No, darling. A lot. He likes you a lot. You certainly don't irritate him.'

Laura smiled, hiding her pain. She didn't want him to 'like' her, or for her not to irritate him. She wanted him to – well, want her. 'I think that counts as damning with faint praise.'

'You must go and talk to him. Tell him that we're depending on him and that we didn't leak the story.'

'So who did? I'm just trying to think who knew.'

'All the literary blogs have got hold of it,' said Eleanora gloomily. 'Why people have to spout on about their doings to the world I can't imagine.'

'Let's have a look at one of the blogs, see if it gives us a hint,' suggested Laura.

'My computer's in my office,' said Eleanora. 'You have a look while I deal with supper. It's a ready meal, I'm afraid.'

'I don't care what I eat, really,' said Laura. 'Where's your office?'

'Room at the end, down the hall. The computer's on.'

Laura typed Dermot's name into the search engine and a whole host of blogs came up. She went through them quickly, ignoring those that referred to his first two novels. Then she found what she was looking for. It was a blog done by Gareth Ainsley – one of the students. Although he styled himself as 'writerfrombeyond' his identity was obvious. And he mentioned the course. The strange thing was, though, she was fairly sure that she'd never mentioned the fact that Dermot was appearing in the festival. She'd been protecting Dermot's privacy so carefully.

As she read the blog, which went on about Dermot's teaching, the other people and the accommodation quite a lot, she realised that this student had probably told the trade press and the gossip magazines before he'd written this. He'd been a very ambitious young writer, convinced of his talent, not entirely erroneously, and had apparently really admired Dermot. So why do this to him? Perhaps he thought it would further his own literary career.

Laura joined Eleanora in the kitchen. 'I've found the culprit, I think. One of the students. But what I can't work out is how he found out that Dermot was due to appear at the festival. I'm ninety-nine per cent sure I didn't tell anyone. I was so careful not to.'

Eleanora tipped the contents of a foil container onto a plate. 'Well, maybe Dermot did. I gather there was a fair bit of late-night drinking.'

Now Laura felt guilty for not being able to stay up late, as well as just feeble. 'There was, and I didn't stay up for it, so Dermot could have said something that gave him away.' She sighed. 'Well, there's nothing we can do about it now. The secret's out, except I'm sure Dermot won't appear now.'

Eleanora picked up the two full plates. 'Bring the glasses and the bottle, darling.'

Laura followed her hostess into the dining room, aware that she had more to say. Suddenly things had changed slightly, and now she felt that perhaps Dermot was better just left alone. The festival would have to do without him.

'To be honest,' said Eleanora, filling two wine glasses to the brim. 'I'm not bothered about the festival. Do start. This won't be delicious hot, but it'll be uneatable cold.' She paused while she contemplated her plate for a moment before picking up her knife and fork and plunging in. She went on, a piece of chicken balanced on the end of her fork. 'Obviously it would be fantastic if Dermot appeared but right now it's him I'm worried about.'

Laura paused, her own fork halfway to her mouth. 'What do you mean?'

Eleanora put down her knife and fork. 'He's a very tempestuous sort of person. If he took all this the wrong way he could . . .'

'What? What are you talking about?'

'Well, I don't suppose he'd actually do away with himself or anything,' Eleanora said slowly, 'but it could easily mean he gives up writing all together, which would be a loss. A great loss.'

Despite her breezy air at times, Laura knew that Eleanora still hoped that Dermot would produce another masterpiece, even after all this time, and not just for her ten per cent. She believed in him, just as Laura did. She felt a rush of affection for the older woman.

A gloomy silence settled over them. Laura sipped her wine, thinking about a world with no more books from Dermot Flynn. 'That would be dreadful,' she said aloud.

'Which is why you have to go there and sort him out.'

Laura replaced her glass, aware that Eleanora was a clever, manipulative person. 'Why me? Why not you? Who better than his agent? You've known him all his writing life. You could be a mother figure to him.'

'I can't be a mother to him. He currently hates me. You're the only one. You did it before, after all. You got him to agree to come to the festival in the first place.'

'Yes, but he hates the festival now! He probably hates me too!'

'Darling child, he does not hate you! Trust me on that. He'll be only too pleased to see an uncritical face.'

'I'm not that uncritical!' said Laura wishing her indignation was genuine.

'I know it must seem a bit too much like déjà vu, or Groundhog Day, or whatever the expression is, but you are the one for this task.' She paused. 'Even if he's not that pleased to see anyone, he'd rather see you than anyone else I can think of.' She looked at Laura, her eyes bright with anticipation.

Knowing when she was cornered, Laura said, 'OK,' and picked up her wine glass again. She felt tired and anxious, but there was a tiny spark of excitement at the prospect of seeing Dermot again.

* * *

The following day, when she was gathering her things for the journey back to Somerby, Laura phoned Monica. Monica had heard all about Dermot, of course. After they'd shared exclamations for a while Laura said, 'Mon, would you come with me to Ireland again? I've got to go and sort him out. Everyone says. I really don't want to go alone.'

'Oh Laura! I can't! I've got a mini-tour coming up. Seamus is coming with me.' She lowered her voice. 'It's going really well between us.'

'Oh.'

'Mm. I haven't actually heard his band yet but I'm sure they're great.' Then she remembered why Laura had rung. 'And really, Laura, this is something you should do on your own.'

'But, Monica!'

'I know, I know, we had such fun before. But it's not going to be fun, is it? Although of course I would have come to support you if I could have.'

'I know. And I also knew it was a long shot. I'm sure it will be very character-forming for me to go on my own.'

'Oh, love, you do sound down about it. Why don't you ask Fenella to go with you?'

'I can't. She's up to her eyes. In fact, even more up to her eyes now.'

'So it's good for the festival, all this publicity?'

'Yes,' said Laura dolefully. 'It's good for the festival.'

She was going to fly to Ireland this time. Eleanora had arranged a cab to pick her up from the airport and drive her all the way to Ballyfitzpatrick. She was also paying for everything. After all, Eleanora had a vested interest, Laura reminded herself.

Personally, because she didn't know what she was going to find at the end of it, Laura would have preferred for the journey to be slower. The flight seemed to whistle by and she was sure the travelling was, in this case, going to be far better than arriving.

She asked the taxi driver to take her to the bed and breakfast where she and Monica had stayed before. She'd booked in there because she knew the people. When Dermot threw her out on to the street she could go to them for comfort.

She had intended to keep her mission secret. Officially she was having a couple of days' break in a pretty part of the world she'd previously visited in winter. She was planning to walk, to relax and enjoy herself.

How long she'd be able to keep this secret, she didn't know. Before she'd even finished registering at the b. and b. she was being asked pertinent questions. 'You were one of the girls who came to see Dermot at the festival, weren't you?'

'That's right. With my friend Monica. We had such a lovely time I wanted to see the place in summer.'

'You'll have heard about Dermot? The paparazzi were on to him. For two days they were there. He hid in his house and wouldn't come out.'

'Poor man. He must have hated it.'

The woman, who Laura remembered was called Marion, clicked her teeth and shook her head. 'Not sure about that. He's stayed indoors ever since.'

'What do you mean?' Marion was obviously dying to tell Laura all about it, so she thought she might as well glean what information she could.

'Well, he doesn't go to the pub. He's not seen at the shop, so God knows what he's living on. No one's seen hide nor hair of him for over a week.'

'Oh.' Laura considered. Would it be best to confide in her? It might make her mission easier, and, she had to be honest, it was unlikely she could do anything without the whole place knowing exactly what she was up to. 'Could I confide in you?'

Marion said, 'Come in to the kitchen. I'll make a pot of tea, and you can tell all. I knew you were here for a reason the moment you made the booking.'

'The thing is,' said Laura, drinking tea so strong she could feel it attacking the enamel on her teeth, 'I've been sent by his agent to check if he's all right.'

'He's not all right. If he was all right he'd be behaving like a normal person, going to the pub, taking his car out, doing his messages.'

'Well, I'm to check on him and report back.' She didn't add that she was supposed to show him the error of his ways, convince him that no one who loved him had betrayed his secret, and that he should definitely come and do the festival.

Marion regarded her seriously, and then handed her a plate of biscuits. She'd already eaten the sandwiches Marion had prepared, but eating seemed to calm her nerves and she took a pink wafer although she didn't usually like them. 'I don't think you should do that.'

'Do what?' The wafer was very sweet and slightly offset the strength of the tea.

'Go and check on him. No nice young woman should go near Dermot when he's like this.'

'Like what?'

'Well! We don't know! But what we do know' – Marion lowered her voice although they were alone – 'is that he has a case of whiskey in there with him.'

Laura lowered her voice too. 'How do you know that?'

'Because one was delivered the day after the paparazzi arrived. It's my belief he's on a bender and no nice woman should go within a mile of him.'

'I think we're both within a mile of him right now.' Laura smiled, she hoped reassuringly. 'I'm sure I'll be all right. He wouldn't do anything to hurt me.'

'Normally, Dermot is charm itself, wouldn't hurt a fly, let alone a pretty young woman like yourself but . . .' Marion paused for dramatic effect. 'I know he likes his pint, but he doesn't usually drink *that* much. It could send him wild. He has a reputation with women. You don't look strong enough to fight him off.'

Laura giggled in spite of the trickiness of the situation. 'I'm sure he's not going to jump on me. He might shout a bit, but that's all.'

'It's still not a fit place for you to visit on your own. Take one of the boys with you if you must go.' She paused. 'I must say folk have been worried. They'd be glad to know if he's all right.'

'So why hasn't anyone looked before now? If he's been holed up for over a week?'

'Scared to. I tell you, he's got a reputation.'

A horrible thought occurred to her. 'He's not armed, is he?'

'Oh dear no. Anyway, if he is, he'll be so drunk he won't be able to shoot straight.'

'I don't think that's very comforting!'

'I'm not trying to be comforting, I'm trying to tell you not to go! But I'm also saying we'd all be glad to know how he is.'

'So you'll sacrifice a stranger to get the information you need?' Laura was fairly sure she'd read a book where this was the theme.

Marion laughed. 'Well, we know him too well to risk it. And besides, we have to live here. If he turns on you, you can fly back to England.'

'Should I have a taxi with its engine running outside?' Laura was laughing too now.

'No, but I'll get Murphy to keep his mule on stand-by.'

After more tea, laughter and for Laura a shower and a change of clothes, she set off up the road to Dermot's house. She didn't feel like laughing now. She remem-bered taking her GCSEs, her A levels, her driving test, and being summoned to the headmistress's office for some unknown reason. None of those experiences had made her feel this shaky.

Chapter Fourteen

She knew the way, although the last time she had made the journey it had been in the other direction. The fact that the village was so small definitely helped. And the fact that on this visit, the taxi had driven past his house, pointing it out to her as the home of the local celebrity. She would have preferred the journey to be longer really, so she could put off the moment of truth, whatever that turned out to be, for a little while. Seemingly two seconds after she'd set off, she was at his gate.

Although she'd been warned it would do her no good, Laura started by knocking at the door and pressing the bell for quite a long time. Inevitably, recollections of what had so nearly happened the last time she had been in Dermot's house came flooding back: the laughing, clinging, shuffling entry into his house, when she was very drunk and he not much better, when they hadn't wanted to be separated for an instant. The memories were not helpful.

Would she ever feel that degree of passion again? When she did finally go to bed with a man for the first time, would she want it as much? Or would losing her virginity just seem like getting rid of something that had become a burden? She knew it was unrealistic but she couldn't believe she would ever have that chemistry – at least for that one night – with anyone else. There was something about Dermot that made every nerve ending alert and tingling. How long would it take to find another, more suitable man who made her feel like that? She could end up a virgin at fifty!

These thoughts kept her occupied until she felt she'd tried conventional methods of entry long enough. It was time for the back-door approach.

The back door was, of course, locked. It hadn't been, she remembered, when she'd sneaked out of it to run back to the b. and b. in the early hours. Now, knocking on it, pushing at it and even giving it a surly kick only indicated it was locked and bolted.

Now what? Maybe shouting. Maybe if he heard it was she, and not some journalist, he might let her in.

'Hello! Dermot! It's me! Laura!' It was not easy for a normally quiet person to make such a noise, to yell her name to the world, but she did her best.

While the neighbourhood might have heard her calls, Dermot obviously hadn't. She'd have to think of something else.

She walked round the house and at last spotted a slightly open window. It wasn't in the best place for an inexperienced housebreaker, but it would have to do. It was the top half of a hopper-type window. Although the curtains were drawn, judging by the position she was fairly sure it opened on to the sitting room. If she could get up high enough and get her arm in, perhaps she might be able to open the bottom half of it with a stick or something. The irony of it all hit her; the last time she was at Dermot's house, she was sneaking out of it. Here she was now doing her darnedest to sneak in.

She dragged the dustbin over to the window, thinking that she had an advantage over normal burglars. She didn't mind getting caught; in fact, if the owner of the house was disturbed that would be a good thing. And if a passer-by spotted her, she could ask them for help, even if she came across as a rabid fan – or possibly a particularly blatant stalker.

The dustbin was a bit wobbly but she managed to wedge it steady with a couple of big stones she excavated from the edge of the flowerbed. Dermot had obviously not been much of a gardener even before he became a recluse so she didn't think he'd notice or even care what she did.

There was a wooden garden chair and she dragged it over to add stability to the dustbin. Once she was sure it wouldn't fall over, she stood on the chair, and then, gingerly, stepped on to the dustbin.

From there she could see the catch of the main part of the window but she couldn't quite reach it, even when she leant right over. But a stick might do it.

It took her a lot of wiggling but eventually she got the handle to unlatch. A lot of scrabbling later she got it open enough to get the stick in the gap. The window opened.

She was almost disappointed that no one had seen her, she felt so proud of herself as she fought through the curtain, got her leg up over the sill and landed in the sitting room.

Once there, she listened, in case her housebreaking had disturbed Dermot. As there was no other sound in the house a sudden panic took hold of Laura. Supposing he was dead! Supposing she was about to find a rotting corpse!

Her thoughts were so confused that for a few moments she didn't know if the thought of Dermot being dead was more terrible than the thought of finding his body. She broke into a sweat while she talked herself into a more reasonable frame of mind. Marion at the b. and b. hadn't indicated that anyone was worried that he was dead, and they would be if his death were at all likely. They just hadn't seen him since he'd been besieged by the press. She decided to hunt him out.

Although she knew, really, that he wouldn't be downstairs, she thought she'd take a look around, to give her an idea of how he'd been living.

The kitchen told her pretty much everything. It was disgusting. It looked like a project for a reality-television programme involving boiler-suited professionals, swabs and mind-boggling quantities of bacteria. There were rows of empty baked-bean cans, their razor-edged lids piled up like a heap of discarded oyster-shells. Every mug, cup, plate, saucer and bowl filled the sink. The floor was piled with dirty saucepans. This was definitely more than a week's worth of mess.

And it wasn't only crockery he'd run out of. There was a pile of dirty clothes heaped up in front of the washing machine. She suspected there'd be more upstairs.

As she looked further she realised that the grime was fairly superficial. There wasn't grease you could write your name in on the walls, it was just that he obviously hadn't washed up for a long time. And judging by the spoons and forks sticking out of the nearer baked-bean tins, he hadn't intended to do any. He was just eating the beans straight out of the can.

'Yuk,' she said aloud, and wondered if it was the first word heard in the house for ages.

As there were no more downstairs rooms Dermot could possibly be in, she bravely went upstairs.

She didn't have to look far, even if she hadn't been able to remember which his bedroom was. She could hear him snoring. Well, he wasn't dead then, she thought, aware of her relief. Although the front part of her brain had dismissed this as a possibility, her subconscious hadn't quite let it go. But now, unless the snoring was really thousands of flies swarming round a rotting corpse, she knew what she would find.

Once in the door of the bedroom she could also smell him. He was lying on his back with his mouth open, deeply asleep. He was wearing a pair of jeans and nothing else. His unshaven state would have meant he had a beard if it had had any shape, but it was just a vast amount of black hair. His teeth glinted white in among the fur although she was willing to bet he hadn't brushed them for a long time. They made him look like some ferocious animal, a grizzly bear or some such.

She cleared her throat. She wanted him to wake up because she was fed up with feeling like a burglar. Once he knew she was there, she could explain herself. But he didn't stir.

She'd been right about the dirty clothes. Socks, T-shirts, shirts, underpants and at least four pairs of trousers littered the floor. What had been going on? Did he usually have a cleaning lady who'd let him down, and he'd been incapable of shoving his own laundry into the machine?

Knowing she shouldn't really, she bundled as much as she could of it together, piled it on to a shirt to make a bag and carried it downstairs. Maybe it was for the best that he hadn't woken. She could get on better without him.

She switched on the radio, tied a couple of tea towels round her waist to save her jeans from getting soaked and set to work.

She should have gone to the shop for rubber gloves, she realised, but as that would involve a lot of questions when she got there, and finding the key before she went, she did without. She certainly couldn't face having to clamber back in through the window again.

Her recycling soul meant she would have to wash the baked-bean cans but there was a lot to tackle before she had to worry about them. She worked out the washing machine and filled it, holding her breath as she stuffed the clothes into it. Once that was chugging away she turned her attention to the rest of the kitchen. She simply couldn't bear to leave it in this state for a moment longer and she might as well make herself useful until Dermot finally woke up. She didn't like to admit to herself she was doing it because she cared.

It was a feat of organisation: finding somewhere to put the dirty things and then the clean ones. No wonder Dermot had resorted to the floor. She opened the window and turned on the hot tap. When hot water did emerge she offered a prayer of thanksgiving, doubled when she also found washing-up liquid. If she hadn't had that she'd have had to go to the shop. Now she'd started, she really wanted the kitchen to gleam before Dermot woke.

When she'd dealt with the kitchen, the bathroom (which was worse than the kitchen, in a way) and had vacuumed the sitting room, she went up to the bedroom and said Dermot's name several times. He still didn't stir. Sighing loudly, she stamped down the stairs. She would brave the shop and the questioning. There was absolutely nothing in the fridge or the cupboards and Dermot was bound to be hungry when he woke up – she didn't fancy the idea of facing a hungry, feral Dermot without food on hand to calm him. It would be her peace-offering – even if she hadn't been the one who'd gone to the press.

She left the front door on the latch and headed down the lane. She was lucky. The shop was full of people, all talking away. She was able to slip among the aisles, tossing things into her basket. The girl at the till rang them up without much in the way of chat. It was possible that she just looked like a woman on holiday, stocking up her holiday cottage.

Back at the house, she had made a nourishing soup, dusted the sitting room and even cut some branches from the garden and put them in a vase when she could stand it no more – Dermot Flynn was going to wake up!

She stood at the doorway of the bedroom thinking what to say when a rasping voice made her heart pound.

'What the hell is going on?'

Trying to give an appearance of calm, she went into the room so he could see her. 'It's me.'

227

A long list of blasphemous expletives issued from his lips but he didn't sound angry, just very, very surprised.

Laura was not impressed. 'It's all very well you lying there and saying all that, but have you any idea what time it is?' she demanded. She was tired, had been worried and was hungry. This all combined to make her angry, too.

She saw his stomach muscles ripple as he chuckled. 'What do *you* think?'

'The time isn't a matter of opinion!' Then she glanced at her watch. 'Nearly five o'clock. Good God! I've been here for hours!'

'How did you get in?'

'Through a window. Dermot, everyone's been so worried about you. Are you ill? Have you been ill? Why haven't you washed, or eaten proper food, or done any washing up for . . .'

'Just over a fortnight.' He was still lying there, showing no signs of moving.

'Listen, get up, have a shower, a long shower, shave, and then I'll give you soup. Leek and potato. I made it myself.'

'How could I possibly resist?'

She stomped out of the room and downstairs. Once in the kitchen she shut the door and sat at the table. Then she did what she'd been longing to do for some time. She allowed herself to weep. What had she done? She'd travelled hundreds of miles, cleaned his disgusting house, made him soup, done his washing, probably got herself drummed out of the feminist sisterhood, and for what?

She'd done it officially because Eleanora had asked her to come, to find out what had happened to him. She also needed to know if he really meant not to come to the festival. That furious text might have been sent when he was at the height of his anger; maybe he didn't really mean it. But in her heart she knew she'd also come because she loved him. That was why she'd cleaned his house and cooked for him. If she'd only come for professional reasons, she'd have just chucked a bucket of water over him or something and retreated to a safe distance, explaining to the neighbours that he was fine, just in a drunken stupor. Eleanora would have expected her to do a bit more than that, possibly, but she wouldn't have demanded she became a domestic drudge for him.

There was no shame in loving someone. Love was a good, uplifting emotion that made the world go round. Everyone knew that. But everyone, even one as inexperienced as Laura, knew that it was best to keep your feelings to yourself until you were fairly sure they were reciprocated.

She could hope he wouldn't realise why she'd done what she'd done. She could hope he wouldn't read the signals that to her seemed as clear as if she'd arranged an aeroplane to trail a banner through the sky saying 'I Love You' in big letters. Men were notoriously dense about matters like this.

She heard movement in the rooms above her and realised she had to get rid of any signs of her tears, or her weakness. She'd blame it all on Eleanora. He might think she had insisted that she dealt with his sordid house and cook for him. He might not identify her as a complete, loved-up sucker.

Her emergency make-up kit in her handbag produced a tiny sample tube of foundation that she patted on round her nose, disguising the redness. Some mascara sorted out her eyes, and by the time she heard him thundering down the stairs she felt quite respectable.

'Laura, dear girl, what are you doing here?' His voice was still a little hoarse, but that didn't make it any less sexy.

'Eleanora sent me. Everyone's beside themselves with worry. They didn't know what had happened to you.

They thought you must have been ill, or gone on a bender or something.' She paused, looking at him questioningly.

'Or something,' he said after an annoyingly long pause, and pulled out a chair and sat on it. He was wearing clean jeans and a shirt that was clean if very crumpled. It was only half tucked in. Part of Laura was grateful that he hadn't run out of clothes completely.

'But you're all right?' Laura ladled soup into a bowl. She wanted an explanation: summer flu, a bad back, something.

She didn't get one. 'Yes.' He started to eat the soup hungrily. 'There wouldn't be a . . .'

She handed him a plate of bread and butter. 'You obviously haven't eaten a thing for ages. Whyever not?'

He shook his head. 'I was not able,' he said through a mouthful of bread.

Silently, Laura added the missing 'to', liking the difference between Irish English, and English English. 'I could make you a sandwich.'

'That would be fantastic.'

Now he'd started eating he didn't seem able to stop. He ate an entire loaf of sandwiches, all the ham, cheese and tomatoes that Laura had bought, and then looked round for more. Eventually he said, 'Aren't you eating anything?'

She laughed at him, sipping her tea. 'Not now, no. I'll go back to the shop for more supplies. Will it still be open?' She wished she'd bought more last time, but she hadn't realised just how hungry he'd be.

'Oh yes, it's open all hours in summer. Have you got money? My wallet must be somewhere.' He got up and started staring around. 'God, the place is clean!'

'Yes. And don't worry about money. Eleanora gave me lots of euros. It'll all come out of your earnings eventually.'

He sat back down in his chair, genuinely horrified.

'Don't say that, for God's sake. When did I last earn her a brass farthing?'

'Don't sound so melodramatic. Your first two books still sell very steadily, as you must know.'

He shook his head. 'I always forget about that. I think in some ways I try to forget I ever wrote those damn books.'

Laura pursed her lips and put her head on one side. 'I don't think so.'

He regarded her for a long time and then sighed deeply. 'God, I'd kill for a cigarette.'

'And would it be me you'd kill?'

He narrowed his gaze. 'Tell you what, if you don't buy me some fags immediately, it definitely will be you I kill.' Then he smiled.

'Oh Dermot,' she said, oozing sarcasm to cover up her melting stomach, 'you surely must have kissed the Blarney Stone, coming out with such seductive phrases. Surely the birds would come down from the trees to do your bidding.'

'Listen, if you don't want to find out, with demonstrations, exactly what the Blarney Stone and meself have got up to, I'd go to the shop in double-quick time.'

If Laura hadn't been so hungry, and so aware that her feelings for him must be so blatant, she might have been tempted to call his bluff. But she didn't. She gave him a schoolmistress's smile, picked up her bag and went shopping again. It was only when she was halfway down the overgrown path that she realised there was no earthly reason why he couldn't have gone to the shop himself.

Her reappearance in the shop so soon caused an almighty stir; she had not been mistaken for a holiday-maker before, everyone had known exactly who she was and whom she was shopping for. It meant she had to tell everyone, several times, exactly how fine he was, and how hungry. She filled two wire baskets with supplies and then just in time remembered. 'Oh, do you know what sort of cigarettes he smokes?'

The man behind the counter reached behind him. He produced a packet of tobacco and some papers. 'He rolls his own but he gave them up in March.'

'Well, he said he'd kill me unless I got him some cigarettes so maybe I won't remind him.'

After her purchases had been rung up and settled into bags the man said, 'Sure Dermot's a lucky so-and-so to find a woman like you.'

'Oh, I'm not his woman! It's just . . . a business relationship.' She didn't want to go into details.

The man laughed. 'I'll tell my wife that. She'll find it very amusing.'

Laura decided not to press the point. She could perfectly understand that the thought of Dermot having a business relationship with any woman younger than Eleanora was a bit hard to credit.

Dermot took the tobacco and the papers from her with a smile that would have melted her heart if it hadn't already happened. His smile was exceptionally sexy. Knowing that every other woman on the planet would probably share her feelings about this wasn't encouraging.

'So,' he said, putting tobacco into a dark-coloured paper and, having seen it properly disposed, licking the paper and closing it. He didn't put the cigarette between his lips but just watched Laura, seemingly for ever.

'So?' Laura caved in, unable to stand another second of the silence.

'So was it you who revealed my story to the press?'

She'd known they'd have to have this discussion and felt more or less ready for it. 'It wasn't "your story" – it was just the fact that you'd agreed to appear at the festival.'

She was pleased that she sounded so calm. 'But actually, no, I didn't. I wouldn't.'

His narrowed gaze and slightly flared nostrils meant she had to keep up the pretence of calm with slightly more effort. 'It must have been Eleanora,' he said, a growl in his voice.

'No! It wasn't. And it wasn't Fenella or Rupert or anyone from the festival. Not even Jacob Stone, who would have dearly loved to shout your name from the rooftops.' Laura felt a growing sense of irritation. How could he think any of them would do such a thing when they'd promised they wouldn't? Did he doubt their word?

This evidence of Jacob Stone's admiration made no impression. 'It sounds as if you know who it was.' He was looking as if he might eat her, whole, in one big bite. 'For God's sake tell me!' he demanded.

She was determined not to let his anger faze her. 'I think it was one of the students,' she said quietly but steadily. 'There's a blog I'm fairly sure was written by one of them.'

'Who?'

'Gareth Ainsley.'

'I'll kill him,' he said, standing up, his fist clenched, his face furious.

The piece of internal elastic that had been keeping Laura functioning, doing the right thing, focused on the task in hand, snapped. She turned on him.

'Oh, for God's sake, Dermot! You are so bloody precious! What the hell does it matter if some poor student of creative writing blogs about you, revealing your not very interesting secret to the world! He didn't tell everyone you were gay! He didn't declare you as a secret heroin addict! Or a paedophile! All he said, in among a lot of sycophantic rubbish, was that you'd be appearing at a tiny little literary festival no one has heard of!'

His eyes blazed and if she hadn't been so angry herself

she'd have been frightened. Part of her was, anyway. 'Well, they've heard of it now, haven't they? This has put it on the map well and truly!'

'And is that such a bad thing? Does it really matter, in the scheme of things, that people know that Dermot Flynn, the "greatest living Irish writer", might appear at a literary festival?'

'It matters if you're Dermot Flynn! Have you any idea how destructive all this attention is to a creative person?'

'No, because, thank the Lord, I'm not a creative person! I'm just the little Jane Eyre character who makes it all possible for you pathetic, irritating, solipsistic, up-themselves "creative people"!' She took a breath. She was on a roll now. She'd had enough. 'Well, I'm fed up with creative people. I think they're a myth. I think you're a myth! A self-created myth who pretends he has writer's block so he can spend the rest of his life doing sweet FA! I think—'

His arms came round her, pushing the breath out of her body, and before she could inhale again his mouth was on hers.

Laura didn't know if she nearly fainted through lack of oxygen or desire. Every feminist part of her should have been kicking, screaming, biting and scratching him, but every womanly part of her refused to do more than moan faintly.

His lips captured hers as if he was going to devour her, the ferocity of his feelings clear. His hands gripped her clothes, pressing her to him, crushing her, making her legs buckle.

The table shot away from under them as they collapsed on to it and she would have landed on the floor if he hadn't caught her and moved her round so he was taking their combined weight. He released her mouth for an instant, but only long enough for them to draw breath before he kissed her again.

Laura was swooning, a tiny part of her registering that although she'd read of this happening in books she hadn't believed it really happened. As a unit, they moved to the sitting room, Dermot kicking open the door, hauling them both through it and on to the sofa. It ejected them on to the floor in seconds.

Dermot pulled her T-shirt out of her jeans and up. He was kissing her tummy, fiddling with the button of her jeans when he seemed to come to his senses. 'Laura? Do you want this?'

'Mmm,' she said, nodding her head urgently, thinking that if he stopped she would die. She knew she had the rest of her life to regret it but she felt she'd rather regret something she'd done than something she hadn't.

Now it was she pulling at his clothes, freeing his shirt so she could feel his skin under her fingers, against her cheek.

'We don't want carpet burn,' he said. 'Come on.'

She wanted to object, sure that if they went upstairs her sanity would return, and she didn't want it to. She didn't have a chance to say anything. He took hold of her wrist and dragged her behind him up the stairs and into his bedroom.

She just had long enough to take in the fact that there was a clean sheet on the bed, untucked, not straight but clean, before he was unzipping her jeans and pulling them down, dragging off her socks before throwing her on to the bed. She started to giggle helplessly, delirious in her happiness.

'We've been here before,' he breathed. 'Do you want to back out?'

'No. I don't.'

'Any time you change your mind . . .'

'I won't change my mind. I'm stone-cold sober, and I won't change my mind.'

'I won't either,' he breathed.

After the first breathless rush they experienced downstairs, Dermot now took his time, removing the remainder of Laura's clothes with sensual care. The rest of his own clothes were pulled off and kicked away.

Laura swallowed as she returned his gaze, serious and tender now. Then, lying on the bed next to her, he supported himself with his arm and continued to gaze at her body. Instead of feeling self-conscious she felt like a flower opening under the warmth of the sun.

'You are so beautiful, darling Laura,' he breathed, and she felt beautiful and so sexy she thought she'd dissolve.

Then he tucked a strand of hair behind her ear and drew his finger down her cheek, along her jawline to her chin before going back to her ear, down her neck to her shoulder.

'Your skin is like silk. Sorry, that's not a very original way to describe it but it's the best I can do at the moment.'

She giggled lovingly. 'It's all right, I don't mind if you don't make love to me in iambic pentameters.'

He kissed the inside of her elbow. 'That's good, I much prefer free verse.'

'And free love,' she murmured, but he may not have heard because he didn't answer.

At first Laura was unnerved by the sensations he created with his mouth, his fingers, his breath. But his honeyed reassurances made her relax and she allowed herself to feel and respond. His skin felt like silk too, but she didn't mention it, just brushed her lips over the curve of his arm, feeling the shape of his muscles.

Later, when he paid intimate attention to her with his lips and tongue, she thought the sensation might overwhelm her and she resisted. And then it overcame her resistance and she almost lost consciousness. This time with pleasure.

*   *   *

Much later she said, 'Goodness me. Is it always like that?'

He laughed, still slightly breathless. 'No, it is not always like that. Chemistry is something you can't fake. We've set a very high standard for your first time.' He sighed deeply. 'I was absolutely determined to give you the very best experience I possibly could but if you hadn't responded as you did, it wouldn't have been anything like so wonderful.' He pulled her a little closer to him. 'You're a natural.'

'Am I? That's nice. I always thought I'd be rubbish at lovemaking.' A memory floated into her mind. 'Monica said you weren't a "novice ride".'

She heard the rumble in his chest as he laughed. 'Well, I don't suppose I am, usually, but you and I do seem to have a special something.' He chuckled again. 'When you tell her all about it, don't forget to tell Monica that I did use a condom.'

'Perhaps I won't tell her all about it.' Just then Laura didn't like the thought of sharing their special secret.

'She'll get it out of you. You don't have to tell her the details.'

'Certainly not!' Recalling some of the details made her blush and go gooey all over again. Had he really done those things? And had she really liked them so much?

'But you haven't forgotten any of the details?'

'No . . .'

'Well, just to make sure you don't, I think we'll repeat the exercise . . .'

Chapter Fifteen

They 'repeated the exercise' on and off all night. Laura woke early. She hadn't eaten much the day before and was now absolutely ravenous. Although she didn't think she'd moved, she must have because Dermot stirred.

'All right?' he muttered into her neck.

'Mm, but absolutely starving!' She sighed happily as she thought about why.

'Mm, me too.' Dermot stretched. 'Is there any food left?'

'I don't think so. I think you ate everything.'

'In which case, my darling, I'd better get up and buy some breakfast. I have this peculiar urge for kedgeree.' He slid out of bed and started finding his clothes.

'That sounds complicated,' said Laura, having decided it was better not to watch him move about the place, stark naked, not if she was going to have to wait before they could make love again. Her hunger was momentarily forgotten.

'Oh, it's not,' said Dermot. 'They have it in a packet. You just put it in a pan, add butter and a bit of cream and heat slowly. They get it in especially for me at the shop. Thank goodness they're keeping their holiday hours or they wouldn't be open yet.' He pulled on his jeans. He was halfway into his shirt when he hesitated.

'What?' Laura was half hoping that he had forgotten his hunger too and just wanted to get back into bed.

'Nothing.' He carried on getting dressed.

Laura watched him, thinking, and then said, 'I've just

realised what the problem is.' She sat up. 'If you go to the shop there'll be an almighty fuss, everyone will pounce on you and you'll be ages.'

He grinned. 'I'll be looking so damn pleased with myself they'll know exactly what I've been up to. They will all want to talk.'

Laura scrambled out of bed. 'I'll go. I can't lie here, starving to death, waiting for you to stop gossiping. Make me a list. Here's an old receipt and a pencil.'

He chuckled and started to write. 'Being untidy has its advantages, you can always find something to write on.'

'I thought writers all kept notebooks by their beds.'

'Not all writers.'

She had got most of her clothes on when she turned to Dermot, who had slid back to bed, still wearing his jeans. 'Can I just ask you something?'

'Anything.'

His look was so full of lust she turned away, smiling. That could come later, when she'd had something to eat. 'Did you change the sheet yesterday, before you came down, because you knew what would happen?'

'I changed it because I knew what I wanted to happen, but I never thought it would. It was also pretty disgusting. I may be a slob but I change my bed linen once a year, whether it needs it or not.'

Laughing, she went downstairs and, having found her handbag, let herself out of the house.

She was fairly sure everyone would know exactly what she'd been up to when she went back to the shop but, with luck, the same people wouldn't be working there this morning. She thought what to add to Dermot's list; she wasn't sure she wanted to eat kedgeree, although it did sound nice. Some more bread and ham would be useful and maybe some orange juice and croissants if the shop had any.

Her head was full of plans about what they'd like to

eat and where they'd like to eat it when she went into the shop. She said a breezy hello without making eye contact and slipped down an aisle out of sight, hoping they wouldn't ask her about Dermot.

All would have been well if she'd been able to find the packet kedgeree he was so intent on having. She had to ask.

While the right place was being pointed out to her, along with a lot of 'You're back again soon. So how was the old reprobate?' type conversation, a tall, thin woman came up to Laura. Somewhat older than she was, with a skin that had been exposed to the weather, she had dark hair tied in a knot at the nape of her neck and wore a crisp white shirt tucked into jeans.

'So you're after Dermot's kedgeree, are you?' The woman looked her up and down. 'You know that's what he always wants to eat after sex?' She laughed, pretending she'd been joking.

'I didn't know,' said Laura, blushing at the mention of sex and because the woman was inspecting her as if she were a horse she was considering buying.

'Oh yes. He says it restores the "vital juices".' The woman's teeth were a little crooked and discoloured and her smile didn't reach her eyes. Never before had Laura felt herself to be so disliked, especially by a complete stranger. The feeling was mutual – there was something about this woman that made Laura instantly bristle.

'Well, I wouldn't know about that,' said Laura, trying to move so she could do her shopping.

The woman barred her way. 'Oh yes. But if you tell him I'm back your services won't be required any more.'

'Oh, are you his cleaner, then?' Laura's inner bitch rose up and snapped.

That did discomfort the woman a little, but not for long. 'No, no I'm not his cleaner. Just tell him I'm back, will you?' Another false smile was directed at Laura.

'You'll need to tell me who you are.' Laura was not going to rise any further to this woman's bait.

The woman laughed again. 'Oh no, he'll know who I am when you describe me. Dermot and I are very old – friends.'

Laura tried hard to fight off all the unpleasant feelings the woman had aroused in her on the way back to Dermot's. She had made her feel like a tart, frankly, and she didn't know if she would ever stop feeling like one. Almost the worst part was she felt that the whole shop knew she had slept with Dermot, and thought she was a tart too. She didn't like the feeling. And what had the woman meant about them being old friends? It was as if she'd been warning her off. And all that about his usual breakfast. She felt cheapened and hurt and used; an overriding desire to get away from this place as quickly as possible overcame her. But when she had checked the availability of the local taxi service and the man had said he'd take her to the airport the moment she gave him the call, it didn't really make her feel any better. He obviously thought Dermot would want rid of her as soon as possible. Her wonderfully happy mood had completely evaporated. Doubts about Dermot's motives were marching in by the double, feeding her growing sense of unease. Had he swept her off her feet because she'd been there, ready and willing? He and his 'old friend' would probably laugh about it all when she was gone.

Right now, though, she had to get through the next hour or so without letting Dermot know how she really felt. She'd be calm and collected, and polite. She certainly didn't want him to see how humiliated she felt.

She put on a smile as she entered his house, and called up the stairs, 'I'm back! Do you want to cook this kedgeree or shall I read the packet and get on with it?'

Dermot appeared a few minutes later, after she'd decided to get cracking with it. She felt horrible. She was a one-night stand and she'd be lucky if she got away without Dermot pressing money on her for her cab fare.

She was stirring the rice mixture into melted butter. 'There was a woman at the shop who said to tell you she was back,' she said as nonchalantly as she could manage, not wanting to look at him until she felt calmer.

'Oh? And who was that, then?'

'She wouldn't give her name. She just said you'd know who she was and that you were very old friends.'

Dermot laughed. 'Oh, that'll be Bridget! She's a case, isn't she? I've missed her. She's been away for months. I expect she'll be round here soon, wanting to see me.'

Laura couldn't bear it. He was confirming her worst fears. And he wasn't even trying to deny it.

'Oh well, she's back now. Would you like tea or coffee with your kedgeree?' She was aware she was being rather clipped but it was all she could do not to break down, and she wasn't going to do that in front of him. Also, a part of her felt angry – at him and at herself for being such a fool. She still couldn't look at him.

'Laura, what's wrong? You skipped out of here without a care in the world and now you're all edgy and anxious. What happened? Was anyone unkind to you in the shop?'

He sounded slightly bemused and just for a second she considered telling him what his beloved Bridget had said to her but then realised she couldn't. Bridget was the old friend; she wasn't. She couldn't say, 'Your old friend, the one you're so fond of, has made me feel like a hooker and that you wouldn't be needing my services now she's home.'

'Oh no, nothing like that.' She stirred furiously. 'It's just I realised my flight is earlier than I thought it was. I have to go almost immediately.'

'But we were going to have breakfast together. In bed, I thought.'

He was still maintaining the act. She managed a breezy

laugh. 'Oh no, I'm afraid not. In fact my taxi will be here at any moment.'

He scratched his head, frowning. 'Have they changed the flight back to England then? It was always in the evening.'

'Oh yes, they've changed it.' She turned off the heat and dropped the wooden spoon. 'I'll just go upstairs and make sure I haven't left anything.'

But she didn't need to look to knew that she'd left two things she couldn't retrieve: her virginity and her heart. Both were gone for ever.

Chapter Sixteen

Unfortunately for Laura, they hadn't changed the flight to England: she had a very long wait at the airport for it, which gave her plenty of time to realise that she'd given her all to a man who just wanted her at that moment, not for ever. He hadn't tried to stop her, or ask her again if anything had happened; he'd just stood there, looking baffled, as if he couldn't comprehend why she hadn't fallen into his arms again, all 'Aren't you wonderful, Dermot' and 'Let me wait on you hand and foot, Dermot'. What's more he obviously had a girlfriend, but being the sort of man he was, since she was away, he'd found a substitute. In other words, he was your classic – albeit charming – bastard. How long would it take her to get over him? Knowing he was a bastard wouldn't necessarily make it any quicker.

Eleanora was going to pick Laura up from the airport, whence they would go to Somerby. Laura was not looking forward to the questioning that would go on from the moment she and Eleanora had located each other. Eleanora would be bound to ask about Dermot and she had rehearsed some suitably bland phrases like: 'He's fine now. Eating well! Seemed quite happy when I left him.' Fenella would ask about the festival and she could hardly tell her that she hadn't actually asked him if he was coming, because she couldn't possibly tell her why not. After the row when he'd accused all and sundry of selling his story to the papers, and she'd accused him of being pretentious, and what happened next, all thoughts of the festival had been wiped from her mind – really amazing sex and subsequent humiliation had that effect.

On the plane, when she acknowledged that she couldn't have him electronically wiped from her brain, and that she would have to see him and deal with him again, she decided she'd send him an email, asking him if he would indeed appear, hoping that he'd at least answer it and say yes or no. Although, he would have to admit, she thought bitterly, she had fully complied with his original conditions and it would be a breach of promise if he didn't.

In spite of her sadness, however, she knew she wouldn't regret making love to him, even though he had set an impossibly high standard for the rest of her life. What had happened afterwards, at the shop, she tried to put firmly out of her mind. She stayed in a state of bitter-sweet reminiscing until the plane landed.

Eleanora kissed her cheek, patted her shoulder and, as Laura had known she would, launched straight in. 'How did you get on, darling? How is Dermot? Is the wretched man going to appear at the festival or not? We're all on tenterhooks.'

Laura appeared to consider, although in fact she'd planned what to say already. 'Well, he's fine, in that he's not ill or anything, but about the festival, I'm not sure.' She felt proud of how normal her voice sounded, despite her inner turmoil.

Eleanora wasted several seconds being irritated and then moved on to more important things. 'No sign of any writing, was there?'

Laura thought back. All that cleaning would have turned up any signs of work and in the bedroom she'd had to use a receipt as a shopping list. 'No, I would have noticed if there'd been anything to see.' She surrendered her bag to the cab driver.

'He used to write in longhand on big foolscap pads, on one side of the paper only. Apparently when each page was finished, he'd throw it on to the floor and only collate it when the work was finished.'

She shook her head sadly. 'No sign of any foolscap pads, let alone any tottering piles of complete pages. The house was in a frightful state but I think if they existed they'd have been obvious.'

Eleanora shook herself as if shrugging off disappointment. 'No change there then. Get in, darling, we should press on.'

When they were both settled in the back seat, sucking mints, she said, 'So why didn't you press him about the festival? A simple "no" would have done.'

'I couldn't really. The time just wasn't right. He was so angry about being outed to the press.'

'He has got a truly awful temper.' Eleanora frowned. 'He wasn't unkind to you, was he? He can be merciless.'

'No, he wasn't unkind.' Although the effect was the same as if he had been. She was sure he certainly never meant to be unkind, or to hurt her in any way – as bastards went, he was a nice one.

'So what will you do about the festival? Fenella is beside herself, wanting to know. She thinks it's going to be embarrassing if all these authors agree to come because of him and then he doesn't pitch up.'

'I'll email him. It's all I can do, really.' She certainly wasn't going to contact him except in the most formal manner. 'But going on the number I've sent him in the past and never had any reply to I think he goes through phases when he never even looks at his emails.'

'You're probably right. But never mind, now the news is out, we can finally advertise him as coming, even if he doesn't.'

'But surely that would be deception, or advertising false goods or something?'

'No. We don't know he's *not* coming.' Eleanora paused. 'Or do we?' she regarded Laura beadily, possibly suspecting Laura hadn't told her everything.

Laura hadn't but she also hadn't lied about the festival. 'Really, I don't know either way.'

'Then it's fine to advertise him. We've hinted enough as it is, after all. Fenella is having some banners made to go over all the posters. Apparently ticket sales have increased like mad. But more importantly, a lot of the big-name authors who wouldn't commit themselves have agreed to come. They're all mad to meet Dermot. And we're the only ones who suspect he might not make it – we'll keep it to ourselves.'

'So when's the big dinner?' Laura asked.

'Oh, the one for all the writers who are appearing? Next Friday, before the big opening. Laura dear, you can't have forgotten. We talked about it. You wrote and invited everyone.'

'Sorry. I'm a bit distracted.'

Eleanora shot Laura a glance that made her blush. Was it possible that losing your virginity and having glorious sex showed from the outside? Laura's blush deepened. Only part of it was because of the glorious sex; the other part was the feeling Bridget had given her: that she was a fill-in for her and no better than a prostitute.

In the end, Fenella was philosophical about Dermot possibly not appearing. She hushed the sea of dogs, led Eleanora and Laura down to the kitchen and handed them both a large glass of wine. Laura suspected that Rupert, now staring into the oven, had been instrumental in calming her down.

'Well, if he comes, he comes, there's nothing much else we can do about it,' she said, shooting Laura a glance that suggested she didn't quite believe her words. 'Have some olives, Laura.'

'He always has been a law unto himself,' said Eleanora. 'That's very good wine, Rupert.'

'Bogof,' said Fenella. 'I got it at the supermarket.'

'Oh. Well, it's very nice.'

'So, Laura, was it very terrifying bearding Dermot in his den?' asked Fenella. 'Eleanora has told us how utterly scary he can be.'

Her aunt nodded her agreement, happy to sip her wine and not interject with a pertinent opinion for once.

'He was a bit tough with some of the students,' agreed Laura. 'And I suppose it was a bit nerve-racking. I had to break into his house.'

Rupert snorted with laughter. 'I don't see you as a housebreaker, Laura.'

'You'd be surprised how good I was at it. I—' Just in time she stopped herself telling him how often she'd sneaked in and out of houses lately. 'I had the advantage of not minding if anyone caught me doing it. I'd have asked any passer-by for help.'

'But there weren't any?'

'No. Never is when you need one.'

'You did exactly the right thing, not pressing him too hard,' said Eleanora. 'I should have gone myself. His childish tantrums don't scare me! Did I ever tell you? Once when we were at the Ivy . . .'

Laura began to relax. No one seemed to be blaming her for not bringing Dermot's promise to appear written in blood and now Eleanora was telling a vivid and amusing story of Dermot in a rage. Her possible failure was being seen as a sensible withdrawal. What Laura couldn't say was that she wasn't remotely frightened of Dermot's temper, although she'd seen a glimpse of it. Once he'd started making love to her she'd just forgotten all about the damn festival.

* * *

The following morning, in the room designated as the Festival Office, Fenella and Laura went through the details. Eleanora was off inspecting some of the venues with Rupert.

'Kathryn Elisabeth has confirmed,' said Fenella.

'Ooh, I must tell my old neighbour. She was a crusty old thing but she got interested in the festival. She'll be thrilled.'

'Everyone is. She's very popular. She's doing a writing course. We've sold fifteen tickets so far, but we can only take twenty, and I've got some people who I'm fairly sure will take the other places.'

Laura was grateful no one knew how she was feeling inside and for being thrown straight back into festival matters.

'Brilliant. We must make sure we have all her back-list. Talking of which, is Henry organised? Has every author who's appearing got lots of copies to sign and sell?'

'He's been ace! Not only has he got books by all the authors we've invited, but quite a few other authors in similar genres. He said you had him very well trained.'

Laura laughed. 'He trained me actually.' She paused. 'So what are we going to do about the authors who haven't confirmed? With only a week to go it's cutting it a bit fine.'

'There is only one of those now.' Fenella took a sip of her coffee, fixing Laura with a stare from behind her mug.

Laura hoped Fenella didn't notice her blushing. 'We'll have to plan events to fill his slots. Remind me what we had planned for him.'

'Apart from the main interview? An "Evening of Irish Music and Literature".'

Laura thought. 'Oh yes. In the pub, to recreate an Irish atmosphere.'

Fenella nodded. 'Except that we couldn't use the pub. We could only have got about ten people in and the publican wasn't keen. And I've got cold feet about the poetry, to be honest. We're a new festival – poetry might not be that popular. Is his poetry wonderful?'

Laura put her head on one side. 'Yes, but not as wonderful as his prose.'

'Shall we scrub it then? Especially as he's quite likely not to turn up?'

'That would be a shame. We could have the music and someone could just read bits of Irish literature. I could choose some pieces. They don't all have to be Dermot's. Have we got someone who could read them?'

'You've got no faith in Dermot turning up then?' Fen asked.

Laura sighed. She no longer had any faith in her judgement. She'd thought she had known Dermot, and then Bridget had appeared before her like a banshee in modern dress and she didn't feel she knew anything about him. 'I just don't know. I think we'd better make elaborate plans for his non-appearance, then he'll turn up just to annoy us.'

Fenella laughed. 'Would it annoy you?'

'If we had gone to huge trouble to fill in for him it would. Who might read the pieces? Do you know any actors?'

'No, but Hugo, Sarah's husband, has got a beautiful speaking voice.'

'We need a bit of Irish, really. Hugo's rather posh, isn't he?'

'We'll think of someone. Rupert can do a brogue, if drunk. He does have Irish blood.'

Laura made a note. 'Rupert, drunk, to read selections of Irish literature. L to make selection. That sounds great! Not!'

'It will be great. Monica's boyfriend's band will be lovely. We'll give everyone free beer, it'll go down a treat.'

'Well, bang goes your profit straightaway. And is Monica's boyfriend's band lovely?'

'It's not all about making money. And I expect so! Monica still hasn't managed to hear them. She's getting a bit anxious about it.'

'Fantastic! A mediocre band plays while Rupert puts on a fake accent and reads out bits of *Ulysses*. I can't wait.'

Fenella laughed. 'You don't have to choose *Ulysses*. You can have funny pieces and Rupert will do it in his own voice. As for the band, why don't you go and hear them? Monica would be thrilled. She rang last night, by the way, wanting to hear how you got on in Ireland. I said you'd gone to bed, exhausted. She seemed to find that quite funny. Anyway, she mentioned Seamus having a gig she can get to at last. She and Grant are going. Give her a ring and arrange to go too.'

'OK, I'll do that. I'm glad that Monica and Grant have become such good friends. I knew they'd get on. Maybe when the festival is over I'll become a matchmaker.'

'Hm. If Monica and Grant are the sort of relationship you had in mind . . . '

'OK, I take your point. So . . .' She made another note. 'All we have to do now is think up some way of filling that big Sunday night spot when Dermot was going to do an interview.' She paused. 'Who was going to interview him? Didn't you have someone in mind?'

Fenella made a rueful face. 'Sorry. I couldn't get anyone that anyone had heard of without being able to say for sure if Dermot would actually be there.'

'Fair enough, I suppose.'

'So I thought you could do it.'

'Me!' Laura squeaked.

'Well, why not? You know more about his books than anyone on the planet and you know him – what?'

'It's just . . . oh, Fenella, you know how shy I am!'

'I know how shy you *used* to be. Besides, as they always say to worried people, "it may never happen".'

Laura had to laugh now. 'Well, that's true. In fact, it probably won't. So what shall we do to fill the space? If people have bought tickets, or even if they haven't yet, we can't have nothing on the Saturday night.'

There was silence as the two women thought hard. 'I know!' said Laura. 'A panel! We'll get a selection of the authors who are coming to talk about their writing practice. It'll be brilliant! Far better than me trying to interview Dermot!' Even the thought of it made her feel weak.

'Fab. I'll email all the authors and ask them. How many do we need?'

'Ask everyone and see how many we're left with.' Laura gave a huge yawn.

'Gracious,' said Fenella. 'You're still tired, in spite of your early night. I didn't realise Ireland involved a change of time zone.'

Laura nodded sagely. 'Oh it does, it definitely does . . .'

Laura had pondered the question about losing one's virginity showing from the outside for some time. A couple of days later, when Monica picked her up in her car, to take her to Bristol, she had her answer. It did.

'So, what was it like?' Monica said the moment they were at the bottom of the Somerby drive. They were on their way to Seamus's gig. Laura was checking the band out to see if it was remotely suitable for a potentially raucous evening with free beer and Rupert, with or without an Irish accent, or as the more cultural backing for Dermot reading some of his work.

'What was what like?'

'Oh, for God's sake! Don't mess me around! Sex with Dermot!'

'Ssh. Keep your voice down!'

'It's all right. We're in a car. No one is going to hear. So tell me!'

Only for a second did Laura consider pretending nothing had happened, but she knew Monica would see straight through her. 'OK. Well. It was amazing,' Laura said quietly, half hoping this would satisfy Monica, and half hoping she'd have an opportunity to talk.

'I don't believe you.' Monica banged her hand on the steering wheel to emphasise her incredulity. 'First times are never amazing, let alone the first time ever. You've spent too much of your life reading romantic novels. Sex is one of those things you have to learn how to do.'

'I accept that. And I know I probably have spent far more of my life reading about sex rather than having it than most normal people, but I'm telling you, it was amazing.'

Monica considered for a moment. 'Well, stripe me pink!'

Laura laughed. 'I think someone already did that.' She indicated the wide pink stripe in Monica's hair. She obviously enjoyed wearing her pink wig so much she'd decided to add a bit of colour to her own hair.

'Laura! I'm trying to have a serious conversation, to help you live through the ramifications of what's happened to you, and you just make stupid jokes.'

'It was you who said "stripe me pink".' Laura pretended to be apologetic. 'But I don't think there are any ramifications.' She sighed. Except a feeling of being used and Bridget, of course, although she wasn't a ramification – she was the bitch from hell but she wasn't going to think about her if she could help it; she had already spoilt something that had been really lovely.

'There will be, I promise you.'

'Well, I hope not.'

Monica hesitated before asking incredulously. 'Are you sure you're not lying about it being fantastic?'

'Yes! I'm not saying that the second and third time weren't even more—'

'Three times!'

Actually, there'd been more than that, but she didn't want to shock her friend. 'Over quite a long period. A whole night.'

'But he's quite old!'

'Thirty-five is not old!'

'I suppose not. So now what? Are you together?'

This was the bad news. She had to keep it cheery, not give too much away – she couldn't face Monica's sympathy. 'I had to go really early the next day to get my flight.' She wasn't going to say that leaving him that morning was the saddest thing she had ever done in her entire life. She knew that it was worth it for the happiness she'd experienced – or it would be once she'd got over the whole Bridget incident – but she wasn't going to mention that either. 'We didn't have much time to talk. But he wanted you to know that he used condoms, every time.'

Monica chuckled, possibly sensing that Laura was trying to make light of the situation. 'You must congratulate him when you next see him.' She paused, glancing briefly at her friend. 'When are you seeing him again?' She wasn't going to let Laura off that easily.

Laura bit her lip. 'I'm not sure. We didn't actually get round to talking about the festival. I don't know if he's coming or not. After all the publicity erupted he said the festival could take a flying jump.'

'Bugger the festival! What about you and him?'

'We didn't talk about when we might see each other again.'

'What?' Monica gave her a quick look. 'Not at all? You just got in the taxi and went to the airport? How often has he been in touch since?'

'He rang me when I was at the airport. Just to see if I'd got there safely.' He'd sounded strange on the phone but that may have been because she'd been very cool with him. She hadn't really wanted to speak to him again, not until she'd got her feelings in order.

'And since?' Monica was sniffing out the bad bits of Laura's story like a truffle-hound.

'Nothing since. Marion – the woman who ran the bed and breakfast we stayed at – emailed me to say he's gone to ground again. But no one's worried this time.'

'But what about you?' Monica was hardly audible, empathy seemed to have affected her vocal cords. 'Isn't your heart breaking? You've done all that with him, given him your virginity, and you don't know when you'll see him again?'

Laura longed to say yes, her heart was breaking, but she couldn't. She thought carefully, trying to express herself in a way that was truthful, but that wouldn't have Monica sending her off for some sort of therapy involving bars, vodka and male strippers, which she would do if she told her everything. No suitable phrases sprang to mind.

'Well?' Monica pressed. She was obviously getting worried.

Laura decided she might as well tell Monica the truth. At least her friend cared. She just wouldn't tell her how *much* it was hurting.

'To be honest, yes, my heart is breaking,' she said. 'But I don't mind, not really. It's hard to explain, but that time with Dermot was so – special, though in some ways, it was just sex.' Although she was the one who'd said them, the words were almost physically painful. 'It was sex with someone I'd admired for years, and years,' she went on as breezily as she could, 'since I was at university. If he wanted – me' – she baulked at referring to her virginity, although Monica had – 'I was more than happy for him – to give myself – oh, I don't know how to put it. I'm just trying to say, I knew what I was doing. I knew nothing would come of it and I did it anyway. No regrets.' She hadn't known quite so well that nothing would come of it until later, but still, the principle was the same.

'What, no regrets at all? Come on, Laura, this is me you're talking to,' Monica pushed.

'I wouldn't have done anything different. I knew what he was like. I didn't expect anything different. And what I had was so fantastic! He took such pains to make me – enjoy it. Really, Monica, I know I'm going to feel a bit sad for a while, but I'm also happy.'

Monica sighed. 'I suppose I do understand. He will have spoilt you for anyone else, you know that.'

'Yes, but there will be someone else. I'm not going to cling to my moment of happiness and not look for more. Obviously, I'm not up for going on the pull any time soon' – she said this so Monica wouldn't suggest the bars and male-stripper cure – 'but I will "love again".' She smiled to highlight her irony and then added, 'After the festival and about ten years have passed.'

Monica sighed. 'If you're sure . . .' And then she snapped out of her romantic reverie. 'OK, that's enough about you. Could you have a look at the map? Are we on the right road? I seem to have got a bit lost.'

They found it eventually. Grant and the rest of Monica's band were already there. It was in the basement of a small club in Bristol. As they fought their way down the narrow stairs, Laura realised that Monica really was nervous. She was very keen on Seamus and they'd spent a lot of time talking about him as they drove along. But his band was a bit suspect. It was, according to Monica,

because of the other members not wanting to play traditional music and not being great at anything else.

'Laura!' Grant hugged Laura long and hard. 'How
great to see you! You look amazing! What have you done
to yourself? New hairdo? No, you still haven't discovered
straighteners. Lost weight? Gained weight? No, you're
still fairly skinny. Must be a new moisturiser. Your skin
looks brilliant.'

Laura avoided looking at Monica who was laughing
in a vulgar way. 'Shall we get some drinks? Grant? You
others?'

She went to the bar hoping she'd remember what
everyone wanted. Monica had ordered a double vodka
to calm her nerves. It was nearly time for Seamus's set.

She got the tray of drinks back to the table without
accidents and squashed on to a corner of the banquette.
'I'm glad I got back before Seamus started,' she said. She
picked up her glass. 'Cheers!'

Seamus and his band didn't seem quite ready so the
audience started talking again.

'Would you want the whole band, or just Seamus, do
you think?' Monica asked Laura. 'It might be better . . .
oh, I don't know. What would Dermot like?'

'Who knows!' said Laura. 'I didn't ask him. I mean, I
think it would work well. Originally we thought of
having him reading his poetry but there's a scene in one
of Dermot's books with Irish music in the background.
It would be perfect. But he's so – I don't know . . .'

'Uncommunicative?'

'Yes. I don't know if he'd love the idea or hate it.
Actually, I do know. He'll hate it. But he might just do it.'

'For you?'

'No. I don't think he'd do anything particular for me.'
Although as she said this she knew it wasn't strictly
true. She remembered some of the things he'd done for
her in Ireland and felt a stab of pleasure. 'Oh, I think

they're starting!' she said, to stop Monica asking any more questions.

The band did start a little later and after the first few bars, Grant and Laura exchanged looks. The first number was a lament that should have had tears of sadness pouring down cheeks; it had the opposite effect. By the end even Laura, whose recent Irish experiences should have meant the words and the music was particularly poignant, wanted to giggle with embarrassment.

Monica sighed, drained her glass. 'Anyone else for another drink?'

'I'll help you carry them,' said Laura, struggling out from behind the table.

'They're crap, aren't they?' said Monica once they were at the bar.

'Well, maybe they just need time . . .'

'Don't beat about the bush, say it like it is! They're rubbish! Bugger! Back to the drawing board!'

'It's OK,' said Laura. 'We'll find a CD with the right sort of harpy-fiddly-drummy-Celtic stuff on it. It might be easier in some ways. Rupert could practise.'

'Don't quite know when he's going to have time to do that,' said Monica. She looked at her friend as her turn to be served came up. 'Do you mind driving home? I think I need another vodka.'

'Do you mind coming home with me? Don't you want to stay with Seamus?'

'I really don't want to talk to him about how it's gone tonight. I'll have to think very carefully what to say.'

While they were being served, Laura said, 'But surely you've heard them play lots of times. You must have known that they weren't all that good.'

Monica explained the reason she hadn't heard them yet was because she'd been on tour, he'd been very busy and what with organising the music festival practically single-handed now Johnny Animal had disappeared off on 'important business' there just hadn't been time.

'Would it be wrong of me to dump Seamus because he doesn't know which way up to hold a fiddle?' Monica asked now.

Laura, her sense of the ridiculous finely honed, giggled. 'Yes it would! Besides, you said he was lovely. Can you manage those bottles? I'll take the tray.'

'You're not still on the voddy, are you, Monica?' asked Grant as Laura doled out bottles of water and spritzers, giving the only glass to Monica.

'God yes, I need something. Laura's driving home. She's so loved up she doesn't need alcohol.'

A look like an interrogation lamp turned on Laura. 'Loved up? Something you're not telling me, Laura?'

'It's Dermot,' said Monica.

'Ye Gods! I might have guessed!' said Grant. 'I always knew she'd lose her cherry to a poet.'

'He's not a poet,' said Laura, eventually, when she'd processed what Grant had said and recovered. 'He's a novelist . . .' And then she gave up. The cat was out of the bag. Luckily Grant and Monica started having an argument about who was the greatest band ever and she was spared any further interrogation.

Chapter Seventeen

Laura woke up on the Friday of the pre-launch festival dinner feeling a mixture of excitement and trepidation. She had had very confusing dreams, including one in which Grant was reading nonsense rhymes while Laura's old school orchestra played in the background. It was a relief to be fully awake. At least in real life one had the impression of having control over events.

As she brushed her teeth she wondered how Monica had got on. She'd been to see what she'd declared to be her final band. Grant had gone with her as a driver, so Monica could drown her sorrows if necessary. The music festival had some good acts, Monica had told her, but was short on publicity. Although Monica didn't dare say it, to her at least, Laura knew Monica wished she had a musical Dermot, to create a bit of useful scandal.

A couple of nights before a group of them had gone to see Monica's band open the music part of the festival. In theory they were supporting a better-known group (which Laura had never heard of), but in fact they had stolen the show. The entire audience had stamped and clapped along and a goodly proportion of them got up and danced in the aisles of the old cinema. Laura had been amusing herself spotting people from the Lindy Hop night she and Grant had been to when Grant pulled her to her feet.

'Come on, girlfriend, let's see if we've remembered anything from when we did this before.' He led her to the front where several rows of seats had been removed (Laura didn't know if this was to disguise slightly low sales figures, or to make room for dancing) and they started to dance. Soon they were joined by Fenella and a reluctant Rupert. Everyone was laughing and clapping – even the boy band kept time, trying to look cool amidst so much overt enjoyment.

'What a fabulous opening night!' Laura said to Monica when they met up backstage, where the party continued, just as exuberantly, only without the dancing.

'There's no greater high on earth than 'a gig going that well,' said Monica, 'except being in love!'

As her Seamus was standing by her, Laura didn't know if Monica was addressing this to her or to Seamus. But at that moment Fenella came up and hugged Monica, and then all her band mates, so Laura didn't have to respond.

Although Dermot was always in the background of her thoughts, leaping to the front whenever there was a nano-second of space between one useful thought and the next, Laura was gradually coming to terms with what had gone on between them.

She realised it had been quite unreasonable of her to expect – even to hope – that Dermot was unattached. Her head had filled in the blanks, even if her heart didn't want to accept it. He was highly sexed and had the free attitude to love and life that great artists often did. If his girlfriend was away there would be a vacuum and he would fill it. Bridget (in spite of her hard-won rationality she could hardly even think her name) would have known this when she went away, pragmatically accepting that being with Dermot meant putting up with his occasional infidelity. Well, good for her, thought Laura, doubting she would have been able to be so adult about it.

Having attempted to sort it all out in her mind she

felt marginally better. She just had to accept Dermot as he was. He'd been a lovely dream. Some irritation remained: even if he didn't want to contact her, he could at least reply to Fenella's emails and say whether or not he was coming. But if he didn't she'd cope. She'd have to.

Laura presented herself to Fenella as soon as she was dressed. It was another glorious day with the promise of more of the same over the weekend. At least the weather was being kind to them.

'So what do you want me to do for tonight?'

Fenella kissed her cheek, partly in greeting and partly in thanks for her prompt appearance to report for duty.

'A seating plan. Sarah's upstairs and she'll do it, but she needs you to tell her who is who. You'll know if people are deadly rivals, at daggers drawn. Damien Stubbs has confirmed. And Kathryn Elisabeth can't come to the dinner but she's fine for her event and for the panel.'

'Oh, that's OK then. But I don't know any of the authors personally, you know.' Laura felt obliged to make this clear, although this wasn't absolutely true.

'Which is how it should be,' said Fenella firmly. 'Any problems, you can ask Eleanora. She'll know exactly who doesn't speak to who.'

'I think maybe that should be "whom",' suggested Laura softly.

'Oh shut up,' said Fenella good-naturedly. 'Sarah's in the dining room. I'll bring some coffee up.'

Sarah had all the names of the guests on place cards and was putting them down and then picking them up again.

'Hi, Laura, how are you? Come and tell me if I've made any ghastly mistakes.'

'That's a lot of people,' said Laura. 'But in spite of what Fenella might have said, I don't really know who's who.'

'But you'd know if I've put a romantic novelist next to a science-fiction writer.'

'Well, yes, but I'm not sure that would matter too much. All the writers of women's fiction I've met have been very down-to-earth and easy.'

'But what about the sci-fi ones?'

Laura considered. 'Ah well – they vary.'

'So where would you like to sit?' asked Sarah when they'd moved the place cards around quite a bit.

'Really, I don't mind. Just fit me in anywhere there's a gap. I'm surprised I'm invited, actually. I feel I should be helping to serve or something.'

'It's being catered. Fen was muttering about her and Rupert doing the cooking but I put my foot down. They're here to entertain the guests, and so are you. Hey, it's good that they got the old dumb waiter sorted, isn't it? Otherwise it would have to be a cold dinner.'

'That will have made a big hole in the budget.'

'What? Fixing the dumb waiter? Not at all. It only needed the cords replacing.'

'I meant having the dinner catered.'

Sarah shook her head. 'Not really. Rupert has provided all the wine from his cellar and has sourced the food. It's being done by this lovely firm of women I know, the Catering Ladies. They're very low key, reasonable and utterly brilliant.'

'Oh well, that's good.'

'You look worried. Is it Dermot?'

Laura sighed. Was it that obvious to everyone? Although she was sure Sarah didn't mean to imply anything personal. 'Not so much him, or at least, not just him, it's the whole thing. I feel we're going to look awfully silly if our star turn doesn't pitch up, however many things we've arranged to fill in the gaps.' She also felt guilty. Although she had emailed him, as had Fenella and Eleanora, she couldn't bring herself to phone. She didn't want to hear his voice. She was just about managing to get her feelings under control; she didn't need anything to undermine that. Anyway, why should she? Why should she even care after he'd effectively used her? And would a call from her make him come when everything else had apparently failed? If several fierce messages from Eleanora hadn't done the trick, nothing would. And should she really sacrifice herself once more for the greater good?

'I don't think once it's started anyone will really notice,' said Sarah, unaware of Laura's internal inquisition. 'We've got the dinner tonight – well, that's not for the punters, but it'll keep the performers happy.'

'And tomorrow's either Dermot, reading with music, or Rupert, pretending to be Irish, reading with a CD.' Laura made a face. 'It doesn't sound very convincing, does it?'

'But there are free drinks, courtesy of the local micro-brewery – we've Rupert to thank for that – so no one will mind if it's not amazing.'

Laura sighed agreement. 'And then the big interview or the panel the day after tomorrow.' She frowned. 'I do see that with free beer Rupert might go down all right, but a panel of authors? Instead of the big star name? I'm really not sure.'

Sarah was firmly philosophical. 'There's no point in worrying about it. You've done everything you can and set up a good substitute event. If people want their money back, well, we'll give it to them.'

'I know, but—'

'Relax, most people will just go to the events they're going to, if you see what I mean. The ticket sales have been very good. Lots of the people on the database you provided from the shop have bought tickets. And the competitions have been very well supported. Trust me, it'll be fine. And Fen says there's a real buzz locally. People stop her in the street and ask about it every time she goes to town.'

Aware that as an events organiser who specialised in weddings, Sarah was a professional soother of ragged nerves, Laura smiled. But she was still worried.

Just then the door opened and Fenella came in with a thermos jug of coffee and a plate of biscuits.

'How are you two getting on?' she said, handing the plate to them. 'These are home-made. The Catering Ladies made them.'

Laura crunched into a lemon-flavoured biscuit. 'Delicious! Couldn't we just have these for the dinner?'

Fenella was just about to tell Laura off when her phone rang. She pulled it out of her back pocket and then walked across the room to where there was better reception. Sarah poured the coffee and she and Laura sipped and ate until Fenella came back.

'You look as if you've either won the lottery or failed your driving test,' said Sarah. 'Which is it?'

'I don't know,' said Fenella, looking from one to the other. 'Sort of both.'

'Tell us then!' urged Laura.

'Well, you know the music festival hasn't been able to get the same amount of publicity as the literary one? Monica's worked really hard at getting it attention but no one seems that interested in giving it any airtime. Maybe it's musicians being even more flaky than writers . . .'

'Cut to the chase, honey,' said Sarah.

'Well, Ironstone – heard of them?' Fenella addressed this to Laura.

'I may be a bluestocking,' she said crisply, 'but I haven't been living in a cave for the past year. They are pretty darn famous.'

'Sorry. Well, they're willing to do a spot—'

'But that's amazing!' said Sarah.

'Yes it is! What's the downside?' Then Laura suddenly wished she hadn't asked. Fenella was looking at her with a sympathy that could only mean one thing. 'Oh don't tell me. It's to do with Dermot, isn't it? They'll come if they can meet the "greatest living Irish writer" da de da de da.'

'I want to thank you for not doing those wiggly things in the air with your fingers for inverted commas,' said Sarah gravely.

This broke the tension somewhat, but didn't stop Laura clenching her fists. 'I'm just so fed up with this! Bloody Dermot! Why is he being so – bloody difficult.' Her pent-up frustration at herself for minding so much was making her crosser than she wanted to be.

'I thought you were going to use a four-letter word for a moment there, Laura,' said Fenella.

'I did in my head. I've just trained myself not to say it out loud, because of working in the shop – or at least not often. But you must see my point! He's been such a – nuisance! I mean, how long does it take to answer an email, even if only to say no! The literary festival starts tomorrow, for God's sake!' She'd even rung Marion, her bed and breakfast hostess, to see if she knew anything, but all she could say was that he was holed up again and no one had seen hair nor hide of him. She didn't tell the others this because they'd ask, perfectly reasonably, if she'd phoned him. She didn't want to have to explain why she hadn't. And anyway, Eleanora had and she was much better at getting mountains to move.

'He did get us a very good sponsor, who hasn't withdrawn his sponsorship in spite of Dermot being such a loose cannon,' Sarah pointed out reasonably.

'He could have lost us it,' said Laura.

'And think of all the authors who confirmed when

there was all that fuss in the press!' said Fenella. 'They were queuing up to come!'

'And if he doesn't turn up no one will ever agree to appear at this festival again!' said Laura. 'They'll say we got people here under false pretences. The press will have a field day . . .'

'He might still come,' said Fenella softly, obviously not really believing that he would. 'Try not to take it to heart, Laura.'

Laura sighed. It was much too late for that.

'And I'm not going to Ireland to try and bring him. Not again. It wouldn't work. It didn't work on either of the other two times I tried it.' Laura took refuge in another biscuit.

'So what shall I tell the man from Ironstone?' said Fenella after a suitable pause out of respect for Laura's previous efforts.

'The truth!' said Laura, still crunching.

'Hang on, let's just think,' said Sarah, tapping her pen on her cheek. 'If they came it would really help the festival?'

Fenella nodded. 'Bloody right! We might get coverage on Radio 1, as well as all the local stations. It'd be mega. We didn't even ask any bands that big, because they're always booked up years ahead. Ironstone just happen to have a gap for some reason. Publicity-wise, it would be fantastic.'

'Well,' said Sarah, after chewing her pen for a few thought-filled moments. 'It won't do them any harm to do something for us. Tell them we can't guarantee that they'll get to meet the great man but we'll do our best. After all, it's what we've been saying to everyone else and they haven't smelt a rat.'

'They will expect the great man to appear,' said Laura, when Fenella had gone away to tell this whopping lie.

'I don't care,' said Sarah. 'Sometimes one just has to be a bit unscrupulous. Other people often are.'

'Quite right!' said Laura, with a very attractive but very unscrupulous-where-women-were-concerned person in her mind.

'So let's get these place cards done.'

'What shall I do with this one?' asked Laura a little later, holding a card with Dermot's name on.

'Put it on the side with the other possible no-shows,' said Sarah. 'A couple of people said they might not be able make it.'

Laura was on duty in the hall. Everyone was due to arrive any minute now. She had the house phone, a list of directions from several local landmarks and a note of which author was to stay where.

The first people to arrive were a couple of women's fiction writers who were very jolly. They'd travelled together, got lost several times and not minded. They'd had lunch at the local pub and were in positive mood.

'I'm Anne,' said one, 'and this is Veronica. To be honest, people who write books like we do don't often get asked to festivals,' she went on. 'And to get to stay in this lovely house,' she added, looking round at the hall, newly decorated with some very pretty *trompe l'œil* morning glories that were concealing something or other that Fenella was worried about. 'That makes it really special.'

'Oh yes,' said Veronica. 'I love that fake pillar. Getting it to look like real marble is not easy.'

Laura laughed, grateful that the party included two such good-hearted people. 'It is a lovely house, and Fenella and Rupert are such good hosts,' said Laura. 'Fenella will be here in a minute to show you to your rooms.' She smiled at both women. 'I've always been a fan of your books.'

Anne Marsh enveloped Laura in a Chanel-scented, silken hug. 'Bless your heart.' She wore a lot of scarves and jewellery and was like a softer version of Eleanora. 'How many writers have you got coming to the dinner?'

Laura considered. 'Well, there's you two, Kathryn Elisabeth couldn't be here tonight but is doing an event in the library tomorrow. There are a couple of literary writers, including Damien Stubbs and a science-fiction writer. We didn't have room for everyone. So that's six.' She didn't mention that there should have been seven, in case there wasn't.

'Well, we're very happy to be part of it all,' said Veronica.

'Hello!' Fenella appeared. 'I'm Fenella.' She shook hands with both women. 'Now, would you like some tea first, or to be shown to your rooms?'

The women exchanged glances. 'Let's find our rooms,' said Veronica. 'But then a cup of tea would be wonderful.'

'I'll organise the tea,' said Laura. 'Would you like it in the sitting room or the kitchen?'

'Kitchen,' they said in unison.

'In which case, you stay here,' said Fenella to Laura, 'and I'll make tea when Anne and Veronica are settled.'

Eleanora appeared and, hard on her heels, a young writer of literary fiction who'd got lost and was not at all happy. Fortunately for Laura, Eleanora gave him a sharp lecture about being grateful for the exposure, and that books like his hardly sold diddly-squat, and that this was a great opportunity.

A couple of men in country clothes arrived. They turned out to be literary editors. They'd travelled together and were extremely pleasant. 'So will Dermot actually appear?' one of them asked Laura.

She shrugged, and then smiled, remembering that they were supposed to be pretending he was coming, at least to everyone else.

'Shall we open a book on it?' said the other one.

Laughing, they followed Fenella to their accommodation.

At last everyone they were expecting had arrived, except Dermot.

'It really is an amazing room,' said Laura, looking around her.

The huge table took up most of the middle, but the room was so large there was ample space for sideboards and serving tables at the edges.

The vast mahogany table shone, set off by the sparkling glasses and crisp white napery. Laura's eye was caught by something and she looked closer.

'It's a darn! In the napkin!'

Sarah laughed. 'It's all antique, from Rupert's family, or from car-boot sales, depending. The glasses are a bit mixed if you look carefully. Fenella's been hunting for nice ones on eBay.'

'But so many of them – the polishing must have been a nightmare.'

'The Catering Ladies really enjoy making everything look perfect.' Sarah chuckled. 'They were a bit horrified when they saw the number of bottles of wine Rupert's put out.'

Laura made a rough calculation. 'That's nearly a bottle per person, no wonder they were shocked.'

'That's just the red wine. The champagne and the white is all being chilled.'

Laura laughed. 'My goodness!'

'Rupert says dinner parties where the empty bottles don't exceed the number of guests are niggardly affairs. And Eleanora says writers all drink like fish.'

'Well, I don't think we need worry about anyone going thirsty!'

'There's masses of soft stuff as well, if you don't want to drink much.'

Laura made a rueful face. 'I'd prefer not to tonight.

Rupert still needs to run through his pieces for Saturday, so we'll have to get up at a reasonable time tomorrow.'

'Rupert's cooking breakfast, so unless it's before dawn, I'm afraid you've missed that slot.'

This was a bit of a blow. Doing something like this without proper preparation could end up the most amateur disaster: hideously embarrassing. Suppressing a feeling of panic, Laura said, 'Oh well, might as well get pie-eyed then!' Seeing Sarah's searching look she added, 'It's all right, I'm joking.'

There was a pre-dinner reception in the long gallery that had, Fenella told Laura proudly, been the venue for a celebrity wedding that had featured in all the gossip magazines. Laura hadn't liked to admit she didn't read gossip magazines, but when she had passed this information on to Monica, she was very impressed.

Monica was sharing Laura's little cottage for the festival while Grant was in a local b. and b. Monica arrived back from sorting out yet another 'slight hiccup' on the music side of things while Laura was ironing her best white shirt.

After hellos, the discussion about opening a bottle of wine or not and the bewailing of Dermot's as yet no-show, Monica said, 'You're not wearing that, are you?'

'Why not? It's clean, freshly ironed, and I've got all the dog hair off my black trousers!' Laura was feeling combative, mainly because she felt she was going to look a little dull next to Monica's glittering pink number that perfectly toned with her glittering pink hair.

'Haven't you got anything else?'

Laura sighed. 'I was going to go into town and buy something, but the time slipped away.'

'OK, let's think. You're a bit shorter than Fenella. Shoe size?'

Laura told her and Monica rushed off. For want of something better to do, Laura picked up a bottle of nail varnish that had fallen out of Monica's make-up bag and began to apply it. Lucky Monica – this was just a jolly dinner for her. It could make Laura look a complete fool.

Monica came back with a hanger on which hung a tiny velvet item that she declared was a tunic. 'But wear it over tights, with these boots' – she produced the long, pale green suede pair that Fenella had been wearing when Laura had first met her – 'and it's an outfit.'

'But it's summer. I can't wear boots, and besides, that – dress is terribly short.'

'Put it on!'

As Monica was sounding very like Laura's mother when getting Laura dressed to visit her grandparents, she did as she was told.

'Fantastic! You look great! Now let me get at your hair.'

'I look like a pixie having a bad hair day,' said Laura when she had manoeuvred herself in front of a mirror, Monica following behind holding said bad hair.

'You won't when I've finished with you. Just stand still!'

Laura was not at all sure she liked the impression she gave but she had to admit that the bits of her legs that showed between the short dress and the long boots did look rather fine.

'It doesn't really matter what I look like anyway,' she said.

Monica made as if to clip her round the ear.

When they got to the house everyone was wearing their finest. There was quite a lot of sparkly black; Eleanora's jewellery was longer and more glittery than ever. The men wore suits or dinner jackets; Grant was wearing a white dinner jacket with a black sequinned bow tie. Laura noticed one of the romantic novelists writing things down in a tiny notebook.

Rupert, particularly dashing in a velvet tuxedo, filled everyone's glasses with either champagne or elderflower pressé that had a few stars of elderflower in it. Then Sarah banged something against a glass.

'Ladies and gentlemen,' said Rupert. 'Fenella was supposed to be doing this opening speech but she absolutely refused, so I'm doing it.' There were polite murmurs and sips of champagne. 'She and I and all the festival committee have worked incredibly hard to make this first Somerby Festival a roaring success, and I'm sure it will be. But one person has done more, gone to lengths far greater than anyone else, to get the literary side of it all going, and that's Laura Horsley.'

Laura blushed so deeply she thought she would spontaneously combust, and vowed to take out a contract on Rupert's life at the first opportunity. The applause was loud and extremely embarrassing. The cries of 'Speech, speech' got so loud she realised she'd have to say something.

'Thanks, Rupert, for that,' she said meaningfully, making sure he picked up the message that she would never forgive her for dumping her in it. 'It's very sweet of Rupert to say those kind words about me, but these things never hang on one person, however much that may seem to be the case.' There was a stage-whispered 'bloody Dermot' from Monica. 'This was a new—' A buzzing sound from the pocket of Fenella's tunic stopped Laura mid-sentence. 'Saved by the bell!' she said gaily and groped for her phone.

An angry Irish voice growled in her ear as she said hello, 'Where the feck am I?'

A beatific smile spread from Laura's lips and ended possibly at her toes. 'Give me a hint and I'll try to talk you in,' she said, aware she was grinning so hard she could barely speak. He was here. Nothing else mattered.

'That'll be Dermot,' said Monica, half cross, half delighted.

'I'll go and change the place settings,' said Sarah.

Laura walked away from the sound of rejoicing and speculation that was going on in the gallery. She went back down to the hall where all her written instructions were.

'I'm in some godforsaken hole with an unpronounceable name,' Dermot went on.

'Right. I think you might be in Wales.'

'Wales!'

'But don't worry, it's not all that far. Are you driving yourself?'

'Who the feck else would be driving me?'

'OK, now what I want you to do is to find a safe place to park the car. I'll send someone to come and get you. You don't sound fit to drive.'

'Feck that! I haven't had a drink for weeks! I'll find the way myself.'

'Don't disconnect! Head for . . .' Laura found the directions she needed and read them out to Dermot. 'Will you be all right?'

'I will be, probably. I can't answer for you, getting me into all this.'

'I'll keep my phone by me. Just ring if you get lost again.'

Laura didn't rush back upstairs again. Just for a while she wanted to keep Dermot for herself. When he arrived he would be common property, everyone would be dancing attendance, admiring, admonishing, wanting a part of him. Now, while she held her phone in her hand, and knew that the last person to have spoken to her on it was Dermot, he was hers: her irascible, ornery, difficult, egoistic, wild Irish writer. She finally admitted to herself that she loved him, even without any hope or expectation that he might love her back. Just loving him was enough for now. And he had come to their festival.

'When do you think he might arrive?' asked Fenella when she went back upstairs again.

'Depending on whether he gets lost again or not, about half an hour.'

'Do you think we should start without him?' said Sarah, who had an anxious-looking woman at her side.

'Definitely. He doesn't deserve to be waited for.'

For some reason, Fenella moved forward and kissed Laura's cheek.

Laura was in two minds whether to wait for Dermot in the hall or to sit down and start eating. She felt fairly sure Dermot would need directions at least once more so she decided to eat. She was seated next to one of the romantic novelists, Anne Marsh.

'I must say, I adore Dermot's writing,' she said.

'I really liked it at university,' said Laura, frightened that she'd shown her feelings for Dermot far too clearly. She quickly steered the conversation away from him. 'But I really love your books. How do you find writing a book a year?'

'Well,' said Anne. 'I'd like it a lot better if every year had fourteen months in it, but lots of writers write far more than I do.'

'And lots write far less.' Her phone went and Laura smiled. 'Far less . . . Excuse me a moment,' she said before connecting.

'How the feck do you get into this place?'

He was downstairs. Barely excusing herself, Laura ran down the stairs and started wrestling with the huge key. 'I can't open it!' she called to Dermot.

'Try pulling it towards you,' he called back.

Laura did, and eventually got the key to turn. Dermot was standing there, looking completely disreputable in an old leather jacket and blue jeans. Her heart clenched at the sight of him. He strode in, dropped a bag at her feet and looked at her. 'Did you dress up as a leprechaun just for me?'

'Don't be silly!' she said crossly, desperate to avoid sounding coy.

She saw him look at her mouth and she felt breathless.

'Are you all right? That key can be quite tricky,' said Rupert coming up behind Laura. Laura wasn't sure if she was pleased to see him at that moment or not. Rupert smiled and held out his hand. 'You must be the famous Dermot Flynn. Welcome!'

'I think you must mean infamous,' said Dermot.

'Either way, it's good to see you. We started dinner, I'm afraid.'

Dermot, who had picked up his bag halted. 'Dinner. Ah. What I need is a shower and a shave.' Then he looked wickedly at Laura and mouthed, 'And a shag.'

She blushed and looked away. Just for a moment she wanted to go with him to where they could be alone for a very long time. Then she mentally shook herself. She wouldn't let him weave his spell on her again. She mustn't.

'I don't want to meet everyone in all my dirt,' went on Dermot, possibly completely unaware of the effect he was having on Laura.

'You don't have to—' Rupert began.

'Trust me,' said Dermot. 'I do have to. For various reasons, I haven't had a shower for a few days.'

'Right. I'll show you to your room then. It has an en suite.'

'And how will I find my way to the party afterwards? This is a huge pile you have here.'

'I'll come and fetch you,' said Rupert. 'In about fifteen minutes?'

'Fifteen minutes is fine. But would you not send the leprechaun?' He nodded his head towards Laura, in case Rupert was in any doubt who he was referring to.

Rupert laughed. 'She'll get more lost than you will.'

'Mm,' said Dermot, looking at Laura in a way that made her just want to smile and smile, 'that might not be so dreadful.'

Chapter Eighteen

Laura went back upstairs trying very hard to wipe the smile of sheer joy at seeing Dermot again off her face. As she got to the door she remembered she could be pleased for the festival's sake, and stopped bothering. There was time enough for her to be sensible and remember he was the enemy and she needed to protect herself – and more importantly her heart – from him.

'He's here!' she announced. 'Dermot Flynn has actually deigned to turn up!'

A buzz of exclamations filled the room. 'What's he like?' said Anne Marsh, when Laura had got back to her place.

'Well, I had met him before—'

'You've met him before? But I thought he was practically a recluse!'

'Not at all,' broke in Eleanora. 'He's just damn difficult to get out of Ireland. Laura did a grand job getting him to come.'

Some man said, 'Did you have to sleep with him to get him to agree?'

Laura looked and saw it was one of the young literary writers. She gave him a withering look. 'As if that would really work.'

'Well,' he said, 'it would for me.'

'Oh,' said Laura, having worked out eventually that he didn't mean that he wanted to sleep with Dermot. She blushed deeply.

'It would be no hardship sleeping with him,' said

Veronica. 'I saw him on television, years ago and thought: Mr Darcy, eat your heart out.'

Perfectly presented portions of Jubilee Chicken were being served over their shoulders. 'I prefer that Sean Bean myself,' said the Catering Lady who had just delivered the chicken.

The young writer ignored this interjection, it being from a motherly soul who was obviously only a waitress. 'You romantic novelists, you're just suckers for an Irish brogue and an easy smile,' he said. Laura remembered he had been shortlisted for some prize or other and one reviewer had likened him to Dermot.

'Oh, it's general,' said Veronica, smiling sweetly. 'All women are suckers for an Irish brogue and an easy smile – don't they come in pairs? You might have to work just that bit harder. Although,' she added kindly, having watched him bluster a bit, 'lots of women are attracted to writers per se.'

Anne glanced at her colleague. The young man, who was now blushing and blustering in equal measures, obviously didn't quite know how to take this.

'I don't know why he's considered such a draw,' he said, sounding resentful. 'He's not J. D. Salinger, is he?'

'Well, no,' agreed Anne. 'But he does have rarity value, doesn't he? I mean, he may not have produced anything for ages, but he was – is so good.'

'And tasty,' added Veronica.

'I'll second that,' threw in one of the literary critics, overhearing this conversation.

'What? That he's tasty?' Veronica raised her eyebrows. 'Something for the gossip columns?'

'My dear girl, I didn't mean that,' he said, 'as you very well know.' He gave her a teasing look. They obviously knew each other. 'What I meant was, we're all here from

279

curiosity. No one from the literary world has set eyes on him for years.'

'And personally speaking, I'm quite happy for him to be the main attraction at the festival,' said Anne. Then she took pity on the young writer who was looking a bit downcast. 'So tell me, Adam,' she said, putting her hand on his and capturing his attention, 'what are you writing now?'

He was thrilled. 'My third novel. I've been working on it for a couple of years now. Just about taking shape.'

'Two years! If it's not a rude question,' said Veronica, sabotaging her friend's attempts to be nice, 'how do you support yourself between novels?'

'I'm a English lecturer.' He looked pained. 'My novels are my work, my life! I don't expect to make money out of them.'

Veronica and Anne exchanged glances and cleared their throats. 'Sorry,' Veronica went on. 'I didn't realise that making money from one's novels was on a par with selling one's daughters into prostitution. It's how I earn my crust.'

Laura chuckled inwardly. Anne and Veronica had swept up the drive to Somerby in a Porsche. Some crust.

'Well, I don't just churn them out, like you do.' Adam took an affronted gulp of his wine.

Anne and Veronica didn't need to look at each other to pick up each other's thoughts. Veronica patted Adam's hand. 'It's all right, sweetie. There'll always be a place in the publishing world for a well-received novel that no one actually reads, let alone buys. You keep on crafting those perfect sentences.'

'I say! That's a bit—'

'Patronising? Sorry,' said Veronica. 'But don't worry, I'll be all sweetness and light from now on, as my reputation requires.' She frowned thoughtfully. 'Dermot managed to do both – write like an angel and sell in shed-loads.'

Laura, satisfied that no blows would be exchanged or

glasses of wine thrown, leant across to Monica. 'You'd better get in touch with Ironstone! And tell the people who aren't here about Dermot.'

'They'll be so pleased! And Ironstone!' She clapped her hands excitedly. 'I must buy new knickers.'

Laura became aware of Fenella trying to say something to her but she was too far away. She leant in and concentrated on lip reading. After several attempts she picked up that Fenella thought it was a pity that Jacob Stone had decided not to come to this dinner.

'He probably didn't think Dermot would turn up!' Laura mouthed back.

Fenella nodded agreement. 'It means I've got to get Dermot to agree to meet him on his own.' She frowned across at Laura. 'Is he very difficult?'

Laura leant further forward, still struggling to hear. 'Who, Jacob Stone? I thought he was your friend.'

'No!' Frustrated, Fenella raised her voice. 'No! Dermot! Is Dermot really as difficult as everyone says he is?'

At that moment the double doors opened. 'Right on cue,' murmured Veronica. 'You couldn't have stage-managed it better.'

Dermot, shaved but still wearing his casual shirt and jeans, stood looking directly at Fenella. Then he smiled. 'Why don't you ask him yourself?'

Fenella got up from the table and walked round to greet him. She hesitated as if not sure if she should kiss him or shake his hand. 'I don't know what to say. In some ways, I feel I know you,' she said.

He just smiled and opened his arms. 'You'd better give me a hug, then.'

Fenella went straight into them.

Laura was aware of a pang of jealousy so deep at first she thought it was actual pain. She'd thought it was fine, that she'd had her magical time with Dermot and now he belonged to the rest of the world. But her heart wasn't clued up to her rationalisation and it hurt. He hadn't hugged her like that.

'I've put you next to Eleanora,' Fenella was saying.

'I don't want to sit next to her. I want to sit by the leprechaun and these attractive women.'

There was an instant shuffling of chairs and people getting up and sitting down. Laura caught Sarah's look of resignation as her carefully planned seating arrangements were tossed into disarray. There was a frantic shifting of cutlery and glasses, too.

'I know perfectly well why you don't want to sit by me, Dermot,' said Eleanora placidly. 'But don't worry, I'll get to you later.'

'We ought to discuss your various events,' said Laura, struggling to breathe properly and working very hard on being businesslike. 'Tomorrow you're supposed to be reading extracts of your books with Celtic music accompanying.'

His look of disgust made Anne and Veronica chuckle.

'Of course, you don't have to do it if you don't want to,' said Fenella quickly. 'Laura's chosen some extracts and Rupert's going to read them in an Irish accent. We have a CD for the music.'

At this his look of disgust was even more extreme.

'Or whatever you prefer,' said Fenella. 'Really—'

'Oh, for goodness' sake!' said Laura. 'I'm sure now he's here, Dermot will do whatever he's scheduled to do.' She smiled sweetly at him.

'For a leprechaun you're very bad-tempered,' he said.

'Not at all. Leprechauns are notoriously bad-tempered. Think of Rumpelstiltskin,' she said, trying to sound sniffy. She was enjoying herself. She could banter with him without fearing for her safety.

'I always thought he was very hard done by,' said Anne to Veronica.

'So did I!' said Dermot, joining in with glee. 'He helps that materialistic woman—'

'It wasn't her fault,' said Anne. 'She was sold into that marriage by her father.'

'And the king wasn't much better,' agreed Veronica. 'He only wanted her for her ability to spin straw into gold.'

'Oh, I think he wanted the girl for her beauty too,' said Dermot. 'He just used the straw-into-gold thing as an excuse.'

Laura channelled her tumultuous feelings into a snappish efficiency. 'Lovely though it is to hear all your thoughts on the subtext of traditional fairy stories, firstly I don't think Rumplestiltskin was actually a leprechaun and secondly, could I just bring us all back to the present day? Dermot has to do an event for which every ticket has been sold. Could we agree what it is?'

'Does that mean we won't be doing the panel?' said Adam, sounding disappointed. 'I was really hoping—'

'For some publicity?' said Anne. 'Surely not!' Her amused expression took the sting out of her words.

Adam glanced at her sideways, as if a full-on look might turn him to stone, and muttered out of the corner of his mouth, 'So how many paperbacks would you reckon to sell?'

'Oh, I don't know,' said Anne. 'If I'm lucky, about a hundred thousand.'

'A hundred thousand? Bloody hell!'

'She's being modest,' said Veronica. 'She sells far more than that.'

'Only because they're in the supermarkets.' Now that she'd demolished him, Anne now wanted Adam to feel better.

Laura was trying to catch Dermot's attention but he was too busy enjoying the interchange between the popular-fiction writer and the literary novelist.

She opened her mouth to try again but Monica pipped her to the post. 'Dermot, do you remember me?'

His charm was like an interrogation light: no one, let alone a woman like Monica, could fail to melt a little under its influence, in spite of how she'd been with him when they were in Ireland. 'How could I forget the woman who asked such searching questions from the floor?'

'Oh? What were they?' asked Adam. 'I always like to plant a few good questions.'

'I don't think you'd want that kind of question,' said Laura, blushing hard, hoping everyone would just think she'd had too much to drink.

'No, but something that allows one—'

'She asked me when I last used a condom,' said Dermot brutally.

'Oh!'

Anne and Veronica both snorted into their wine, unable to hide their amusement.

'But Dermot's not going to hold that against me,' said Monica. 'Are you? I want to ask you about Seamus.'

'And I don't think—' said Laura.

'What about Seamus?' asked Dermot. 'Who is Seamus?'

'He's a musician,' said Monica, fighting for her man. 'I just don't think – I mean, possibly—' She stopped. 'You might know him?'

'Just because they're both Irish, doesn't mean they know each other,' said Adam. 'Hi, Dermot, may I introduce myself? Adam Saint.' He leant over and stuck his hand out towards Dermot.

'What's his surname?' said Dermot, having smiled briefly at Adam, ignoring the proffered hand.

'O'Hennessy. He lives—'

'Oh God, *that* Seamus! Of course I bloody know him! Don't tell me he's made you pregnant? I'll knock him down for you.'

Becoming hysterical, Monica began to laugh. 'No! He hasn't! Anyway, if he had it would be my responsibility. He just wants to play—'

'Monica,' Laura implored. 'His band was dreadful! You said so yourself.'

'What does he want to play, and why?' demanded Dermot.

'His bodhrán. Behind you as you read out pieces from your great work.'

It was Adam Saint's turn to laugh. Dermot made a face at Laura. 'Did I agree to this?'

'I probably didn't get round to asking you,' she admitted. 'I got distracted!'

Dermot smiled. 'So you did. So what precisely would you have been asking me to do if you hadn't . . . got distracted?'

'To read from your work to the accompaniment of Irish music,' Laura muttered. 'It's to link the music and the literary bit of the festival together. I know you hate the idea, but don't worry, we can do Rupert's thing.'

'With the fake accent and the Celtic Twilight bollocks?'

Anne and Veronica were loving it. Even Adam Saint seemed content.

'Yes,' muttered Laura, concentrating on getting a bit of sweetcorn back into the rice it had escaped from with her fork. It was wonderful to be so close to Dermot but also agony. It was making it so much harder to keep her feelings in check. Unrequited love was so painful.

'Well, I'll do something, if only to spare us that. And Seamus can play, as long as it's *not* the fiddle.'

'Oh Dermot, thank you!' said Monica, reaching across three plates of chicken to kiss him, and narrowly missing some curry-and-mango-flavoured mayonnaise as she did so.

'So who's going to do the big interview on Sunday night?' asked Adam. 'Everyone's going to be really interested to hear that.' Something in his tone suggested *schadenfreude*.

'I'm sure they are,' said Dermot lazily. 'Did I agree to do a big interview? Or did you slip that one by me too?' His gaze wandered over Laura in a speculative way that made her feel weak and angry with herself and consequently cross with him for having this effect on her. He obviously thought they could pick up where they'd left off. That he only had to look at her and she'd willingly leap into bed with him.

'Oh, for goodness' sake, stop being such a prima donna. Of course there'll be a big interview! This is a literary festival! It's what happens!'

'So who's doing it?' Adam pressed on, possibly hoping for the hardest-hitting, most incisive, unkindest interviewer around – the Jeremy Paxman of the literary world, if not *the* Jeremy Paxman.

'I am,' said Laura, more sharply than she had intended.

'Oh,' said Adam. 'Bit of a pushover that will be for you, Dermot! Can't you face a proper interviewer, then?'

'I'll have you know that the leprechaun here is very proper, or she was until I got to her, and I'm sure she'll ask some very searching questions,' said Dermot.

'I will indeed,' said Laura, hoping to goodness she'd be able to think of more than the three she'd scribbled down in her notebook late one evening. 'We couldn't book anyone famous without knowing if Dermot was able to attend,' she said to Adam.

'You see? It's all my fault,' Dermot said. 'Laura dear, is there any chance of getting you on your own?' He raised an eyebrow and Laura flushed. Did he really expect to claim his 'shag'? While the mouse was safely back in Ireland, the cat could claim his prey. Humph!

'Oh, you can't nobble her,' said Adam. 'That would be entirely unsporting.'

'I'm not entirely sure what you mean by "nobble",'

said Dermot, 'but that was the very last thing I had in mind.'

'Here's the pudding,' said Veronica quickly, sensing trouble. 'Banoffee pie. I think I've died and gone to heaven.'

Laura caught her eye and smiled her gratitude. She knew Dermot had been going to say something outrageous and realised Veronica had too.

'No really, I insist,' went on Adam. 'It would be unethical for you and Laura to talk before the interview.' He paused. 'Because it seems to me that Dermot can twist any woman round his finger and he'd just talk her out of asking anything remotely tricky.'

'I assure you what I want to say to Laura is of an entirely private nature,' said Dermot. He was serious now; no more suggestive looks.

Sweat prickled along her hairline as she realised what Dermot might be going to say. He was probably going to 'explain' about Bridget, make it clear that what had happened between them had been delightful, but it was a one-off and she mustn't think of it or him any more, but how about a shag for old times' sake, Bridget need never know. She could almost hear his lovely sexy voice saying the words. She couldn't bear it. 'I think you're quite right!' She said this so vehemently, people looked a little startled. 'I mean,' she went on, trying to sound more rational, 'I think it should be like the bride not seeing the bridegroom the night before the wedding.'

Dermot was frowning and apparently somewhat confused. 'Well, if that's how you feel, Laura.'

'I do! I think I'd feel better about interviewing you if we hadn't talked beforehand. I could approach it in a more professional way.'

'And a writer of your experience, Dermot,' said Veronica, 'shouldn't have any problems with Laura here. Oh, I do realise she'll be a lot tougher than she looks in that tiny dress and those heavenly boots, but she's not going to hang you out to dry!'

'No,' Laura agreed meekly, 'definitely not.' The ache in her heart had returned with a vengeance.

Dermot sighed. 'For feck's sake! But if you insist!' He looked around the table and then got up. 'If I can't talk to the person I want to talk to, I'd better go and see my agent. Is there any chance of any brandy, do you think?'

The happiness that Laura had felt on seeing Dermot again had turned to the depths of despair. She managed to stay chatting to Veronica, Anne and Adam for a few moments longer and then she excused herself on the pretext of seeing when the coffee might turn up.

Fenella was in the kitchen on the same errand, much to the irritation of the Catering Ladies who had it all in hand.

'Are you all right, honey?' said Fenella.

'I'm fine, or rather I will be. I've just suddenly realised what Dermot turning up means. I'll have to interview him, unless there's anyone else.' Frantically she mentally scanned the authors who were around. She couldn't do it, she just couldn't. 'Maybe—'

'No,' said Fenella firmly. 'It has to be you. You know his work, you won't take the limelight away from him, you are the one.'

'You know, there are at least two song titles in that sentence,' said Monica, appearing behind Laura. 'But Dermot is utterly lovely.'

'You know, you're sounding very Irish these days,' said Laura. 'Maybe you're spending too much time with Seamus.'

'Well, you're right there,' she agreed happily, 'but isn't it just darling of Dermot to let Seamus play behind him?' Monica seemed to have forgotten Dermot was the bad fairy who had broken her friend's heart.

'He doesn't know how bad Seamus is, obviously,' said Laura.

'He can't be that bad,' said Fenella.

'And he knows him,' Monica said. 'Anyway, Seamus isn't bad, it's the band that's awful, and Dermot probably knows exactly how bad – or even good – he is. It's a great chance for Seamus.'

'If you ladies would either like to take up some jugs of coffee, or get out of the way, we'd be very grateful,' said one of the Catering Ladies.

'Oh, sorry,' they said in unison, and moved out of the way.

What she needed, Laura decided in the shower the following morning, was time to go away by herself with Dermot's books and think up some really insightful questions. But she had a busy day ahead of her and even her time alone in the shower was limited; Monica needed to get into it.

'Do you want toast and stuff here, or to go across to the house for a cooked breakfast?' she asked a still-damp Monica a short time later. 'I wouldn't mind checking in with Veronica and Anne. I'm taking them to their event later.'

'Won't Dermot be there?' Monica put a large dollop of something smelly on to her hair.

'I'm allowed to see him, just not alone,' said Laura primly.

'Are you all right about doing it, though?' Monica said, sculpting her hair with the product.

'I would be if I had time to think about it, but I won't have a moment to think up anything until about ten minutes before it happens.'

'It must be extra hard for you, seeing that you're sleeping with him.'

'I'm not! It was just that time!' She sighed. 'But of

course it is harder. I can't treat him just like any other writer.' And I don't want to treat him like the man who's broken my heart.

'What you need to do is to work up a good old grudge against him,' said Monica, plugging in her hair-dryer, unaware of the depth of Laura's anguish. 'Think how badly he's treated you and get your revenge.'

'But he hasn't treated me badly, really.' Laura kept feeling an impulse to confide in Monica about Bridget, then realising she didn't want to drag it all up again. She was coping as well as she could, she thought. Don't rock the boat. Monica knew she was upset; she didn't need all the sorry details.

Monica wasn't having this. 'Oh, for Jaysus' sake! From where I'm standing, he may be lovely and charming and a God's gift to the literary world, but he had his evil way with you and never phoned! In my book that's not gentle-manly behaviour. How much more badly could he treat you?' She obviously still felt loyal towards her friend and for that Laura was grateful.

'I should think a lot worse. He could have made me pregnant and then left me.' Then, wanting to change the subject, she said, 'Now, what about breakfast? Cooked or toast?'

'Cooked, I think. I want to see Dermot, even if you don't.'

'Monica, don't start interrogating him . . .' But Monica was already out of the door.

The Somerby kitchen was full of chatter, clattering and the smell of bacon. Rupert was wearing a huge apron and had three frying pans on the go and a separate pan full of scrambled eggs. Dermot wasn't there.

'He, Rupert and Eleanora stayed up into the early hours,' Fenella reported to Laura, obviously annoyed. 'They'll be fit for nothing later, and Dermot's got to do his thing with Seamus.'

'Have you eaten anything yet?' Laura asked.

'No she hasn't,' snapped Sarah, equally tetchily. Everyone was obviously a little anxious now the literary festival was officially open and the first proper day of events was before them. She took Fenella by the shoulders and guided her to an empty seat. Then she put a big plate of food down in front of her. 'Get that down you. I'll fetch you some tea.'

They all chatted for a while about nothing in particular, and Laura had just begun her own breakfast when Dermot and Eleanora appeared. Eleanora demanded a full English and Dermot just some toast and black coffee. Anne and Veronica, who were tucking their chairs neatly under the table, exchanged glances. 'I love it when people act out of character!' one of them whispered as they left. 'You'd expect Eleanora to gnaw on dry toast and Dermot to have a huge fry-up!'

As soon as she decently could, Laura returned to her little house to sort herself out. She had come back to see if Anne and Veronica were ready when she met Sarah in the hall.

'This could be a bit awkward,' said Sarah. 'There are several journalists here. Would you be a love and run back down and see if Dermot wants to speak to them? Otherwise, I'll get rid.'

Laura went back down. Only the hard-core coffee drinkers and smokers were left: Dermot, Eleanora and Rupert, who'd blagged a roll-up from Dermot and was looking guilty.

Feeling like a prefect disturbing a midnight feast Laura made her announcement. 'But Sarah will send them away if you don't want to speak to them, Dermot.'

'I think you should see a select few,' said Eleanora, 'and then the story comes from you, instead of being a lot of invented rubbish.'

'Should I send for Max Clifford?' asked Rupert, only

half joking. 'Or don't we need a publicity person? We have got Sarah, after all.'

'So what shall I tell her?' asked Laura, having turned from one person to another, no longer feeling like a prefect but like a child who isn't really allowed to join the adults.

'OK, I'll see a few, until I get bored,' said Dermot, getting up and giving Laura a wicked grin. 'Don't tell Fenella Rupert had a fag, will you?'

Laura tossed her head and tutted, reverting to prefect-hood with gratitude. 'I won't need to tell her, she'll smell it a mile off.' Then she gathered up some dirty crockery, leaving Dermot to face the press.

Chapter Nineteen

Laura didn't have time to worry about how Dermot got on with the journalists. She had to take Veronica and Anne to their venue, where they were doing a joint talk, followed by a signing. Then the two authors were adjudicating a short-story competition that they had already judged, before going to a local café for a 'Tea with Two Authors' event. They were good sports and didn't mind working so hard, but a great deal had been asked of them and Laura felt a bit guilty. When she'd suggested them as adjudicators for the competition, she hadn't realised it would mean running from place to place in quite the way it had worked out. Fortunately the cakes at the café were extremely good and Laura insisted they be allowed to eat a couple before the questions began again.

She was just contemplating a Jap cake, a wonderful old-fashioned confection involving coffee icing and crushed meringue, when her phone rang. She went outside to take the call. It was Fenella.

'Sorry to bother you, but Dermot asked me to call.'

'That's OK, but he could have phoned me himself. I know I said I didn't want to speak to him, but I only meant—'

'It's not that. Dermot's been giving interviews all day. Eleanora is thrilled! She doesn't know why he's being so obliging, but never mind that. He hasn't got time to choose readings for his event tonight and wonders if you have any ideas?'

Laura had thought about this when she very first had the idea of combining music and readings. 'OK, I've marked some places. If you go into my house, on the bookshelf are copies of both Dermot's books. The passages I think are best have paperclips on the pages.'

'You're amazing! I bet you're glad I never got round to borrowing them after all, or we'd never find the books, let alone some good bits.'

She wanted to retort that Dermot's books were all 'good bits' but just said, 'Glad to be of help.'

Laura went back to the tea shop and decided Jap cakes were no longer optional, but essential. She was frantically thinking about when she was going to have time to plan what to ask Dermot the following night. Tomorrow she was touring the countryside for the 'Festival in the Community' with authors in the back of her car, taking them to visit old people's homes. Still, there should be time between getting the authors back to Somerby and being on hand again in case she was needed to get them to Dermot's musical event. With luck, she shouldn't have to do that at all, and then she'd have plenty of time. Well, an hour or so, anyway.

When she and Fenella had been planning the festival they had welcomed each new suggestion and set it up gleefully. The programme was full of events at venues all over the area. Everyone had taken up the ideas with enthusiasm. It was only now, when the festival was actually happening, that they realised quite how much running around was involved.

It was quite late by the time they got back to Somerby as Veronica had insisted on visiting a local garden centre and Laura felt she could hardly say 'there's no time'. Grant and Monica were waiting for her on the doorstep of the main house. She had forgotten they were all going to have a drink together before Dermot's event. She'd have no time to write down her questions this evening. She sighed.

'Laura, I can't believe you've been taking these lovely authors round the country in my old banger,' said Grant as he and Monica helped Veronica and Anne out of his old car.

'It's been fine,' said Anne, taking his arm and heaving herself out of the back of the car. 'It's just we're women of a certain age.'

Veronica, in the front, who had got out unaided, humphed. 'Women of a certain arse, more like!'

Grant regarded them both. 'I don't know if I should laugh at that joke or not!

'Right!' he went on, once Anne and Veronica had been shown back to their accommodation and supplied with tea and whisky. 'Let's go back to yours and have a glass of wine. I've been saving myself. I want a full update. Didn't you pack just a bit too much in to the literary festival, Laura?'

'Mm. We did,' she admitted as they set off towards her cottage. 'The thing was we didn't realise how everyone would leap at the chance of having an author, or a writing competition, or even a "Stitch and Bitch with Books" event so avidly.'

'So, what's a "Stitch and Bitch with Books" then?' asked Grant.

'It's like a Stitch and Bitch, when women get together and—'

'It's all right, I worked that out.'

'Well, in this instance, someone reads aloud, so there's no bitching really, and everyone knits squares for a blanket. It's happening on Monday morning. Fenella's providing the cake.'

'Come on you two, never mind Stitch and Bitch,' said Monica. 'I'm going to the event early with Seamus to help with the sound check and things. We need to hurry.'

Upping the pace a bit, Laura said, 'What's your b. and b. like, Grant?'

'Lovely, but a bit bucolic. There are cows right outside my window.'

'What do you expect in the country?' asked Monica.

But Grant forgot his objections to rural life when he saw where Laura and Monica were staying. This was the first time he'd been over. 'Oh, this is charming,' he said. 'Really nicely done.'

'It is, isn't it?' Laura agreed, retrieving a bottle of wine from the fridge. 'You go first in the shower, Monica. You're in a hurry.'

'Only the same hurry you're in,' said Monica, pausing en route, looking at her friend suspiciously.

'I don't have to go early like you do.'

Monica gave her a beady glance.

Laura inspected her nails. 'I may not go tonight. I need to plan my questions for tomorrow.'

'You can't not go to Dermot's event,' Monica protested. 'He'd be so upset.'

'No he wouldn't be!' Laura was equally adamant. 'He wouldn't care at all, if he even noticed.'

'But, Laura!' Grant was appalled. 'You can't miss it! You've loved his work since you were a baby—'

'Not quite a baby,' she protested quietly.

'You can't miss hearing him read,' Grant went on. 'You'd never forgive yourself.'

After being stared at by two indignant friends for several seconds, Laura sighed. 'I suppose you're right, Grant. I've heard enough lesser writers read their stuff. It would be silly to miss the best.'

'Let's get out the wine,' said Grant.

'Monica can't have a drink if she's driving,' said Laura, feeling bullied and wanting revenge.

'It's OK, I'm not driving,' said Monica. 'We've got

a driver. We're picking up Seamus on the way. It's such a shame he's not staying at Somerby.'

'Somerby is filled to the gunwales,' said Laura. 'Some authors have had to stay in bed and breakfasts.' She paused as a happy thought occurred to her. 'You could go and stay with him, if you want.'

Monica shook her head. 'No. I need to be on-hand really, for the music festival stuff.'

Laura sighed, contrite. 'I'm sorry, Mon, I keep forgetting about that side of things. How's it going? Did you tell Ironstone? Will they be there tonight?'

'Some of them, definitely, but it's a sell-out. Seamus is bricking it.'

'We have got the CD fall back position if he's that scared.'

'No! Dermot has vetoed that, remember.'

'Come on, Mon, never mind all that, do you want a glass of wine first, or a shower?'

'Both of course! Haven't you heard of multi-tasking?'

Grant and Monica both insisted that Laura came early with them, not trusting her turn up unless they took her to the event by force.

'It is a shame we couldn't organise the pub to host this event,' said Monica.

'Yes, but apparently it couldn't fit in nearly enough people so they moved it to Fenella's cinema,' said Laura.

'Fenella's cinema?' said Grant.

'Not her personal cinema. She loves the building and wanted it used for everything.' Laura paused. 'It's also the biggest venue around. It's where Monica did her gig, remember?'

'Oh. I thought it was just a theatre.'

'Poor Seamus! He's going to be so nervous!' said Monica interrupting. 'He'd have been much happier in a pub.'

Monica sat in the front next to the driver on the way to pick up Seamus. Grant and Laura sat in the back, squashing up when Seamus got in. Laura was also feeling nervous. She so wanted it to go well, for Seamus's sake, and, of course, for Dermot.

Sarah had asked her if she should photocopy the pages of the book and enlarge them for Dermot to read from. They had discussed it and decided it could do no harm, but Laura said that laminating them wasn't a good idea. Apart from anything else, if he dropped the pages they would skid all over the place. Laura had the sheets; Dermot had the books.

'It's like members of the cabinet not travelling on the same flights in case there's a plane crash,' Sarah had said solemnly. 'There's a back-up position.'

Laura wasn't sure if being made to laugh was helpful or not. It did relieve a bit of tension, but now she was worrying about Dermot's driver, a very steady ex-policeman called Reg, getting into an accident on the way to the venue.

The venue functioned as a cinema most of the time except when the local amateur-dramatics group put on productions, or the village panto was on. It was a very pretty building, kept up by massive fund-raising activities. This time, all the seats were in place so as to have as big an audience as possible. Although they arrived a good hour before the event, there were already people gathering outside.

'Kerrist!' said Seamus as the driver slowed down, looking for a place to stop. 'There's bloody loads of them here!'

'It's all right,' said Grant. 'They're here for Dermot. You don't need to worry.'

'That's not very kind!' said Monica, shoving Grant's arm. 'Of course they're here for Seamus!'

'They're here for the event,' said Laura diplomatically. 'And I'm really nervous too!'

'And me,' said Grant. 'I'm really worried that someone will forget their lines or something. I feel like a mum at a kid's play. Let's get in there. The bar should be open, shouldn't it?'

'Yes,' said Laura. 'The idea is to make it feel like an Irish pub as much as possible, given that it isn't one. With music and crack, and porter.'

'Crack?' said Monica. 'I thought this was a nice sedate music festival.'

'It is,' said Grant. 'It's the writers who might let the side down.'

'Shall I drop you here?' asked the driver, who'd been chuckling quietly to himself. 'And you've got my mobile number? Ring me when you want to go home.'

'Could that be now?' asked Seamus.

'No,' everyone chorused, and they all got out.

The first person they saw when they got inside was Adam. 'I came with Dermot,' he said, implying he was doing a useful task. Laura, who normally would have had sympathy for the young writer, found this rather annoying. 'He doesn't want to be swamped with fans,' Adam went on. 'Or to discuss tomorrow's interview. He needs to focus on tonight's performance.' He glared at Laura as if she was a door-stepping paparazza looking for scandal.

Laura didn't respond. Adam had obviously appointed himself as Dermot's minder – a task that Fenella or Rupert had been allocated. But as they were busy, they'd probably been happy to let Adam do it, and presumably Dermot hadn't objected. As for discussing tomorrow's interview, it was the last thing she would have ever done. It was a bit ironic that all Adam's original resentment of Dermot had somehow morphed into hero worship and a fierce protectiveness.

Monica took Seamus up to the stage and was already giving orders to the sound crew. Dermot was sitting on the stage, on a chair, reading, a well-thumbed copy of one of his books in his hand. He had a tall glass by his side.

'Let's go and get a drink,' Grant suggested. 'We're not needed here.'

The bar was already buzzing. The usual volunteers had been supplemented by staff from the local pub, there not usually being much call for draught stout at the theatre. There was a young man in black jeans, black T-shirt and a ponytail instructing a woman in her sixties how to pull the perfect pint.

'I'm not sure if I should drink,' said Laura when Grant asked her what she wanted.

'Oh, for God's sake! You'll never get through this sober! I can tell, you're far more nervous than Seamus is. Have a large whisky.'

By the time he'd got back to their table, the place was packed. Laura was relieved. A good audience, and no chance of Dermot being able to spot her in the crowd. It couldn't be better. But she still planned to sit right at the back, behind a pillar if she could find one.

Laura wasn't surprised that Dermot was a star; he read beautifully, captured the audience and held them, totally enthralled. She was momentarily surprised that Seamus was so good. He didn't play the bodhrán he'd been so miserable at, but the guitar. Very, very softly, he played traditional Irish songs: 'She Moved Through the Fair', 'Down by the Salley Gardens', 'The Lark in the Clear Air'. And Dermot read.

In deep, dark brown tones he described a small boy watching through a window as his mother kissed his father and feeling excluded, a windy morning in spring, a blackbird's song and a feeling of expectation that had no cause; falling asleep on a hard, leather-covered banquette in a pub while the wedding party caroused.

There wasn't a cough, a murmur or a fidget to be heard. Even Grant was listening intently.

Laura knew she was what was popularly known as being 'tired and emotional' but the words were so evocative, so poetic without being sentimental, and the music was so touching that she felt tears smarting in her eyes.

She concentrated on keeping them very wide open and then occasionally blinking, so a big tear splashed down. This way she could blot up each tear with her hand, and hope no one noticed how overcome she was. Not that anyone would, she realised. They were all transfixed.

She and Grant were right at the back. On Laura's insistence they had delayed going in as long as possible. She had said she wanted to get back as soon as the event was over, to prepare for her interview, and to avoid Dermot until she could face him calmly and unemotionally the following morning. Now she was even more glad she had. His reading had brought up every feeling, every longing – not that they were buried that deep beneath the surface, but with each sentence all her love and admiration for him rose up with renewed force.

Dermot closed the book and Seamus rested his fingers on his guitar strings to silence them. It was over. For a moment there was silence, as if no one wanted to break the spell Dermot had woven around them. And then the theatre erupted.

There was, inevitably, a standing ovation. Laura slipped outside, too overwhelmed to be able to join in. Damn the man for putting her in this turmoil, she thought. But wasn't he wonderful? Walking up and down in the road on her own, her heart began to sing. He was a star; he wouldn't regret coming to the festival. And however painful it was to admit it, she loved him with all her heart.

'Are you OK?' A friendly male voice addressed her.

'It's me, Hugo. I'm Sarah's other half and a friend of Rupert and Fenella's.'

'Oh yes, of course. Hello again. I'm fine,' she insisted.

Hugo studied her thoughtfully. 'Do you want me to run you home? Escape all the crowds? You're interviewing the great man tomorrow, aren't you? You might need some time away from the furore.'

'That would be brilliant! Can you do that?' Laura felt relief course through her and she almost stumbled.

'What, drive you home? Yup, and be back before anyone notices I haven't been here all the time. Come with me. The car's here.'

Having asked Hugo to tell Monica and Grant she'd gone home, she left a note for Monica and then fled up to the mezzanine and went to bed. She couldn't think of any questions tonight: she was too wrung out. After ten minutes she came back downstairs and made some hot chocolate. She took it back up to bed with her and hoped she'd get to sleep this time. Surprisingly, she did.

On Sunday she had very little time either to think about the interview later that day or dwell on the emotions Dermot's reading had stirred up in her the night before. She'd joked to Fenella and Sarah at breakfast about needing time to lie on her bed with slices of cucumber on her eyes, but really she was worried that if she didn't have time to prepare, Dermot would make her look a complete fool. And while it was how Dermot performed that mattered, his reputation wouldn't be enhanced if he was asked obvious questions by a slip of a thing with wild curly hair who was totally unprepared. She owed it to herself, too.

Sunday's schedule was genteelly packed. As soon as they'd had one of Rupert's famous breakfasts, Veronica and Anne plus Maria Cavendish, a crime author, squashed themselves into the car and Laura set off towards the first of their destinations. The 'Festival in the Community' had been a very popular idea – one Laura now wished she hadn't had, although perhaps it was the distraction she needed.

At the last place, a very grand home for retired gentle-folk, she was about to get out of the car when Veronica said, 'You stay here and prepare your interview. We'll be fine. Honestly.'

Grateful, Laura agreed that she would, but instead she found herself daydreaming.

A tap on the window jolted her out of her reverie. She realised she had actually fallen asleep. All this emotion was wearing her out.

'Never mind, you'll be better for a nap,' said Veronica, when they all got back in the car and discovered Laura in dreamland. 'I'm a great believer in catnaps.'

'But you don't want Dermot to run rings round you,' said Anne. 'What time is the event?'

'Seven. We're having an early meal. Maybe I should skip that and think up some questions then.'

'Really,' said Maria Cavendish, who'd only joined the group that day and wasn't as friendly, 'you should have thought up your questions weeks ago, when the event was first arranged.'

'But she didn't know if Dermot was coming,' explained Veronica. 'There was going to be a panel of authors instead.'

'Oh? Is that why that was cancelled? Hmph. I could have come tomorrow instead.'

'But the old ladies loved you!' said Anne. 'It's amazing how many of them read really gritty crime.'

In between navigating back to Somerby and telling the writers how brilliant they'd been Laura tried to pull her disparate thoughts together. By the time she finally delivered her literary load, all she'd come up with was 'Did you like school?' Then she remembered she'd asked him for his Desert Island book. He'd said *Ulysses*. She could get him to talk about James Joyce for a little bit. It would ease them both into the interview. Once she was back in the quiet of the cottage, she noted both these questions down in the back of her diary, ready to transfer them to something more substantial. Sarah had asked her if she wanted a clipboard, but Laura felt some notes on a sheet of A4 would be easier.

Laura's teeth were chattering and she felt sick. She had managed to think of a list of questions and written it out, and she could tell, just by looking at her hand-writing, that she was terrified. Not that she'd been in any doubt but the spiky, uneven strokes revealed the turmoil going on inside. She was slightly disappointed that Dermot hadn't even tried to see her. But then she'd been busy and so had he and they had said they wouldn't. He'd sent one text saying 'Go gently on me' which she'd decided not to reply to. On reflection she was grateful she hadn't seen him after last night.

And she decided that she'd feel better about the whole thing if she controlled the one thing she actually could control: her hair. On hearing this, Sarah, who'd come to see why she hadn't been at the meal, bringing a sand-wich with her, went to find some straighteners. When she brought them, she insisted on staying to do Laura's hair for her.

'I'm not a hairdresser,' Sarah explained, gathering up a strand of Laura's hair, 'but I have seen lots of brides getting their hair done. It's a shame I didn't book Bron. She's my hairdresser friend I've worked with a lot. I just didn't think of it.'

'If I didn't have mad hair it wouldn't be a problem. I don't usually think about it much myself—'

'But this is a big occasion. You want to look your best. It's natural.'

Sarah was getting on quite well with the hair straighteners. Laura sat quietly for a while, enjoying being looked after for once. It was strangely comforting. Then she said, 'What do you think I should wear?'

'You looked lovely in what you wore last night, unless you want Dermot to see you in something different.' She frowned. 'Not that he would have seen much of it.'

'I can't care what Dermot sees me in!' Laura's anxiety turned this into a bit of a shriek. Hearing herself she added, 'I do hope that didn't come out as if I cared what he thinks.'

Sarah laughed soothingly, taking up another lock of Laura's hair. 'No, it just came out as if you want to look professional for the audience, how Dermot feels about it is neither here nor there.'

'That's excellent! That's just what I meant. How did you know?'

'Oh, I spent a lot of time kidding myself about my feelings too,' Sarah went on. 'Now, are you going to clip your hair back? Or just let it hang?'

'I think a clip.' Laura scooped up a hank of carefully straightened hair and held it up. 'What do you think?'

'You look about twelve, but adorable. Are you going to wear make-up?'

'A bit. Some mascara. Anything else always ends up under my eyes in seconds. Will that be enough, do you think?'

'And some lipstick.' Sarah supervised the clip, the mascara and the lipstick. 'There, now you look at least fourteen.' She paused. 'Have you got any notes? Questions?'

'Mm.' She picked up her sheet of A4 and noticed it shaking. 'I need a file to put this in.'

Sarah noticed it too and smiled reassuringly. 'I'll give you one. And do you want me to drive you to the theatre? Or will you travel with Dermot?'

Laura's mouth went dry at the thought of travelling with Dermot. 'Oh no. I'd rather go with you.'

'Then I'll make sure I don't have to give anyone else a lift.'

'Gosh, thank you, Sarah. You've been amazing.'

'I haven't done anything, actually. But *you* really will be amazing. I promise you.'

Somehow Sarah's words stayed with her as they drove to the venue. Her parents had never had much faith in her but other people had, and Sarah reminded her that she had done difficult things in the past and done them well. She thought of everything she had achieved since the whole festival thing had begun, from Lindy Hopping to speaking to schoolchildren to talking would-be authors through their manuscripts. Asking Dermot a few questions, allowing him to talk as much as he liked on the subjects that came up shouldn't be as hard as any of that. And yet somehow it seemed, much harder.

Sarah stayed with her, keeping her calm and bolstering her spirits until it was time for her to go on to the stage behind the drawn curtain.

The stage was set with a low table covered with a cloth and two chairs. On the table were two glasses of water and a carafe. Dermot was already there. He smiled at Laura. 'Maybe we should shake hands before we start, like boxers.'

His smile made her stomach turn over. 'I'm interviewing you. It's not a confrontation,' she said, and heard her voice tremble. And she didn't believe it, really.

Dermot had a file of papers propped against his chair. 'I know you didn't want us to talk but I feel I must. We haven't had time – you rushed off and—'

She put up her hand. 'No really, there's no need for you to say anything. It's fine. I do understand.'

Sarah called from the wings. 'It's time. Are you guys ready?'

'Not quite,' said Dermot. He was gazing at her, a puzzled look on his face.

'Oh yes we are.' Laura was firm. She felt if she waited any longer she might actually be sick.

'We must find a moment to talk,' he began. 'What happened in Ireland—

'We don't need to talk about that. In fact, we don't need to talk about anything except – oh, the curtains are going back,' she said with relief, even if it meant her next ordeal was about to begin.

Rupert introduced them and, staring beyond the lights, Laura could see the place was packed. She glanced at Dermot, to see if he was shaking too, but he didn't seem to be. He was looking out at the audience; how he felt about it was a mystery to her.

When the applause had died down Laura took a sip of water so her mouth would work. This was it.

She recited the phrases of introduction she had prepared and then turned to Dermot with the first question.

'So, tell us, Dermot, were you happy at school?'

The question surprised him but after a few seconds he was off, describing how bad he was at so many subjects, how he read Proust under the desk and that the whole school thought he was a complete idiot until he won an essay competition. He captured their interest, he made people laugh, and everyone loved him.

'And now, something I always want to know about writers, what's your Desert Island book? If you could only have one book, for the rest of your life, which one would it be?'

His eyes smiled and for a moment she was transported back to the day on the headland when they first really talked. 'God, that's a hard one. Fortunately, I've been asked it before and so I know the answer.'

She nodded, smiling.

'It's *Ulysses*.'

'But many people find James Joyce impenetrable.'

'He is, but infinitely rewarding.'

He went on to talk about Joyce for a little longer and then turned to Laura expectantly.

Her next few questions were as insightful as cocktail party small talk, she knew, but fortunately Dermot answered them brilliantly. Whether this indicated that he had at one time gone to a lot of cocktail parties, or that the small talk down at the pub in Ballyfitzpatrick was very similar, Laura didn't know. Either way, the audience was in turn laughing hysterically or leaning forward to pick up every nuance.

Having warmed him up she felt she had to ask her proper question now. It was a slightly risky one but any interviewer worth his or her salt would have asked it. Another sip of water, a deep breath and she launched in, 'So, Dermot, it's been a few years since there's been any new work from you. Would you like to tell us why?'

She felt like Judas and couldn't look at him, but she could imagine the flash of anger he must have been shooting at her.

'Actually, Laura' – it sounded very personal, although it was addressed to the audience too – 'there has been some new work.'

As she expected this answer – it was his usual front – she decided to push on. She'd got this far, she couldn't back out now. 'Well, have you got it with you?' she asked.

'I have.' He picked up his folder and put it on his lap.

'Oh.' She certainly hadn't been expecting this answer, but now came the real challenge. She was curious as to how he'd respond. 'So then would you like to read some of it? Or shall we go straight to questions from the floor?' she said.

'Read!' came the reply from the audience.

Dermot smiled at them and then turned back to Laura. 'It's a short story.'

'That's nice,' she said, not wanting to reveal her mounting excitement. He really did seem to have something new. 'Would you like to read it?' She felt as if she was encouraging a small child.

'Are you sure you don't want to ask me some more questions instead?' he asked teasingly.

Was the man mad? He was offering to read a short story, thus putting an end to the agony that was this interview and make literary history in one simple action!

'Well, let's ask the audience again, shall we?' she said, confident that they'd back her up.

The 'yes' from the audience was deafening, but Dermot kept his gaze on Laura. She sneaked a look at him but she couldn't guess how he was feeling.

'Then that would be lovely,' she said, as if accepting a second cup of tea.

'OK then. Here goes.'

'It's wrong to play a game when the other person doesn't know the rules, but somehow we find ourselves doing it all the time.'

His voice was so beautiful, and so sexy, at first Laura just enjoyed listening to the melodic sound of each eloquently expressed phrase without really taking in what he was actually saying, but gradually the story took shape in her mind and she listened more attentively.

'At what point in the game do you confess? In the middle? Or at the end, when success feels like defeat? And hurting someone is inevitable?'

As he read on about commitment and letting someone down gently, Laura's mouth went dry, blood coloured her cheeks scarlet and she thought she might faint. Was he talking about her? Had he written a short story about her, and their relationship, if it could be called a relationship?

The rest of the story passed through her ears without fully connecting with her brain. It was a defence mechanism, she decided, when she realised she couldn't capture his words any more than she could catch thistledown. The odd word floated through slowly enough for her to grasp it. '*Betrayal . . . passion*', and, cruelly, '*hero-worship*'.

The more he read the more she felt a chill clutch at her heart. He'd written about her, about them, about unrequited love and letting someone down gently. And he had read it out loud, to a room full of people. Why couldn't he have just sent her an email? At least she could have read it in private.

She sat on the stage waiting for the torture to end, grateful that the audience was so enraptured by Dermot that none of them was looking at her. Thankfully no one would connect the story with her, there was no reason why anyone should. That helped. She felt now she could finish the event with dignity even if she felt like crawling away and hiding from the world for ever. She realised a small part of her had still hoped, but he couldn't have been clearer. How could she ever face him again? A glance at her watch told her there'd be no time for questions. She knew Dermot would be glad of this.

When his story came to an end the audience got to its feet, thundering applause as loud as possible. She was vaguely aware of mobile phone cameras clicking and even some flashes. Had some press got in the event? She knew they weren't supposed to be there, but how could they be stopped really?

Dermot came to the front of the stage with his hands held up to silence them. Laura crept off the stage into the sanctuary of the darkened wings.

Chapter Twenty

She knew that however much she wanted to, she had one more task to do before she could head for the sanctuary of the cottage. Seeing her old boss Henry in the book room was a lovely surprise. It shouldn't have been, of course. She knew he was supplying books for the festival but it was the first time they'd caught up with each other. His dear old face was a welcome sight after what she'd just been through.

'Sweetie!' he said, leaping to his feet, then added, less enthusiastically, 'You're looking rather tired.'

'Hardly surprising,' said Laura, smiling widely, hoping he wouldn't spot the effort it took, 'we've been fantastically busy.'

'But hugely successful,' Henry said approvingly. 'All the literary world is here and listening to every word Dermot utters.'

Laura shuddered and then hastily turned it into a shrug. 'His events have been very well attended, but so have all the others. Now, am I really needed here? Or shall I get back?' She so wanted to creep away to a darkened room.

'You're needed here.' Henry was firm. 'You've just interviewed the star of the show. That means you're a bit of a star yourself. Ah, here's Eleanora.'

Eleanora swooped down on Laura in a cloud of black sequins, shocking pink bugle beads and marabou. Her earrings bit into Laura's cheek as they kissed. 'Darling, if you're even dreaming of escaping before Dermot's done his signing, forget it. He's having a late supper with Jacob Stone, but right now he's fighting his way through the autograph-hunters. He'll be here in a minute to sign books.'

'I hope some of this vast crowd buy books,' said Henry. 'Trouble is, when there's nothing new—'

'There IS something new,' said Eleanora triumphantly, 'and I can't help thinking that Laura had something to do with it.'

Laura sat down suddenly on Henry's recently vacated chair, her knees weak. She felt hot and cold all at the same time. For a moment she thought Eleanora had guessed. 'I really don't think – I mean – I think he must have been writing obsessively before I . . .' Aware she was in danger of revealing what had gone on after she'd discovered him in Ireland she stopped.

'Oh, darling,' Eleanora would have none of it. 'You're so bloody modest! Take the credit! He's produced nothing for nearly fifteen years. You walk into his life and he's writing again! And you were so professional out there. Now, just for a moment, be happy!'

'But I'm not—'

'You'll never get her to take the credit for anything,' said Henry, producing a glass of wine from behind his table and handing it to Eleanora. 'Best not to pester her.'

Laura was about to protest some more when he handed her a glass of wine too. 'Just sit there and relax. You've had a long day.'

Laura sipped the wine, missing her quiet days at the bookshop and Henry very much. Just lately life had been far too exciting for a bluestocking.

Monica came rushing in. She bent and hugged Laura hard. 'That was so lovely! So tender, so utterly beautiful.' She sniffed. 'I've been crying my eyes out!'

'Why? What?' Laura narrowly missed spilling her wine as she disentangled herself. Surely Monica didn't suspect either? She was in danger of sobbing into her friend's chest.

The thought of everything she and Dermot had shared reduced to a story – albeit a brilliant one – made her want to cry. She knew for the sake of the literary world she should be thankful he'd lost his writer's block, and if she'd helped in any way then she should be proud to have been of service, but right at this moment she could only think of herself and the tragedy of it all and just hope no one thought to ask whom the story was about. She couldn't bear to be exposed to the examination of the world. She would just die of embarrassment if word got out.

People were beginning to come through to buy books now, but no one was looking in her direction as if to say 'poor you'.

And then the great man himself arrived, flanked by admirers and press alike. Their eyes met briefly and Laura saw in his a tender concern that told her everything she felt she needed to know: the story *was* about her. The reason he'd wanted to talk to her in private was so that he could explain it to her and she hadn't let him. He probably knew she was in love with him. She wouldn't have been the first down that particularly rocky road, after all. And with her naivety, it was pretty inevitable, given what they'd shared. He, being basically kind, didn't want her hurt. But her feelings were not returned. She just wished he hadn't put it all into a story and read it out so publicly. He of all people should know the value of privacy. And if he felt that way why had he even joked about a 'shag'? She was so confused.

But she smiled at him, every cell of her body trying to convey that it was all right, she wasn't in love with him, didn't think the story was about her. In fact, she wanted him to know that everything with her was fine and dandy. She was asking a lot from her smile, she was well aware, but she did her best.

Then, making a heroic effort, she moved her way through the crowd until she met him, halfway to his signing table. 'Well done, Dermot!' she said bravely. 'That was fantastic! I hope you don't mind if I go back now. I've got a splitting headache.' The fact that this part was true lent veracity to the rest of it. 'I'll see you tomorrow.'

He looked back up at her, frowning a little as his pen hovered over a book. 'Will I not see you later?'

Laura shrugged. 'Oh yes. When I've got rid of the headache I'll come over. Probably.'

She didn't wait to see if he'd accepted this, she just fought her way out of the room and then the cinema, hoping she'd come across someone who could take her home.

She spotted Reg, the driver who'd brought Dermot to the event. She knocked on the window. 'Any chance of a lift back to Somerby? Dermot will be ages yet. I've got a frightful headache.'

He wound down the window. 'Jump in. I'll have you back in no time.'

So far so good. She'd take aspirin, drink hot milk and go to bed and worry about having to face Dermot, possibly over breakfast, in the morning. She'd cross that bridge when she came to it.

Another note to Monica, apologising for her 'copping out', and Laura climbed the stairs to the mezzanine level and fell into bed. She was genuinely exhausted but it took her a little time to relax enough to sleep. She knew that everyone else involved in the festival was just as exhausted and she was dipping out, leaving them to carry on. It wasn't fair, really. But although she felt guilty, she didn't feel guilty enough to get up again and go over to the main house and help. She had to think how she was going to get through the next twenty-four hours.

Laura awoke full of determination. She would go to breakfast at nine o'clock and face Dermot like a grown woman, not a lovesick teenager. She'd had her night of heartbreak, now she'd face 'Real Life' head on. She would not let anyone, most of all Dermot, see how hurt she was.

She would have liked to have had Monica with her, but as she'd suspected she might, she had a text instead, saying that Monica was staying with Seamus and would be back sometime the following day and that Grant had headed off to his aunt's for the day.

Oh well, thought Laura, trying to find something to be positive about, it means I can spend as long as I like in the shower. She was determined to turn up to breakfast looking fabulous. No one would know she was heartbroken and felt betrayed, least of all Dermot. She would sweep in on the tide of the success of the festival and eat sausages, eggs and bacon with pride! She was seriously tempted to put a fabric rose Monica had left lying about behind her ear.

'Good morning,' she cooed as she opened the kitchen door, sounding worryingly like a primary-school teacher addressing her flock.

She looked quickly round the room and realised Dermot wasn't there. Relief and disappointment raged for a moment and disappointment won. She chided herself. Even now her heart was in danger of ruling her head. She pulled out a chair next to Veronica, who was reading the paper. Veronica lowered the *Daily Telegraph* a little and gave Laura a warm smile over the top of it. Fenella was yawning into a cup of coffee; Reg, the driver, had a piece of fried bread and was cleaning up every scrap of egg yolk with it; and Sarah was writing things down in a notebook. Hugo, next to her, appeared to be composing a sonnet to the piece of sausage on his fork. Eleanora was sipping mint tea with her eyes half closed. Although there were several people in it, the big kitchen felt rather empty.

'Laura!' said Rupert from the Aga, wearing a striped apron and wielding a fish slice. 'What will you have? A bit of everything? A kipper?'

'No kippers, thank you. But I'll have everything except black pudding,' she said. 'Thank you.'

'Black pudding is full of iron you know, darling,' said Eleanora, 'but I'm glad to see you've got an appetite. You look a bit peaky.'

The appetite vanished. Why did Eleanora say that? Why was she surprised, or commenting on her appetite? She must stop being paranoid.

Laura reached for some toast. 'Well, you know how it is, I didn't eat much last night.' She took a breath. 'Dermot not up yet?'

'Oh no!' Eleanora was suddenly bursting with good humour and news. 'I forgot you didn't know. He went off to London last night so he can do breakfast telly today.'

'But I thought he was having a late dinner with Jacob Stone?'

'He did, and then the two of them went off to London in Jacob's helicopter,' said Fenella. 'We've recorded the show,' she went on. 'It was on horribly early. But I think he's doing another couple of shows, isn't he, Aunt – I mean, Eleanora?'

'*Loose Women*,' said Eleanora. 'Excellent programme.'

Laura, feeling bewildered, looked round the table for clarification.

Sarah, who had closed her notebook and was now gathering plates in the corner, helped her out. 'It's a lunchtime show where a group of women discuss current affairs, and gossip.'

'It sounds right up Dermot's street,' said Laura, just as Rupert put a sizzling plate down in front of her. 'Oh, that looks delicious!'

Reg got up, taking his plate with him. 'It was. Now if you don't mind, I've got things to do.'

Now that Reg had left, it seemed that everyone else apart from Laura had had their cooked breakfast and were now just reading the papers, eating toast and drinking coffee.

Everyone was behaving so naturally she didn't need to pretend to be her usual cheery self. And with Dermot out of the county there was no danger of her bumping into him and being forced to see the concern on his face all over again.

Fenella came and sat down next to her. 'So it's just Damien Stubbs's event tonight, and then we've done the big stars. The event is sold out and that man from *The Times* is arriving at lunchtime. Plenty of time for Damien to miss his train and get the next one.'

'You're not very confident of Damien's time-keeping,' said Veronica, having put down the paper. 'It's the trains I worry about, which is why Anne and I came by car. Fortunately we live quite near to each other.'

'What time –?' Fenella stopped, belatedly aware that it wasn't polite to ask when people were leaving.

'In about half an hour,' said Veronica reassuringly. 'The car's packed already and Anne's just taking some photos of your lovely wild garden.'

'We make sure it's tamed in time for the wedding season but it soon grows unruly again. Everyone seems to prefer it that way,' said Fenella.

Vernonica agreed that wild was wonderful.

'Anyone need a lift to the station or anything?' asked Laura. 'No? Then when I've finished this, I'll get upstairs to the office, start sorting out thank-you letters and things.' She turned to Veronica. 'You won't go without telling me? You and Anne have been so brilliant.'

Veronica patted Laura's shoulder as she got up. 'Well, any time you want me – us – again, just say the word. It's been a cracking festival, it really has, well done!'

After Veronica and Anne had been seen off in a throaty roar everyone drifted back to the kitchen.

'It's been really odd, hasn't it?' said Fenella, sliding the kettle on to the hot plate. 'We've spent most of the festival wondering if Dermot was going to turn up. Then he whistled in, did two amazing events, and was helicoptered out again. It's as if he was never here, in a way.'

'Sort of,' said Laura, feeling that in some ways her life would have been easier if he hadn't whistled in.

'But he made the festival such a roaring success. And all down to you, Laura.' She paused. 'You've been such a star, getting Dermot here and everything. Jacob Stone's said to give you a bonus.'

'Oh, you don't need—'

'Then I explained that we couldn't, so he's given you one instead.'

Laura was mortified. 'You mean, after all that, we didn't make a profit?'

'Well, we did,' said Rupert. 'But not a huge one. Jacob emailed me to say he was going to give you two thousand pounds, on top of your fee.'

'That's amazing!' said Laura when she had taken this in. 'That's so kind of him!' She realised she hadn't really given much thought to where her next pay cheque was coming from.

'Dermot told him how much you'd personally done to get him here, before he went to California.'

Laura swallowed, hoping he hadn't done this in too much detail. 'Oh. So Jacob Stone's gone to California?'

'No, Dermot has. A film deal. Eleanora says it may not come off, but apparently lots of people have been interested for ages and he's never entertained the idea before. It's for his first book.'

'Oh, yes. It would make a lovely film. So what's changed? Why is he willing to have it made into a film now?' That was it – she'd never see him again. A part of her wept, even if it was probably for the best.

'It's losing his writer's block, so Eleanora said.' Fenella frowned. 'You did know that, didn't you? It wasn't just the short story, he's writing a novel as well.'

Laura felt sick. 'No I didn't know that. That's brilliant news.' It was but she couldn't help feeling like a discarded shoe. She'd been useful and now she wasn't needed any more. And why hadn't he told her? The fact that he'd hardly had a chance to tell her and that that was mostly her fault was small consolation. Maybe that's what he'd been trying to tell her on the phone. She'd deleted a couple of messages before she'd even read them. She asked herself now if she'd rather have Dermot, writing and happy but away from her, or with her and blocked. At first it seemed like a Faustian pact she was glad she didn't have to make, but the more she thought about it, in the grand scheme of things his happiness seemed more important than her own. That was love for you.

'We were saying – weren't we, Rupert? – that we must have a party with everyone who's been involved in the festival. Once we're not doing back-to-back weddings. We could plan what we're doing for the festival next year.'

Laura laughed, grateful for the diversion. 'How you can even think of another festival? This one isn't over yet.'

The last two events felt a bit anticlimactic to Laura. Everyone was very tired and although the Somerby hospitality flowed as ever, even Fenella was losing her enthusiasm for it a bit. But at last it was just Laura, Rupert and Fenella, back in the kitchen.

'So, have you got any plans?' asked Fenella.

'What? After writing all the thank-you letters, you mean?' Laura managed a cheery laugh. In fact she had no idea what she would do now. She thought she might go and stay with Grant and look for jobs and flats in his area.

'Mm.' Fenella was looking at her rather intensely and Laura felt it must be because she was yearning to have her house to herself again.

'Well, I thought—'

'Can I offer you a job? You can have your converted cow shed for as long as you need it.'

Laura got up and put her arm round Fenella's shoulders. 'You've been brilliant and are so kind, but . . .'

'Books are your thing?'

'Told you,' said Rupert. He was doing the crossword as was his habit.

'I thought it was worth a try,' said Fenella, 'but if you won't work for me, you must ring Eleanora. She said you were to if you seemed jobless and at a loose end. Are you?'

Laura laughed. 'I suppose I am, really.'

'Then she's got an idea.' Fenella said this as if the idea might be on the wackier side of totally insane.

'Oh, hasn't she gone to the States with Dermot?'

Fenella dismissed this idea. 'Oh no, she says she's too old for California. A little light shopping in New York is fine, but Dermot has an American agent as well as an agent for his film rights, so he doesn't need her.' She took a breath. 'Does the thought of ringing her horrify you? You never know with her. Sometimes her ideas are terrific, but sometimes they're just mad. She suggested that Rupes and I went crocodile-hunting for our honeymoon.'

Laura giggled. Bless Fenella, she was going to miss her. 'I'll give her a ring. There's no harm in finding out what she has in mind. And I'll call Grant as soon as I've done that. Finding a flat will be so much easier, thanks to Jacob Stone's bonus.'

'Well, ring Eleanora first,' said Fenella.

'Darling!' said Eleanora, when at last Laura was put through. 'Come to lunch tomorrow. There's someone I want you to meet.'

'Um . . .' This could mean anything from a nearly blind date to a job opportunity. As Fenella had said, Eleanora was capable of anything.

'The Grove, at twelve-thirty. That OK? Trains fit in? Don't try and drive, darling. There's nowhere to park.'

Laura rang Eleanora's office a few minutes after this brief phone call to find the address of the restaurant. Eleanora's advice to Laura not to drive was unnecessary; the thought of a five-hour drive twice in one day made her feel weak. Add lunch with Eleanora and she'd be on her knees.

'You don't know what she's got in mind, do you?' Laura asked Fenella while the three of them huddled down one end of the kitchen table and ate tinned tomato soup with white bread.

'Not a clue,' said Fenella. 'But she was fantastically impressed by all you did with the festival. Maybe she wants you to run another one.'

'Let me get over this one first. I—'

'Hey!' Rupert shouted. 'Look at this! There's a full-page article about us!'

Instantly they were all jostling to read it.

'And it's not just about Dermot!' said Fenella proudly, when she'd read a bit. 'Listen. *Somerby is to festivals as those delightful boutique hotels are to big chains. Add a literary star who seemed to have dropped out of the firmament to the mix and you have something really special.*'

Laura grabbed the paper now. 'We need to buy lots of copies and make a scrapbook. Other papers might have articles too. It'll be so good for next year. We can put extracts in the brochure.' She felt herself brightening despite her heartache.

'I'm so glad there's going to be a next year,' said Rupert, patting Laura's shoulder. 'As long as you run it for us.'

Laura laughed. 'And in the meantime, I've got Eleanora!'

Chapter Twenty-One

Fenella had been firm; Laura was to take a taxi to the restaurant from the station. If it meant she was a little early, well, she could wander round the streets for a bit, as long as she didn't get lost. The restaurant was in Mayfair so the surrounding shops were only for looking in, not actually entering, but Laura did manage to find her way back to the restaurant when she finally decided the time was right – five minutes after the time for which she was invited, to give Eleanora time to arrive.

Except that Eleanora hadn't arrived, although when Laura asked for her at least her name was recognised. She was shown to a table and asked if she wanted anything to drink.

'A glass of white wine and some fizzy water please.' This way she could have an encouraging slug of neat wine, and then turn it into a spritzer if she wanted to.

The restaurant was full of people who seemed to have very little interest in the food. They were talking business to each other at a hundred miles an hour. There were no couples looking into each other's eyes, girlfriends exchanging confidences, or mothers and daughters having meaningful talks. Everyone here was working. Laura enjoyed people-watching, and would have had more fun with it today had she not been anxious about the lunch.

What was Eleanora up to? She'd given Laura what had turned out to be her big break, introducing her to Fenella and Rupert and the Somerby Festival.

Maybe, as Fen had said, this really was another job opportunity.

As she fiddled with her napkin and adjusted her perfectly aligned knife and fork, Laura reflected on all she had learnt since that first meeting. Up until then all her life's learning had been through books, fiction mostly. Since then it had been real life, sometimes painfully real.

She deliberately turned her mind away from Dermot. One day she would look back at her time with him and smile, see it for what it was, a lovely introduction to sex and, for her, love. Now it was an aching wound, poisoned by a growing sense of betrayal. Once her feelings of embarrassment and humiliation had lessened a little, a sense that he hadn't really been mindful of her feelings despite all his 'concern' had gradually built inside her. It didn't make her love him any less or take away the pain but it strengthened her resolve to make every effort she could to get over him, as quickly as mending a broken heart ever could. Having plenty of distractions like lunch today helped.

At last Eleanora appeared with a man probably in his late thirties or early forties in her wake. Laura relaxed. She'd long ago stopped feeling nervous about the actual meeting. She was just worrying about Eleanora not turning up. Now she was here, she relaxed.

'Darling, this is Gerald O'Brien, another Irishman, but don't hold that against him.'

Laura had to smile and allowed the man to take her hand. 'How do you do?' he said formally. 'In England people seem awfully keen on kissing each other when they're introduced, but I'm a bit old-fashioned.' He smiled apologetically and Laura was touched.

For a few seconds she searched for traces of Dermot's voice in Gerald O'Brien's, but she couldn't find any. Of course there were hundreds of accents and variations of accents from Ireland, but part of her had hoped for some connection with the accent uppermost in her mind.

'I am too, I think,' she said, shaking his hand. 'A bit old-fashioned, I mean.'

Eleanora, having kissed Laura, plumped on to her chair with a little puff of air as if she had descended from a height. 'I see you've started on the wine already, good girl. Let's have a bottle. I know drinking at lunchtime has quite gone out with the younger crowd, but I still enjoy a glass or two with my lunch.'

She perused the wine list with concentration. Gerald O'Brien and Laura exchanged shy glances. He was not your stereotypical Irishman, thought Laura. He was quite charming enough but he had none of the easy blarney that seemed to ooze from Dermot. She pushed down the familiar ache.

The ordering didn't take long. Laura had had time to change her mind several times while she was waiting and both Gerald and Eleanora were decisive. The wine came and was poured and Eleanora put her elbows on the table like a woman about to make a statement. Then she caught sight of someone over the other side of the room. 'Oh my God!' she said. 'So sorry – got to table hop although it's frightfully bad manners – but it's Susie Blanquette. And she's with Hubert von Trapp! How dare she? She promised she wouldn't look at another publisher until she'd finished her novel and had something to sell! We were going to have a beauty parade and now it looks as if she'd going with Hubert. Excuse me. Must stop this!'

Laura found herself smiling. Only Eleanora could leave two quite obviously shy people on their own, at their first meeting, before they could even pretend to know each other well enough to make conversation.

She swept off on her mission leaving Gerald and Laura to look anxiously at each other, both determined to make an effort. 'So what do you do, Laura?' asked Gerald.

325

'Oh, I – um – well, I've just finished helping to run a literary festival,' she said. She still didn't know if Eleanora had set them up for a date, in which case she should think of something to say about herself that would make her sound interesting (but unavailable), or a job, in which case she'd definitely want to appear interested and efficient (and possibly available).

'That sounds interesting.' Gerald's polite but genuine response gave her no clue. 'My wife worked as a volunteer at the Cheltenham Festival once, when she was a student.'

He had a wife, so he wasn't a potential date. This was a relief. She relaxed a bit more.

'It *was* interesting, and quite challenging too, actually. It is amazing how many things you need to be able to do. I had to talk to groups of schoolchildren which, I have to say, is one of the most frightening things I've ever done in my life.'

'I can imagine! In fact, I can't imagine anything more terrifying!'

His horror made Laura laugh and she felt herself relax even further. 'Well, they were supervised and I didn't have to talk for long. Der— a friend had given some hints on how to tackle it and it went quite well. I almost enjoyed doing it at the last school.'

'I still don't want to do it. You must be a natural teacher.'

Laura shook her head. 'Oh no, I've never done any teaching.' She paused. 'Although come to think of it, I sort of did, when I helped someone run a writing course.'

'You are a woman of many parts,' said Gerald gravely, but with enough of a twinkle to tell Laura that he had a sense of humour.

Eleanora swooped back. 'Nipped that in the bud. But honestly! What is the point in having an agent if you don't do what they say?'

There was a moment's pause and then Gerald spoke. 'I can promise you, Eleanora, if you were my agent, I'd do exactly what you say.'

'Oh, are you a writer?' asked Laura.

Gerald was horrified. 'God no! The boot's on the other foot! I'm a publisher.'

'Oh.' Laura was spared having to wonder why the thought of being a writer was so ghastly, or to think of a proper reaction by the arrival of the starters.

'Yes and he needs you, Laura dear.' Not even the arrival of a miniature sculpture made from shellfish, seaweed and something bright red put Eleanora off her stride.

Gerald and Laura exchanged appalled glances. 'I don't think—' they began, more or less in unison.

'Yes you do, you just don't know it yet.' Having checked that Gerald's soup and Laura's tian of baby vegetables had arrived, she picked up a mussel. 'Laura has always wanted to be an editor.'

'How do—'

'I met that Grant? Lovely boy. He told me.' She put down her fork. 'I am a bit of a fag hag, I must admit. But I never know if it's because I'm stylish or wear too much make-up!' Eleanora was off on one of her tangents again.

Neither Gerald nor Laura felt able to help her here, so kept silent. 'Anyway,' Eleanora went on, 'that's neither here nor there. I'm determined to put you two together.'

The two in question exchanged glances, aware they lacked the moral fibre to withstand Eleanora once her heart was sent on something. 'I don't think—'

'I don't want . . . The thing is,' Gerald went on more decisively, 'I can't afford to pay a full-time editor and I must have someone in Ireland.'

'And I need full-time work and I don't live in Ireland.' Laura borrowed determination from Gerald with gratitude.

This time the glances they exchanged were almost triumphant.

Eleanora was having none of it. 'Goodness me, how negative you both are! These are tiny details! You're made for one another!'

When the waiter offered to refill her wine glass, Laura accepted gratefully.

Chapter Twenty-Two

Eleanora didn't give up. She told them both how good Laura would be. 'Think about that writing course! You got through those manuscripts, knew what was wrong, how to put it right. You were brilliant. She was, Gerald, Dermot said so.' She sipped her wine. 'I even took on one of the poor dears, though in this market . . .'

'Are you talking about "The" Dermot? Dermot Flynn?' Gerald cut through what could have become a long lecture on 'the State of Publishing Today'. He turned to Laura. 'Did you work with him, then?'

'Yes.' She couldn't think of much else to say on the subject. It was just as well she didn't want the job, she was doing very badly in the interview. Of course, had the job been in England, she would have been much more enthusiastic.

'And her organisational skills are second to none. The festival was fantastic! All down to Laura.'

'And Fenella, and Sarah and Rupert and countless others,' Laura said.

'You got the star to appear.'

'What star?' asked Gerald politely.

'Dermot, of course. She went to Ireland and brought him back, kicking and screaming. Didn't you read about it in the trade press? Quite an amusing little article.'

This was news to Laura and not particularly welcome, but if Gerald hadn't read about it, others might not either. He was now really interested. 'Is he out of contract? He must be, surely, he hasn't produced anything new for ages.'

Eleanora laughed. 'Don't even think about it. Way out of your league. Very, very expensive.'

'But he'd turn my little Irish publishing house into a giant.'

Eleanora shook her head. 'Takes more than one, darling, you know that as well I as I do. You're the publisher, damn it. Talking of Dermot . . .' She turned to Laura, 'He's been calling me, saying you won't return his calls. Do for heaven's sake ring him, there's a dear, he's driving me mad.'

Laura nodded as if in agreement, but although she knew full well that Dermot had been trying to get hold of her there was no way she'd ever return his calls. She had nothing to say to him.

Eleanora glanced round the room again. 'Oh, sorry. Just seen an old friend. Back in a min.,' she said and she was off.

'I knew it was a long shot but I thought I'd try.' Gerald narrowed his eyes. 'Hey, if he's calling you, I don't suppose you could persuade Dermot—'

Laura shook her head sadly. 'No! I assure you I have no influence over him.'

'Then how did you get him to appear at the festival?' Gerald persisted. 'He's famously difficult to budge out of his "little grey home in the West".'

'That was just a one-off,' Laura explained. It was agony for her to talk about him. If she kept it general she could just about cope. 'Just for the festival. And anyway, it's one thing getting someone to pitch up at a literary festival and quite another to persuade them to join a publisher that's far too small for them.' She looked around. 'Where is Eleanora? I can't believe she's really seen an old friend.'

Gerald also turned round. 'She has. She's over there. She seems to know half the room. I think this is where she always has lunch so she's bound to get to know everyone even if she didn't before they came. So tell me really, how did you get Dermot Flynn out of Ireland to come to this festival?'

Laura now realised she might be asked this question again and again; she'd better think of an answer fit to print, or at least say out loud. She smiled to give an impression it was down to serendipity and therefore not really anything to do with her efforts. 'Well, let's just say alcohol was involved.' They needn't know it was on her part more than Dermot's. 'And I didn't bring him between my jaws, like a Labrador, and drop him at Eleanora's feet. She just makes it sound like that.'

He laughed. 'It sounds impressive even if you didn't.' Laura decided he was rather sweet as he leant forward, sounding really interested. 'So, have you really always wanted to be an editor?'

This was one question she could happily answer, with genuine enthusiasm. 'Oh yes.' She sat up straighter. 'That's true. I really have no desire to write anything myself, but I would really enjoy polishing someone else's work so that it really shines. When I worked at the bookshop and used to read as much of the stock as I possibly could, I came across books – self-published ones mainly – that obviously hadn't had much editing. It really showed me how important editing is. I'd think: this bit would be so much better here, or the writer needed to introduce this character or that much earlier. And then, when I was doing it for the writing course, well I loved it. I see editing as like being a master jeweller: you take a wonderful but uncut stone and polish and work on it until it really shines. The original stone is still the main thing, but now everyone can see its beauty.'

Gerald seemed apologetic. 'To think I dismissed you because you didn't live in Ireland! You're just what I need.'

'And to think I dismissed you, just because you did! Although I think to begin with the thought of moving to another country seemed like a big thing, but now – well, I might as well live in Ireland as anywhere else.' A horrible thought made Laura bite her lip anxiously. 'You don't just want me because I know Dermot, do you? If I joined you, would you constantly be badgering me to get Dermot to sign up?'

This time he laughed. 'Indeed no. I was just trying it on with Eleanora. I know my place. But would you really consider it?' He ran through what would roughly be involved: two to three new authors a year, editing, potential to grow. Laura grew more and more excited as he talked. She couldn't help herself. It did sound pretty much like her dream job. Before long Laura *really* wanted to work for Gerald, even if it was in Ireland. After all, Ireland was quite a big place and Dermot would probably spend all his time in the States or somewhere now. But even if he didn't, they could both live there and never meet up. It would be fine. And somehow despite everything she still felt a soft spot for the country she'd lost her virginity in. 'But your office is in Dublin, isn't it?' she asked.

He acknowledged that it was.

'And that's a really expensive place to live?'

He nodded. 'Yes, but you don't have to live in Dublin, as long as you could get there once a week or so. You'd need to meet the authors in the office occasionally.'

Laura considered her carbon footprint for a moment. In theory it would be possible to fly to Dublin once a week and still live in England, but she didn't really want to send half her life in an airport. No, she would take a chance and relocate.

It sounded almost perfect. There was only one thing that was concerning her now. 'But I'd still need full-time work, not just part-time.'

'I'm sure I could make it full-time. I'd need to check my finances but the more I think about it, the more I realise I've needed someone like you for a while. It's time I took on someone full-time.'

She felt flattered. She may have lost her dream man (if she'd ever had him in the first place) but it looked as if she might just be on her way to securing her dream job – or at least the distinct possibility of it. But would she be mad to take it? She had a bit of money: would it tide her over until the work picked up? Moving to Ireland didn't seem as daunting as it might have once done. She was a different person now. But it was still quite an upheaval.

Seeing Laura's doubts, Gerald put his hands on the table in a triumphant gesture. 'I've just had an idea! I don't know why I didn't think of it before. I own a couple of holiday cottages on the west coast—'

'Where on the west coast?' Laura's self-preservation antennae went on red alert. If he said Ballyfitzpatrick she'd say no, however wonderful the deal was.

'Ballymolloy. It's a really beautiful spot. You might not have seen it though. It's not very near where Dermot comes from.'

Suddenly it sounded perfect. She smiled broadly. 'I'd love the chance to see a bit more of Ireland!'

'Well, the thing is, the holiday cottage isn't quite ready for visitors yet. There's still a bit of work going on, decorating and suchlike. If you wouldn't mind being there while it's finished, I'd let you have it rent-free.'

She'd once heard that things that sounded too good to be true usually were. 'That's a very generous offer and it's very tempting, but wouldn't it lull me into a false sense of security? Living rent-free, I'll get to think I can manage on the money.' But she was used to living frugally: maybe she could make it work. It was such a great opportunity. And why not – if it didn't work out she could always come back to England, no lasting harm done.

Gerald was determined to reassure her. 'By the time the building and decorating is finished I'll probably have full-time work for you and I've got friends in the business who might use you too. Editors tend to be freelance in Ireland. It's a much smaller market than in England.'

By now Laura's enthusiasm was pushing aside her natural caution. 'And I could always get a job in a pub, to make a bit of extra.'

Gerald became solemn. 'I don't think I'd like to think of you working in a pub. Tell you what, I'll undertake to get you all the editorial work you need, be it from me or other publishers. Although you might have to do a bit of copy-editing, too – you can handle that.'

'I'd need to go on a course for copy-editing, wouldn't I?'

He nodded. 'Possibly, but you could do it by mail order.'

She laughed. 'Don't you mean by correspondence?'

'As near the same thing as makes no difference.'

Her moment of levity vanished. 'I've just thought of something. If I've been living in your holiday cottage say for . . .'

'Three months.'

'And if I've made any friends, I won't want to uproot myself again. Is there likely to be anywhere to live in Bally— what you said? Or is it just a holiday place?'

'Oh no. It's also full of commuters. Lots of young families live there. It's a great place. It has a real buzz to it.'

'It sounds brilliant!'

'So you'll come?' Gerald seemed eager.

'Well, what's to stop me? And if there's a house thrown in – well.' She smiled reflectively. 'This morning I was about to be jobless and homeless and now both seem to be sorted out, in the best way possible.'

'Oh, good girl,' said Eleanora who Laura now suspected

334

might have been listening to a good bit of the conversation. 'You're sounding really positive now. Shall we have a bottle of champagne to celebrate? Waiter!'

'I hope it's not all too good to be true,' said Laura to Monica on the phone three weeks later. She'd already thrashed out all the pros and cons with Fenella and Rupert and there seemed to be more of the former than the latter. This was the first time she'd had a chance to run it all past Monica, who'd been on tour. 'The thing is, while I'm living rent-free I can decide if I like it over there, and if I don't, well, I can find something back in England. Now I've done that copy-editing course Eleanora arranged for me, I could get work here, possibly.'

'You have been busy since I've been away.' Monica was impressed. 'When did you do that?'

'Last week. It was only for two days, although they were quite intensive. I feel I've learnt a useful skill. I stayed with Eleanora and I'm surprised I've got any liver left, frankly, the amount we drank. I'd totter in through the door, she'd give me a huge whisky, then I'd fall asleep until suppertime. Then we'd have wine.'

Monica laughed. 'Well, I'm definitely coming with you to check it all out. Seamus is on tour – he's so much more confident these days since that reading. Anyway, if you're going to live in some godforsaken island, bloody miles away, I want to make sure it's not just some hole in the hedge.'

'Mon, this is Ireland we're talking about! You love Ireland!'

Monica's anxiety subsided. 'I know I do, but I'm going to miss you.'

'And I'm going to miss you! And everyone! It is all quite scary for someone like me.'

Now Laura was revealing her nerves Monica felt she could afford to be reassuring. 'Oh, you'll be fine!'

'I know I will when I get there it's just the going part.'
She paused, sounding a little plaintive. 'You can come
and stay as often as you like.'

'And I will! And we'll drive over there together. But
we must have a farewell party before you go.' She paused.
'Have you heard from Dermot?'

Somehow she didn't want to tell Monica about the
unanswered calls.

'Of course I haven't. Why would I? I don't even want
to hear from him!'

'Sweetie, this is me, Monica, you're talking to. You
don't have to pretend.'

'I'm not pretending anything! I don't want to speak to
him. I will admit to you that I'm in love with him, but
he's not in love with me, he never was. Everything we
did was just a wonderful, passing, temporary thing.
Speaking to him would only make it worse. I've just got
to get over it, and I'll do that better if I don't have any
contact with him.'

She'd had a hard time convincing Eleanora that she
wasn't to divulge her address or land line or her new
mobile number – she'd changed it just in case – or
anything to Dermot, especially as he'd already been
trying to reach Laura through her. But she had eventually managed it by confiding in her. Eleanora had
obviously led an exciting romantic life and the scene in
the shop with Bridget was somewhat familiar to her.
After that she said, 'Fine. I absolutely understand and I
won't say a word.'

And Fen was on board too, although she just thought
it was because Laura didn't want to get roped into any
more slave labour as far as Dermot was concerned.

Monica was silent for a bit. 'OK. I do see your point.
Now, what shall we do for a farewell party?'

'Well, I would really like to do something for Fenella
and Rupert. I thought about a picnic. We can have it in

the grounds so we're not too far from cover if the weather lets us down. They've got a lovely patch of meadow by a stream. It would be perfect.'

'Oh, I'll help you and Grant will probably, too. There's a shop near me that does brilliant pork pies.'

'And I thought I'd order some sausage rolls and bits and pieces from Sarah's Catering Ladies – the ones that did the food for the festival dinner party. Then we just need some bread, a bit of salad and some strawberries or something.'

'And champagne. I can't wait.'

The weather didn't let them down. A small gathering made their way down from the house carrying rugs, cool bags, chairs, cushions and bottles. Rupert insisted on bringing a mini barbecue down to the water's edge and he and Hugo cooked lamb chops, sausages and steaks. Despite it also being a thank you to Fen and Rupert, they'd insisted on organising most of it themselves. Henry, Laura's old boss from the bookshop, and Eleanora were the only ones allowed steamer chairs, whence they presided over the proceedings and gossiped about the book world, enjoying themselves hugely.

Fenella, Monica, Grant and Laura became a little nostalgic towards the end as they talked about the festival and how much fun they'd had.

'Of course, we've forgotten how much hard work it was,' said Sarah, who was less emotional, 'but I think you should definitely do it again next year, Fen.'

'Only if Laura agrees to come and run it,' insisted Fenella, dipping a strawberry in a bowl of cream and eating it.

'Oh I will!' Laura said, this time with genuine enthusiasm. 'After all, we've learnt so much from doing it this time, it would be nice to use the experience.'

'So what would you do differently?' asked Grant.

Laura lay back and closed her eyes for a few minutes. 'I can't think of anything really.'

'It would be better if the star act hadn't been so elusive,' said Monica, 'but in a way that added to the fun.'

'I thought we weren't supposed to mention the D word,' said Grant.

'No one did, until just now,' said Monica, pushing Grant's elbow and causing him to spill his mug of tea.

'It's all right,' said Laura. 'He is the elephant in the room, after all.'

'Jaysus,' said Monica, putting on her best brogue, 'I've heard you call him a lot of things, but never an elephant before.'

It was a wonderful afternoon and Laura felt sad when it was time to leave, but she was soon off on her own adventure and everyone had promised to keep in touch.

Two weeks after the picnic, Laura and Monica set off from Somerby to Ireland. They were going to travel to Fishguard on the daytime ferry, spend a night in a bed and breakfast on their arrival, and then set off again in the morning. They planned to reach Ballymolloy in the afternoon.

'I'm so glad you're coming with me,' said Laura as they turned out of the drive into the road. They were in Monica's VW Beetle again, Laura having sold her car. She felt it was a sign that she was committed to making her new life in Ireland work and she wouldn't really need one over there. She went on, 'Now it's actually happening, I'm really nervous.' She paused. 'I haven't lived in many places in my life.'

'It's a big step for anyone,' agreed Monica.

'I know! I mean, it's more like emigrating than moving.'

'What do you parents think about it all?' asked Monica after a suitable pause.

'Full of their usual lack of enthusiasm for yet another

of my madcap schemes,' Laura said dryly. 'I do feel a bit guilty about them actually. I meant to go over and visit them but there just wasn't time, what with the course and everything. And Fen and Rupert needed a bit of help with a wedding and after all they've done for me, it seemed the least I could do. I'll come back and see them when I'm settled in and can reassure them a bit. But this suited Gerald best. He's got lots of work waiting for me, apparently.'

'Your parents should be thrilled for you,' said Monica indignantly. 'It's your ideal job.'

'I know. But they don't do "thrilled". And they worry about it being part-time, and freelance, and in another country. All that stuff. It's only natural.' Although she found her parents intensely negative and irritating, Laura was aware a lot of it was caused by genuine concern, and she didn't want others to think badly of them.

'Well, I'm thrilled even if I will miss you.'

'We haven't known each other long, have we? And yet I feel we've been best friends all our lives. I'm going to miss you terribly.'

'It's because we were girls on the razz in Ireland all those months ago. It bonded us. And now we're going to be on the razz in Ireland again!'

Laura laughed gently. 'I wonder whether, if I knew then what I know now, I'd have "razzed" quite so much.' But only a moment's thought told her that despite everything she regretted nothing.

Dermot seemed to fill her every waking thought, even when she was concentrating on something quite different, and knowing that she might never see him again was intensely painful. But less painful, she decided, than seeing him while knowing he would never be hers. And she wouldn't turn the clock back: the pain she was now going through regarding Dermot was worth it. She truly believed she was happier to have known Dermot and be left with possibly a lifetime of heartbreak, than to be living a more contented life without the memories of that mad, ecstatic time.

'It was great,' said Monica, also pensive. 'For both of us. I'm just sorry it hasn't—'

'It's OK. It wasn't destined to "work out".' She chuckled. 'Can you really see me married to a great literary lion like Dermot? Nor can I!'

Monica said something with her head turned away which sounded a bit like, 'I can, actually.'

Laura ignored this.

'You know,' said Monica, sounding tired and not just because they'd been travelling for what felt like hours. 'I always thought those jokes about Irishmen saying, "You can't get there from here" were just jokes! But they're horribly real!'

'We're here now, thanks to Gerald. Our call to him got us back on the right road. It's just a matter of finding the house, which shouldn't be too difficult.'

'I hope to God this house of yours has the electrics done, or I'm checking in to the nearest hotel. And taking you with me.'

The house definitely had had its electrics done, as all the lights were on when they finally found it and pulled up outside. The door opened and Gerald stood there to welcome them.

'Hello! How was your journey? I wanted to be here when you arrived, to make sure everything was all right. Besides, Cara – that's my wife – insisted. Said it was only fair.'

Warmed by his concern, Laura kissed his cheek and introduced Monica. 'She came with me—'

'Just to see she wasn't living in a sheep pen or something,' Monica finished for her with a smile.

'It's not that bad although there are some floors still up and the kitchen's not finished yet,' said Gerald.

'Come in while I bring your bags. When you're a bit settled, we'll go out for dinner.'

'Well,' said Monica some hours later, when they were back in the house, 'I think you've fallen on your feet here. And Gerald is sweet! Imagine! Coming all the way from Dublin when he could have just left the key with a neighbour and let you sort yourself out!'

'It was kind.' Laura flicked the switch on the kettle. The kitchen may not have been finished, but it was going to be very well equipped eventually. 'He has another cottage here he wanted to check out, so he didn't come all the way from Dublin just to welcome me.' Still, Laura had been very touched.

'And don't forget he's arranged a little drinks party on Sunday so you can meet some of the neighbours.'

'That certainly is kind. Do you want tea? Or hot chocolate? I'm not sure I want anything now I've boiled the kettle. I think I'll just fall into bed.'

'Mm, me too. It's been a long day. Fun though.'

'Yes,' said Laura. 'A bit of a big day, but definitely fun.'

It was difficult saying goodbye to Monica early on Monday morning – she was flying off to visit Seamus, on tour in Germany – but not as hard as it might have been had Gerald not been so thoughtful. She stood on the doorstep, sensing a hint of autumn in the air, waving her friend off in the taxi. She couldn't help remembering another trip to the airport in a taxi, and she fought back her melancholy with an effort.

But Gerald had made things as easy as possible. Apart from greeting her and Monica, and arranging a party so she could meet her neighbours (which Monica had agreed had been a 'gas'), he had also left her with quite a lot of work. It was this pile of Jiffy bags, lurking in a corner, that stopped Laura slumping into a heap; it was her new job, she had to get on with it. And she wanted to – she felt ready for the challenge. As soon as she'd waved Monica off, she went to the room she and Gerald had designated her study, and had a look at the pile.

Gerald had admitted that he'd been neglecting his slush pile, waiting for her to come. Her first job was to go through everything, decide if there was any merit in any of it, and write a report on anything she liked. Although she'd spent enough time with Eleanora to know that slush piles rarely threw up anything interesting, she couldn't help a slight feeling of excitement as she picked up the first parcel. She had found her scissors and was attacking the staples that held it together when there was a ring at the back door, swiftly followed by a cheery 'Halloo!'

Her heart soared and descended in a sickening way as she hoped, and then stopped hoping, that it was Dermot. She'd told everyone not to tell him where she was after all. She got up from behind the table to meet the first of the builders.

The builders were, they told her, 'snagging'. There were two of them. They were in their thirties and brothers, and were there to go through the long list of little things that hadn't gone right the first time round. There was a radiator to move so a door would close properly, there were skirtings that didn't fit, taps that dripped and generally things that weren't right.

'That Gerald,' said the older brother. 'Stickler for detail.'

'Gerald's fine. It's his wife who's the real obsessive.'

'Quite right too,' said the younger one. 'If only they'd got us in in the first place, they wouldn't have this long snagging list. The first builder went off abroad before the job was finished,' he explained. 'Which is why your man got us in.'

Laura was just about well versed enough in the vernacular to realise that this was a general term, and that the building brothers didn't think that she and Gerald were connected in any way except as employer and employee, landlord and tenant.

'So how long will it take you to get through the snagging list?' she asked.

The brothers exchanged glances and then took on the slightly anxious look that builders will when asked how long anything will take. 'Hard to say,' said one of them. 'We've got the decorating to do when we've done the carpentry and plumbing. Could take a while.'

Laura smiled. 'Well, that's fine with me. As long as you're here, I'm here rent-free. So take your time!'

Another glance was exchanged and then the older one said, 'It's not often you hear that in the building game.'

'Well, obviously,' Laura went on, feeling guilty about Gerald, who'd been so kind to her, 'don't take too much advantage . . .'

'We'd call that "extracting the Michael",' said the younger brother. 'And don't worry, we won't. We'll try not to disturb you too much. Now, would you like a cup of tea? I'll bring it in for you if you've work to do.'

Later Laura emailed various friends with a description of these unusual builders and instantly Fenella came back with one asking if the builders would travel, but then said she was only jealous.

Laura got through the slush pile quite quickly. Lots of it was so far off publishable standard she knew a simple rejection slip would deal with them. Others were better, and on these she wrote a report, but she knew they too would be rejected. In fact there was nothing that sang to her and told her it was the book the world needed next. Gerald's last words to her with regard to the slush pile had been, 'Remember we're looking for an excuse to turn a book down. Taking one on means a lot of work and possibly no return.'

Laura had refrained from asking him why he was a

publisher if that was his attitude, because she did understand. Her experience with the writing course had taught her a lot. Manuscripts could be promising, good even, but still a long way from being something the public would want to read. But Laura's bookshop experience, however, told her that lots of the books that did get through this process were still not, in her opinion, actually good.

Gerald had told her to ring him when she'd done the slush pile, so after a couple of days, she did.

'Laura! You're a wonder! I'll have to send Eleanora flowers to thank her for putting us together.' He paused. 'Are you doing anything on Thursday night? Cara and I were thinking of coming down. We can have a look at the house and I can pick up anything you might have to give me.'

'I don't think so, but I have to say, and it's all down to you, I have been invited out for meals several times already. People have been so kind.' She had been dreading feeling lonely at the end of her working day, far away from home and family, but she hadn't had a chance to, and as books had always been her friends, the odd night on her own had been welcome. But somehow, being in Ireland made putting Dermot out of her head harder than ever. She missed him dreadfully. How long did it take to get over a broken heart? At least she was busy, she had a social life and she was surviving.

'You're kind too,' said Gerald. 'And people are curious. They want to have a look at the new arrival in the area.'

After he had put the phone down, having arranged to come up to collect the manuscripts, insisting that she was going to be taken out to dinner by him and his wife, a sudden thought struck Laura. Did all the people who had been so kind to her know about her connection with Dermot? Had Gerald told them, or hinted at something? There had been that mention in the trade press but ordinary people didn't read that, did they? Or was that why they were all being so nice? Then she realised she was being neurotic. No one had mentioned his name to her. Just because he was on her mind every minute of every day, it didn't mean other people were similarly afflicted.

Although she almost craved time alone, she resolutely accepted all invitations. Later on she could decide whom she really wanted to spend time with and whom she didn't, but she was keen not to get a reputation for being unfriendly. Her heart sank a bit when she was asked to join a book group, though. She'd enjoyed running the book group attached to the bookshop, but this might have been because she was usually the one who got to choose the books.

'Oh well,' she said now to Shona, who seemed to be the social engine of the community, 'I'd love to come another time but I'm not sure I'd have time to read the book.'

'Oh God, we don't worry too much about that! At least, I don't. Just come for the crack and the cake and the wine.' She paused. 'Crack is conversation, you know, I wouldn't want you to think . . .'

Laura laughed. 'It's all right, I know that.'

'Then come along. You can keep me company if you haven't read the book. We can ask pertinent questions – or at least you can.' Shona paused again. 'You can tell I'm trying to convince you that we do actually talk about the book, at least for part of the time.'

'I wouldn't like to come if I haven't read it, but what is it?' She didn't like to say she'd read most of the books groups tended to choose. 'I used to work in a bookshop so I've read a lot.'

'That's why we want you to come!' said Shona cheerfully. 'And the book is *The Willows* by—'

Laura's heart had started to race before Shona had

345

got halfway through the title of Dermot's second book. 'I – I have read that,' she managed after a few dry-mouthed seconds. Typical. She was reminded of him at every turn.

'Oh well then, that's grand. You must come. You probably understand all that highbrow stuff. It was Jocasta's choice. She likes all that literary fiction. I prefer a good raunchy read myself.'

Laura didn't know if she wanted to laugh or cry. To hear Dermot's great work described as 'highbrow stuff' was partly satisfying: he might have caused her much heartache, but she did think it was one of the greatest books of the current time and she wanted to defend it. But could she bear to sit and listen while people declared they 'couldn't get through it' and 'felt it was a bit obscure'? She'd never chosen his work for her own book group, it was too special and personal to her. And that had been before she'd met the man and fallen in love with him.

'What night is it you meet?'

'It's the second Wednesday of the month. It's usually the first one, but we missed it. Someone had a fortieth.'

'That's tomorrow, isn't it?'

'It is so. Can you come? You can easily walk from your house, but I'll pick you up so you don't feel lonely when you arrive. I'll be with you just before eight.'

'Did I agree to that?' Laura asked her half-built kitchen a few seconds later. 'No, I didn't think I had.'

But she was glad enough to be going out by the time she had to get ready. Although she loved the book she was now working on, getting it into some sort of order was like herding cats. The main character was wonderful but she kept going off to other places in her head and it was hard to decide if these flights of fancy should just be severely cut or if they valuable insight into the protagonist's mind.

Shona was on her doorstep at a quarter to eight. 'Do you mind if I come in and have a look around? I've been dying of curiosity about what your man is doing to these houses.'

Glad she'd thrown all her dirty washing into the bin when she'd got ready, Laura laughed, and obliged.

Chapter Twenty-Three

'These women scare the bejaysus out of me,' said Shona as they walked up the drive to one of the big houses that Laura looked out at every day. They had views of the sea and lots of them were converted to holiday flats. This one was still a big family house. 'They all have degrees, or are going back into education or something.'

'Now you tell me! You made out they were a friendly lot who just drank wine and ate cake.'

'I know. I lied. I thought if I brought you it would give me a bit of credibility, having a clever friend.'

Laura had to laugh.

'Honestly,' Shona went on. 'They only tolerate me because the book group was my idea.'

'I'm sure that's not true.' Laura sounded convincing but she was wondering if she'd made a horrible mistake coming. Her own academic qualifications were fine but she'd always tried to keep her book group open and accessible to everyone. She hated it when people scored academic points over the people who were there because they loved reading.

A slim, elegant woman in a white linen dress opened the door. She had cork wedges on her perfectly groomed feet and her tan, be it fake or genuine, revealed not a single streak. Her hair was blonde, short and beautifully cut. The highlights could have been put in strand by strand. All this perfection was set off by the hall behind her: pale, hardwood floors, inset lighting and one stunning piece of glass at the end of the hall.

'Hello, so glad you could come.' A dazzling smile, with teeth to match, was directed at Laura. Its brilliance dimmed slightly as it moved to Shona. 'Shona, I do hope you've read the book this time. You know we made a rule, three non-reads and you're out. You're on your fifth.'

Shona tossed her head defiantly. 'Who cares? Anyway, it's you lot's fault for choosing such boring bloody books. Reading is a leisure activity not designed to improve the brain.'

'I'm Jocasta,' said the woman, ignoring this denial of a sine qua non as she would have undoubtedly phrased it, and putting a perfectly manicured hand into Laura's.

'I'm Laura. It's very kind of you to let me come.' The hand was cool and Laura was aware that hers was hot and anxious-feeling.

'Well, we are a closed group really, but when Shona explained that you're new to the area—'

'And I said I'd never make cake again,' put in Laura's champion.

'We felt it would be churlish of us not to let you come,' finished Jocasta. Then she studied the woman she'd been so generous to. 'Laura? That's a pretty name.'

'Thank you.'

'I long for something more ordinary – Jocasta is from the classical Greek.'

'So is mine, Laura that is. It means laurels.'

Jocasta laughed. 'Oh. I don't think mine means anything. But do come in. Most of the gang are here.'

They were ushered into more perfect space: cream walls, cream sofas, a cream rug on the blond floor, a massive abstract painting. Surprised, Laura noticed some wooden frames with pictures of children in them on a side table. Were they hers? If so, how did she keep all this so pristine? Maybe they never came in here.

Laura was introduced to the half-dozen women already there. They were all well dressed and probably went to the same hairdresser as Jocasta as their hair had that sleek every-three-weeks look. Unlike the one that Laura had run, this book group didn't seem to have the young mums who ran out of the house with baked beans on their clothes, desperate for a bit of adult conversation and having to fight to get it.

She sat down on a sofa next to one of the other women. Some dog hairs on her black trousers, brought with her from Somerby, made her suddenly yearn for it, as if it were home. She wasn't exactly untidy herself, but she felt out of place, like a pigeon in a flock of parakeets, in this elegant, magazine-like setting. She needed a bit of mess to make her truly comfortable.

There was a low glass coffee table in front of them and on it was a pile of books.

'I'm doing some decluttering,' explained Jocasta, handing round glasses with an inch of chilled white wine in the bottom. 'So do help yourselves to anything you'd like. Otherwise they'll go to the charity shop.'

Laura recognised most of the books. Not one of them would she describe as a 'good read'; all of them were a 'virtuous read': the kind of books you could boast of having read at dinner parties.

'I can never get rid of books I've enjoyed,' said one woman, picking over the selection. 'But maybe you didn't enjoy these?'

Jocasta was now handing round olives the size of bantam eggs. 'Of course I keep the serious literature, but this is just light reading.'

Laura heard Shona snort into her wine.

'I could sell the books, of course,' Jocasta was saying now as she swayed her perfect figure on to another sofa that was not only cream, but suede and pristine. 'I spend a fortune on them. I love to support writers.'

'Don't sell them to a second-hand bookshop then,' said Laura, wishing she hadn't opened her mouth before she even started. 'The authors don't make a penny and it's their intellectual property.'

'Oh.' Everyone was staring at her. She really did not want to get into a discussion about how authors were paid. 'So if you've excess books,' Laura said, 'you should give them to a hospital or something.'

'Or a charity shop?' asked one woman.

'Or that.' Laura had a feeling this wasn't the perfect solution for writers either, but she couldn't remember all the arguments that had been dinned into her by an author once when she worked at the bookshop.

There was some low-voiced chat and the books were picked over and some claimed. Eventually Jocasta took charge. 'Can I call us to order? Has everyone got a drink?'

'I'd quite like a top-up,' said Shona boldly.

'And me,' said a couple of the other women. 'We all walked here, so we don't have to worry about drinking and driving.'

You could tell, thought Laura, that Jocasta only poured very small amounts into the glasses not because she was mean, but because that was how you should pour wine.

'OK, we've all got drinks,' Jocasta expressed her disapproval very subtly. 'Who would like to go first?' She looked round the room. 'Well, shall I? Because I chose the book?'

'Why not?' said one of the women.

Laura began to feel even more tense. Supposing they didn't like Dermot's book? It felt utterly personal to her, and she thought it would have done even if she hadn't met him – let alone all the other stuff that had gone on between them.

'OK, well, I chose it because I'd read an article about

351

the writer in the paper. And of course I read it to the end,' said Jocasta, 'because I'm one of those people who, if I start a book, have to finish it.'

'Did you not like it, then?' asked Shona. 'Because if you didn't, for once, I have to agree with you—'

'Shona?' Jocasta was disappointed more than annoyed. 'I shouldn't have to remind you. We wait until one person has finished speaking before we move on to the next.' Laura was reminded of Bill Edwards and smiled to herself.

'Sorry,' said Shona, feigning meekness.

Jocasta gave her an irritated look. She had a copy of the book in her hand and was looking at it, as if it could help her express herself. 'I thought this book was wonderfully lyrical. The characters were marvellous. The descriptions of the scenery were superb.'

Although Laura should have loved hearing Dermot's work praised like this there was something about Jocasta's enthusiasm that seemed a little forced. Jocasta looked at the woman on her left and said, 'Your turn, Fionnuala.'

Fionnula's opinions echoed Jocasta's fairly closely. She praised the writing, the characters, the scenery. It seemed to Laura that they had all missed the point; they were admiring the book from a distance, they weren't getting into it, living it and, alas, loving it. Was it their fault, or was it the book's? Laura yearned to bang the glass coffee table and demand, 'But did you like it?'

Maybe Shona was telepathic because while she didn't bang the table, she did ask the question.

'Oh of course! I loved it!' said Jocasta. 'After all it's one of Ireland's most important books – from recently, anyway.'

'Not that recent,' objected Shona. 'It seemed to me to be set in the Dark Ages, although I didn't finish it.'

'You never finish the books, Shona!' It was not only

Jocasta complaining now. 'You should have more intellectual rigour.'

'I'd rather have a life,' she said, unrepentant.

'Well,' said Jocasta, 'perhaps we can hear from Laura now? Any questions you'd like to ask? We find having someone with us who hasn't read the book can promote some interesting discussion – except Shona, of course, who's never read it!'

Shona laughed good-naturedly, immune to Jocasta's reprimands. 'I did read quite a lot of this one. I might even finish it now,' she said.

'So, Laura?'

Laura was overcome with a desire to rush out of that beautiful room and jump in the mud and then come back in and roll on the rug. Fortunately before the urge overwhelmed her completely, the 'Minute Waltz' tinkled out of someone's handbag, growing louder as the owner of the phone hunted around. While Fionnuala apologised and moved away from the group, Laura decided if she went to the loo, they'd have forgotten all about her by the time she came back.

She was directed to a downstairs cloakroom of such grandeur it made her wonder what the family bathroom or Jocasta's en suite would be like. She confirmed there were children in the house because there were gold imprints of two little sets of hands and feet, mounted and framed, decorating the walls.

As she washed her hands in the glass basin, inevitably splashing the glass tiles, she speculated that no non-organic product would ever pass Jocasta's children's lips and that Jocasta's bedside table would perfectly reflect those one read about in feminist literary magazines. There the celebrities only seemed to have fresh flowers, incense and a couple of literary novels, one of them in French, by their beds. Not for them the radio, the clock, the pile of half-read tomes, the face cream and the dusty bottle of water.

She patted her hands dry on the back of the towel, so as not to mar the perfection of the room, which in real terms was a downstairs loo, but in Jocasta's was another opportunity to reveal her perfect taste. Laura was ashamed to realise that had Jocasta raved about Dermot's work with a proper amount of passion, she wouldn't have been having these bitchy thoughts, she'd have been admiring her taste and her perfect minimalist style.

She went back into the room, hoping that Jocasta had forgotten about giving her time to ask questions about a book she knew almost by heart. Perhaps by now they'd be talking about childcare, builders and bonuses. Laura knew nothing about any of these subjects, but she didn't care about them either so she didn't need to be anxious. But they were still on the book and Shona was getting the third degree.

'What do you mean you don't understand why the father was so angry?' one of the women was demanding. 'It's an Oedipal thing. Oedipus made love to his mother and murdered his father! It's blindingly obvious!'

'You spotted that too?' Jocasta seemed delighted to find a fellow intellectual. 'I thought I was the only one. The author was drawing an exact parallel to the Oedipus myth!'

'But that's disgusting!' said Shona. 'I don't want to read books with things like that in them!'

'It's not in the book in actuality,' explained Jocasta kindly. 'It's symbolic! It's what's behind the author's thinking when he put that bit in.' Seeing Laura return to the room she said, 'I do think you should give this book a try if you have a moment. You might find what we've all had to say about it quite illuminating.' She paused. 'It's a bit of a meaty read so take it on holiday with you, when you've got a bit more time and can really concentrate.'

She meant well, Laura could see that, but she was cross with Jocasta and the others, not only for not enthusing about her favourite book, but for patronising Shona. 'Oh I have read it, years ago. And I must say I think it highly unlikely that Dermot – the writer, I mean – had even heard of Oedipus when he wrote it.'

'How can you possibly say that?' Jocasta exchanged glances with the woman who'd made the reference. They didn't want their insight questioned by Laura who was not only new to the group, but English to boot.

'Well, I can't say for definite, but he was in his early twenties when he wrote it, he hadn't been to university and came from quite an intellectual backwater. When you meet him—' She didn't know if she'd intended to reveal that she knew Dermot, to discommode Jocasta and her scary friends, or if it was an accident, but whatever, she was stuck with the result. Unless maybe she hadn't actually said that out loud? She crossed her fingers and prayed.

But she had said it out loud. Everyone started plying her with questions.

'You've met him? Do you actually know him? What's he like? He was so gorgeous as a young man, God, I'd have slept with him no matter how boring his books were.' The comments came flying at her and she took the opportunity to think up what to say when everyone fell silent, which eventually they did.

'I do know him, a bit. He attended a literary festival I helped to organise.' Talking about him made her miss him even more.

'He can't have done,' said Jocasta knowledgeably. 'He never goes out of Ireland. It's a well-known fact.'

'But he did,' said Laura.

Jocasta shook her head. 'I think you must have been mistaken. We know our Irish writers in this group and—

'Actually,' spoke up one of the women. 'There's been

a bit about him in the papers recently. One of them mentioned a festival. Didn't you see that one, Jocasta?'

Jocasta's eyelashes fluttered while she hunted for a reason why she hadn't been completely on top of all the Sunday papers.

'Jocasta! We usually rely on you to tell us all that's going on,' said one of the women who lived near enough to walk.

'It must have been the week when Rickie had a green fit,' Jocasta said, 'and wouldn't let us buy any Sunday papers. Trust him to make me miss out on such important news.'

'Not important, really,' said Shona. 'It's just celebrity gossip. You wouldn't mind missing out on that, would you?'

'This is literary gossip!' said Jocasta. 'It's different! It does matter!'

'It did matter to the literary festival,' said Laura, chuckling a little. 'And he did come and it caused quite a sensation in the literary world. I think he's still in America, talking about film rights.' She didn't know for sure. Eleanora had been rather vague.

'Well, I know you're wrong there,' went on Jocasta, on firmer territory now. 'There was a big feature some time ago when he said he'd never let his books be filmed. And he hasn't written anything new for years and years.' She paused. 'I looked him up on Wikipedia.'

'Not a terribly reliable source, if I may say so,' said one of the other women.

'Tell you what,' said Shona, possibly taking pity on Jocasta. 'I think it's time for a socking great bit of chocolate cake!'

Jocasta wasn't grateful. She broke into the general agreement with, 'Sorry, we don't do sugar and fat in lethal combinations in this house, although we know Shona's cake is to die for.' She smiled in a way that almost earned her a slap. 'But I have made some flapjacks with millet and just a little organic honey.'

'How do you know it's organic honey?' demanded Shona, who felt slighted in so many ways. 'Do they tell the bees not to go near flowers that have pesticides on them?'

'I don't know,' snapped Jocasta, getting up. 'I just buy it. OK!'

While she was gone the other women gathered round Laura. 'So what about the real Dermot Flynn, then? Is he anything like as wild as they all say he is?'

Laura realised it would be so much easier if she could say, 'Tell you what, girls, he was a ride!' Being unable to admit she'd slept with him – for all sorts of reasons – and tell them what a fantastic lover he'd been, she just said, 'Well, he has a great sense of humour.'

Laura didn't like being the centre of attention and cursed herself several times over for not keeping her mouth shut. And she went on being unable to keep it shut, too.

'The thing about Dermot's books,' she heard herself saying, 'is the passion. Never mind the symbolism, the beautiful writing, the prose, just think of the young man's journey. Do you want to go with him, or not? If you don't, toss the book aside and read something else.'

'I couldn't do that,' said Jocasta, who'd come back into the room with a tray of herbal teas and a cafetiere of coffee for those rash enough to ingest caffeine so near to bedtime. 'If I start a book I have to finish it. I feel it's my duty.'

'Me, I'm with Laura,' said Shona, happy to be able to associate herself with the one who knew Dermot Flynn personally. 'If I don't like a book I just read another one.'

No one else confessed to sharing this cavalier attitude to books and the subject moved on.

'So,' said Jocasta a bit later, 'do you think you could get Dermot to come and talk to us, as a group?'

'No,' Laura said bluntly. 'I'm not in touch with him any more and even if I were, that is the last thing I'd ask him to do.'

'But you could get in touch with him, via his publisher,' Jocasta persisted. 'And if you got him to go to England, you could surely get him to come a few miles up here.'

'No! He'd hate it!'

'How do you know? How well do you know him?'

She didn't really know he'd hate it. He might absolutely love being idolised by all these yummy mummies, but however much he'd love it, she wasn't going to track him down and invite him. 'Not all that well.'

'So! And he can't be that precious if you got him to attend a literary festival in England!'

There was just a hint in Jocasta's voice implying that if Laura, not a formidable opponent, had got Dermot to attend the festival, Dermot must be the sort of genial guy who'd go to a book-group meeting for the promise of a glass of wine and an organic canapé.

Laura was fairly used to this reaction by now. 'He had his own reasons for attending the festival. I can't tell you what they are' – well, she could have done but she wasn't going to – 'he's a law unto himself.'

'Still,' said Shona. 'You must be proud of yourself for doing that. It's still a great feather in your cap. And knowing him personally – it'll make you a great dinner-party favourite in these parts.'

Although it was sweet of Shona to credit her so, the thought of being a dinner-party favourite made her shiver. She got up. 'I think I'd better be going. No, you don't need to come with me, Shona, I know my way home and it's not dark or anything.'

Jocasta rose to her feet to show her out. 'I have to say, Laura, I think you're going to be a real asset to our book group. And not only that – I'm having a few friends round next week. Nothing formal, just a bite to eat and some good conversation. I'd be thrilled if you could join us.'

'When's that?'

'Next Friday?'

'Oh, that's a shame! I've arranged to go back to England to visit my parents for a long weekend. I didn't get a chance to say goodbye properly when I left, and they're anxious to know how I'm settling in.'

The thing about lying, she'd learnt, mostly from reading fiction, is to keep it as close to the truth as you possibly could. When she'd got home she went straight on to the Internet to look up flights. Then she telephoned her parents.

Laura wished she felt more enthusiastic about this visit. She loved her parents, of course she did, but she was aware she seemed like a cuckoo to them, a small, undemanding cuckoo, but still not really one of their own.

They had arranged to meet her at the airport and were there when she came through the gate, looking out for her in their matching his-and-her beige anoraks.

'Oh, it's so kind of you to come and get me!' she said, feeling a rush of love and hugging first her mother, and then her father, who patted her awkwardly.

'There's no sense in wasting money on taxis,' he said, taking her bag. 'Have you only got this?'

'Mm. I didn't want to check anything in. To save time.'

'Well, come along,' said her mother. 'We don't want our parking ticket to run out.'

As she went with her parents to the car park she realised how deflated they always made her feel. If anyone else had collected her, Monica, or Grant, say, they'd have been plying her with questions about her new life, full of enthusiasm for her great adventure, or saying how much they missed her. But no, her mother was more concerned about overstaying her time in the car park.

Always she hoped that this time it would be different, and always it was the same. However, she was pleased to be seeing them again; it saved her having to talk about Dermot to people who were only interested in her because of her tenuous connection with him. Not that it had been tenuous, but at this remove, the whole Dermot thing felt like a dream, or as if it had happened to someone else and hurt just a little bit less.

'Oh, you've changed that flowerbed!' she said as they walked up the path to the house. 'Didn't it used to have roses in it?'

'Yes, but they kept catching your father's clothes as he went through to the garage, so I put lavender there instead.'

'How lovely! You must smell it as you brush past,' Laura said.

Her father turned to her as he put the front-door key in the lock. 'Can't say I've noticed.'

Laura followed her parents into the house, trying to fight the feeling of depression she always felt when she visited them.

'I think I must have grown!' she said brightly. 'Everything seems to be smaller!'

'I don't think so, dear. Everything's the same as it was. Once you've got the house how you like it, there seems no point in changing it.' She put the kettle on. 'Would you like tea? Or shall I open the bottle of wine I bought?'

A glance at the kitchen clock told her that at Somerby the wine would have been opened at least half an hour ago. She felt horribly disloyal. These were her parents, this was the home she'd grown up in, and she was comparing it unfavourably with what was virtually a stately home. She knew that children did sometimes change when they left home and went to university, but she hated herself for doing it. On the other hand, as she warmed the pot, making tea for her parents, she wondered, if she had changed, really, or if she just had never fitted in.

'So what have you been up to, Mum?' she said, finding knives and forks so she could set the table.

'Nothing much, dear. We lead quiet lives really. You know that.'

While she put three table mats on the kitchen table she waited for her mother to ask her what she'd been up to, in return. But she didn't. Laura fetched the cruet from the sideboard in silence. Surely her mother must be a bit curious about Laura's new life? Apparently not.

'Can you call your father? It's ready and there's a television programme I want to watch later. Have you got a television now?'

At last, some expression of interest! 'Um, yes. There is one in the house I'm staying in.' She waited for a question about the house. None came. 'And I can get English channels too, but I don't watch it much. I'm not in the habit of it. Besides, I've been really busy since I moved to Ireland.'

'I never miss an edition of *Midsomer Murders* if I can help it. Oh and I like that one with the two gardening women as well.'

'I'll go and get Dad,' said Laura.

Her father was a bit more interested in her life than her mother. 'So, are you going to manage on the money?'

'Oh yes, I think so. Of course being freelance isn't as secure as having a salary—' It was out before she could stop herself. Her father pounced on it.

'Then why did you take it on? Why did you want to go to Ireland anyway?' His jaw went from side to side as he chewed, adding emphasis to his disapproving tone.

Hoping (unrealistically she knew) that it was just that: her father didn't like the idea of her being so far away, she ploughed valiantly on: 'Jobs like that are quite hard to get into. In England you have to work your way up. After the literary festival, and I told you how successful that was—'

'But it didn't pay very well, did it?' persisted her father.

For some reason she didn't quite understand she hadn't told her parents about her bonus. 'I didn't do it for the money, I did it because I love working with books and writers.' Why couldn't her father ever just be happy that she was doing what she enjoyed? Why did he always have to bring money into it? It wasn't as if she ever asked them for a loan or anything. 'Anyway, I met this woman who put me in touch with my new job.' She felt too deflated to tell them about Gerald in detail.

'But why go off to Ireland?' insisted her father. 'There are plenty of jobs here.'

'But this is an opportunity to do what I've always wanted to do! Ever since I left university, I've wanted it. I'm a copy editor, and editor – a permanent one if that's the way the work goes.'

'In my day, sorry if that makes me sound like an old codger' – he didn't sound at all apologetic – 'we didn't do "what we'd always wanted". We did what would put food on the table and pay the mortgage.'

Laura sighed and put her hand on his where it lay on his rolled-up table napkin. 'I know, Dad, and I'm really grateful that you did all that so you could keep Mum and me, but I haven't got to keep anyone else except myself.'

'Forgive me for saying this, Laura,' he went on, removing his hand, 'but it strikes me that young people nowadays are all me, me, me.'

Defeated, Laura turned her attention to the shepherd's pie, which was delicious.

'I've got pineapple upside-down cake for pudding,' said her mother. 'I know that's your favourite.'

It had been her favourite when she was nine years old but she'd never felt able to tell her mother her tastes had changed.

After she and her mother had washed up, which didn't take long as her mother was a very tidy cook, they spent the evening watching television. There was a documentary on about world poverty and the arms trade. Tears she hadn't allowed herself to indulge in for a while slid silently down Laura's face. Everything came back to her in a rush. Dermot; her overwhelming love for him, not returned . . . She could hardly bear it.

'I'll just watch the news and then I'll make us all a cup of tea before bedtime,' said her father.

'Oh, we never opened that wine,' said her mother.

'Never mind. Tea's fine.'

No wonder I spent all my time reading, thought Laura when she was back in her old room.

All her old childhood favourites were there, marking the progress of her growing up. There were the pony books that she adored until she moved on to Georgette Heyer in her early teens. Then there was her D. H. Lawrence phase, Iris Murdoch, Edna O'Brien, and then Dermot's two slim volumes. She'd bought these second-hand and loved them. When she went to university she found she could study them and bought new copies. It was these copies that she had taken with when she left home. She sighed, wondering how her life would have turned out if she'd never read his books. She laughed forgivingly at her old self, and congratulated her new one. She'd come a long way!

Now, she burrowed in her bag for the book that

Veronica had signed for her at the festival. She'd been saving it for emergencies: a time when only a really good page-turning, romantic read would do. This definitely qualified as an emergency.

Chapter Twenty-Four

The Saturday morning routines were not altered because Laura was there. The three of them went shopping, and then went to a café for lunch. Here they each had a bowl of soup, a bread roll and a sandwich. Then Laura's father had steamed pudding with custard and her mother had a small portion of vanilla ice cream. Feeling terribly rebellious, Laura had a cappuccino.

'I never could get on with coffee,' said her mother, seeing Laura stir in some sugar. 'It gives me a headache.'

'It does make me a bit buzzy sometimes,' said Laura, 'but I thought it would make a change.'

'From what?' asked her mother, puzzled.

'I don't know really,' Laura said apologetically. 'Shall we get out the paper and start on the crossword?'

'Not till we're home,' said her father. 'I don't like the paper to get all creased.'

'Besides, it rude to read at the table,' said her mother.

Laura's flight was for Monday morning but she was seriously considering changing it to Sunday, to end the agony a bit sooner. But what reason could she possibly give?

On Sunday night she and her mother had just joined her father in the sitting room, having washed up the supper things, when there was a banging on the front door. Laura was calculating that there were over twelve hours until it was time for her to leave. She was really looking forward to the number being in single figures.

'Oh my goodness, who can that be, at this time of night?' said her mother.

'I'll go,' said Laura. 'I'm on my feet.'

'Keep the chain on,' ordered her father, getting up. 'I can't imagine who'd be knocking so loudly. If they were a neighbour, they'd just ring the bell.'

Laura, feeling she'd welcome in an army of Jehovah's Witnesses just to relieve the monotony, went into the hall, unlocked the door, leaving the chain on, as instructed, and opened it.

'Hello?' she said tentatively. 'Can I help you?'

'Is that Laura? Jesus-Kerrist-on-a-jet-ski! Am I glad to see you! I've been over half the world trying to track you down!'

Sure she was about to faint, Laura fiddled with the door chain but her sweating fingers skidded over the fitting.

'Who is it?' demanded her father, coming up behind her. 'Who are you letting into the house?'

'It's me, Dermot, you silly—'

Just then, Laura got the door open. Dermot was on the doorstep wearing his old leather jacket, a pair of filthy jeans and three days' worth of stubble.

Laura's father acted quickly and had the door shut again in seconds.

There was a roar from outside and then more banging.

'Dad, it's Dermot! He's – well, he's a friend of mine.'

'I demand to see Laura!' came Dermot's voice. 'Or I'll break the door down.'

'Better let him in, Dad. Think of the neighbours!' Laura hoped this old mantra would work as it always had before.

'Shall I call the police?' said Laura's mother, who had joined them.

'Good idea,' said her father. 'I think the man must be drunk.'

'I don't think so, Dad.'

'I've never dialled nine, nine, nine before,' said her mother. 'I'm not sure how it works.'

'You don't need to dial it!' insisted Laura, wrestling with her father for control of the door. 'He's not a burglar! He's someone I know!'

'He's not coming into my house!' said her father. 'Making all that noise.'

'Mum, you don't want the police round. The neighbours! What would they think? Or say?' Laura had been threatened with the wrath of the neighbours all her life. Why weren't her parents thinking about them now, when it would be quite useful?

'I'm not letting him in. He sounds quite mad to me,' said her father. 'And Irish!'

'That's racist!' said Laura, fighting harder now and getting her fingers on the door chain long enough to pull it back.

'I am Irish, and I am mad,' said Dermot unhelpfully, grinning at them and certainly looking the part. 'But I'm not drunk and I undertake not to break the furniture.'

A neighbouring front door was heard to open. Laura hissed at her mother, 'People will wonder what on earth's going on! Let him in!' As she said that, she got the door open and took hold of Dermot's sleeve. 'Get in, quickly!'

'Have you any fierce chihuahuas in there?' he asked, obviously relishing the situation.

'No!' Laura pulled him in. 'They're Dobermanns!' She shut the door and leant on it, panting for a few seconds, and then regarded her parents and Dermot, who were all looking at her. She swallowed. 'Mum, Dad, this is Dermot Flynn, the one who came to the literary festival I organised.'

Her parents stared at Dermot warily.

'Maybe we should go through to the sitting room? I'll put the kettle on,' Laura persisted, convinced that the

narrow hallway was not the best place to be in the circumstances.

'How do you do, Laura's mother.' He took her hand.
'Laura's father. I'm Dermot Flynn and I've been trying
to trace your daughter for some time.'

'They're Mr and Mrs Horsley,' said Laura, beginning
to see the funny side but trying to hide it with irritation.
'Now do go and sit down, everyone. I'll make tea.' Her
heart sang at the sight of him, even if she didn't want
him to see just how pleased she was to see him. He had
a lot of explaining to do.

'No!' her mother squeaked, suddenly aware she and
her husband would be left with this terrifying Irishman
if Laura made tea. 'I'll do it!'

'Now listen,' said her father, bracing up to Dermot and
seeming to Laura suddenly very old and frail. 'I don't
know—'

'I'm sure he'll explain in a minute,' said Laura,
suddenly protective of her parents to whom Dermot must
seem like a creature from another universe. 'If we all just
sit down where it's comfortable, we can talk.'

Feeling like a corgi nipping at the heels of beasts much
larger, she chivvied her father and Dermot into the sitting
room and her mother into the kitchen. She virtually pushed
the men into chairs and switched off the television.

'Well, Dermot,' she said into the silence, frightened
that she might laugh, 'fancy meeting you here.'

'To be honest, Laura, and hoping I'm not being rude –'
he glanced at Laura's father, who was looking very wary
and ready to spring up at any moment, should Dermot
look like doing anything unexpected ' – but I'd have
preferred to meet you somewhere else.'

'Oh?' She would too, obviously, but couldn't say so.

'Yes, I've had the devil of a job finding you.'

'So, how do you two know each other?' her father
asked.

'The literary festival. I did tell you,' said Laura.

'I was one of the writers,' said Dermot.

'The star writer,' said Laura, to punish him a little.

'I've never heard of you!'

'You never read novels, Dad. But he was one of my set texts at university.'

'Was I?' Dermot was very amused. 'Did you ever tell me that?'

Laura winced. That sounded so intimate – it made Dermot seem more than just a writer she'd met. She was always meeting writers when she worked at the bookshop. With luck her parents wouldn't notice.

'So why were you banging on our door in the middle of the night?' demanded her father.

'It's only half past nine,' put in Laura. Although she wanted to kill Dermot for about a hundred good reasons, she was really very pleased to see him. He had at least put a stop to the boredom.

'I was looking for Laura. I've been looking for ages – ever since I came back from America – but no one would tell me where she was. And she wouldn't return any of my calls.' He looked pointedly at her. She shrugged.

'Why do you want her?' asked her father.

'Who told you I was here?' asked Laura, suddenly intensely curious. 'No one I know knows I'm here.'

A glance at her father, and Dermot decided to ignore his question. 'I eventually tracked down Grant.'

'Grant?' said her father. 'That chap you used to work with?'

Dermot nodded. 'It's a long and complicated story. Eleanora – my agent – wouldn't tell me where she was.'

'I told her not to,' said Laura.

'Nor would Fenella and Rupert.'

'Who are all these people?' demanded her father, as if trying to pick up the plot of a long-running soap opera.

'Friends of mine,' said Laura. 'Oh good, here's Mum with the tea.'

Mrs Horsley had got out the best cups and saucers. Pouring and distributing tea took an inexorably long time, but it did mean her mother had accepted Dermot as a guest, thought Laura, which was a start. She'd have to hope her father thawed soon or they'd be in for a very tricky evening.

'So how did you get on to Grant?' Laura was touched by her friends' efforts to obey her entreaties not to give away her whereabouts, even if a part of her had secretly wished one of them might have disobeyed her.

'Via Monica's website,' said Dermot. 'She said she was sworn to secrecy but she didn't think that Grant was, and so gave me his email address.'

'Oh.' Good for Monica! She knew when a woman was lying to herself and her friends.

'Sadly for me, his email was down for a couple of days. He said he had been told not to tell me anything but that he thought I had a right to know. So he gave me your address.'

'It's all very complicated,' said Mrs Horsley, nibbling a ginger nut to aid her concentration.

'So I went there,' Dermot continued.

'Where?' asked Mr Horsley.

'To where Laura lives in Ireland.'

Some hint of what might have happened, given what had gone on earlier, occurred to Laura. She blushed retrospectively. But joy at the enormous trouble Dermot had gone to find her was starting to warm her heart like sun on the first spring day.

'I was banging on your door,' he went on, 'although to be honest, I could tell there was nobody in.'

Laura was sweating now.

'Eventually a girl came up to me and asked what I was up to. She recognised me and went mad. Flung herself

370

at me and said, "Oh my God! We didn't believe her when she said she knew you, but she does! Fantastic!" Stuff like that.' He frowned slightly at Laura. 'I didn't realise you'd be proud enough to know me that you'd tell your new friends about it.'

'It was forced out of me,' Laura explained. 'It was at a book group. They were reading *The Willows*. They said you'd put in the Oedipal bit consciously. I said you didn't. I did not say I knew you well!'

Only Laura saw the laughing message in his eyes, referring to just how well they did know each other. 'Thank goodness for that.'

'So what else did Shona say?'

'She asked if I'd go and talk to her book group and I said hell would freeze over first.' He paused. 'Unless, of course, you'd like me to? I didn't know it was your book group too, at the time.'

Laura thought she might cry. It wasn't a declaration of love but it was a very, very kind thing to say. She shook her head.

'Anyway, after a bit more banter, I asked her if she knew where you were. She said you'd told a friend of hers that you were going to visit your parents in England.'

'So you'd left your address with your friend in Ireland?' suggested Mrs Horsley. 'How sensible.' She regarded her daughter as if surprised she had shown so much intelligence.

'No,' said Laura. 'I didn't.'

'I got back to Grant. Fortunately I had his mobile number by then.'

'He's only been here once. He's usually hopeless about remembering addresses,' Laura said.

'He remembered the name of the town,' Dermot explained. He looked at Laura's father. 'Thank God you're not ex-directory.'

'Hmm. Well, you never know when someone might

need to get in touch with you,' said Mr Horsley, as if he had foreseen this very occasion.

'So here I am. If the flights had been a bit more frequent, I'd have been here sooner.'

The clock on the mantelpiece struck ten.

'Where are you staying?' asked Mrs Horsley.

Dermot looked at Laura. 'To be frank with you, I only had one thought in my head, and that was to find Laura. I didn't think about booking anywhere to stay.'

'There are no hotels in town,' said Mr Horsley.

'It's too late to book in at a bed and breakfast,' said Mrs Horsley. 'Although I suppose I could ask Sheila if she's got vacancies, but I don't really like—'

'Couldn't he stay here?' asked Laura, fighting to keep the edge of hysteria out of her voice.

'No. The spare room is full of your stuff, Laura,' said her mother reprovingly, the silent subtext being: if you'd wanted your friend to stay you should have done something about it.

Her father said, 'We took it all out of the loft when we had the extra insulation put in.'

'Oh, for goodness' sake! He can have my bed!' said Laura. 'I'll sleep on the sofa.'

'No,' said Dermot firmly, 'I'll sleep on the sofa.'

Laura's parents exchanged worried glances. What had happened to their safe, familiar Sunday evening? Their daughter, who'd never been much trouble, even if she had been difficult about her studies, had inflicted this wild Irishman on them. What was the best way to react?

'Is there really nowhere he could stay in town?' Mrs Horsley asked her husband.

'No, dear.'

'Mum! It'll be all right.' Laura tried to be patient. She did understand her parents' anxieties. 'Really it will. It's only for one night.'

'I'll be quite happy on the sofa,' said Dermot. 'I've slept on plenty of them in my time.'

'No, you must have Laura's bed. We can't put a guest on the sofa. I'll go and find some clean sheets.'

'Really, Mrs Horsley.' Dermot was firm. 'There's no need to change the sheets just for one night. It's not worth all that washing.'

'I've only slept in them two nights,' Laura pointed out. 'They'll be fine for him.'

'Really—' her mother protested.

'Really,' Dermot repeated. 'They'll be fine.'

'Shall I make some more tea?' said Laura, feeling the argument about where Dermot should sleep and the sheets could go on all night if some kind of full stop wasn't put to it. Tea was the ultimate full stop, she felt.

'And maybe you would like some sandwiches?' asked her mother, making Laura send a wave of gratitude towards her. She wouldn't feel so grateful to Dermot if he accepted them, however. She didn't know why he'd really come to find her and she just wanted the evening to end. Perhaps everything would seem clearer in the morning.

'No thank you, Mrs Horsley, I ate some fish and chips somewhere along my route. Can't remember where.'

'If you want good fish and chips you have to go up north,' said her father, whose own family came from Lancashire.

'I'll make some more tea.' Laura disappeared into the kitchen to be joined by her mother seconds later. It was obvious her parents had no intention of retiring just yet. Usually nothing would stop their nightly routines.

'Darling, who is he?' she whispered, although it was unlikely she could be heard through two doors and quite a long corridor.

'I told you!' replied Laura, also whispering, finding mugs, the best china being still in the sitting room. 'He's a writer who came to the literary festival I helped arrange. I did tell you, about the festival, I mean.'

'But why has he gone to so much trouble to find you? You're not . . .' she hesitated '. . . an "item" or anything?'

Laura put her arm round her mother and hugged her, just for using the word 'item'. 'Of course not,' she said calmly. 'I expect he just wants me to do something for him. I helped him run a writing course.'

'I don't think he would have made such an effort just for that,' said her mother, refilling the kettle. 'I think he likes you.'

These thoughts had been running through Laura's mind like a tape on fast-forward. Why had he take such pains to track her down? Could it possibly be because he did like her? But was that enough for her to risk everything for? There were still so many unanswered questions she needed to ask before she even dared to hope that. 'Well, maybe . . .'

'And I wouldn't blame you if you liked him,' she confided. 'I've always had a soft spot for wild Irishmen.'

'Mum!'

'Just as well I've got your father, isn't it? Otherwise who knows what might have happened? Shall I just put milk in here? Or bring them through with the jug on the tray?'

Laura was reeling from her mother's confession. It was not just that they shared a previously unsuspected predilection; it was the fact her mother had told her about it. 'Oh, let's just put the milk in here.'

Dermot gave up arguing about which of them would sleep in Laura's bed and which on the sofa when he realised that the sofa option involved Laura's single sleeping bag. He did not, he stated, relish sleeping like a sausage in a skin.

Laura had rearranged the cushions on the sofa for

what seemed like the hundredth time but was still not comfortable. She suspected, however, that it was not the cushions or the sofa that was making it hard to sleep, but the thought of Dermot sharing the same three-bedroom semi as her and her parents. Him turning up like that was like a miracle, or a film, or a romantic novel . . . or something.

Why had he chased her all over the British Isles? (Well, England and Ireland. Did Ireland count as the British Isles?) Surely he wouldn't have done that when presumably he could have just gone home to Bridget? Could their night of passion possibly have been more than just amazing sex for him, too?

Ever since she'd worked out, at the festival, that he'd been frantically writing, which was why he'd stopped contacting the outside world, even her, she'd wondered if their subsequent passion was just some sort of release for him, as soldiers high on adrenalin after battle need.

But surely he wouldn't have gone to all that trouble to locate her unless she was more than a woman in the right place at the right time? No. He hadn't just jumped on her, he'd made love to her, tenderly, thoughtfully, taking account of her inexperience. He'd made sure she had a really wonderful time.

She'd blocked a lot of this out of her mind since her meeting with Bridget. She'd made her brain reject the messages her heart might have given her if she'd let it. But now she allowed herself to remember the intimate details; how he'd used his skill and experience to give her pleasure. It made her sigh blissfully but it didn't help her sleep.

Then she heard a noise at the door. It could have been her father, checking up, or her mother, come down for a motherly chat. But somehow she knew it was Dermot.

'Hello?' he whispered.

'Yes?' she whispered back.

'May I come in?' he asked, still whispering.

'Yes, but don't wake my parents. Not that they're asleep, probably. They'll be worrying.'

She heard him come in and bring the door to behind him. 'Will they? Why?'

'In case you're doing what you're doing now!' She sat up, but she was still encased in the sausage skin.

'I couldn't sleep a night under the same roof as you without . . .' He paused.

Torrid and frantic thoughts of what he might be about to say made her breathing become rapid.

'What?' They were already whispering but this was hardly audible. He either heard her or guessed.

'I had to put my arms round you.'

He scooped her up and enveloped her, pinning her to him. She couldn't breathe. His shirt collar was sticking into her cheek, but she didn't care. She didn't want to breathe, really, she just wanted to go on being held by him for ever, even if his clothes dug into her.

And then she pulled back. However much she wanted to let her emotions take over, there were things she needed to know before she could give in to her feelings. She had to be able to trust him. She drew her knees up to her chest, still in the bag.

'What is it?' He frowned and then he smiled at her ruefully. 'Oh, don't tell me, I think I know. It must seem as if I've been a bit of a bastard.' He sat back and sighed.

She so wanted to forgive him everything but she had to suppress her smile at this understatement. 'Just a bit.'

He cleared his throat, got up and moved away from her. 'Can I tell you how it was from my point of view?' he said, as if asking for her permission to continue.

'Please do. I need a change of viewpoint.' Nerves were making her flippant. Whatever he had to say she needed to hear it.

He smiled slightly at this but then became serious.

'I think I fell in love with you way back in January. You were so sweet, so different, so pretty, so—'

'Enough with the flattery.'

'It's not flattery, it's the truth. And after we met I suddenly found I was able to write. You were the key. You were the reason I offered to do that writing course.'

'Oh, was I? If that was the case, why didn't you – I don't know – make any kind of move?' Her voice cracked with remembered hurt.

'There were a few reasons, really. One was that I didn't think I could do more than kiss your cheek without wanting to take you to bed and I couldn't take you to bed in those circumstances. It was too public and I needed to be really sure . . . I mean I was sure but I didn't want to risk hurting you.'

He looked at her, holding her gaze until she turned away, a wave of longing washing over her. She didn't say anything; it was important he told her everything, if she was ever to truly trust him. She nodded for him to go on.

'And back in Ireland,' he continued, 'well, I was well into a book, a book that was pouring out of me. I felt I had to finish it, or as near as damn it, and then pursue you, so I could do it properly.'

He came and sat back down beside her, taking her hand and stroking it. She didn't move any closer but she didn't take her hand away.

'Oh God, I thought I might never see you again, touch you, get the chance to tell you how much I love you, how much I need you.'

She shifted slightly in her sleeping bag, but let her hand continue to rest in his. She still had some questions she wanted answered.

'Just a few other things, if you don't mind,' she said. 'I need to know about Bridget. Why didn't you tell me you were together?'

He frowned. 'What do you mean? Bridget and I were never anything but friends, drinking companions.' He paused. 'You didn't think . . . Oh God. She means nothing to me, nothing.' He tried to pull her closer but she remained slightly distant, even though every part of her was longing for him to take her in his arms again.

After a pause he went on. 'I'm sorry I ravished you in Ireland. I was furious with the press, angry with everyone and I'd been working every hour there was, not eating properly, drinking, smoking, doing anything that would help me get a few more words down on the page. I was mad with writing – seven thousand words a day sometimes.'

'I didn't see any sign of it when I went there,' Laura said

He chuckled. 'No, I hid it all under the bed. But when I saw you, I knew I had to have you, had to put all the care and intensity I put into my work into making things all right for you.'

She blushed and smiled – he was so passionate. 'Well, you did.'

'I might have held back a bit longer if you hadn't been in a temper. There's something about a woman stamping her foot that is irresistible.'

'Hmm. You mean in a "Come here, you little fool, don't you know that I love you?" sort of way?' She felt she could dare to tease him as things started to become clearer.

'I don't know! I just knew I had to have you.'

'And you did.' He'd explained about Bridget and she did believe him but somehow she still wasn't quite satisfied; she still couldn't get rid of the feeling that he'd used her, even if it had been unintentional.

As if he'd read her mind, he said, 'Sweetheart, I didn't just want you because I wanted sex and you were there. You didn't think that, did you?' He seemed horrified by this thought. All the while his fingers were caressing hers.

'No, I didn't feel that at the time,' she replied honestly. 'But when you didn't get in touch with me afterwards—'

'But you were so cold! Running away almost before we'd had breakfast.' He paused, reluctant to reveal his gentle amusement. 'You must have sat at the airport for ages.'

'I did,' she admitted. 'It was because of Bridget.'

'I told you there was nothing between us.'

'I know, but she said—'

He interrupted her. 'What did she say?' he pressed.

'She said something that made me feel you'd . . . used me.' She couldn't look at him; all the hurt and humiliation she'd felt at the time came flooding back.

He sighed and sat back again, his hands now in a fist on his lap. 'That woman!' he said in frustration. 'But I wish to God you'd said something at the time.'

'I couldn't! I was too humiliated,' she protested.

'Well, I didn't know what had happened. One minute everything was wonderful and the next you'd become an ice maiden. I felt a bit humiliated too. I got to feeling that you'd just used me to get rid of your virginity. I tried to put you out of my mind and got back into writing. Now I can understand why—'

'Don't.' She took his hand again and held it tight. He pulled her into his arms and hugged her tightly and they stayed like that for some time until he drew away once more.

'I wanted to explain about the obsessive writing at the festival but you wouldn't give me a chance,' he said quietly.

'I couldn't bear the thought of you explaining that what we'd had was very precious but – I've read so many damn novels, I know all the expressions – but that you and Bridget were getting married or something.'

Even though she knew for certain this wasn't going to happen now, the pain it would have caused her made her flinch inwardly. 'And then there was the story.'

'What about the story?' He was confused.

'I thought it was one of the most beautiful Dear John – or maybe that should be Dear Joan – letters ever written.'

'Dear God, you're a terrible one for getting the wrong end of the stick. The story was fiction! And if it was about anyone, it was about Bridget. I never knew how she felt about me until she came up to see me after you'd left.'

Laura sighed deeply, collapsing a little with the weight of her misunderstanding. 'I just never thought you could really love me. As much as I—'

'Well, I can,' he cut in. 'And if you're not very careful I'll prove it to you.' He enveloped her again and then his mouth found hers and she heard him sigh before their lips connected. It was heavenly.

After a while, she said, 'I'm sorry, I can't let you make love to me on the sofa in my parents' house, when they're probably not even asleep.'

He was breathing hard. 'It's OK, I knew you'd feel like that. It's why I didn't get undressed. We have the rest of our lives to make love to each other. I'll go back upstairs to my room but first I need to thank you.'

'Do you? Are you grateful to me for bringing you to England and to the attention of the literary world once more? You should be! It'll make you rich and famous. Notorious maybe.' She felt she could tease him now she definitely knew he loved her.

'Well, of course I will give you a cut of my earnings – if not all my earnings – from now on in but that's not what I meant.'

'No?'

'No. You did something very much more important.'

'What? What could be more important than fame and fortune?' She spoke lightly but she really didn't know what he could be talking about.

'As I said before, you cured me of writer's block. When you came into my life I'd got jaded and cynical and you – well, you showed me that there were still sweet, pure things.' He kissed the top of her head.

Tears clogged the back of Laura's throat and she waited until they'd gone before saying, 'That makes me sound like an organic pudding, if I may say so.'

He laughed, hugging her close. 'Oh God, you're so adorable. When I'm being soppy and sentimental, you're sharp, like a drop of lemon juice.'

'OK, now I'm an organic lemon pudding.'

He suddenly paused, gazing at her, an earnest look on his face. 'Darling, have I made it clear to you how much I love you? That I want to spend the rest of my life with you?'

'Not exactly, no.' Her heart fluttered.

'Well, what do you need me to say?'

She laughed, bolder now, her heart singing with joy. How could she have forgotten how much she loved being in his company, teasing him? 'Dermot Flynn, I am not going to put words into your mouth. You have your own silver tongue to help you.'

'Laura Horsley, I do solemnly declare—'

'I think that's plagiarism.'

'Don't care. I do solemnly declare that I have never loved anyone as much as I love you. And that I will love you until the Mountains of Mourne stop going down to the sea or some other very unlikely geological event takes place. And I want to take you home to Ireland and keep you safe by my side for ever. And the little ones, when they come along. I'll keep them safe too. What do you say?'

Laura's insides were melting. 'Did you ask me a question?'

'No. I just wanted your general opinion of what I just said.'

'Apart from the plagiarism?'

'Apart from that.'

'I think they most be the most beautiful words you've ever invented.'

He seemed pleased. 'And to think I just said them off the top of my head.'

Laura put her hand up to the top of his head and pushed her fingers into his curls. 'I expect our children will have curly hair.'

'That's all right. Curly-haired children are my favourite kind.'

They had just snaked their bodies so there was as little space between them as possible when they heard movement overhead.

'You'd better go back upstairs,' said Laura. 'Otherwise we'll never be able to face my parents over the All-Bran.'

Epilogue

'Are you sure you're all right carrying that bag?' asked
Dermot as they prepared to set off.

'Of course. It's only got a few things in it. You seem
to have equipment for an entire Boy Scout Jamboree in
that rucksack. We're only going to have tea.'

'Not at all,' he said dismissively.

They were at the farm, preparing to go for a repeat of
the walk they had gone on together, back in January, when
they had only just met. It was now October and the sort
of autumn day that made Laura want to quote Keats: there
was a hint of mist and veils of dew-spangled cobwebs on
the fuchsia-filled hedgerows. Part of their picnic was apples
from the tree in Dermot's garden and there was the promise
of hot sun later. She had moved into Dermot's house ten
days earlier, after he'd had the entire house repainted.
Every morning when she woke up to hear him snoring
beside her, she thought she'd die of happiness – that was
if he didn't wake her first, pulling her to him and holding
her tight prior to making love to her so thoroughly she
was sure everyone could tell how she'd started her day
just by the glow that surrounded her.

'Where are the dogs?' she said now.

'I asked the farmer to keep them in.'

'Oh, that was very kind of you. I would have coped.'
Now that she and Dermot were together she felt nothing
could daunt her, certainly not a few noisy collies.

'I didn't want you having to cope with anything, not
today,' he said firmly.

When they had climbed over the gate, Dermot assisting Laura in a way that involved his hand on her bottom and her giggling for quite a long time, they set off walking.

After a little way, Laura said, 'I can't quite believe we're preparing for my parents to come to stay.'

'We should have that spare bedroom in a good state before they get here.'

'What I really can't believe is that you invited them.'

Dermot had behaved like a perfect gentleman the morning after he had burst into the Horsley household and by the time he and Laura left (by taxi – very extravagant) her parents had seemed quite happy that he was now taking charge of their daughter and her journey back to Ireland.

'I thought it was only fair that they should see their only child was being properly looked after,' he explained. 'And I've been thinking, we may want to sell my house.'

'But you've lived there for years?'

'I've always had a fancy to build one where you can see the sea. There's a plot up here I might persuade the farmer to sell.'

'Oh!' This sounded exciting – it was the most beautiful place. He'd obviously been giving it quite a bit of thought. And knowing how much Dermot was adored in the area, even more now he was known to be writing again, a film was to be made of *Mountain Road*, his first book, and he was bringing in more than a trickle of wealth along with his fame, she felt fairly sure the farmer would willingly sell him a field. She suspected the local planning official would also grant planning permission for it if he possibly could.

'I thought we'd have our picnic there and maybe make a few sketches of what we might want.'

It sounded like heaven and Laura was ridiculously pleased with the way he so easily and readily said 'we' these days, but she didn't comment. Anything too enthusiastic would cause Dermot to kiss her and then they might not get to their picnic destination by teatime.

They walked on in silence, Laura reliving everything that had happened since they'd last climbed the hills together and looked out over the sparkling sea. She was now working full-time as an editor, mostly at home, so she could indulge herself by cooking for Dermot when he wasn't cooking for her. They were a very modern couple. There were times when Laura still couldn't quite believe it wasn't all a dream. Then she would pinch herself and know that it was all deliciously real.

Bridget had left the village, returning to where she'd been when Laura first arrived. Although no one said anything, during the couple of times she and Dermot had gone to the pub together, she got the impression people were relieved that it was she and not Bridget who had captured the heart of their favourite bachelor.

Dermot had started a fourth book. He had turned one of the bedrooms into a study. It was a room she hadn't been in when she'd found him after he'd disappeared from the world. It was where he had been writing, writing, writing the book he had hidden under the bed that was now being fought over by several publishing houses. Now his writer's block was cured, he couldn't seem to stop, as if all the unwritten words of the previous years had been dammed up and were now flooding out of him.

When he'd finished a long stint, he'd find Laura, who was using the dining room as an office, and snatch her up wanting to make love to her. If she really had to finish a piece of work he'd go off into the kitchen and start cooking, finding recipes on the Internet and then charging off in the car, hunting for esoteric ingredients in all the neighbouring shops. Their local store was considering having a section labelled 'Dermot's Follies' in the hope that his influence might encourage others to buy shiitake mushrooms, truffle oil and capers.

'I think this is the perfect spot,' he said.

'For the picnic or the house?'

'Both.'

They stood together, arms wrapped round on another, their hands in each other's back pockets, staring out to sea.

'Imagine pulling back the curtains to that view every morning,' said Dermot.

'On a day like today it would be bliss, but what about when it was stormy and grey?'

'Then we'd pull them shut again and not get up at all.'

She tried to look disapproving but a smile kept tugging her mouth into the wrong expression. 'Let's have tea. Have you got the kettle?'

'Of course.' Dermot opened the neck of the rucksack and started pulling things out. 'Volcano kettle – you've got the *Irish Times* in your bag. Matches, you've got those too. Oh, and tea. I think you've got that. In a paper bag? Have a look.'

After a bit of rummaging, Laura found a brown paper bag with something that felt like tea in the bottom. 'Here you are.'

'Could you just check it is tea?' Dermot seemed a bit odd suddenly, edgy almost.

'I don't think it could be anything else. There's only just the cake and biscuits in here.'

'Just have a look in the bag. Here . . .' He spread a rug on to the short turf. 'Sit down first.'

Shaking her head at her loved one's madness, Laura sat on the rug.

'Now look inside the bag.'

She looked. 'It's definitely tea. There's no doubt it isn't coffee, hot chocolate or cannabis.'

Dermot collapsed down next to her and took the bag.

He peered into it, and then poked in his finger. 'Here, have another look.'

Obedient but confused, Laura looked. In among the tea leaves was a ring. Her heart missed a beat and a smile spread across her face as she put her hand in the bag and took it out. For some reason she couldn't speak; she was overcome with a rush of emotion. She studied the ring. It was a ruby, set in gold, with tiny diamonds round it. It looked old. And there was no way that this was anything other than an engagement ring.

Dermot was looking at her anxiously. 'If you don't like it, we can choose another one – together,' he said.

'I love it,' she whispered, looking up at him.

'Try it on then,' he urged.

She shook her head. 'I'm superstitious about putting rings on that finger unless . . .' She hesitated. Although she'd seen the love in his eyes, saw it every day, knew what this ring symbolised, she couldn't quite bring herself to take it all for granted.

'Here, let me.' He took hold of her left hand and then, taking the ring from her, he slid it on to her finger. It was a little large but she thought it looked lovely. Before she could admire it for long he took it off again.

He was already kneeling but he put one leg behind him so that he was on only one knee. Laura stifled a giggle. It was all so hopelessly romantic and he looked so serious.

'Laura, dear heart, love of my life, will you marry me?'

Sighing and smiling, she said, 'Well, I just might.'

'Just say yes, would you, woman!'

'Yes,' she said, her voice strong and clear.

'Yes, Dermot, I will marry you?' he said, holding her once more beringed hand tightly as if he was afraid she'd scamper off.

'Yes, Dermot, I will marry you.' But she'd hardly got out the last word before he had taken her in his arms and they were rolling on the rug together, kissing and laughing.

'Now we can tell your parents when they come to stay.' He reached across to the rucksack and produced a newspaper-covered bottle. 'Let's have a mug of champagne.'

'I thought we were going to have tea!'

'Bollocks to tea. We'll have that afterwards. Now, we're celebrating!'